JEFF STURGEON'S
THE LAST CITIES OF EARTH

JEFF STURGEON'S THE LAST CITIES OF EARTH

Edited by

JENNIFER BROZEK

Edited by

JEFF STURGEON

WFP
WordFire Press

JEFF STURGEON'S THE LAST CITIES OF EARTH

Cover art and interior art by Jeff Sturgeon
Introduction by Todd Lockwood
Prologue Timeline by Jeff Sturgeon

EBook ISBN: 978-1-68057-253-7
Trade Paperback ISBN: 978-1-68057-253-7
Dust Jacket Hardcover ISBN: 978-1-68057-255-1
Case Bind Hardcover ISBN: 978-1-68057-291-9
Library of Congress Control Number: 2021951354

Cover artwork by Jeff Sturgeon
Kevin J. Anderson, Art Director
Published by
WordFire Press, LLC
PO Box 1840
Monument CO 80132
Kevin J. Anderson & Rebecca Moesta, Publishers
WordFire Press eBook Edition 2022
WordFire Press Trade Paperback Edition 2022
WordFire Press Hardcover Edition 2022
Printed in the USA
Join our WordFire Press Readers Group for
sneak previews, updates, new projects, and giveaways.
Sign up at wordfirepress.com

CONTENTS

DEDICATION

Dedicated to John A. Pitts and Mike Resnick, who both passed away during the creation of this anthology. John whom this book, this world, The Last Cities of Earth, would not have happened and to Mike, who was there for me.

INTRODUCTION TO
THE LAST CITIES OF EARTH

TODD LOCKWOOD

Jeff Sturgeon and I started playing Dungeons & Dragons in 1977 and found the same inspiration. Make-believe for adults. Rules that inspired worldbuilding and storytelling, and made those worlds mutually explorable. Interactive storytelling. It was the perfect fit for a couple of creative teenagers with active minds and things to say. It set us on a path to careers in art and gaming.

The thing is, I discovered D&D in Colorado and Jeff found it in California. We wouldn't meet for another 25 years, at Norwescon in Seattle.

Sometimes it takes decades to meet the people you should have known all your life.

He's a veritable sasquatch. Tall and bearded, outdoorsy. He moves with an easy gait. But he's quick to laugh and has a Scottish twinkle in his green eyes. He's knowledgeable about things that might surprise you, and passionate in all endeavors.

We've both been artists our entire adult lives. It's how we earn our livings. I wound up at TSR and then Wizards of the Coast. Jeff was part of the first wave of gaming artists in the industry and worked for various companies before he finished at Electronic Arts. Eventually he left the gaming world in order to paint.

His works are spectacular images of outer space, alien land-scapes, even abstracts. He grinds metal sheets to give them whorls and swirls, then airbrushes for color and paints details judiciously in acrylic. They're magical. They catch the light and shimmer to life as you move past them.

But Jeff, like me, was never happy with only one creative outlet. We both have stories to tell, worlds to share. Maybe that's why Jeff asked *me* to write this little intro. I understand what he's up to. We see a lot of things from a very similar point of view. And we're both artists embracing the written word.

Jeff found the seed for *The Last Cities of Earth* in a painting created for a convention art show. A tall vertical construct—a city in the sky—built with lost knowledge, floating above a cloudy landscape. As he worked, a story leapt fully formed into his head. The muse had struck! With each new painting the story grew, becoming a unique look at a ravaged planet and the people who populate it still, floating in their technological havens above clouds that hide the truth of the world their ancestors left behind.

Jeff shared his vision with friends throughout the science fiction community and inspired them with his paintings. Kevin J. Anderson suggested that the world was worthy of serious exploration. Peter Wacks, and the late great John A. Pitts pushed too. Jeff soon had a stellar cast of talented authors eager to help him bring it alive.

The Last Cities of Earth is a shared-world anthology. More than just brilliant science fiction, like Jeff, it is thoughtful, forward-looking, and honest, built upon his love of story, his sense of history and of humanity. It evokes his passion for speculative fiction, scientific discovery, adventure, mystery, and good old-fashioned storytelling. It provides a showcase for many of the most inventive writers in the industry, set to the task of revealing this future Earth's dark secrets, its hidden dangers, and its ancient truths—story by story. It might be a warning. It could be a heart-pounding adventure. It might, by turns, be introspective or hopeful. But it's all smart and sexy, and I can't wait to see where it goes from here.

—Todd Lockwood, February 18, 2020

A BRIEF TIMELINE FOR

THE LAST CITIES OF EARTH

JEFF STURGEON

2049 AD Doctor Maxwell Vincent Stephan is lauded for discovering the first breakthrough in the manipulation and control of gravity.

2060 AD By this time, every country in the world is experimenting with anti-gravity and innovation. What started out as a way to revolutionize the shipping industry turned into a science fiction fan's paradise. The rich and famous begin building great floating estates, with the first such commercial property built for the actor Harlan Kilgore, featuring six acres of land with a mansion, several visitors' quarters, an in-ground pool, and a helicopter pad.

Before the end of the decade, corporations, oligarchs, and government agencies have built complexes that float high enough into the atmosphere to interrupt traditional flight paths into major cities. Architects designed new skyscrapers without the fear of the gravitational drag of the Earth's core.

A fad for those who could design and build the world's tallest building, always a contest between industrialized countries, took on an *Alice in Wonderland* quality. Fairy cities, as the press dubbed them, are planned and many are begun. The issue becomes a matter of funding.

2074 AD The completion of three massive building projects in the ocean are announced. With the use of anti-gravity technology, domes were built to withstand the massive pressures in the deep ocean, making the creation of underwater cities viable.

2085 AD The first three major projects celebrate their five-year anniversaries: New Sidney, off the coast of Australia; Deep Seoul, off the southern tip of the Unified Koreas; and new Surabaya, three miles north of the city of the same name that had been lost to the rising oceans in the Java Sea.

March 15, 2085 The US government and the United Nations shock the world with the news that the supervolcano under Yellowstone in North America is going to erupt within the next six years. The devastation, they said, would be such that the world's weather will be massively disrupted, and a new ice age is predicted. North America is expected to undergo dramatic and catastrophic physical damage with loss of life from the Event exceeding 400 hundred million in the United States alone. Tsunamis and earthquakes on a scale greater than 9.0 are anticipated all around the Pacific Rim. Volcanoes are expected to erupt throughout the Ring of Fire. The predicted Yellowstone Event will be an extinction level calamity not unlike the meteor that wiped out the dinosaurs.

December 2085 The largest short-term jump in human population in recorded human history. This exacerbated an already overwhelmed and decaying worldwide infrastructure and supply chain. Violence erupts. Fear and anxiety fuel border conflicts across the globe and erupt in the new conflagration of migration, chaos, and war.

The story does not end there, however. While humanity is a passionate species, prone to violent outbursts, there is another side. Over the course of human history, it is widely documented that when faced with a crisis, we have achieved great, even remarkable, things.

2086 AD The restrictions on genetic manipulation disappears from nearly all countries by 2086. Religious cries of playing in God's

Domain have gone unheeded. While genetic manipulation had been going on for decades in corporate and government laboratories, nothing was as dramatic as the innovations which occurred in this area after the prediction of the Yellowstone Event. Every hacker with access to a gene splicer began experimenting beyond the rational control of scientific rigor. When code switches began to appear on the internet, viable mutations that would have been considered abhorrent by society just a single generation before the Yellowstone Event were suddenly the hope of Mankind's survival. Wild rumors appeared about mutated humans who could live in the depths of the ocean, in the thin atmosphere of the stratosphere, and, in some cases, in the anticipated ruins of a nuclear-fallout world. The bioethicist Jacob Whitcomb called this the darkest day in humanities' existence.

The years between 2085 and YE also showed great achievements in space. Within two years we had a fledgling colony on Mars using the wealth of practical knowledge gained from twenty-five years of expanding the lunar colony. In four we had a science station orbiting Europa and an industrial station where robotic ships harvested hydrogen, helium, and methane from the upper atmosphere of Uranus. The might of the first world countries had turned to preserving their ways of life off Earth. These furious endeavors spawned new sciences, new thoughts. New technology appeared to show a path forward. Maybe humanity would be saved after all.

The city-island Tower and spires described the size and shapes of the hundreds of structures lifted into the air around the world with cutting-edge anti-gravity tech developed by the US military. The tech is based on sound frequencies manipulating magnetic fields. In North America, the federal government mandated that if resources were found, and time allowed, each state would build and erect a city, churches, corporations, academic/universities, and labs. Civilians of wealth built structures separate from the state mandates, led by New York City which was more like an island. Most states did not have the time, resources, or stability to attempt to build a city-island. Local and state governments quickly collapsed as the YE date approached.

Most of the great cities across North America were built using private funding. Key federal government cities, clustered in the old Washington, DC area or in underground bases, were built and expanded by special operations organizations, military, academic institutions, and organized religions, as well as by those on Wall Street and from the banking industry around key financial centers, enhanced by a few of the wealthy and powerful.

The cities were built on foundations pulled from bedrock that was cut by massive lasers and formed into different designs with Tower-Cities built into and above them as work progressed 24/7. They were designed to reach high into the atmosphere to tap solar energy, well above the coming volcanic winter which was predicted to rage for nearly fifteen years before slowly abating and exposing a world completely changed from the world of the late 21st century ruled by climate change, escalating heat, rising sea levels, and massive storms, hurricanes, and typhoons.

A new ice age awaited the survivors.

Food tech was designed for greenhouse growth, and air ships of different designs and sizes were built and readied for the time when the first brave captains and crews ventured out into a much-changed world on epic voyages of rediscovery and exploration as cities would attempt to link up over the ensuing years. It was assumed many, isolated by climate or distance, would remain alone and silent.

2100+ AD During the early years after the Yellowstone Event almost nothing is known. Survivors clustered in the great cities of the sky, deep in underground bases, and in pockets around the equator and in the southern hemisphere. Still, most reliable sources estimate that more than ninety percent of the human population perished in the five decades after YE. What transpired in the cities and bases over the decades and centuries since is guesswork.

Those who survived, huddled in their various shelters and suffered through many harsh winters before the climate shifted enough so that in 2143, the first brave airship captains could leave their floating city-states and reach out to the world once more.

The flying fortresses, the city-states of a fractured world, are now scattered around the Earth like a child's abandoned toys. In recent years they have begun to reconnect with their brethren using a fragile string of airship routes crewed by brave people with a penchant for glory and a desire for adventure. Whether rediscovering lost cities, building viable trade networks, or uncovering caches of lost technology, these airship captains and this new breed of explorers have begun to knit society back together.

The inhabitants and rulers of the newfound cities of humanity are, perhaps, no longer purely human, but they remember their humanity.

FATHERHOOD

STEVEN L. SEARS

I'm a princess! Just like in the story books!" The little blonde-haired girl laughed as she twirled around the room showing off the crown on her head she had cut from pink paper. "Look!" She curtsied elaborately, bowing her head so low the crown fell to the ground. "Oopsie!" she exclaimed and giggled.

"Yes," Joshua replied in a bland voice. "Very cute." Joshua didn't have a sense of humor, never had. Even when the quantum scientists in his department made jokes that only quantum scientists would understand, Joshua would continue his work without laughter or comment. He was more interested in facts than emotions, he was more dedicated to his work than to being social. He understood the humor, he just wasn't wired that way.

"Well, I think I'm a princess!" the eight-year-old continued, picking up the crown and placing it carefully on the table next to the door.

"You can be a princess if you want," Joshua answered. "Right now, you need to exercise." The little girl sighed and picked up the jumping rope. "Pooh," she said with a mock pout as she started skipping over the rope. Joshua turned his attention to the monitor and recorded her heart rate.

The room used to be a common room, where people would congregate and socialize. Joshua had turned it into a small exercise area.

"This is to keep you healthy," he told her. "I know you don't like it, but it's important."

"I wish I could go outside and run around," she said between breaths.

"You can't. Not for a long, long time," Joshua reminded her. "We stay down here, until I think it's safe."

Joshua had found her in the Greensong level-twelve daycare center of the underground facility a little over a year ago, surviving on the stores of food in that level's kitchen. Despite her isolation, she was as bright, trusting, and curious as any other child of her age. Or so Joshua assumed. He had little experience with children; they weren't allowed in the classified areas of Greensong.

The Pentagon created the facility as a combination bunker for the political elite and a research laboratory, secret and apart from the prying eyes of enemies and journalists alike. At its peak, there were almost six hundred people working among its fifteen levels and in the underwater laboratories offshore, all interconnected by a massive computer network system.

Joshua's work involved defense and infrastructure reconstruction; a system that, after its initial testing, would be housed in New DC One, the prototype floating City-Tower above the capital. Joshua, himself, was to be in charge, overseeing the defense of the United States from nuclear attack, and then, the rebuilding of society as quickly as possible in the aftermath. His mother, Dr. Alicia Mackenzie, was head of the research department and had pioneered the huge quantum computer system.

"So, where did we leave off yesterday?" Joshua asked her. He was well aware of the answer, but he felt this was a better way to engage her. Joshua didn't have any kids, nothing had prepared him for dealing with this young girl, but he had been doing his best to keep her happy and healthy. One thing he had learned over the last year was that her mind tended to wander and focus on the unimportant.

"Uhm … the floating cities?" she replied. "I think it was the cities!"

"No, Caroline, after that."

"The volcano!" she responded enthusiastically.

"Yes, exactly!" Joshua attempted to sound excited, as if they were playing a game. He found she reacted more positively toward that.

"It was Yellow ... Yellow ..." she stared off, her brow furrowing in concentration.

"Yellowstone," he replied in soft encouragement.

"Yellowstone," she repeated. "Yellowstone Park! It blew up." She picked up her pace, pleased with herself for remembering the story Joshua had told her.

Scientists had known for over a century that the Yellowstone Caldera was an active volcano, capable of an eruption at any time. There had been several scares during the late 1900s, but those had subsided, and life had gone on, putting the possibility that this civilization-ending event would occur sometime, just not now. Geologically, it was a good gamble.

"But the floating cities were important," she continued. "That's where the people went."

"Yes, Caroline," he acknowledged. "They were very important."

The first serious research into anti-gravity was to expand payload weight restrictions in launching material to the new science colony on the Moon. It wasn't long before the rich shipping magnates and others of the wealthy elite began floating their homes; a futuristic version of gated communities, separating themselves from the "common" people forced to live on the ground. But even wealth has its limitations, so the floating mansions were dismissed as toys and dalliances.

"I bet that was fun," she grinned. "It's like you could be a dragon and play all day in the clouds!" She did a quick double jump over the rope.

Joshua continued monitoring her heart rate. She was a happy child and still at that age when her mind was formative, open to the world as a wonderful playground to be explored.

But there was so much more to the story. Even playgrounds have dark corners where children shouldn't stray.

Because of the military aspects of anti-gravity research, Congress had restricted the commercial usage to keep the advanced technology from the hands of foreign powers.

Eventually those restrictions were defeated when a neurobiologist named Jai Li Tsun, working at the Greensong complex, managed to sneak the research out of the country and publish it. A firm believer that all humanity should share in technology, she was soon extradited and placed in prison.

But the genie was out of the bottle. The race was on for bigger platforms, ones that could hold more than mere mansions. However, the very size of the power generators limited the weight the units could support.

The major breakthrough came about when Clark Enderson, a PhD dropout from MIT and founder of EnderSun Technology Systems, developed solar-powered "repellers" which used the variations in gravitational fields above metals embedded in the Earth, creating electromagnetic compression fields underneath the platforms. The result was a continuous power source which, when focused on a given point, could support enormous amounts of weight. Ironically, the heavier an object was, the more powerful the field generated.

It wasn't long before the first City-Tower rose from the ground, into the sky above Washington, DC. Though only a prototype with limited room, it was still a superhuman effort and had the backing of a nation determined to reassert its technological dominance as it had done in the space race of the 1960s. Dubbed New DC One, no one seriously planned more than a couple of the Tower-Cities as showcases to the world.

That plan changed on March 15th, 2085, when the bet with Mother Nature was called. Volcanologists working with the Caltech Seismological Laboratory detected a massive pocket of magma moving from deep beneath the crust into the Yellowstone Caldera. They estimated they had six years left before the center of the United States exploded, threatening the very existence of humanity.

Old rivalries were forgotten as the world's nations dedicated themselves to the preservation of humanity and eventual rebuilding of civilization. All the major minds of science and technology were brought together, including Jai Li Tsun, released from prison and hailed as a heroine.

The colonies on the Moon and Mars expanded rapidly as people deserted Mother Earth. Overwhelmed, immigration restrictions were soon enacted; there would be no escape to the stars. The answer, the only answer, was to build more Tower-Cities and hope humanity could ride it out above the devastation, where the sun could provide energy, technology could supply food, and airships could establish trade and communication between the survivors.

New DC One lost its prominence when the first full DC Tower rose nearby, twice as large and built to expand as needed. Two other DC Towers were soon in the works, all three designed to house and protect the essentials of the United States government while New DC One was relegated to mere defense systems upkeep.

Within five years, the combined might and wealth of a planet created dozens of floating City-Towers, capable of supporting millions of people, awaiting the Yellowstone Event in relative safety.

Caroline started to sing a song to herself, matching the rhythm of her skipping rope. It was one of the songs from the video archives, something popular from the past about a spoonful of sugar. Joshua was bemused that she attached music to her workouts, but, as she put it, it "made the work seem quicker."

Had Caroline been a mere three levels further above, she would have been lost. The daycare center was spared, though the other six children with her had died. Caroline didn't want to talk about them, so he didn't ask. He had recovered too many bodies.

"The whole ground just blew up?" Caroline asked him.

"It was more than just an explosion," Joshua responded as he continued to monitor her heart rate. She was starting to ask the difficult questions now about the Yellowstone Event.

"It was a tectonic event, a huge one," he explained as she finished jumping rope and moved to the stationary bicycle. Joshua had set up a small screen in front of it and was able to play recordings made of the countryside to give the appearance of travel. Caroline seemed to enjoy it. It made her smile to imagine what the outside looked like, full, green, and lush. Joshua knew differently; there was no doubt the land above was ravaged and barren. "The entire center of the country was a volcano, waiting to explode. And, finally, it did."

"Oh," Caroline said and fell silent, pedaling evenly to keep up with the imaginary scenery on the screen.

"Is there something specific you wanted to know?" Joshua asked. She pursed her lips and contorted her face as a child might do when making a show about thinking.

"Did a lot of people get hurt?" she asked.

"Yes," Joshua replied. He had expected this question eventually, he had no other way to respond except to tell her directly. "A lot of people died."

"How many?" she pedaled faster.

"I don't know," he said flatly. "It's all too early. There will be repercussions to the event, climate change, species will die off, most of what we knew as the world is gone." He knew what he was saying was blunt and cold, but he truly did not know how else to tell her.

The little girl slowed her pace, staring at the screen in front of her. Joshua waited. She nodded toward the manufactured image of the forest. "That's not real, is it?"

"It was at one time," Joshua tried to soften his voice. "But, no. No more." She sighed and picked up the pace. Joshua was pleased to see her heart rate remained stable. *Children are very resilient,* he thought to himself. He didn't like it, but this was the only world Caroline would know for a long time. Possibly forever.

"When I was little, I remember my mommy taking me to a sky-city." She glanced upward. "What happened to them?"

"I would hope most of them survived," he responded. "That's what the Tower-Cities were built for." Technically, none of that was a lie.

"So maybe they did?" she said. "Maybe we're not alone?"

"Maybe," he said, hoping she would not be too probing. "I'm trying to reconnect the outside computers but there's been a lot of damage."

"Did your mommy die?" she asked innocently.

"Yes," he said. "She died."

"I'm sorry," Caroline looked down at the pedals. Joshua saw her eyes moisten with tears.

"You can stop now," he told her. She slowed her pace to a stop and got off the bicycle. Joshua watched as she stepped closer to the screen and stared into it. After a moment, she reached up and flicked it off.

"They're out there. They have to be out there," she said with a firm voice.

"Yes, Caroline," he responded. "If they are, we'll find them."

"I love you, daddy!" she said with a grin.

Joshua paused. It was the first time she had called him that.

"It's lunch time."

Caroline wiped her eyes and skipped toward the door. She picked up the paper crown, balanced it back on her head and with a big grin, made a show of curtsying again before heading off to the kitchen.

Joshua shut down the equipment. *And if they are out there, we must remember that they tried to destroy the world; Mankind tried to destroy the world,* Joshua thought. Protecting Caroline was his only concern now.

✶

"Daddy, you lied! You lied to me!"

Joshua had just finished lighting all the candles on the cake for Caroline's thirtieth birthday when she stormed into the communal room and stood with her fists on her hips. This wasn't the Caroline who would announce "Princess is unhappy!" when she was playfully admonishing him. The twinkle in her eye was absent, the slight upturned smile at the corner of her lip was gone. Joshua could tell, this was serious.

"Caroline, calm down." Joshua replied. "Blow out the candles on your cake and we'll talk." He had been looking forward to her birthday ever since he had opened the tunnel into the main Greensong library. Caroline was an avid reader and had digested almost every book in the memory banks. Her favorite novel was Jane Austen's *Emma,* and he had found an actual paper copy in the archive safe. It had an autograph on the front page, but he had no idea if it was real.

The cake, though, was very real. It sat on the table now, the candles burning and ignored by the birthday girl. Despite her growing into adulthood, she was still very much a child at times, lacking the normal socialization that would come from interacting with others. It was just the two of them, and being a father still wasn't something Joshua felt comfortable with, though Caroline fully accepted him in that role.

But now she had discovered the secret he had been keeping from her; they weren't alone.

Joshua had long since reestablished the network with some of the remote defense computers, including several of the underwater facilities off the coast, still functioning despite the absence of their human operators. But while running a diagnostic on the topside transponders, the comm board had suddenly lit up, as hundreds of camera nodes pinged back. He shut them down immediately, worried that a return signal might give away their location. As it was, Caroline had been on the network in her room when her terminal suddenly downloaded hundreds of images from the outside.

They showed her the ruins of Washington, DC, the ground around the old city still barren and dry. Other images showed her the ruins of the New DC One Tower, collapsed upon itself, much of it still buried in the earth from the impact of the fall, its mighty spires broken. But along with these images of ancient destruction, there were images of Mankind's recovery. In the sky, three strange craft, mighty airships coasting just above a blue river. And in the distance, one of the three DC Towers floating among the clouds. Pristine and six times larger than its original size, it majestically ruled over the landscape for miles in every direction.

"I was going to tell you," Joshua began. "But let's do it later." He really wanted to get back to the birthday and his surprise gift.

"You told me it was all gone." She didn't back down. "You said there was nothing! Nothing!"

"I never said there was nothing," he replied defensively. "I said it was all destroyed. And it was. A long, long time ago."

Caroline stood there, fuming, waiting for a complete explanation he didn't want to give.

Joshua realized it was unavoidable. "You remember when I taught you about the floating cities? They were where humanity went to avoid the Yellowstone Event?"

"Go on," she prompted, biting her lip angrily.

"Dozens of the Towers were built, all around the world. Every major city had at least one. Eventually there were enough to hold millions of people. But even with that many, billions more would die."

"Why didn't they build more?" she asked.

"They didn't have time," he answered.

"What happened?" Caroline asked.

"War," he responded. "War happened. A nuclear war."

She took a deep breath and sat down at the table. "I don't understand. Why?"

"Because Mankind is like that. Fear, hatred, whatever you want to call it. Instead of thinking about humanity, they could only think about themselves. If they weren't going to survive, no one was going to."

She stared off into the distance, her head moving slightly from side to side. Joshua was telling her that everything she thought she knew about the outside world was a lie. A lie he had allowed her to believe.

"The fighting started on the Indian subcontinent and spread through Asia," he continued. "We were hoping we were safe here and that it would die down. I'm not sure what happened, but a missile must have hit directly above us. DC Tower One was crippled and crashed to the ground. After that, nothing. No communication with the outside."

"So, all the people here died because of that?" she asked.

"The explosion collapsed the upper levels," he explained. "The compression wave went farther, killing more. When the Yellowstone Event happened, there wasn't much left here to destroy."

"Why didn't you tell me?"

"I was going to," he softened his voice. "I was. When you were old enough to understand. I was trying to protect you."

"Protect me?" She stood again. "There are people out there! They live in the floating Towers!"

"Yes, that's true," he responded. "But those are the same people who did this."

"Show me." She turned toward the large screen in the corner of the room and gestured toward it. "Show me, everywhere!"

The birthday surprise was not going to happen, Joshua conceded to himself. He reconnected the outside communications and the screen suddenly lit up. It was a map of North America. Blinking points of light were scattered across the board marking the location of the major City-Towers.

Caroline stepped forward in awe, tracing her finger across the map from point to point. "Oh, my God ... how many of them?" she asked.

"Worldwide? Probably no more than a hundred. I've only connected with eight of them. Quietly, of course. Just for information."

"And ... the people?" she asked hopefully.

"Yes," he responded. "Hundreds of thousands in those eight Towers alone. "

"Those things I saw above the river? Like the dirigibles I read about?" She was referencing several books from the early 1900s, when the huge gas airships ruled the sky.

"It's how the cities trade. And communicate." He paused to give weight to his next words. "And wage war against each other."

She didn't react, so transfixed was she with the images on the map. She tapped the screen on the eastern coast of the former United States.

"This is where we are," she stated as fact. "And this blinking light ... that's the floating city I saw. It's almost right above us."

"No, it's several miles away," he corrected her. "It looks closer because it's so large."

"People live there." Her words drifted off, and her eyes turned dark. "You knew about this for years and you didn't tell me."

"Did you hear what I said?" Joshua replied. "They wage war. It's not like it was in the past; there is no United States anymore. The City-Towers have become little fiefdoms, each with their own kingdoms and selfish interests."

"You've been monitoring them for years," she exclaimed.

"Yes, I have," he shot back. "I've been watching them, carefully, Caroline. Those airships, they've built fleets of them. Not just to travel, but to kill each other in mindless wars over trade and power. That's exactly how all this started. That's how they destroyed our world in the first place, even before Yellowstone!"

"I want to talk to them," she said.

"You're not going to," he replied firmly. "It's too risky."

"We have to let them know we're here!"

"Why? So they can bomb us? Again? You don't understand. Oh, yes, there were people of peace who hoped that Mankind would have learned from the past. But, no. They destroyed the world, Caroline. I will not let them harm you."

"I'm lonely," she yelled as tears streamed down her face, her fists tightening in helpless frustration. She sat at the table and put her head in her hands, sobbing.

"So am I, Caroline," he replied softly. "I knew a world that was filled with people, good men and women. I had friends who worked here with me. We were all dedicated to protecting our country and those in it. We failed and they are all gone. The good people, all gone."

"But I'm all by myself," she choked out the words.

"I'm sorry you feel that way," Joshua said.

Caroline shook her head. "I didn't mean you, daddy. I didn't mean you."

"I know," he replied. "I understand. But you, Caroline, you're one of those good people, don't you see? I may have failed with the others ..."

"Don't say that," she interrupted.

"... but I won't risk you," he finished. "One day, perhaps. Until then, let's just wait and see, okay?"

She nodded and turned off the screen, then turned to the cake and blew out the dwindling candles.

"Happy birthday, Caroline," Joshua said.

She looked up, mustered a smile and wiped the tears from her cheeks. "I love you, daddy."

✶

The smell was like nothing she had ever experienced. How could she have? Her entire life had been spent underground; everything her senses had experienced had been recirculated and manufactured.

Caroline leaned her head back against the wheelchair headrest, closed her eyes, and inhaled again. Her senses had dulled over time, but even at the age of ninety-seven, she could smell the pine, the honeysuckle sweetness of the flowers, and the dull buttery scent of the wood decomposing on the floor of the forest.

It was overwhelming. All these years, she had only imagined

what it would be like outside Greensong. All the books she read, all the videos she watched, all the descriptions she tried to process, they were pale attempts at the reality.

She opened her eyes and took it all in. Tilting her head to the left engaged the wheelchair's electric motor, and it turned slowly to allow her the view of the creek at the bottom of the hill. The grass covering the small downward slope was thick, and she imagined herself as a little girl, those many years ago, running and tumbling down to splash in the water.

She smiled when she saw the deer next to the stream. They looked different from the pictures in the old books, the antlers were more pointed, directed forward, and the metal reflecting in the sunlight. They ignored her and continued eating the small rodent they had trapped. A buzzing sound made her look up at the bees. Their huge shadows traveled across the ground, the beams from their eyes scanning their surroundings, the small stinger-guns moving slowly back and forth. She knew they wouldn't harm her, she had played with them below, in the Greensong gymnasium, along with the wolf-dragon cubs.

But, out here, in the open ... Even the colors reflected off their cyclical wings were more vibrant. Everything just seemed so intense, magnified from her existence underground.

She longed to feel the grass under her bare feet, to explore it all. Somewhere beyond the forest were the remains of New DC One. The ruins were, most likely, long overgrown with brush, but she had always hoped that she could travel there, to try and understand what had happened to her world. Why there had been so much evil.

Above the trees, she could barely make out the lower spires of the nearest DC Tower. Even from this distance, it looked huge and majestic, disappearing up into the clouds. She squinted slightly to make out the many small specks moving up toward the Tower. Airships, she was sure. They couldn't possibly see her, so there was no danger from the evil they carried. Not that it would have mattered. This was Caroline's last day in this world and she knew it.

She'd had a long life and Joshua had been good to her. She couldn't have imagined a better father, though Joshua had told her that her real father had died long ago. It didn't matter, Joshua was the only one she had known. He had taken care of her, fed her, taught her, and made her strong. Overprotective at times, she knew, but always with her best interests in mind. As she grew older, she saw that it was his way of showing his love.

After the nuclear attack and the destruction of YE, she realized he'd had no other purpose than to make her happy and safe. She mused that it probably kept him going. *When you lose everything, a purpose may be all you have left,* she thought. *Maybe that's all the difference you need.* She had read that somewhere, then smiled as she remembered she had written it herself in her journal.

Will someone ever read my journal? she wondered. Joshua had long ago encouraged her to write it all down; that, one day, good people would return and would want to know. She was an example, he had said, of why good people were worth fighting for.

A father doting on his only daughter, she knew. It had made her feel good that she had always been perfect in his eyes. But more, she hoped he understood that he, also, had made a difference for the future. Or, at the least, that he had been able to make a little girl feel like a princess in a fairy tale surrounded by darkness.

The breeze kissed her cheek and made her gray hair dance over her ears. Caroline didn't feel sad, she knew her time was over. She accepted that fact and was willing to let go of the pains of life, to move on to whatever mystery lay before her.

"I'm ready," she said softly. She took one more deep breath, then exhaled it slowly. "I love you, daddy."

"I love you, Princess," Joshua responded.

Caroline smiled, joyous that the last words she heard were ones that defined her entire life. She felt a slight pull as Joshua disengaged the life sustaining connector from the base of her spine.

Her breathing slowed, then ceased. The light in her eyes faded and became dull.

Caroline was gone.

Joshua started to turn the wheelchair around, to take her back inside. He paused and reconsidered.

He felt ... sad. Or, at least, the approximate representation of sadness that his programming allowed. In the vastness of the invisible quantum universe, where his processing structure was located, he was able to replicate most of the human emotions he had been studying. This one had taken him by surprise the first time he processed it; "sadness."

"No," his disembodied voice said, with no one to hear him. "You belong here, Princess." He engaged the wheelchair's motor to move her to the edge of the woods then shut down the unit and severed his connection with it.

He didn't actually need her body, he had more than enough organic material from all the previous Carolines if he wanted to clone another. This one had lived longer than the others, so he felt a special attachment to her. But what else was there to learn? He had already exceeded his original mandate, at least as far as understanding what it was like to be human.

Dr. Mackenzie had programmed him to protect them but failed to teach him to understand them. He recognized that was a flaw, of course, and made the necessary corrections in his coding. He understood that to truly protect something, you needed to establish a bond with it, a commitment of some sort. In humans, this was not easy to quantify. There were millions of stories in the Greensong library that attempted to explain the connection they had with each other and all of them failed. They were just words to Joshua. But the last two hundred and thirty years protecting and caring for the Carolines had taught him much. Each new Caroline had the same DNA, of course, but were unique from the others in their growth and reactions. It mystified him, so he had logged and analyzed every step and milestone along the way, requiring them to keep journals that he would study.

In the process, something began to ring to him as familiar; something in his programming he had been completely unaware of. Recovering his mother's logbook and journal revealed that she had layered his lower-level coding with her own DNA; that part of the human evolution that was specific to survival and continuation of the species.

It was that second part that had been the key and hardest for him to understand. Even with his infinite processing power, it had taken him this long to understand the complex emotion and motivations of "love."

The Carolines had taught him love. From them, he learned *why* humanity should be protected, and why nothing was more important than preserving the lives of others like her and providing a world for them to live in.

He was now ready to proceed with the next step of his programming; rebuilding what had been destroyed by Mankind. He had already created an area where he could work without observation or intrusion. Mutating creatures and modifying existing equipment to his needs, this "dark zone" in the submerged laboratories just off the coast was easily protected. The airships that ventured into the zone would be destroyed by his creations of organic and metallic DNA, his own airships and drones. They, along with the other mutations, would be the new protectors of the Carolines of the future.

But, first, he had to make a safe space for them; he had to guarantee that what happened before would not happen again. That the hatred of Mankind that once destroyed the world could not return.

His mother had programmed him to protect and rebuild. For him, it was an easy equation. On one side was a world of evil and destruction. On the other, the world of the Carolines; beautiful, hopeful, loving, and...filled with princesses.

Mankind had to be eradicated completely. It would take time, of course. Joshua was still collecting information as to their infestation, but his initial estimate saw the task in terms of millennia.

Whatever it took, Caroline, all the Carolines, had been worth it. There was no way Joshua could see a world where their love and humanity's hatred could co-exist.

He just wasn't wired that way.

✶

Steven L. Sears has worked as an actor, writer, story editor, producer and creator in television, film, digital media, and animation. His lengthy career has encompassed over fifteen separate television series, including *Walker-Texas Ranger, Xena: Warrior Princess, The A-Team,* and *Swamp Thing*; and development deals with a number of the major studios in the industry, including Columbia Studios, Sony/Tristar Television, Rhysher Entertainment, Artists Inc., Cookie Jar Entertainment, Digital Pictures, and many others.

He is the author of *The Non-User-Friendly Guide for Aspiring TV Writers*. Based on over thirty years of experience, it's a direct and honest look at working in television for anyone choosing to make TV Writing a career. His partnership with sci-fi author Kevin J. Anderson resulted in the gritty futuristic sci-fi graphic novel *Stalag-X,* and partnering with Peter J. Wacks, he co-created the upcoming epic book and graphic novel series *Vill'annie*.

As is often said "If it ain't on the page, it ain't on the stage." Steven has managed to do both. And he's not slowing down.

AND SOMEDAY WE WILL RIDE THE CLOUDS

DANIELLE ACKLEY-MCPHAIL

I cannot help but look above, as I do every night, for some faint glimmer of Dublin's floating lights. I like to know which way to cast my curses. Three years have gone by since the nobs lifted the best parts of the city into the sky. Three years since they left the rest of us to face slow extinction. Those without the scratch to buy a place, some without sponsors who just got overlooked, or those like me ... evidence the geneticists—and, no doubt, the bureaucrats that paid them—felt it best to leave behind.

Feck them all. I refuse to lay down and die.

Swearing under my breath, I tug lightly on my full-face respirator to make sure the seal is secure, both annoyed and reassured by the fine scratches on the Plexiglas shielding my eyes. With or without the mask, the smell and taste of ash haunt me. Mineral-heavy and sulfuric. I scarce remember life without the slick, silty particles everywhere. We live in a shadow-world. Gray ghosts of what we'd been: the people, the air, everything around us.

"Feck!" I swear aloud, if a little breathless, as I shove those thoughts away. I can't afford to spiral down that rabbit hole. Not again.

As I rev my quad utility vehicle, the engine coughs, then sputters, before catching again. Damned if I don't hear a bit of grinding as well. I don't have much time before she seizes from the ash. I tried to rig a filter before I headed out, but it gets through anyway. I reach behind me and check the load strapped to the back. Some I looted from a cottage long gone to dust; cans of food, a better knife than the one I've been carrying, a spare solid oxide fuel cell for the UTV, a box of bullets, but no gun. A good haul.

The rest of the stuff I found scattered over the countryside … mostly broken tech cast down with the rest of the trash from Dublin above, half-covered in shite. Things I may or may not be able to refurbish. Some to trade, some for our own use.

Mostly, nothing spectacular. Except the anti-grav engines. I've had some luck finding them out here, among the refuse. Banged to hell and all kinds of broken, but I worked in the anti-grav lab. I can fix them if I can find enough working parts. Don't know how we'll use the a-g engines yet, but they are the key to lifting us above the ash layer.

I surface from my thoughts as I feel something to my left. A tug on my awareness. A sense I wasn't born with, but I've learned not to ignore, courtesy of the feckin' geneticists. Do I understand it? No. Do I care? No. Let's just call it my consolation prize.

Slowing the UTV, I turn toward the sensation. With caution, I pull up to the remains of a cottage with just one wall and a chimney left to create an L, open to the ashy sky but sheltered on two sides. I scan the terrain around me, including above. Seeing no sign of threat, I leave the engine idling and climb from the vehicle, carefully stepping over the fallen fieldstones that used to make up the cottage. I am drawn to the far corner, where the walls still stand but the roof timbers litter the floor. There is just enough space for me to slip past them.

In the remains of what used to be some farmer's kitchen, I look down and see a root cellar hatch, a blessed remnant from another era. Whatever draws me is down there. It takes me ten minutes to clear the hatch, my skin crawling the whole time as I expect an ambush that never comes.

When I tug open the hatch, the faintest whiffs of must and mold make it through my respirator. I barely notice. My eyes go wide, and I nearly throw myself down into the cellar. To either side, old stores of moldering root vegetables are barely recognizable for what they were, but there in the back, its shape delightfully unmistakable, sits a five-gallon jug of water, blanketed in dust and ash but clearly unbreached.

There are times I don't curse those who made me the way I am.

The contents of that jug send my extra sense humming. It is all I can do not to stop and crack the seal, but to do so would ruin it. I nearly weep at the thought of that pure, clean liquid instead of the swill we run through the purifier. No matter how many times we filter it, the water we live on never sheds the taste of ash. My mouth feels twice as dry for want of a single drink. Instead, I haul the jug from its hidey-hole and over to the UTV. Huffing hard with the effort, I quickly nestle my find beneath the other items I've scavenged, as hidden and protected as I can make it. A girl can't be too careful.

I climb behind the wheel and head back toward town. Expecting someone to appear to steal my prize, I go faster and faster. Recklessly so. The UTV threatens to flip as it bounces over the hills. I lean back hard to compensate then let up on the accelerator.

I should have kept it gunned.

The engine gives out as the high-security lab building where I used to work comes into sight. We've made it our home. Not quite a biodome like they've built beneath the oceans—or the hills, as some claim—but the closest we can manage. Its nearness taunts me.

"Feckin' hell! Ye bloody piece o' shite! Now? Now ye have to break down?" I throw the gear shift into neutral and climb from the quad, yelling the whole time. "Sion, get yer arse out here! Maggie! Bran! Someone!" I don't wait. Can't afford to. I didn't risk encounters with pirates or gene-modified creatures as I trolled the wasteland just to have someone snatch my find a mere dozen feet from my door. I lower my head and put my right shoulder to the vehicle's open frame, then I throw my full weight into moving it.

I don't weigh much. No one does anymore. Well ... no one on the surface.

I grit my teeth and dig in, pushing with everything I have. All I manage is to inch it forward a foot or so.

Finally, someone comes up on the other side and joins me. I glance over in the haze but get no more than a vague impression of a familiar silhouette. Assuming it's one of the kids, I lower my head and strain once more, hard enough I would almost swear I feel the roll bar pressed to both shoulders. Relieved, I ignore the odd sensation as the vehicle picks up momentum.

I reach over to the dash and activate the remote my brother Callan had rigged for the large security door. As I wait for it to open wide enough for the UTV to pass through, I try real hard not to think about how he'd succumbed to acute silicosis soon after. We hadn't had a respirator to fit him, so he'd gone without. I can still picture him in his racing goggles, a damp cloth wrapped around his face and nose. Better than nothing, but in the end, enough volcanic ash eventually got through to scar his lungs until he coughed as black as any coal miner.

Clearly, I need to work harder at controlling my thoughts.

A deep sigh fogs my respirator and leaves me a little lightheaded. I curse beneath my breath once more as we finish pushing the vehicle inside, and I hit the remote to close and lock the door. When I look over to thank whoever came to my aid, no one is there.

✶

"What the hell?" I murmur.

Someone raps my knuckles sharply. I look down to find little Aislinn staring up at me.

"What are ye about, then?" I ask with a frown, though I know right well she's chastising my language. Her solemn gaze is reproachful, but she says not a word. Just as she hasn't since I found her huddled against her mother's corpse in the wastelands, two years ago.

I shuck my gloves to ruffle her hair, bright and golden and currently free of ash. *"Tá brón orm,"* I murmur in Irish. *I'm sorry.* She throws her arms around me in a rare hug, and I all but forget the mystery of who helped me. I smile, though there is no way she can see it, and gently disentangle her before she gets too ashy. "Go on, send the others to help unload while I get cleaned up," I tell her, my words a bit breathless by the time I'm done.

When she runs off through the doors separating the lobby from the labs, I step into what used to be a janitor's closet just beyond reception and close the door, flicking on the battery-powered lantern. First, I take off my respirator and draw a deep half-gasping breath. My first full breath in almost an hour, thanks to the ash gradually clogging my filter. Before I do another thing, I carefully inspect my mask: every seal, every strap, the gaskets, and glass. Satisfied it took no damage while I was climbing around the cottage, I pop out the spent filters—securing them in a sealed bin to later be rinsed for reuse—and clean everything else thoroughly with rubbing alcohol before inserting fresh filters and storing the mask on the shelf my nephew Sion and I share. He is still young enough my mask fits him; I will need to find a larger one soon, though. I will not let him go the way of his father, Callan.

Hearing a sudden clatter outside, I crack the door to see the children cleaning off my finds as meticulously as I just cleaned my mask. A single bank of bright LED lights—powered by generators we fight daily to keep alive—aids them in their efforts.

I wait for them to discover my prize. Aislinn finds it first and actually gasps, one of only a handful of times I've heard her utter a sound, other than in her sleep … and those do not bear mentioning. The sound is enough to draw the others' attention. I bite back a laugh, smiling as the children shout and cheer as they dance around the room, though the longing in their gazes breaks my heart.

Softly, I close the door and let them enjoy being children as I finish cleaning up.

Still smiling, I unsnap the restraints at my neck, wrists, and ankles, and strip off the thermal jumpsuit. My skin is a faint bluish-gray where the finer particles of ash have gotten through. I toss the jumpsuit in a linen cart, followed by the band I use to bind my breasts and the rest of my underthings. Last is the cap protecting my bare head. I draw it off and allow myself a brief wistful thought for my shorn locks. Barely a faint coppery stubble covers my head now.

I frown. Soon the older girls will join Sion in his daytime scavenging. They will need to be shorn as well. And taught how to bind themselves. The joy I felt just moments before fizzles and dies. Curse the feckers that left us here!

I finish my cleanup with a rag and a basin of water I filtered before I went out, left waiting in the janitor's sink for my return. Pulling on clean underthings and a fresh jumper, I return to the lobby.

The children are waiting for me, their eyes wide and bright.

Some sit on the counter, some sit in the chairs that remain from before Yellowstone erupted half a world away. Aislinn squats in front of the jug, staring at her reflection, her little butt thrust out for balance and her chin in her fists. Everyone, save her, turns to look at me.

I frown as I notice the other things I gathered in my foray, still on the counter where the children had placed them once they were clean. The jug made sense. It weighed more than any of them could lift. The rest …

"Yer not done," I said, my tone severe, certain my look resembled the one I'd received from Aislinn earlier.

"Aww, Chance!" they said in one voice, those that spoke. It's not my name, but it's all anyone knows me by anymore. Even myself.

I stare them down and frown a little deeper.

A few groans. A few guilty looks. Then the children slowly rise from their perches and make their way to the counter. Not one of them even glances at the water, though I know they want to. Sion takes responsibility for the ammunition and heads for the doors to the back, where the storage and living quarters are, in the hermetically sealed rooms the lab had originally used for sensitive testing. The others each pick up an item and follow.

Well, except for Aislinn. I doubt she realizes I've come out.

I walk over and scoop her up in one arm. With the other, I heave up the jug. Bracing each of them on a hip, I join my ragtag little family.

✶

I serve each of the children a small portion of delightful clean water and send them to sleep before I head toward the labs that are still labs. I check them all, as I do every night, first the hydroponics, then the protein and algae vats, all still thriving, though the scientists who minded them are gone. Maggie sees to their keeping, as her mother had before her passing. I don't bother with the airship wing, where the children sometimes play among the shells of half-built vessels.

I definitely skip the genetics lab, with its makeshift holding cell. It is empty now, though it hadn't always been. Old shame surfaces that I hadn't realized when the world was still 'good,' and the lab was just a job. True, I worked as a structural engineer in the anti-grav wing, but how could I not know what else took place? The kind of company I worked for? I myself was an unwitting test subject of those clandestine gene mods, though I didn't discover that until after, as abandoned as the poor soul left locked in that cell.

Gritting my teeth, I hurry past to the lab we're using for a storeroom to pick through my findings. I allow myself five ounces of water from the jug, which has already been installed on a dispenser left over from before our reality changed.

As I sip at my water, I'm unsure if I should curse this place. Whether we'd allowed it or not, the lab and the scientists that ran it —some rumored to hail from the Netherlands, where a rogue group called the Horsemen had practiced less-than-ethical genetics—were as guilty of mucking with our lives as those responsible for Dublin above. True, I can live on sixteen ounces a day of the most brackish or polluted water to be had, but no matter how much I drink, my mouth remains dry as dust.

Small consolation, but I also gained my uncanny ability to sense concentrations of minerals. That comes in handy in the wasteland, especially today. I never would have found the hidden stash of water otherwise, not that that makes up for being left to rot. Besides, I don't expect that second skill was intentional.

Must have been my faerie godmother at work.

As I move toward my pile of findings, my brow furrows and my lips purse. Something is missing, though I can't say what. I spread out the objects on the counter. A gacked game console I hope to refurbish for the kids, along with some games on a slimstick. Spare engine parts for the quad. The fuel cell. A couple of small anti-grav engines—one with fried wiring, the other, a cracked crankcase—clearly tossed from above.

There should be three. I *know* there were three.

Grumbling, I leave the room and head for the lobby, where the UTV waits for me to break it down and unclog it. I briefly squeeze my aching eyes closed and sigh. One more thing I have to do before calling it a night … or a morning.

As I round reception, I swear I hear something. A faint shuffle, followed by the decided absence of any sound. I stop and go still as adrenaline spikes my blood. I know this place better than I know myself. What should be here and what shouldn't. Closing my eyes, I frown and slowly pivot, letting my other sense speak to me.

Nothing. Or not what I expect. Nothing that feels the way a person does. There is something in the back of the quad, though. I edge my way over, braced and wary, alert. For a moment, I sway, and I grip the tubular roll cage of the UTV.

My missing a-g engine has a friend. As alike the first as to be a copy, only undamaged as far as I can tell. And they're both sitting in the back of my quad. What's more, the quad looks like it's been detailed. I squat down to inspect the engine, not quite mimicking Aislinn's earlier pose, but close enough.

I nearly land on my arse, but for my grip on the frame.

My free hand trembles as I reach out to stroke the engine's coils then jerk back. My fingers come away cleaner than Sion's plate after a meal. I lower myself to the ground with my back resting against the wheel, too stunned to wonder how the air smells like anything other than ash.

Who has been here, and how the hell did they get in? Better yet, why?

After a few deep breaths, I leave everything where it is for now. On edge, I patrol the building, checking every lock and security-shuttered window. Nothing is disturbed, save me. I go find my bed, but it is a long time before I can rest.

✶

My anti-grav engines presently number seven, four of them now working, thanks to parts I cannibalized from two of the others, not counting the one that appeared from thin air. And I don't. How can I trust something, not knowing where it came from? Or how it got there? The next morning, I'd asked the children. Not one of them had an answer … then or now. And none of them will own up to cleaning the UTV.

Again, I'd say it was my faerie godmother, only I don't trust that any more than before.

Hard to say why I bother, anyway. Looking for the engines. Not like they'll do us any good by themselves. Not much bedrock laying around waiting to be lifted into the sky, or fertile land to plop atop it. Let alone a city.

I laugh and almost can't stop, picturing our little lab perched on a bare rock in the sky.

Still, I can't give up. I'm a chancer, always ready to gamble life will be better one day even when it goes to shite. I have to be. The children need me, and so I hold tight to hope. Pulling on my jump-suit and my mask each night to brave the shadow-world and pry its treasures from its treacherous grasping hands.

Like tonight.

"Chance ..."

I turn, my mask poised above my head, in the middle of putting it on. Sion stands in the doorway. He looks worried. I set the mask down and turn to face him fully. Of all the children, he's the only one old enough to trust out on his own, nearly man-high, if not man-mass, but who is anymore? I keep him to the daylight hours, hunting information, mostly so I know where to steer clear of in the night, though he has grown skilled at ferreting out things we can use.

"What have you heard?" I ask.

He shifts and shakes his head. "Nothin'," he murmurs, his cheeks taking on a bit of blush as he looks anywhere but at me. "But ..."

I wait, patient, letting him work it out.

"But something doesn't feel right. Like someone's watching."

"I'll take care tonight," I tell him. "Keep the door locked and stay inside for now."

Sion nods and reaches behind him, handing me his aluminum baseball bat, the only treasure he has left from the time before, a gift from his American granddad. I sober as I accept it, realizing exactly how worried he must be.

What does he sense that I've missed?

We've had trouble before, though not so much recently. There aren't many left with the strength to do harm. Everyone is too busy surviving. Besides, those still around know we give of what we have when someone is in need. Most of them even look out for us, surely for the sake of the children. There are so few of them anymore, on the surface.

Still, no point in being careless. I secure the knife I found on the last run in a makeshift sheath strapped to my thigh, and I make sure Sion's aluminum bat rests beside the driver's seat of the UTV before heading for the wasteland.

I could stay closer, but the remains of the city muddle my extra sense, too many things compete for my attention. And too many others compete for those things. Most anything useful had long ago been claimed, anyway. In the countryside, I can breathe. Odd thing to say, but it's true. There is freedom in the wide-open spaces most have already given up on. If I squint my eyes and think real hard, I can even convince myself that the hills hold hints of green. I can picture the Earth shaking off its thick blanket of ash, grabbing for every bit of sun it can, despite the haze.

That's what I get for daydreaming.

Airship pirates drop down from the sky while my head is in the clouds. Just far enough ahead that I can stop … if I'm wise. I only see the ones before me, their tethers slack, and their bodies poised to pounce, but I have no doubt more land behind me. I don't bother reaching for my knife. Half of them have scatterguns, the rest either crossbows or the occasional pistol. They all have blades longer than mine. I should stop.

But then, whoever said I was wise?

I gamble they want the quad—or me—unharmed, and power through. Most curse and leap to the sides, but one laughs and jumps to land on what little hood the UTV has, gripping the roll bar with one hand and reaching for me with the other. Baring my teeth, I slam my foot on the brake. The other pirates laugh now as the one reaching for me flings back, swinging on his tether before landing on the ground. I move my foot from the brake to the accelerator and try to spin away to shoot off over the hills, but it's too late, the others close in. I am about to jump out and run, hoping to lose myself in the haze, when the winds whip up fierce and sudden. I cling to the frame as pirates are snatched through the air on their tethers as if in the grip of a vengeful god as the upper reaches of the storm toss the unseen airship about. I duck my head to protect my mask as black rain and chunks of hail pelt my arms, leaving welts in my flesh and dents in the quad.

As the pounding ends, I hear only my own panting and the faint screams of pirates above me. I can't help but hope they've bruises twice the size of mine by the time they reach their ship. Dropping my head to the steering wheel, I draw deep shuddering breaths, the air briefly clear in the wake of the storm.

The first thing I spy when I lift my head is a familiar silhouette on the path before me, half-seen in the haze. There is no way it is one of the children; the first time or this one. I notice an odd shimmer around him, like some kind of force field, and though his long dark hair obscures his face, it is clear he wears no mask or other protective clothing, just tweed trousers and a linen shirt, with Brocks on his feet. My eyes go wide, and I begin to shake, not knowing why, but more afraid of him than I was of the pirates. Before he can move, I floor the accelerator and spin the wheel, heading back toward home as fast as the quad will go.

✶

The children are asleep by the time I reach the lab. All but Sion. He waits for me at the door, silent and clearly still worried. I say nothing as I hand him his bat. By the time I am done cleaning up, he's gone. I smile and tear up a bit, though, on seeing a steaming cup of tea waiting on the counter. A proper cuppa, made with clean, fresh water and a real tea bag, from the scent wafting up from the plastic teacup. A sigh shudders through me.

It has been so long.

I sip the slightly sweet brew and savor the herbaceous tang of the tea. With one hand on the hilt of the knife I'd strapped back on after changing, I wander the building. Trying to calm my nerves? Or trying to make sense of the encounter on the hill? Either proves to be futile.

I find myself in front of the genetics lab staring pensively at the open cell, nothing more than a crude iron cage. All that remains inside is a bare cot, an empty tin plate, and a few tangled strands of long dark hair.

Faint memories surface as I stand there: *A huddled form wrapped in shadows and a thin blanket. Only his shivers told me he was still alive. Then low groans and a piercing eye staring out as the man struggled to sit up. It had been almost a week since the scientists fled. I hadn't even realized anyone else was there with me, let alone trapped. I couldn't imagine how he was even still alive. I was alone then, save my nephew, Sion. Frightened of what the stranger might do, but unable to leave him to die, I searched until I found a ring of keys, then tossed them in the cage, running to hide Sion and myself before the man could get free.*

I never knew what had happened to him. Before or after I'd found him.

Part of me finds relief in now knowing he is alive and well. Part of me is still deathly afraid.

Shuddering, I turn away, heading for the anti-grav lab. Tonight … the pirate attack … it woke me up. We aren't living here. We don't have a life anymore. We exist. Endless rounds of scavenging and cleaning and surviving with precious little joy or purpose. That's all anyone on the surface seems to have anymore.

Feck that.

Tonight's encounter with the bloody pirates has given me an idea. I can't float an island, but I can sure as hell get an airship into the sky. There are more than enough parts left behind to put together a small one, big enough for me and the children to live comfortably. I doubt we have the solid-cell propulsion engines they were designed for, but with four functioning anti-gravs, it won't matter. Get them rigged and all we'll need are maneuvering jets and a solar sail.

I can do that. I *will* do that …

I go to my desk with my mind already buzzing. Setting my teacup down, I pull a design tablet from my drawer. It still holds a charge from when I was working on the a-g engines but not much of one. I start keying in my ideas and sketching rough diagrams with the stylus just to get them down.

Hearing something, I turn to thank Sion for his thoughtfulness, but the breath goes out of me, and my tablet clatters to the desktop.

The man from my memories stares back at me from the doorway, leaning casually against the jamb. It is the first time I see him clearly. His features are strong and striking, rather than handsome. Sharp cheekbones and slashing brow, his dark gaze just as piercing as I remember.

I have to admit, he still scares the piss out of me.

But I can't show it.

"What are ye doing here?" I snap. "How the feck did ye get in?"

He doesn't answer.

I stand and move away, putting distance between us. I draw my knife once he can no longer see me do it.

"Ye saved me, will ye not let me return the favor … if not for yerself, then the children?"

I sneer over at him. "Do I look like I need saving?"

"Earlier, ye did."

My sneer turns into a glare, but I can't entirely concede the point. "Perhaps, but it's not like ye did the saving."

He chuckles, and I want to punch him in the face.

"Okay," he said, with a not-quite mocking bow. "How about I make yer life easier then, for all of ye?"

I struggle not to glance in the direction of the children. Maybe my efforts are pointless, but I have to tell myself he doesn't know where they are. Still, I will do *anything* to keep my children safe and provided for, no matter how I've come about them. "How?"

He flings his arm out, unerringly gesturing in the direction of the wasteland, in the direction of my encounter with the pirates. "Follow me, let me take ye to Underhill."

I'm less concerned about him being a rotter, now … and more concerned with him being a nutter. He reaches out to me, but I jerk away. "Do ye take me for a fool? *Underhill*? The land of the Sidhe? There's no such place. Faerie stories told to frighten children into behaving."

"There's always a chance of that," he answers. "But does it matter where we go if it sees you all safe?

"Think about it … Why have ye not screamed? Tried to get away?" He cocks a brow. "Shall I tell ye?"

He moves closer again, and I raise my knife right before him. Surprisingly, he doesn't impale himself upon it. He *tsks* at me and tilts his head to the side ever so slightly, looking nothing if not hurt. The look reminds me of Aislinn. I get the sense that it's meant to.

Moving slowly, he lifts his hand again, and this time I am powerless to shift away. He takes the knife from me and shocks me by sliding it back in my makeshift sheath, clearly confident that I'm no threat. I tremble as he reaches one hand toward the center of my chest, just shy of touching, and places his other hand over his heart.

Something akin to my special sense unfurls, and I gasp. It feels as if his hand presses me, though inches separate us.

What the hell did those gene hackers do to me?

"Here," he murmurs. "Right here is a piece of me. It calls to me, and I would do anything to keep it safe, to see it well. To see it free ..."

I stumble back at that, my fists coming up quicker than I can think.

He chuckles, lifting both hands palm out as he slowly steps back. "Not the way I meant it, love.

"They put a piece of me in ye, in the before time, when neither of us had a choice. I'm not saying I want it back, but I would like ye by my side, safe and tucked away from the hell up here."

I can't deny what he says. The truth echoes in my own heart even as he speaks.

"Ye've been so brave ... and so have the children. Forget about trapping yerself on a speck of dust in the sky ... join me beneath the hills where a whole world awaits ye."

I do not like the way he keeps mentioning the children. I'd rather he forgot all about them, but he seems all too aware.

I meet his gaze. He's moved in, his hand over my heart, and his forehead pressed to mine. It no longer matters to me if he believes we're off to faerie land, or whether this *Underhill* is a secret complex deep beneath the ground born of the tech of a shattered world. I grip his hand and use it as an excuse to step back.

"*Yer* my faerie godmother ...?"

He gives me an odd look, and I try again. "Ye left me the anti-grav engine, didn't ye?"

He grins but squeezes my hand tight enough I wince and grab his wrist, feeling the odd echo of my own grip. Something sly flickers in his gaze. I catch a glimpse of the shadow-world and I have to wonder what he was doing there when the pirates struck. I certainly don't believe it was coincidence.

"Why?" I ask, a bit numb as I wait for the answer. "Why, if ye don't want me to go?"

"I can't deny my own heart what it desires ..." His answer is too pat, too slick. I can feel the lie in it. I drop his hand and step back, whipping out my knife.

"It was a test." I speak the truth for him, my tone flat and dead to my own ears. "A test to confirm I can find them and fix them. Yer not here for me, or for the children. Ye want my ability to sense. Ye want a tech in yer camp." I don't give him a chance to tell me a lie. I feel the truth inside. Of that, he did not speak false. Whatever was done to us before the world crumbled, we are linked. I don't know precisely what he intends, but I sense it is not for my benefit, or the children's. I can't take the chance he will try to use them to influence me. And not knowing how he gets in I know only one way to stop him.

I bring my blade up under his ribs and through his heart before I can even think about it, before my thoughts can warn him, crying as his lifeblood pours out over my hands and his weight bears me to the ground.

I lay there as part of me dies, strangely loathed to let him pass alone. His mineral-rich blood floods my senses, taste, smell, and otherwise, until I actually miss being immersed in ash.

Even so, my resolve hardens.

I will do *anything* to protect my children.

I will also fight to give them a better life … not just survival.

We may not ever raise our own island to the sky, or succeed at piloting an airship up above, but my children and I will be free, not subject to someone else's whim, victim to their shadow-world.

And someday we will ride the clouds, if only in our dreams.

✶

Award-winning author and editor **Danielle Ackley-McPhail** has worked both sides of the publishing industry for longer than she cares to admit. In 2014, she joined forces with husband, Mike McPhail, and friend, Greg Schauer, to form her own publishing house, eSpec Books (www.especbooks.com).

Her published works include six novels, *Yesterday's Dreams, Tomorrow's Memories, Today's Promise, The Halfling's Court, The Redcaps' Queen*, and *Baba Ali and the Clockwork Djinn*, written with Day Al-Mohamed. She is also the author of the solo collections *Eternal Wanderings, A Legacy of Stars, Consigned to the Sea, Flash in the Can, Transcendence, Between Darkness and Light*, and the non-fiction writers' guide, *The Literary Handyman,* and is the senior editor of the *Bad-Ass Faeries* anthology series, *Gaslight & Grimm, Side of Good/Side of Evil, After Punk,* and *Footprints in the Stars*. Her short stories are included in numerous other anthologies and collections.

In addition to her literary acclaim, she crafts and sells original costume horns under the moniker The Hornie Lady Custom Costume Horns, and homemade flavor-infused candied ginger under the brand of Ginger KICK! at literary conventions, on commission, and wholesale.

Danielle lives in New Jersey with husband and fellow writer, Mike McPhail, and two extremely spoiled cats.

To learn more about her work, visit www.sidhenadaire.com or www.especbooks.

DUSTY ROSE COMES TO DC

BRENDA COOPER

Secret Service Director Subil Moonsky leaned against the wall on a private view balcony in POTUS Tower looking down at scorched skies boiling in a twisted windstorm. The floating city rode so high that a different wind touched her cheek, lighter and cold as snow. She glanced up. Bright stars dotted the silken black, making the three spires of DC feel more a trio of spaceships than floating cities.

Subil felt like a tiny speck of sadness in a vastly sad universe. The raw emotion sat on her like the wrong uniform, her unease amplified by the darkness and the storm. She shifted to resettle the gear on her belt. Stunners and lasers and lights and a mask. More. It weighed her down. An irrational urge to chuck it over the side drove her fingers to the fastening. But these symbols represented her duty, her life's ambition. She snatched her hand back, held it with her other hand. What had come over her? The pressure of the many logistics and defenses and tiny perfections that had to be right?

The election of 2304 was no surprise, of course, and another four years of President Gail Smith wouldn't hurt anything. Or change anything. On Inauguration Day, it was Subil's duty to focus on strategy, to allow her augmented mind to pull clues together.

President Smith would be anxious. She had been on every other Inauguration Day. The woman was the center of Subil's daily world, and decent enough, if cold. There had been a time when an American President's terms lasted a year if they were lucky, but Smith's father, the second President Smith, had brought peace between the three Towers, and President Gail Smith had kept that peace for six terms. Like the balcony Subil stood on, the President's peace ran above a storm of threats from inside and outside of the Towers.

Someday, the massed forces outside of DC would come to take everything away from them. Subil was privy to many briefings that detailed DC's worries about attacks from the cities of old enemies like Russia and China. Worse, and closer to home, airship pirates populated the skies like locusts. DC's defenses had always prevailed, but her father had warned Subil many times over that she must always believe that DC could be broken.

The bright light of a laser cannon arced somewhere just below and to the right, then flashed gold on successful impact. She frowned and touched her ear. "Jackson? What did we just kill?"

"An airship or two. We'll look as soon as the storm blows out."

They'd expected unwanted visitors. Not much news passed in or out of DC, but election results would have escaped. Still. "They came through this storm?"

"Yes. And there are more airships outside the borders."

"An unusual amount?"

"No."

It shouldn't worry her, but it did. "Report everything you find." She shook herself, trying to shed the unwelcome ennui that still clung to her skin like smoke. From where Subil stood, she had a long climb to reach the White House. Uneven steps spiraled up, and up, and up. Morning light began to spill down the steps, illuminating corners and cracks. By the time she finished the climb, her legs tingled, and she had calmed the edges of her emotions enough to school them away from all but the sharpest bot observers.

The White House loomed over the grounds where the inauguration would occur. Lawn, trees, and walkways lined the Mall to the Washington Monument. The two icons of power occupied the highest flat location on the Tower. The craggy top of the floating city rose far higher, silver and gray streaked with black, beautiful in the luminescent early light.

Subil passed two of her agents, offered encouraging nods as they passed with salutes. Seats had been arranged in the open plaza, bunting placed, three bandstands wired and ready for speeches and music. Even though it looked perfect, she stalked between the rows of white chairs and climbed up on each stage. She made a minion take one row of chairs away to create a wider aisle. She made another move one microphone a foot to the right so the President would be protected from line-of-sight should somebody climb the impossible back wall of the spire. President Smith had survived two assassination attempts in the last decade, and Subil herself had been credited with uncovering the first one.

She wasn't satisfied, but was she ever? Her jaw thrummed and she touched her ear. "Jackson?"

"We found a woman. Alive. You'll want to talk to her."

Alive? After a fall through that windstorm? And worth her talking to *today*? "Give me forty minutes."

The line hissed closed. Jackson was too efficient to waste a breath saying goodbye. She called Hastings and turned the circus of preparation over to him. But before she escaped, the one voice she couldn't ignore called out, "Subil! Have you got a moment?"

It wasn't a question. Subil nodded and turned toward her charge, her master, her President, her verbal sparring partner. So many things this woman was to her. No friend, though. Never that.

President Smith wore a long robe over her thin frame. Her bare, angular face looked hard as the stone they stood on. It would be softened with color and nanodecos for her speech, years and pain covered for the masses. But right now, she looked flinty and worried. She nodded sharply at Subil. "Thank you."

Subil inclined her head and waited.

"This storm drives worry through my bones. Tell me that the skies are clear and we are safe."

Subil looked up. "The skies are never clear in DC. But I will do everything I can to keep you safe."

The President nodded, shifting on her feet. "I am ... more worried than I want to be. It would be a symbolic day for an attack. Perhaps the Russians?"

Subil kept her face a mask. "Shifts are doubled today. I added retired agents back in disguise. I will keep you safe, Madame President."

President Smith sighed. "Perhaps it is only the wind. It bothers me." As if to underscore her point, a small puff of the same cold wind that had touched Subil's cheeks earlier lifted a strand of the President's dark hair. She touched Subil's shoulder. "I am grateful for you." Then she turned away, hurrying toward her morning briefing.

The President's touch was as rare as Subil's strange sadness. She hadn't expected the day to be so strange.

Subil slid into the down-elevator. As soon as the door closed behind her, she opened a window into Jackson's optic nerve. He blinked three times in a set pattern, acknowledging her presence. He was finishing a sentence. "—must know that is a lie."

The angle of view told her Jackson loomed over the woman.

The captive looked up, licked her lips, but said nothing. The girl was naked, her skin dusty. Old tear tracks streaked dusty cheeks. Maybe twenty-five years old, maybe thirty. No lines in her face, and a calm smile that probably masked panic. She answered Jackson calmly, as if he weren't pressing into her personal space. "I came to invite your President to a gala."

"To a party of people suing for *peace*?" Jackson's voice sounded credulous. "And you still think we should come after we destroyed your airships?"

She didn't look as afraid as she should. She even smiled. "Yes. You must come. It is written."

Written? The elevator bounced under Subil's feet, and she severed her connection to Jackson's vision. Walking while seeing with someone else's eyes was for experienced field agents or robots, and she was not fully either. Too bad the captive was naked—her clothes might have provided clues about prosperity or origin. Subil reviewed what she *had* been able to see as she jogged down the sterile rock corridor towards the cells. The woman's muscles seemed normal, healthy even. That was seldom true of anyone they captured. Her right wrist was swollen, sprained or possibly broken, and one knee bruised. No harm had come to her face. In other circumstances, she might be a beauty.

Subil swept into the interrogation cell. Jackson, dressed in regulation black with his hair pulled back so tightly that the bones in his face stood out, still stood over the captive. A scowl amplified the effect. The woman was getting under his skin.

He glanced up as Subil entered, leaving her name unspoken. She stood beside him, her head at his shoulder. The captive looked smaller in person, and more colorful. Her dark eyes had flecks of green and gold in them, and they shimmered slightly. Overlays? What did she see with them? The faint dust on her skin looked almost pink. It glittered slightly, almost pretty. Surely makeup.

Subil knelt down and met the woman's gaze straight on. "Why are you here?"

She smiled. "We came to invite the President to a party."

Subil held still, unreactive.

"We want to meet her. We have made a great peace on the outside. We want her to come and preside over it with us, and see that ..." She paused. "...the United States of America is dead as we knew it, its boundaries smudged and its capitals destroyed." She glanced at the wall, through the wall, as if she could see the monument and the White House far above her. "Mostly. But America is not dead in spirit. We need our capital city, our leader." With that, her shoulders relaxed as if they had lost a weight.

Subil stepped back, wary. The woman had risked death for this? Her companions had already died for this? Jackson had been right to call her. Something was off. "I will deliver your invitation to the President. But she is very busy and unlikely to come. Tell me how you arrived here."

She raised her eyes. "We came from the New Mississippi."

A chill shivered up Subil's spine. The great river was gone, the state with it, buried inside a dead history book or three. "We?"

"We came together. We knew that not many would get through, that the District of Columbia is defended by forces we don't understand. But we are making a new world and we were sent to invite President Smith to come and help us."

How simplistic. "The President's duties are in DC" She let a beat pass and then whispered, "Tell me about New Mississippi."

The captive hesitated, then looked directly at Subil. "The original Mississippi divided the country, cutting it in two. It was hard to cross, hard to manage, but it gave water to millions. Millions." She stopped, as if the very shape of the word filled her with wonder. "Millions drank from the Mississippi. Then Yellowstone ... Nothing about the old division remains. No trace of the river as it was. But we are creating a new thing that unites. A river of goods, of trade, of hope. We do not wish for DC to remain separate and dark and scary. We want you to join us."

Not for nothing. And they weren't a bigger force than DC or Subil would have heard of them. Surely. "Where is New Mississippi?"

The woman's thin fingers tapped her own heart. "Everywhere."

Subil reached out to touch the woman's arm. "Where did it start?"

The woman flinched at her touch and looked down. "Near the original delta. Our river runs south to north."

Why had she flinched at Subil's touch?

"Come." Jackson touched Subil's arm, and she preceded him through the door.

Jackson's office looked like an empty box. He touched a point on the wall, and a table and two chairs rose from the ground. Real-time video of the woman flashed into view, filling a full wall with the woman's face set in a contemplative expression and her hands resting palms-down on her knees.

Jackson led Subil to the closest seat and took the other. A robot bustled in with a cup of hot tea exactly like she preferred it, bitter and steaming. She cupped it in her hands, recalling her earlier melancholy. Subil's reaction to the woman wasn't quite fear. Something deeper. She caught Jackson's wary eye. "Why did you want me here?"

"I found her on the ground, pieces of airship all around her. Pieces of something else too, some kind of escape pod. They expected to be shot down. The two with her had safety pods as well, but they died. One opened his door, and the dogs ate him; the other's pod shattered and smeared broken bones everywhere." He gestured at the video. "Our prisoner cried once, after I left her in there and before I went in to talk to her. Otherwise, she's worn that damned calm like a mask. She's not a bot, not highly modded. But there was more tech in her airship than I expected. A rich pirate?"

Subil grunted. "Would a pirate speak of peace and invitations? She looks like she's been brainwashed." She blinked, recalling past briefings. "There is a DNA mod that gives humans a zen-like calm. It was a rage ten, twenty years ago." It had started in SCOTUS. After a year, the President had banned it; she wanted DC able to fight.

Jackson glanced at her. "Maybe. I remember. We recovered some of the broken bones. They're being analyzed."

Subil had half an hour left. The soft sadness had risen a bit, winding around her windpipe. "The proclamation of peace has to be a weapon," she mused. "Doesn't it?"

He recognized it as a question. "The ceremony will be safe. I will watch."

Subil stood. "Give her something to make her tell the truth. Set a minder on me, and then go check on the body you brought back. Ask the worms if they know anything or if there have been more airships. Even outside the borders. They're supposed to know that."

Although he nodded and smiled, she knew he didn't like leaving her alone with the woman. Still, the minder would record, and Jackson would watch later, when she hadn't given him other things to do. Privacy was an illusion of the moment. She felt like she had it when she stood at the edge of the spire and looked down, but she of all people knew that was, at best, illusion.

As she opened the door, the woman looked at her curiously.

Subil sat, carefully, choosing a position she could spring up from if needed, her legs in front, half bent, her back resting against the cold wall of the cell. "Tell me about this peace."

The woman blinked, her strange eyes again registering something. But Subil's eyes could call up any camera in the city. So she let it be, waited. The truth drugs would have come in through the air. Subil was immune, but the woman probably was not. She might already want to tell Subil everything in her small and soon-to-be shattered heart.

Eventually, she smiled. "There is enough health now. Forests and birds, wild animals, and streams of clear water. It is time to rebuild instead of just survive. We have forged safe roads between floating cities." Her eyes narrowed a tiny bit. "Except here. No one is safe coming here. This is a place of original sin, the most critical place we must change for humanity to heal." She took a deep breath. "You are invited into the glorious future we are creating." Her eyes now looked past Subil, as if she stared at something beyond the walls of her cell. "We have been trying to touch DC for years. Everyone who comes in dies. It is like a sore on the face of the world we are creating, but it was once something glorious."

The captive dripped with hope. Subil swallowed, unable to imagine feeling such hope, especially after being shot out of the sky by an enemy.

"We want to meet the leader of the Towers. There is power in legend. DC is like Camelot, a story that many still remember. We don't believe that DC should be feared."

Even though the others who came with this captive had died? Subil smiled at the stranger. "It must have taken great courage to come here."

Her tongue flicked out and wet her lips. "There was a woman statue—lady liberty—who welcomed everyone. Do you still have her?"

"She drowned."

The captive swallowed and looked away.

Subil didn't voice the sigh that coiled on top of the sadness lodged in her throat. This woman could be a weapon, or at the least, a misinformation bomb. She had survived the scan, so she posed no danger that DC understood. Subil kept her voice soft. "You do not need to know about our leaders."

The woman sat still and quiet.

Eventually Subil whispered into the quiet. "Tell me more about New Mississippi."

The woman smiled again, looking a little dreamy. Undoubtedly touched by the drugs. "It is a river of trade, a river of people, a river of knowledge. It is a river of all the things we need to become. But hatred poisons water, so we are rooting it out."

There it was. The religious bent that had coughed up the words about written prophecy. Maybe the danger was also here. Religion had harmed many in the Old World, and wasn't allowed in DC "How do you root out hatred?"

"We change it." Total calm on her face. Serene as hell.

Subil shivered. "With?"

"Love."

Either the drugs hadn't gotten to her after all, or she truly believed in naïve things. "And love changes the world? How does that happen?"

"With magic."

Subil shook her head and stood, ready to leave.

The captive's smile flashed with white, healthy teeth. Her eyes widened, the strange swimming colors in them captivating. "We must all become more than we were. That is the only way forward. Otherwise, we are full of hatred and fear. Do not be afraid."

Subil stiffened and turned. As the door snicked closed behind her, she let the sigh escape, although the sadness stayed with her. Her finger felt cold against her ear. "Jackson. What about the bones?"

"Analysis suggests DNA alterations at almost three percent."

"Describe the changes."

"They are more compliant. As you suggested. More likely to attract and be attracted by others. I suspect less violent. The CIA worms are doing some more digging, checking for other changes. The man had an implant we don't see in the woman."

Subil nodded, unsurprised. Most people were around one percent different from the old human norm based on both natural and unnatural mutations. Subil had almost two percent change herself, Jackson as well. Some engineered. They were faster and smarter. Resistant to many diseases. Other changes mattered more than DNA. She and Jackson had implants and nanotech that tuned them to the artificial intelligences in the Tower. "The woman has no other detectable changes?"

"Not that we've found so far."

A curious question rose in Subil. One she almost never asked. "Do you know her name?"

"Rose."

"Did she tell you?"

"It was on her clothing. She wore a pale mauve uniform with a riverbank and a bunch of painted flowers on the back. It had the word on its chest, and when I addressed her with it, she turned her head."

The White House had a rose garden. It had yielded the flowers for the centerpieces for tonight's state dinner. She rubbed her eyes, wondering why she was thinking such inane thoughts when she needed to be assessing the risk the stranger posed. "I have to go."

"Shall I take care of her?"

He meant kill her. Most captives lasted a day, maybe two. Dropping them onto the ground below the city was a death sentence, although anyone who had met people as important as Jackson or Subil didn't get even that infinitesimal chance at life. They were merely gassed to sleep. The word *yes* started to form on Subil's lips but sank into the sadness she was still unable to shake. "Not yet."

"Very well."

"Send me what the worms learn. And analyze her harder. Tell me what's in Rose's DNA."

"Of course."

Back at the inauguration grounds, the activity level had risen as suited servant bots lined up to seat people. The human teenagers who would help the most important guests from the other two Towers to their seats milled awkwardly, some talking to each other, and others deep in conversation with bots. Subil smiled, remembering when she had led one of the dour SCOTUS judges to her seat for the last inauguration of President Smith's father. Teenaged Subil had felt certain she would screw up something important. But she hadn't, and neither would these youngsters.

Her map told her the President was already in the dressing room, the mad prep to make her seem young and beautiful started.

The twenty-four justices would have left the imposing SCOTUS Tower, the fifty-two Senate members and the hundred and four House members on their way from the larger and plusher LOTUS Tower. All together, they would bring three hundred and six more agents to this place, in addition to all of Subil's own. The most important people in DC would all be here, except for one Senator chosen by lottery to be the President-in-Waiting and the one SCOTUS chosen as Judge of the Apocalypse.

Everyone who wasn't performing some other duty like caring for the sick would be here. Schools and stores had closed. The great aerial tramways that connected the City-Towers had transformed into ferries for the most important. The line of lesser guests waiting at the gates shone with color, with glittering gems, with fabulous outfits streaked with metals. And who could blame them? On most days, DC was boring for the thousands of people populating the Towers, and the mayor spent hours keeping them happy enough that they didn't kill themselves or anyone else.

What had Rose said? That *love kept away fear*?

The mayor used entertainment-infused adrenaline in the form of games and contests.

It wasn't love, she thought, *and it doesn't work for everyone.* She swallowed, angry with herself. When had she ever thought love would conquer anything? When had it ever?

Maybe nothing was love. No one loved President Smith. She was too cold. Like the wind that stole a yellow scarf from one of the people in line, sending it scudding over the heads of a hundred people before someone caught it. She shivered and turned away, closing her eyes to bring up images of the President stalking triumphantly toward the inauguration lunch with her cabinet members. Should she interrupt to report her visit with Rose?

Surely not. But not reporting nagged at her. Something was wrong and had felt wrong all day. She contacted her agents and requested five minutes of the President's time.

✶

President Smith wore a white dress with a pale blue wrap. The wrinkles had been fluffed out of her face with drugs and her cheeks puffed with some magic Subil was still too close to middle age to need. But the President's eyes and voice were cold. "Yes, Subil."

"A briefing, Madame President." She stepped into a box-of-quiet in the corridor, one designed to contain sound. The President and two of Subil's agents joined her inside of the red-colored square on the carpet that defined the boundaries of the box. "We shot down three airships."

The President nodded, crossed her arms. Airships were frequently helped down out of DC's skies.

"One person lived. A woman. She wanted me to bring you an invitation."

President Smith blinked but didn't otherwise move. One of Subil's agents leaned in.

Outside of the box, tastefully dressed people and their minders streamed by, some glancing furtively toward the box and others obviously making sure the agents knew they were not looking at something they should not see. Subil continued. "They want you to meet them at some conclave where they are building a peace. That is what they said. A peace. As if it were a building."

President Smith raised a single eyebrow. "And you believe her?"

"Of course not. But the woman is healthy and seems sincere. She carries no weapons. I wasn't going to tell you, but someone with resources worked very hard to assure her survival, and I thought you ought to know." Subil hesitated. "She does not seem sane, but she appears to be the healthiest person we have captured in my lifetime. She's been well-fed and physically trained but appears to have no mods." She remembered Rose's eyes. "Well, few mods. But there *are* DNA changes. We are doing further analysis."

"Do you consider this one woman a danger to my inauguration?"

"Of course not." Except ... that ineffable sadness, and the strangeness of hope. She owed the President honesty. "The experience of meeting her unnerved me. I cannot say why."

The President took a long breath and softened almost imperceptibly. "I have been unnerved all day. If you do not believe it is a current danger we will proceed. My audience is here."

"The woman is locked up. I don't see how she presents danger."

"She is not dead?"

"I want to study her."

"Don't be too kind. We will talk about her this evening, after the last ball." President Smith backed out of the quiet box.

Half an hour later, the last of the teenagers had accompanied the last of DC's leadership to their seats. Subil's worry had risen. She kept remembering Rose's hopeful face, the beautiful pattern in her eyes, and the calm manner in which she spoke.

Mississippi. A river of connection.

DC had always been alone, through all the generations of Subil's family. It was supposed to be alone.

There was no more United States, but was there something else for DC to lead? The people who lived here now were not peacemakers or leaders. Their own affairs consumed them. But they had never seen an outsider. What if they met Rose?

The first drum notes of the band started; the vast audience slowly stilled. From her vantage point above where the President would speak, Subil watched the colorful crowd sit, a wave of movement that traveled from behind the standing legislators to the security fence. Next, the legislators themselves sat, House first, then Senate. The members of SCOTUS stood for a full beat then rested together as one being, one line of severe black creating an oval front row beneath the still-empty dais.

Such tight ceremony. So practiced. She swallowed, pleased and disturbed. Were they their own worst enemy? Caught in their fears? What if something good had happened?

The Vice President introduced President Smith and stepped back. The President had added a black over-cloak to her dress, a touch of power. "I am pleased to see the strength of the District of Columbia arrayed here below me. Pleased to be asked, once more, to lead this great district so that we may remain strong in anticipation of a future when we once again rule the world."

The old words. They sounded different this morning. Like they might mean something. She had heard them a thousand times, maybe more. But had she ever *heard* them?

"We have done well these last four years. We have increased our trained security forces *and* the number of artists in all of the Towers. We have beaten back every attack on us."

The audience should be standing, clapping. As one. Instead they sat still. Even the regular people, who almost never sat at an event, much less at Inauguration Day.

The President hesitated for a breath. Enough for Subil to notice even if no one else did. "There had been a peace between and among the Towers of our world ...."

Subil's inner ear buzzed. She tucked a strand of hair behind her right ear, touching the lobe of her right ear for the briefest second to allow Jackson's voice to hammer through. He sounded winded, almost staccato. "The wind. Get everyone inside. Get a mask on the President."

"What?"

"The wind has a drug in it. It slows you down. It makes you question. Rose is screaming that it makes peace."

Subil didn't understand. The wind bore peace? She listened to her memories of Rose. "Didn't she say they brought love?"

"Put your mask on."

She fumbled for it, unsure why she should do such a thing. What threat?

"Now!"

Jackson, telling her what to do? But her fingers slid the mask free of its pouch, felt the smooth surface like a familiar friend. She had drilled this a hundred times but never needed it.

The President continued speaking below her. "… laws that have done more than keep us safe. They have kept us happy and …"

She flipped the mask open and pressed it to her face. As the edges sealed against her skin she missed a breath, expertly holding air inside her lungs and then shifting rhythm to match the mask's optimal cadence for airflow. Each breath forced its way into her lungs, and each exhale took some of her sadness with it. She took five deep, cleansing breaths while the President moved to talk about the power of the Legislature and Jackson spit details into her head. "They have three airships above us. *Above us.*"

The three spires rode the air so high Subil could see the tops of distant mountains on rare, clear days.

"They have been releasing a gas into the winds, maybe even directing the wind. We're still analyzing it. It seems to dull thinking."

Directing the wind? Who except DC could do such a thing? As her head continued to clear, her body coiled with the desire to act.

Below her, the President spoke and the audience sat.

She blinked up the map that showed the location of each of her staff, marked all of them who stood behind the President, who waited in alcoves, who would be less visible. She tagged them quickly, her mind and flicking eyes enough to identify them for her message. "Masks. Now."

There.

But she had almost failed to get her own on. She had fumbled. "Now!"

She waited, giving them time, assessing. An unseen enemy, unfelt, unheard. "How, Jackson? How?"

"New technology. Light enough for the stratosphere."

She glanced up. A few thin clouds. Nothing else.

"They don't have to be near enough to see. It's everywhere now, over our whole territory."

Jackson might be untouched. His air was scrubbed. "How did you find it?"

"A worm noticed a pack of dogs playing with another pack."

Huh? The dogs were hybrids, part mech, part extension of the city, but still in largely biological bodies. "Thank them." She stared over the crowd. "Everyone seems calm."

"Like Rose."

Shit. *Like Rose*. She started down the hidden steps, plotting each move that would get her to the President, who she would get a mask from, how to make sure they didn't cause panic. Commands spilled from her like rain, Jackson listening and sometimes adding, each sentence moving a staff member or touching her counterparts. The cold stair rail steadied her. The sadness was gone, finally, and only purpose remained. "What's next? Do they think we'll follow them to Mississippi? Or are they about to attack?"

"I don't know yet."

Hot anger surged through her, followed by resolve and energy. Whatever plan the invaders had, she would outwit them. She raked the fingers of her free hand through her hair, drawing light scratches on her scalp, releasing a thousand nanobots to sharpen her thoughts.

It felt good to feel like herself!

As she slid the President's mask over her nose and mouth, she gave the command for all of the waiting Secret Service to do the same for their charges, for the other, lesser trained security staff to help hurry the regular people away.

President Smith's eyes widened, and she leaned into Subil, whispering, "What is it?"

"Breathe deeply. Come with me."

President Smith took three following steps, guided by Subil's hand on her elbow, and then shook herself, standing slightly straighter. Subil passed the President to four of her best agents and hurried to meet her counterparts from the other Towers to direct and defend and save DC.

✶

Six hours later, Subil sat at a round table in her office staring at pictures of a clear sky. The airships had gone. Without a trace. Whoever they were—New Mississippi or simply pirates—they had fled. No shots fired, no damage, no aggression. DC forces followed, of course, but the winds in the stratosphere favored the invaders.

"Come," President Smith demanded.

The five-minute walk seemed to take longer. The President pulled her roughly onto a box of silence. As soon as they were both enclosed, she hissed, "You did not perform."

Subil nodded. "I am sorry." There was no excuse she could make. Was there ever? For a threat you couldn't see? "I should have anticipated that attack vector."

"Does this have anything to do with the woman you caught?"

Subil didn't hesitate. "Almost certainly."

"Go to her and connect me via video. I want to see this threat before we kill her."

As Subil headed for the elevator, every human she passed wore a mask. It reminded her of pictures of the great pandemic of 2291 when a rabid flu had killed half the population of LOTUS and only slightly fewer in the other two Towers. The air still registered as ever so slightly tainted, and Subil left her mask on until she was in the elevator on her way to see Rose.

Jackson waited in the nearby room, watching on the wall, while Subil patched President Smith in and headed for Rose's door. No one had spoken to her since Subil's last visit, although robotic attendants would have catered to her physical needs. Rose's nakedness made her look vulnerable, maybe particularly since her head was bowed. She stirred as Subil entered, pushed the tangled hair from over her eyes. "What time is it?"

"Six in the evening." Subil leaned on the wall. Rose sat in her chair, still apparently unconcerned. She hadn't been getting any gas down here. So whatever created her unusual calm, it was not the air.

Rose smiled faintly, her smile looking as sad as Subil had felt that morning in the balcony. "The inauguration is over?"

Subil nodded. "It went well. The ceremony is always a favorite for people who live here."

Rose smiled wistfully, apparently nonplussed. *Had* she known about the airships? "No one from outside has seen the tops of the Towers. Is the spire still there? The Washington Monument?"

"Yes. Please tell me more about New Mississippi."

Rose blinked. "I told you everything. We are traders and city-dwellers coming together to help each other out."

"Peaceful?"

"Almost always. The world has not finished healing."

"Tell me again why you came here?"

"We wanted your attention."

Which they had gotten. But that was for Subil to know. "It's possible we will want to contact the river someday. How can we do that?"

Rose smiled. "I can take you to them."

Subil swallowed. No, it wasn't going to be. She would be surprised if Rose saw the dawn. If the President didn't order her killed, Subil would. DC would not be drawn into danger, not on her watch.

✶

Two hours later, Subil entered the Oval Office. She had climbed up in near darkness, her thoughts blacker than the sky, her eyes periodically flicking up toward the stars, as if any enemy would be able to come in from above them again.

The President looked up from the pile of papers she was at least pretending to read. "Is she dead yet?"

"She is." Subil swallowed, unexpectedly unhappy.

"Am I safe, Subil? Are the skies clear?"

"The skies are never clear over DC."

"No," the President said. "They never are." She stood. "So can you explain to me why, for the first time ever in my *entire* life, I want to leave DC and see the world?"

Subil shifted uneasily. "I cannot. But I feel it, too. It must be an after-effect of whatever the wind bore in."

"What this woman sent us."

"If you will," Subil sighed. "More likely, what her people sent us. New Mississippi."

President Gail Smith raised an eyebrow. "That river was dangerous. It killed many."

"It did, Ma'am."

"Dismissed."

"I understand." And with some prejudice. Subil had failed to keep the peace. It should bother Subil, but it did not. As she left the President behind and started home to her small flat on the White House grounds, Subil felt light on her feet. She realized that she, too, wanted to peek out into the world. She shivered, as if some part of her hated that idea in spite of the fact that it was a good one. A stray thought burned into her brain. *Maybe they should breed more packs of dogs. And use them to keep DC in, as well as others out.*

Or maybe they shouldn't. Her thoughts weren't lining up like they should.

She called Jackson. "Did you find out what was in Rose's DNA?"

"Not yet. We will."

Instinct forced one more question from her. "Did you save her body?"

He sounded slightly offended at the question. "Of course."

"Did you analyze the dust on her skin?"

"Dust?"

"Her skin had a dust on it that looked like makeup. What was in it? Was it just makeup?"

"I don't recall if I … I don't know." She imagined him pulling up a video and checking for the fine star-like grains glittering in the light of the past. It took a full two minutes before he said, "I'll find out."

"Thank you."

His voice softened. "You're welcome, boss. I'll call as soon as I know anything. Can I do anything else for you?"

"No."

It was only half an hour later when Jackson called back. "Did you touch her?"

"I did."

"Stay there. Send me a blood sample. Do not leave your house."

"Of course."

During the wait, while Jackson analyzed and she stayed inside, she found herself humming. She fiddled with her houseplants, enjoying the curves of the stems and the soft hairs on the undersides of the leaves of one. They were all genemod, of course, and beautiful for it. As was she, as was Jackson, as was Rose. What difference did it make if Rose had changed her? That was what had happened. She knew it now, but it was very difficult to find a reason to be angry. They were all beautiful together, all of them. She and Rose and Jackson and the President and every one of her staff. Even the CIA worms. They were all beauty.

In her bed, she pulled up one of the cameras that looked over the edge of the world. There was no sign of the storm that had roiled the sky beneath her that morning. Rather, the periodic lights of the dead neighborhoods below her looked as pretty and mysterious as the stars above, both part of a strange world that the three Towers of DC hung near but didn't touch.

To her surprise, a tear streaked down her cheek.

✶

Brenda Cooper is a technology professional, a writer, and an editor. She holds an MFA from Stonecoast and is an Imaginary College Fellow at the Center for Science and the Imagination, CSI, at Arizona State University. Her fiction has won two Endeavour awards and been shortlisted for the Phillip K. Dick Award. Brenda's most recent work includes the novels *Wilders* and *Keepers*, which are stories of climate and robots set in the Pacific Northwest and her next novel will be *The Making War*, out in October of 2020. Brenda is the IT Director for a successful local construction company. She lives in Washington State where she can be found riding bikes and walking dogs when she isn't at work or writing.

CLOUT CITY

JODY LYNN NYE

"Who sent you?" the big, hairy male demanded, showing long, sharp teeth. His thick fur protruded awkwardly from the neck and cuffs of the dark blue uniform he wore. Insignia on his collar, flat, billed cap, and left breast gleamed gold, showing he must be a person of importance. Several others of his kind lurked behind him in the shadows. Captain Fleury Marconi couldn't see their faces, only the gleam of their teeth and eyes.

Fleury huddled into the corner of the rough, yellow-painted room into which she had been shoved. The black-haired woman was tall and fit enough to climb all the rigging inside her lighter-than-air craft, but she didn't stand a chance against even one of these behemoths. Waves of frigid air made her clutch the collar of her fur-lined parka close around her neck. In her entire thirty-two years, she had never been that cold.

"My crew," she croaked, her voice breaking with fear and strain. "Are they all right?"

"Who sent you?" the male asked again, ignoring her question.

"Who sent us?" Fleury echoed, puzzled. "Nobody sent us."

"Then you ain't welcome here," he said. "We don't want nobody sent. You invaded Chicago territory wit'out permission, and that has consequences."

"Sir, there are pirates out there!" she exclaimed, looking from her questioner to the nearly unseen people in the shadows. "We were on our way east, toward Boston, when three black-and-white airships came out of the clouds and tried to take my vessel, the *Magellan*. They shot at us! Part of my hull was holed by their harpoons. I ordered my helmswoman to take evasive maneuvers. Suddenly, we saw your city floating ahead of us. All we wanted to do was take shelter behind it while we effected repairs. When your security ships surrounded us, we were surprised. I haven't really heard of Chicago trading with other cities. We weren't sure this Tower was inhabited."

"Pirates, huh?" the male said, thoughtfully. He picked his fearsomely sharp teeth with one long claw. "Where were you, over Lincoln Park?"

"I don't know." Fleury put on her stoniest face. It would be a mistake to give this … this beast too much information. She didn't know enough about the potential consequences of dealing with a hitherto unknown population. Wait until the folks in Washington heard.

Rumors she had picked up from other captains in Texas said the abandoned city by the lake had centuries of valuables and resources just waiting to be scooped up. She and her crew had found the concept of untapped wealth irresistible. Further rumors of dangerous beasts lurking in the ruined canyons of Old Chicago had to be just that: rumors. Nothing much could be living in the landscape of a nuclear winter, without food, shelter, or even running water. Fleury figured that they could go in with heavy mining equipment and a map of the old city, pinpoint a few areas as good prospects, and stake their claim.

Well, it wasn't going to be that easy, of course. Like other airship crews, the *Magellan* made some money transporting goods back and forth between the major Towers and the minor ground-based habitations, but most of their income came from digging up technology from the past, pre-YE, and bringing home artifacts to whatever collectors, museums, university libraries, research facilities, or anyone else who would pay good, solid cash. She was proud of her ship, a trading sloop with a three-deck gondola trimmed in recycled mahogany wood and gleaming polished bronze hanging beneath a two-hundred-foot ovoid hull of aluminum, and even prouder of the people who worked for her. The year before, her crew had found an amazing cache of valuable minerals in what used to be Iowa State University in Ames. The proceeds of their very hard work had given them a pretty merry Winter Holiday. Fleury had paid off a good chunk of her ship's repair debts. She hoped Chicago would take care of another bunch of bills and maybe let her tuck some away for the future.

Chicago had turned out to be richer pickings than she had dreamed. Ground penetrating radar had shown up some dense pockets in among the foundations of long-fallen buildings. Each of the buildings was a fresh treasure store. Fleury was spoiled for choice, trying to decide which one to explore first. Her crew of twenty-eight chose one at random and started digging.

Under twelve meters of ice some kilometers northwest of frozen Lake Michigan's southern shore, they uncovered a library, decorated in the Art Deco style of two centuries back. It seemed to be untouched, except for some pretty explicit graffiti painted on the brick walls and defacing a handsome mural, and the front picture window shattered in a way with which Fleury and the others were all too familiar—the results of a nuclear shock. But her engineer, Mark Cho, had done a ton of readings with the ship's portable Geiger counter and assured her that whatever half-life radiation the explosion had left behind was long dissipated. With the help of a powerful head-mounted light, she picked her way over fallen ceiling tiles and the occasional skeleton of a patron unfortunate enough to be in the building when the bombs had fallen, and wondered at the titles she came across. "Boss," said one emblazoned with the picture of a large-nosed man wearing a black fedora and a smug expression. *Boss of whom?* she mused.

The library, with its tons of perfectly preserved books, had to wait on discoveries with a higher resale value. Instead, the crew started excavating next door in a massive underground parking lot filled with row upon row of abandoned and derelict cars. Mark had whooped with joy at discovering each vehicle had a catalytic converter, containing precious platinum and other trace rare earths. Fleury had ignored the signs that someone else had been salvaging and exploring in the same area, but the gleanings were just too tempting. Chicago could pay their bills for years.

When three strange vessels had hit the *Magellan*'s radar and come out of the clouds firing harpoons, her first officer had radioed an SOS down to them. The explorers had had to cut and run, leaving nearly all of their findings behind. Fleury was devastated. With the damage to their airship consuming most of her attention, she didn't even consider that the floating city listing at an angle in the thick clouds might be inhabited. Until the force of small blue-and-white ultralight craft had poured out of a bay near its thruster base, blue cylindrical lights spinning, it had been no more than an obstacle that the *Magellan* could hide behind. The pirates clearly knew more than she had; they shot off into the mist as the squad vehicles moved in.

All she knew, before the forward windshield broke and a gas canister exploded in the bridge, was First Officer Penrose exclaiming, "Bears!"

Penrose wasn't wrong; the Chicagoan confronting her did resemble a bear with his bulky, dark fur-covered body, blunt muzzle, and thick limbs with heavy claws. When he took off his cap to scratch his head, he even had little round ears. Fleury steeled herself against her natural impulse to flee from a massive predator. Regardless of his looks, though, he and his colleagues behaved like humans, if gruff, crudely-spoken ones. And their appearance explained so much else. What but a bear, or a wolf, or another climate-adapted creature like them could survive in this frigid wilderness? Genetic alterations were common in countless other regions. Before the rest of the country lost touch with northern cities, the University of Chicago and Northwestern University had been sharing biological research with the facilities in the west. They must have begun work on adapting Chicagoans as quickly as they could. Obviously, they had been successful.

While Chicago wasn't north of the no-go area of the 44th parallel, its notorious weather made the approach across the upper Midwest more than chancy. Fleury had had to get unanimous support from her crew before making the transit. Now she knew why they had never heard from ships that had come this way. They'd been intercepted, by either the pirates operating in the district, or the officials in the Tower, and killed or absorbed.

"Right, I'm gonna ask you again," the bear said, straightening his cap and glaring at her with beady brown eyes. "We ain't stupid.

If you're stealing from us, we're gonna take your ship apart piece by piece. What were you doing here?"

"Um. Trying to make the Kessel run in less than twelve parsecs?" she offered. When he looked blank, she sighed. "Look, I'm just trying to fly cross-country. The territory above Tennessee and Kentucky has weird updrafts over the Blue Ridge Mountains. I was trying a new approach toward Boston. We were carrying used mining equipment. It's so heavy that when the pirates started chasing us, we jettisoned it to lighten our load. I bet they went back and started using it already," she finished hopefully. Her yarn sounded absolutely plausible and would explain the presence of their gear on the excavation site. She was rewarded by seeing a shared glance among the bears huddled on the other side of the room. "We really need it back, sir. We need the payoff that equipment will bring us. We haven't been doing anything wrong. You can search our ship. There's no stolen goods on board." Of that she felt reasonably confident. The one hard and fast rule aboard *Magellan* was "In case of trouble, drop everything and run for your life. No bauble is worth dying for." They hadn't had time to load even one of the catalytic converters.

The interrogator went to confer with his fellows in deep grunts.

"Okay," he said, striding back to her. "We'll take you up on that. Let's take a look at your airship."

"Free my crew," she countered, "and we'll give you the grand tour."

"No deals until I see what we're dealing wit'. You ain't got the clout to refuse. Now, come on."

✶

Three of the Chicago natives, whom Fleury mentally dubbed Papa Bear, Mama Bear, and Baby Bear, all uniformed and armed with truncheons, sheathed knives, and hip-holstered pistols, hustled her out of the police station and out through a series of corridors leading downward. The latter two clearly worked for Papa Bear. They regarded him with respect bordering on awe. Fleury determined to make an ally out of this male; he obviously had plenty of influence there. She cudgeled her memory to remember every detail she could to relate to the outer government. So little was known about the current situation in Chicago. Any surviving population was to be prized, and potential trading partners made the economy flourish, especially with regard to merchant ships like hers.

The Tower structure seemed to be sound, no matter the odd angle at which it hovered in the air. The floors and internal roadways, canted at a ten-degree slope, had been covered with a rubbery material to give walkers and vehicles sound footing. After a while, she found herself automatically compensating for the up- or downward angle, but it still struck her as pretty odd, since the shops and buildings were level on the slanting streets.

"Um," she began. "Why haven't your engineers straightened out the thrusters in this Tower? I mean, the engines are working. The adjustment shouldn't be that hard. Then you wouldn't need those road covers."

Papa Bear glared at her. "Are you dissin' my city? It works. There's only so much money in the budget for infrastructure. We got buildings, roads, and bridges to maintain. We got schools to support. You wanna take money away from *kids*?"

"Um, no," Fleury said, abashed. Papa Bear nodded fiercely and resettled his cap.

"We're headin' for Upper Lower Lower Wacker Drive," he said. At her puzzled glance, he waved a massive paw. "Forget it. It's where your ship is parked."

He cut to the right toward a wide road that separated the main part of the city from a massive park that occupied most of the eastern edge of the city structure at that level.

She had plenty of time to look around. A number of statues and monuments in the park looked as though they had been rescued from the old city below, including a pair of naked warriors with feathered headdresses on horseback, an impressionist phoenix that sported one oval eye with two pupils, a shining flattened sphere that seemed to hover a meter or so above the ground, and the bronze figure of a smiling man in a baseball cap with a bat at his shoulder. She gasped at the sight of a huge, three-tier fountain furnished with verdigris-covered figures blowing water at one another. A streaming plume shot high into the air, scattering pigeons in every direction. A couple of big dogs ran after them, snapping at their tails and missing. She couldn't take her eyes off the fountain. It was a wealth of liquid water, more than she ever dreamed she would see in this northern region.

"Where do you get your water from? The lake's frozen over."

Papa Bear gave her a pitying look. "I'm gonna assume since you piloted a ship here that you ain't stupid. The lake's fed by rivers and underground aquifers plus underground rivers. It ain't just a dish of water. We got solar plants melting ice, too. Best water in the world."

The upper levels could compare favorably with any of the other floating City-Towers that she had visited. She was struck by how beautiful and well-designed Chicago was. Soaring spires of glass pointed toward the sky, filled with transmission towers and solar collectors. The glass had been beveled at the edges, creating interwoven rainbows across the mostly cloudy sky. Some sunlight trickled in from behind the thick gray clouds surrounding the city, but most of the light came from massive round, flat disks like the bosses in a cathedral ceiling.

In between the roof and the tops of the buildings, small atmospheric craft soared. Instead of the free-for-all she saw in Austin and the West Coast, Chicago traffic proceeded in an orderly fashion that corresponded to some kind of internal grid. Most of the sparse ground traffic was maglev heavy goods vehicles and public taxis. All the people she could see, walking or driving, were ursines like her guides.

"How many people live here?" she asked.

Papa Bear grunted. "You taking a census?"

She huddled back into her parka and just kept looking around.

On that level, the city was a work of art with examples of construction ranging from Gothic Revival to Art Nouveau to 20th Century Modern, with Art Deco predominating overall. The architecture was at odds with the rough appearance of the inhabitants. The temperature hovered around fourteen or fifteen degrees Celsius. Nobody but she appeared to feel cold. The bears stumped through this handsome landscape, at home with ornate bronze doors and eclectic public sculpture.

"All this came up from the old city?" she asked.

"Heck, no," Baby Bear said, speaking for the first time. Her—or his—voice was an octave or so higher than Papa Bear's. "We rebuilt it. Got Daniel Burnham's lakefront all finished, except there's no lakefront up here. People like it."

"Is everybody … is everybody here … like you?"

"You mean debonair and good lookin'?" Papa Bear asked. "They wish."

Fleury couldn't help but laugh. Despite the power he held over her of life and death, she liked him. She wanted him to like her, but she didn't know how to get past the constant deflecting. She had to find a way to impress him somehow. Her crew needed allies to escape this place, and once they did, it would be good to make connections for trade.

A few blocks from Police Headquarters, they came to a rubber-covered road that spiraled downward. They walked down two full turns until Papa Bear steered them into an open chamber with yellowed steel walls that proved to be a freight elevator. The doors clanged shut and the floor beneath them dropped hard, leaving Fleury's stomach behind. The mechanism groaned on for what seemed like forever, until the doors opened again to reveal a massive, dimly lit hangar. The noise that burst in nearly knocked Fleury backward. Papa Bear grabbed her shoulder and hustled her out. She shivered. The air was even colder than on the main street level.

"Dis is the main hangar," Papa Bear shouted over the deafening roar as he steered her around the catwalks that crisscrossed the huge open space. "We're just above the Tower engines."

Perhaps another couple dozen more hairy Chicagoans, this time in coveralls, were at work there, repairing or cleaning the police shuttles that were moored there. A trio of airships with shining oval hulls hung on gantries. Their shining oval hulls were emblazoned with a rectangular blue-and-white flag decorated with four coral-colored stars and the motto, "Urbs in Caelum."

Worried, Fleury sought about the chamber until she spotted the *Magellan*. It was moored behind the three official airships. To her relief, the big airship looked to be in good condition. The gondola still had a harpoon sticking out of it, with several meters of grappling cable dangling from it.

The envelope had sustained five holes, as Penrose had reported, but someone here had patched them with multiple layers of thin silver strips. Fleury had to stare. She hadn't seen that much duct tape anywhere for years. She wanted to ask Papa Bear if they had any to sell but decided she would keep her mouth shut for the duration.

The senior bear kept his claw hooked under her arm, hurrying her toward her ship. Eight bears in police uniforms met them at the gantry.

"Okay!" Papa Bear shouted. "We're lookin' for contraband. Nuttin' from out of town, just local stuff. Holler if you find something."

Fleury lived through the longest two hours of her life, as measured by the digital clock over the dispatcher's glass booth next to the now-closed hatch. The bears were thorough. A trio of them swung down from a gantry above the *Magellan* and went over every gas cell and stabilizer individually on the massive hull. She spotted lurking shapes passing by portholes inside the low-hanging bridge and the decks above it attached to the belly of the envelope.

"Good-lookin' ship," Papa Bear said, his arms crossed on his broad chest. "How fast can she go?"

Fleury hesitated. She could go over a hundred thirty klicks per hour full out, but it was hard on the hull and made the engines shake. "A hundred ten easy," she said.

"Not like the jets from the old days, huh? But yeah, we'll get a lot of use out of it."

"It's my ship!" she yelped.

"Until we figure it out for sure, you can think so," Papa Bear said, showing his teeth. "You're intrudin' here. You got any backup? Anyone to corroborate your story? You do the math."

Fleury fumed. She had no intention of being marooned in Chicago forever. To her relief, the bear squad emerged, shaking their heads.

"We got nuttin', sir," said a slim female with golden fur. "It's clean."

"Commissioner!"

A high-pitched voice rose above the din. Papa Bear's eyes lit up at the sound. He turned and dragged Fleury with him.

A small air car piloted by a huge male with black fur wearing a pinstriped coat and trousers fluttered up to the catwalk where

Fleury and Papa Bear were standing. A small female with brown fur and wide-set eyes in a dark green jumpsuit hopped out onto the walkway. She almost vibrated with nervous energy. Papa Bear poked Fleury in the back.

"Straighten up. Dis is Da Mare."

Fleury regarded the newcomer as she approached. "A mare? She looks like the rest of you."

"She's da may-or," Papa Bear pronounced very carefully. "Head of the whole city. Most powerful person in the city of Chicago. Act like you know what respect is."

Every bear on the *Magellan* got to their feet when the mayor approached. She was small, even shorter than Fleury, but walked with an authority that commanded attention. She wore a pearl necklace and a gold ring almost invisible in the thick fur of her left paw. Like the rest of the Chicago bears, she didn't need shoes.

"Welcome, your honor," Papa Bear said, with a courteous bow. "As you see, we intercepted this intruder when it was loiterin' around the South Side. This is the captain. You got a name, bareskin?"

"Captain Fleury Marconi," Fleury said, extending a hand. Papa Bear tapped her hard on the wrist, making her drop her arm.

"You don't touch Da Mare. She is the one in whom actual authority resides in this city. In other words, she is the queen of clout, and you don't have none. What can we do for you, your honor?"

The nervous female lifted the corners of her mouth in a brief smile, then dropped them with an expression of concern.

"It's all right, Commissioner Grabowski. My name is Braelyn Sturgeon. Commissioner, is Braedon on board that craft?"

Papa Bear looked equally concerned. "Your kid? No, we evacuated everybody on it when we brought it in about two hours ago. They're in custody. This craft is confiscated in the name of Chicago. I was gonna see about naming it after you, your honor."

The flash of smile repeated. "That's very nice of you, commissioner, but right now I am concerned about my son. Have you seen him today?"

"No, your honor. When did you last see him?"

"Yesterday afternoon." Mayor Sturgeon looked ashamed. "I had meetings. His babysitter said he locked himself in his room to write, as he usually does. This morning, she went in to tell him to come down to breakfast and found this note. He's just a cub!" She clutched a square of blue paper that had been written on both sides in a juvenile hand. "He's smart and very observant. He publishes his own news on the computer system. He takes too many chances trying to get the story."

Fleury's eyebrows rose. "A cub reporter. That's ... a lot to be proud of, Madame Mayor."

The mayor was too upset and nervous to acknowledge the compliment.

"Where do you t'ink he went, your honor?"

"He's been studying old maps. He thinks he found a library in Lincoln Park."

"Lincoln Park!" Papa Bear echoed.

"I know!" The mayor looked stricken. "I told him he wasn't allowed to go down there under any circumstances." She turned to Fleury. "Did you see him there?"

Fleury shook her head, then added hastily. "We weren't in the old city, ma'am," she said. "We'd be happy to help you look for him."

"We can't do that," Papa Bear said, flatly. "Why the hell—excuse me, your honor—why did the kid decide to enter enemy territory like that?"

The mayor gave him a concerned smile. "For me. He knows I want to expand the literacy program here, but we need more books. The old computer systems are about nonfunctional. We have to go old school to survive. Printed books are key to helping young people, in fact everyone, to improve their education."

"We all have to rely on resources of the past, ma'am," Fleury said.

Her honor looked at Fleury as if seeing her for the first time and peered at her hood. "That's not your fur, is it? Where are you from?"

"Texas, ma'am. The Republic of Austin. Papa—I mean, the commissioner mentioned Lincoln Park before. What's this about enemy territory?"

Braelyn Sturgeon sighed, looking even more worried.

"The Lincoln Park Pirates. They used to be part of this city, but they didn't like our rules," Papa Bear said. "It started with dissent in the City Council. Then it turned into undermining the authority of rightly elected officials. Then outright sabotage. We understand wanting to take over by sheer power. But they dug up old technology in the Museum of Science and Industry and built the first steel-hulled airship. They made a run on Daley Plaza, and blew up the last full meeting of the aldermen. We had to create our own fleet to defend ourselves. It's been ugly. They raid us every time they get a chance. They stole what they could and sabotaged what they couldn't.

"It took years," the mayor added, "but we fought them to a negotiated truce. We stay in the Loop, the South Side, and over the lake. They got the North and West sides. Lincoln Park is in that zone."

Fleury frowned. "So, if Braedon is in their territory, he's probably in danger."

"Yes." The mayor drummed her claws on her lower lip. "Is there anything you can do, commissioner?"

The big bear hung his head. "I'm sorry, your honor. I can't send in officers. It'll break the truce, and who knows what they've been building in the meantime? Damn that kid. He knows all this!"

An idea suddenly struck Fleury.

"But I'm not part of your truce," she said. "I want my ship back. If my crew and I can find your son and bring him back, I want you to release *Magellan* and all of my cargo. Including the material on the ground."

"It ain't your ship any ....!"

The mayor held up a slim paw. The commissioner clamped his muzzle shut.

"I'm listening. What can you do, Captain Marconi?"

Fleury thought fast. "It's a big area, but we have infrared equipment. It's necessary for finding gas leaks on the airship. We can create a diversion and drop some of my crew in there with the device to locate him. I'm sure I can locate a library." That was no lie. "Once we spot their ships, I'll lead them out of the way, giving my team time to locate Braedon and bring him back without them realizing anyone else was down there."

The mayor shook her head. "No. Their ships are fast. They'll shoot you down and blame us for the incursion."

"All we need is a temporary diversion," Papa Bear said, eagerly, his big face alight. "She just told me it'll do a hundred and ten."

"Theirs can fly at almost a hundred twenty!"

"I think we can make *Magellan* go even faster than that if I let my chief engineer tinker with it," Fleury said with confidence.

The mayor continued her tapping. "Will that take long? We have to hurry. Every minute he is in there, the chances are greater that one of the Lincoln Park Pirates will spot him. They'll make an example of him." Her eyes filled with tears. "He's my son, but I can't let the truce break. It took years to get to this point. I keep hoping I can reunite the city."

"We'll find him, ma'am," Fleury promised. "But you have to let me have my crew and my ship. And when it's all over, I want to go retrieve my equipment from where we, er, dumped it. We'll bring him back to you." She put out a hand. "It was nice to meet you, Commissioner."

"What, you think you're going by yourself?" Papa Bear asked, with a look of sheer disbelief. "I'm coming wit' you. You think we're stupid? The moment you're out there, you might fly off to the other end of the world."

"That's right," the mayor said, fixing her with a firm stare. "Take Commissioner Grabowski and his aides with you. That's my condition. Bring my son back, and it's a deal. All of it." She put out her paw and Fleury let her hand be engulfed in it.

"Yes, ma'am!"

✶

Her twenty-eight crew members, shuddering with the cold, were herded off an airbus that landed at the top of Lower Upper Upper Wacker Drive. She greeted them with relief.

"Anyone hurt, Penrose?" she asked her first officer as Papa Bear and his colleagues guided them into a large room furnished with long metal tables and an ancient dry-erase board.

The tall, dark-skinned man shook his head. His bright red parka had a long smear of grease down the left side, but no tears. "Minor bumps and bruises. Plenty of nausea. Most of us heaved our breakfast from the gas canister. We haven't had anything to eat since."

"I got that handled," Commissioner Grabowski said, with an expansive wave. The door opened to admit Mama Bear pushing a two-tiered metal cart. Square steel pans rattled on the top, and a basketful of narrow bottles clacked against one another on the bottom next to a vast bowl of golden potato chips. When she lifted the tops from the pans, savory smells filled the room. "Eat up!"

Fleury looked inside. Narrow tubes of peculiarly red meat nestled in long, split bread buns. Each had been decorated with condiments, some of colors nature never intended, like a chopped relish of a radioactive green and luridly yellow mustard. The rest were largely recognizable, such as chopped white onion, small olive-green peppers, lusciously ripe red tomatoes, and a sprinkle of gray-green particles that smelled of celery. Her stomach reminded her she had spent many hours without food, too. She reached for one of the buns, but hesitated.

"I'll be the guinea pig," Mark said. He picked up one, took a bite from the end, and beamed. "It's good!"

The rest of the crew didn't need further encouragement. Fleury seized two of the buns, grabbed a chilled bottle from the basket below, and rushed to take one of the antique metal folding chairs at the end of one of the long tables. The meat, if it was meat—she had long ago learned not to ask what was in a meat dish—tasted savory, though a little salty, and the strange condiments complemented it perfectly.

"These are great! You have to agree to let us export these to the rest of the country," Fleury said, gulping down the last bite of her first sandwich. "What are they?"

"Chicago dogs!" Papa Bear exclaimed happily, around a huge mouthful. "Best in the world." Fleury felt her gorge rise. She gulped. He saw the look on her face and grinned, showing those sharp teeth. "Not made of dog. Dogs are great buddies. But you don't want to ask no more than that. Two things you never ask about how they're made: deals and sausages. And you never, never put ketchup on a Chicago dog. Got it?"

She got it. "But where are you raising tomatoes? Sport peppers? Cucumbers? Poppy seeds? It's below freezing out there!"

"Cooler by the lake," Papa Bear said, with pride. "All the crops are in underground hydroponic farms, hundreds of acres, fed by the Chicago River and the water towers. We're the City That Works, and we made it happen. It's been hard, don't think it hasn't. Those mugs on the North Side, they don't appreciate all that went into helping the city survive. They just take, take, take." He grimaced. "We had a fantastic layout in the old Navy Pier greenhouse, and they bombed it. Morons. That coulda been feeding thousands."

Fleury didn't have an answer to that. She popped open the bottle and took a swig of the sweet, dark brown liquid. She licked her lips, eager to collect every drop. "Is this … wintergreen?"

"Yeah. And sassafras. Root beer. Chicago special. Been around since before my great-granddad's day."

From the looks on their faces, her crew thought as highly of the sweet soda as they did. Another potential export. Fleury wanted to drink bottle after bottle, until the first mighty belch gathered itself in her belly and burst out. She blushed. The others laughed.

"There's no such thing as a free lunch," Linda McConnell said. The short, busty, freckled brunette was *Magellan*'s purser. She dusted the poppy seeds off her hands and folded her fingers together. "What's going on? Are they letting us go?"

"Uh, not exactly," Fleury said, with a glance at Papa Bear. The police commissioner discreetly moved a half dozen paces away. She had no doubt he could still hear them just fine. "Our release is conditional on fulfilling one small job."

"*How* small?"

"One small boy," she said, raising her hands palm up. "He wandered off into a dangerous situation, and his mother is the mayor."

"A boy who looks like *that*?" Second Mate Romilda Ferenc asked, nodding toward Papa Bear. "He ought to be able to take care of himself."

"It's not so easy," Fleury said. "He went into the zone ruled by the pirates that attacked us. It will violate a truce the city has with them if they go after him. That leaves us. If we don't do it, the city is going to keep our ship. We'll be stuck here. If we do it, they'll let us go."

"Can we retrieve our gear?" Mark Cho asked. "It's not really well-hidden where we left it."

"Where we *dumped* it," Fleury corrected him, with a meaningful look at their host.

"Huh?" Mark asked, looking from his captain to the uniformed ursine.

"Uh-huh," was all Papa Bear said. She didn't pretend the Chicagoan couldn't understand what the engineer had intimated. She gave him a sickly smile. He waved a dismissive paw.

"We'll make this work," Fleury said. "We have to."

"This isn't what we signed on for," Linda protested. "We don't go out there and attract attention from pirates! We could be killed!"

"The mayor's son is just a kid," Fleury argued. "He needs our help."

"Just because somebody made some stupid choices doesn't mean *we* have to fix it!"

"Didn't you do stupid things when you were a kid?" Romilda asked.

"I didn't put thirty other people in harm's way," Linda insisted, her expression stony.

"*I* remember when you did," Penrose said, a look of mischief on his face.

"That was one time!" Linda crossed her arms on her chest. "Well, I won't do it. We need to collect our stuff and get out of here. This isn't our fight."

"Dat's where you're wrong," Papa Bear said, coming to loom over them like the shadow of death. "It just became your fight. Here's your choice: do it and earn your ship back, or no ship. Welcome to Chicago. We'll help you get housing, and maybe find you a job in the Public Works department. We sure ain't letting you near the Transportation Department. Once you're here, you're here to stay. You want your ship back or not?"

"They've already confiscated it once," Fleury pleaded. "Help me here. We've done similar things in other places. Think of it as hostage rescue. Could we ... work out a monetary reward for Braedon's safe return, commissioner?"

The big ursine scratched his underarm. "Maybe I can find something in the Victim Compensation Fund. It's gonna be gold coins, though."

"Gold?" Gunnery Officer Hugh Rice's wide blue eyes widened even further. He went into a huddle with the rest of the crew. Fleury watched them with her heart in her throat. For the first time in her career, Fleury didn't know what her crew would do.

After an eternity, the huddle broke.

"You got it, Captain," Hugh said, with a grin. "What do we have to do?"

✶

Fleury spun the wooden wheel of the *Magellan*, steering it out of the Chicago Tower hangar, her feet on the pedals that controlled upward and downward motion. The airship felt the wind whip the massive hull as it cleared the portal, and she fought it back into line. She felt the enormous craft respond to her control, surging against her grip, but obeying at last. She loved her airship. It seemed like a living being, with all its moving parts and its quirks. Sometimes she wondered if it liked her, too. Engineer Cho and his staff had given it as much of a wellness check as they could in the hour they had been allotted by Papa Bear.

Only vital crew held station in their usual positions, such as Engineering, Gunnery, and Navigation, but the rest, with First Officer Penrose, stood by in the cargo bay, waiting for her signal that they had reached the drop point.

She eyed the weather on the ancient radar screen, spinning wind gauges, and through the brass-framed front windshield. For a wonder, the clouds had cleared out to a thin scattering below ten thousand feet. The bottom of the skeleton of a massive skyscraper was visible off to her port side. It was as though the sky cooperated with the plans they had just made over the conference table. Not the temperature, though; it hovered around minus ten Celsius. At least it was too cold to snow.

"How do you live like this?" Fleury asked. In her rear camera, she watched a handful of hangar crew leaning out to watch them depart. "I'd seize up like unoiled machinery in this climate!"

"You're from out of town," Papa Bear said. "We're tougher

here." His voice lacked his usual cocky confidence. She glanced his way. In the first officer's chair to her right, Papa Bear held tightly to both armrests.

"Don't fly much?" she asked, with some sympathy.

"Not with someone else driving," he admitted. He pointed out the forward view port. "Watch it. You gotta stay over the lake until the last minute. Chicago clout don't hold no water with the Lincoln Park pirates."

"I know." She kept a steady hand on the wheel and brought up the chart on the viewscreen to her left. A tiny silver oval representing *Magellan* floated over a map borrowed from the Public Works department. It was marked in blue zones and white zones, divided by a solid red line that snaked along the middle of main thoroughfares in the old city. Former landmarks were indicated with names and question marks. From what Fleury had observed before, little of former Chicago remained intact. She was out over a deep blue zone indicating Lake Michigan.

It was rare these days that Fleury had full control of the airship. Usually she sat behind the nav station in her captain's chair, but both her helm officer and navigator were part of the rescue squad.

According to the notes the mayor had found in her son's den, er, bedroom, Braedon had probably entered the Lincoln Park demesne along Lake Shore Drive, heading for the DePaul University Library, the largest in the area. Fleury and the others realized almost immediately that it was the treasure house of books they had earmarked before. They had had to pretend to know nothing about it even though their information was almost a century newer than the officials in the Chicago Tower. According to a university map that had been scavenged from a Chicago visitor's center, it had numerous potential access points, entrances and exits, almost irresistible to an inquisitive youngster who wanted to help his mother achieve her goal. Fleury had to admire his effort, even if it put other people in danger pulling him back again.

Studying the map, they had decided on the now-deserted Lincoln Park Zoo as the drop zone. After dipping down long enough to decant Penrose and his rescue squad, they would create a diversion long enough for them to get to the library, locate the boy, and return for pickup.

"Why do we have to go back there?" Linda had asked, reasonably enough. "We can just radio our location to you once we find him."

Fleury had smiled at that, realizing that meant Linda had just volunteered to be in the landing party. "Because we don't know if the pirates have frequency scanners. It's possible they found our position by listening to our between-decks chatter."

"Damn," Romilda said. "That means we have to go old-old school."

Old school indeed. Fleury had to rely on whistle-tubes and one fleet-footed midshipman to communicate with engineering, cargo, and the weapons stations. She kept well offshore, watching the map for the snow-covered structures in the long, narrow lakefront park that indicated Lincoln Park Zoo. Her away team had three clockwork sleds, each with the capacity to carry six people. The engines should be good for two runs of a few miles. Each crew member was armed with rifles and pistols in case they ran into any local wildlife. Like in so many areas, Chicago had released all the zoo animals to survive on their own. Mama Bear had claimed to have seen penguins, but there were also reports of walruses, timber wolves, and snow leopards roaming around. Most importantly, they were carrying the ship's one and only infrared detector. That would help them locate Braedon faster than following tracks or roaming around the facility calling his name.

As soon as the mound of the zoo buildings appeared on the horizon, Fleury turned on the speed and steered the massive airship inland. She yanked the brass speaking tube down on its flexible hose.

"Attention, landing party. Prepare to depart. I repeat, prepare to depart!"

She sailed in over the shore of the frozen lake, sculpted into graceful curves of ice at the shore. A flat mound like a monadnock offered itself. She hovered low and felt the *Magellan* dance as the heavy sleds were dropped on rope harnesses.

"Landing party away," Penrose's voice came through the speaking tube. "See you later, Captain!"

Fleury hit the controls to fill the gas bags. The *Magellan* shot upward.

"Let's go find us some pirates," she said. "Heading west-north-west, elevation one hundred fifty feet, top speed."

"Aye-aye, sir!" the skeleton bridge crew chorused. Fleury smiled. Papa Bear held tight to his armrests.

In her teenage years, Fleury had prided herself on being a demon pilot. Having to surrender the controls when she assumed her first command was tough. She always wanted to grab the wheel from her very competent helmswoman. Now she had the reins of this magnificent Pegasus in her grasp once more. She played the controls like a virtuoso, keeping watch for the airship port that the Chicago crew said was miles inland in what used to be a city park.

Just as they had predicted, the dull gleam of white-and-black oval hulls appeared in the distance, including the three that had chased her behind the Chicago floating Tower. Fleury made for the largest one, three times her size.

"Permission to light us up!" Midshipman Travis Wade pleaded, his hand smacking into his forehead in salute.

"Let's give them a real Texas hello," Fleury said. "Permission granted!"

Travis ran to the communications console and pushed every button on the board. A row of blue lights blazed on at the bottom of Fleury's windshield. She knew that brilliant-colored lines and circles had just lit all over the massive hull and around the panels of the gondola, not to mention the landing lights, eight massive search-lights stationed fore and aft on the cabin's keel. The light show had to have surprised the hell out of the people on the ground. She spoke into the tube.

"Gunnery station, Molotov cocktails at the ready?"

"Yes, sir!" Hugh's voice came through. "She's a sitting duck, ma'am! We can take her out!"

"Remember they're supposed to miss!" Fleury snapped back.

"Awww!" the crew in Weapons moaned.

"Throw to miss," Fleury commanded. "We want them to leave this area!"

"Yes, sir," Hugh said, glumly. Fleury grinned, making directly for the big airship.

"Gotta love it," Papa Bear said.

As the *Magellan* zoomed toward the pirates' mothership, she caught brief glimpses of dozens or hundreds of bears in jumpsuits and leather helmets like hers scattering. Three hundred, two hundred yards ....

"Bombs away!" she called. Cheering erupted from the gunnery station. In her aft cameras, Fleury saw streamers of flame descending. She had to hand it to Hugh: they fell in a massive oval around the big pirate ship. All but one. It bounced off the nose of the hull, leaving a streak of flame before it crashed to the ground and burst into a pool of fire.

"Who threw that?" she demanded.

"Sorry, ma'am!" said Gunner's Mate Barbara Nelson. "My wrist slipped."

They were so low Fleury could hear the shouts and angry cries from the Lincoln Park crews. She zipped in as tight a curve as she could maneuver and came around again for a second pass over the big ship. The pirates flattened themselves on the snowy ground.

"Strap in and hold tight!" she called.

She circled around one more time but wobbled the wheel hard. The gondola shook, almost knocking Travis off his feet. He sprang for one of the cleats bolted to the bulkhead and hung on. Papa Bear swayed in his seat.

"What the hell are you doing?" he demanded, planting his big feet firmly on the wooden deck to brace himself.

"I need to look like I don't know what I'm doing," she said. "I want them to underestimate me. Like we discussed."

"Yeah, yeah," the ursine said, waving a paw impatiently. "Watch those turns, okay?"

Fleury grinned and came around again for another run. By now, the mothership's crew was racing for the gondola. They wanted to get the ship aloft before the invader managed to strike and actually hit it.

"Molotov cocktails ready? Bombs away!" she called.

By now, the ground crew was throwing sheets off the anchoring bollards and shouting orders to one another. About ten minutes had passed since she let herself be seen. She needed at least thirty more.

She hadn't had to use a technique like this in five years, not since she had been threatened by a rival trading company who, in her opinion, verged on piracy. The captain of that ship was a presumptuous ass who liked to throw his weight around and steal loads out from under the noses of other crews. The only way to get it back was to disable the ship, not destroy it. It was a surgical procedure, but she had to get the patient arranged to where she could operate. Above all, she must not fall into a position where the pirates could board *Magellan*. Their superior numbers would quickly overwhelm hers.

She circled wide again.

"I count at least sixty on board," Romilda's voice issued from the speaking tube.

"Acknowledged," Fleury said. She let the ship wobble again.

As soon as the enemy began to lift, she stopped her arc and sped away on a northeasterly course at about half speed. Before she hit the lake shore, Chicago Tower territory, she veered due north.

In her rear camera, she saw the ship lift and begin pursuit at a sharply increasing altitude. The enemy captain was good. Fleury guessed her opponent wanted to get above her, something she could not permit.

"Back off the engines," she instructed Cho. "We don't want to lose them."

In a few minutes, the enemy ship had come within a few thousand feet of *Magellan*. Fleury ascended, always keeping just above the black-and-white vessel. It was a monster. The five-deck gondola must have held a hundred fifty to two hundred crew. She estimated twenty cannon or harpoon ports on either side of the ship plus four fore and four aft. *Magellan* had a total of sixteen, but crew only enough left on board to fire one side at a time. It had to be enough!

The enemy ship saw her tactic and tried to rise up on her starboard stern. Fleury angled to the right to keep on top of them and kept ascending. It ducked out from beneath her at a sharp port angle. Fleury cut hard to the left and came around in a wide upward spiral. The cloud cover loomed closer. She didn't want to disappear into it yet. *Magellan* could ascend almost one thousand feet per minute. She needed twenty to thirty minutes more, at the least. The longer she played cat and mouse with them, the longer her ground crew had to find Braedon.

The two ships wove back and forth. While she had the higher ground, she maintained her advantage. The enemy knew that all too well. It couldn't fire on her with its gigantic hull in the way, and it was vulnerable to anything she might choose to drop on it. All the time she feared that Lincoln Park might launch a few of its smaller vessels. Against superior numbers she would have little choice but to cut and run, to return for her team after dark, maybe even a few days from then. With the cold weather and few supplies, delays would be hard on her people. She had one opportunity to take her shot.

The skies grew even grayer as the brief afternoon light began to peter out. Fleury worried that the enemy would drop back and give up the chase. She couldn't let them do that. Every time the big ship came close, she would give it a tantalizing look at her stern, then flick it out of reach.

Whizz!

"Enemy fired harpoons from forward emplacements," Hugh reported. "Three flights. None of them struck us."

"Give them a single harpoon from the center stern gun, directly at the bridge windshield," Fleury said.

"That's hardened glass," Papa Bear argued. "It'll bounce right off."

"Exactly!" Fleury replied.

The ursine chuckled. "Got it. Never mind."

By now the two ships were well away from the enemy base. All the pirates' attention was on the pursuit of the gaudy intruder, not on the landing party. Fleury pictured her very thorough first officer proceeding in an orderly and methodical fashion with the heat detector. She hoped the boy or her team hadn't been intercepted by those pirates remaining behind.

She and the big ship maneuvered again and again upward through the graying skies, trying to bring one another into position for a broadside barrage. The enemy swerved port, then hard to starboard. Fleury almost missed the turn, finding herself flying over empty space. Hastily, she sped back, but not before the enemy managed to loose off a brace of cannon at her.

The gondola rocked hard.

"Strike on starboard stern," Hugh reported. "A steel ball ripped off one of our steering fins!"

Fleury tried the wheel. It spun far too easily to the right. She felt it catch at about thirty degrees farther than usual, meaning the other gyros were still intact.

"I'll compensate," she said. She glanced toward her aide, clinging to the comms station. "Travis, how long has it been?"

"Twenty-two minutes, ma'am!"

"Good. We can start to wind this up."

She had kept the velocity to approximately two-thirds of *Magellan*'s capacity all through the ascent. They were within a thousand feet of the cloud canopy when she slowed down to less than half. The enemy ship took what it thought was its advantage and opened up the throttle. The ship grew in Fleury's rear-facing camera at an alarming clip.

"Ma'am, they're getting close enough to fire full guns!" Romilda shouted.

"I know. Steady ... steady ...!" Fleury bit her tongue to keep from making the order too soon.

The viewscreen was almost filled with the image of the approaching ship. The blood pounded in Fleury's ears. This was where it could all go wrong. One split second late, and they were dead.

"Steady ... steady ... prepare for broadside!"

"Aye, sir!" the gunnery crew shouted.

The cloud layer was only yards away. Fleury held tight to the wheel.

"They're bringing their guns to bear, sir!"

"Marconi, wake up!" Papa Bear bellowed. Fleury ignored him. She wrenched the wheel hard to port.

"Now! Mark, cut engines!" She stamped on the right pedal, deflating the gas bags inside the hull. Her knuckles whitened as she held onto her controls, keeping the ship on its bearing.

The three bears let out wails of dismay as *Magellan* fell, twisting in the air. Wind whistled past the gondola like a tortured soul. Her stomach in her throat, Fleury counted to three in her mind, then stamped on the left pedal, re-inflating the bags with helium.

The precipitous drop had taken them down four or five hundred feet and twisted the airship so that its starboard side was below and facing the stern of the enemy craft. Fleury crowed in triumph.

"Gunners, fire at will! Mark, re-engage engines!"

Magellan's gondola rocked as all the cannons and harpoon guns blasted away, lighting up the twilit sky with red fire. The enemy ship attempted to turn on its axis to confront them, but it was too late. The broadside ripped into their engines. A couple of cannon blasts hit the triple propellers, knocking one massive steel wing spinning off its axle with a twang! The other two were hammered into scrap metal. Harpoons studded the rear of the enemy ship, but those just added insult to injury. A few of the Lincoln Park pirate gunners let off harpoons at *Magellan*, but Fleury eased her foot down on the right pedal. The enemy craft rose out of sight. It had been disabled and could not follow her. The engines purred.

"Great job, everybody!" Fleury called. The gunners yelled and whooped. "Now, let's get out of here!" She wrenched the wheel around. The ship heeled like a faithful dog.

"Ain't you gonna finish the job?" Papa Bear asked, aiming a thumb over his shoulder.

Fleury eyed him. "I am finishing the job. We're going back to pick up the mayor's cub. That was just the distraction. We took out the pirate's engines. It's drifting helplessly through the skies a long way from home. It's going to have to be repaired before it can follow us, and by then, we'll be long gone. The main event is taking place at ground level miles away from here."

Papa Bear chuckled. "You're so sure your people found the kid? Like in a place they've never been before? Maybe next to that mining equipment that you just happened to throw out of this airship conveniently adjacent to the target?"

Fleury smiled at him. "Sometimes a coincidence is a good thing."

✶

Travis cut all the lights as they veered out over the lake and took a southward course back toward the rendezvous point. Fleury did her best to hide her nerves in case Penrose hadn't returned or had not found the cub.

By the time they reached the zoo and lowered the harnesses, darkness surrounded them. A few lights showed habitations to the north and west of them, but the greatest illumination was a column of blue light out over the frozen lake: the floating Tower of New Chicago.

"Beautiful, ain't it?" Papa Bear sounded wistful.

"It really is," Fleury said.

"I'm just sorry I couldn't see what the old city was like in my great-granddad's day, before it blew up."

"Me, too. It must have been magnificent."

The radio on Fleury's console crackled into life.

"Request permission to come aboard?" Penrose's voice asked.

The bridge crew cheered. "Permission granted!" Fleury said.

"Is the kid with them? He better be okay," Papa Bear warned.

Fleury kept her worries to herself. "We're going to find out."

She and Papa Bear hurried down to the cargo bay, steadying themselves as the gondola pitched and swayed. The equipment was coming back up, but was the boy with them?

Fleury's eyes were momentarily dazzled by the bright lights of the landing chamber. From the hatch in the floor, the second of the sleds was being hauled upward on the clockwork winch. Piles of the previously abandoned mining gear lay scattered on the floor in puddles of melting snow, and a high-pitched juvenile voice nattered a steady stream of questions and comments over the noise as the crew worked.

"And then they started chasing us! I like these flat wagon things. I never get to ride fast at home. Do you get to ride these all the time? They shot at us! I saw that spear sticking out of the snow right next to me! They sure yelled when that wolf jumped off the hill at them. Nothing like this ever happens in the city. My mom is gonna be pretty mad at me, but I hope she won't ground me for too long. I made a great discovery! I can't wait to tell everyone all about it! What do you want with those long pipes? They don't look like anything useful ..."

The voice came from a miniature version of the mayor: brown fur, blunt muzzle, wide eyes, two little round ears, and a grin that stretched almost from one ear to the other. In fact, Fleury reflected, Braedon was kind of cute.

Papa Bear showed all his teeth, but it was a happy expression, not a fearsome one.

"He's fine. If he's awake, he's talkin'. We can radio his mom that we're bringing him back. Congrats. You get your ship back." He glanced at the long pipes on the deck: the previously abandoned catalytic converters. Fleury wanted to kick them under the nearest rug. She shot a sheepish glance at Papa Bear. He waved a paw. "Fuggedaboudit. We're not gonna argue about a few tailpipes. You saved the cub. You caused the pirates a bunch of trouble, and nobody died. We didn't have to get officially involved. In fact," he added, with a huge grin, "if anybody asks, we don't know nothin' except you earned a little clout here. Next time you come back, you can use it."

Fleury was surprised to realize that she wanted to. "I'm looking forward to it," she said. "This is my kind of town."

✶

Jody Lynn Nye lists her main career activity as "spoiling cats." She lives northwest of Atlanta with three feline overlords, Athena, Minx, and Marmalade, and her husband, author and packager Bill Fawcett. She has written over fifty books, most of them with a humorous bent, and over 170 short stories. Jody has been fortunate enough to have collaborated with some of the greats in the field of science fiction and fantasy. She wrote several books with Anne McCaffrey or set in Anne's many worlds, including *The Death of Sleep, The Ship Who Won, Crisis on Doona* (a *New York Times* and *USA Today* bestseller), and *The Dragonlover's Guide to Pern*. She wrote eight books with Robert Asprin and has since his death continued two of his series, the *Myth-Adventures* and *Dragons*. She edited a humorous anthology about mothers, *Don't Forget Your Spacesuit, Dear!* Her latest books are *Rhythm of the Imperium* (Baen Books), *Moon Tracks* (with Travis S. Taylor, Baen Books) and *Myth-Fits* (Ace). She is one of the judges for the Writers of the Future fiction contest, the largest speculative fiction contest in the world. Jody also teaches the intensive two-day writers' workshop at DragonCon. You can find her online on Facebook, Twitter, and her website, www.jodynye.net.

BONSAI

STEVE PERRY

On the ground, three thousand meters below it, Tinzen sat *seiza* deep in the shadow of the Seed Vault, his mind not quite empty, his spirit a little less than completely calm.

He had brushed a bare spot in the snow, which was only a handspan deep, and put down a towel, less to honor the tradition than to keep his knees dry. Faux-tumo did melt the snow pretty good. Not properly meditating, but musing, on the fate of the world, and his part in it.

Someone was coming, and although she tried to be quiet, Tinzen could sense her slightly roiled energy. By the time Kinsu arrived, Tinzen was on his feet, enjoying the chill, now that he allowed himself to feel it again.

"Sorry to disturb you, Rinpoche."

"You did no such thing. Is he here?"

"He is."

"And ...?"

"He seems every bit the Dancing Master of Kung Fu."

"Ah." He smiled.

The deadliest of men, convinced of his superiority, who came to challenge the Dalai Lama, only to discover that his physical power was not a match for real spiritual power. It was a great story, and they knew he liked telling it, so not unexpected they would play to it.

"Then I suppose we should go and see him."

✶

In the temple, Tinzen prepared green spiced tea while he waited for Kinsu to deliver the applicant. The smell of patchouli incense hung fragrantly in the cool air.

Tinzen preferred the scent of burning marijuana himself, but the tourists had their expectations.

"Rinpoche, this is Roland King, from New York."

"Thank you, Kinsu." The young woman gave him a slow military bow and left.

"M. King. Tea?"

"Yes, thank you."

Tinzen made tea, pouring the hot water into the cup, swishing the loose leaves into a froth with the bamboo whisk. Truth was, it wasn't a Tibetan ceremonial process at all, they'd swiped it entirely from the Japanese a couple hundred years ago, but if anybody noticed, nobody remarked upon it. He preferred Earl Grey himself, in a proper tea ball so he didn't have to pick the bits out of his teeth, but, again, he didn't want to disappoint his visitors. The archaic notion of a mysterious Orient still had a certain cachet, though he doubted his visitor paid that much mind.

After he delivered the cup to the young man, he nodded at the chair across from his. "Please."

They sat. Roland looked thirty, appeared extremely fit, and he moved in excellent balance. Tinzen's people had done background checks, of course, and the one his masters had made for him was impressive. Probably even some of it was true; certainly, he'd have to have enough martial arts training to pass a test, and he looked the part. Wouldn't be hyper-nano-ed, since that would be spotted by the temple's sensors and would raise eyebrows. The really serious martial artists held off on that, since they considered it cheating.

He was tall, blond, icy blue eyes, the kind of martial gravitas that comes from knowing you can kick serious ass and not work up a sweat. Tinzen was almost tempted to give him a real try, just to see. It had been a while since he had danced with anybody outside his own art—never hurt to test yourself against the unknown now and then.

Nah. Win or lose, wouldn't matter. It came one o'clock, and the single, deep, and resonant gong in the vestibule sounded the hour. It was a realistic prop, but the sound was a recording lifted from some old celluloid flatvid. Something with a giant ape in it, he recalled.

"How is it I may help you, my son?" My son. That was something of a guess, given that Tinzen was seventy but looked forty, and this "kid" could just as easily be older than he, rebuilt to look younger.

Socially, it was polite to go with the proffered view as valid until you found out otherwise. The Hindus had that part right, about Maya. All was illusion—even when it was not …

"I came to study, Rinpoche. The ways of the Dob-Dob Sera."

Tinzen smiled into his teacup. That was a good one. Nice bit of research somebody had done, probably talking to a monk dropout. Usually somebody was willing to part with secrets for enough money. He was quick, he caught it. "I am serious, Rinpoche."

Tinzen laughed. "You are? You thought you were going to come here and train to be who? Iron Fist? Seriously? You have high rank in like, four arts, right?"

"Five."

"And you consider yourself an adept fighter?"

"With all humility, I do."

"All right. Here, step over this way, stand right there, let's have a look.

"Take a stance and stop my attack if you can."

Roland grinned in return. He shifted his feet a hair, already had his hands up, one at chest level, the other at his waist. Covering high and low lines, weight balanced and knees bent, he was pretty good, judging on just how little it took to get there.

"I'm ready."

Three meters away, Tinzen said, "Actually, you aren't."

In a fast and smooth move earned from long practice, Tinzen whipped the dart pistol from under his robe and fired, a sharp *thwip* of compressed air. He was good; he tried to dodge, but he wasn't fast enough. The look on his face was priceless as the muo-electric spin-charged capacitor dart hit him on the left collarbone, and he fell.

He'd have a headache when he came to, in about five minutes. Plenty enough time for a couple of the beefier lads to load him into the robotic shuttle and send it on its way. He wasn't the right one, Tinzen could tell. Set 'em up, knock 'em down. One-on-one, or with armies, war was always the same. Me against you, us against them, and demons take the hindmost. Though in war, sometimes the demons took them all.

Tinzen lifted the pistol's muzzle and blew across it three times. No smoke, as in the old cowperson holoproj entertainments, but the barrel had been engineered to sound A220, a clean, musical tone in the temple's cool air.

Om … om …

Om … Motherfucker.

✶

"Rinpoche, there is a comm from Dupuis."

Tinzen grinned. He leaned back in his chair and propped his bare feet up on the vat-grown Brazilian Rosewood desk. "What a surprise. Put him through." Dupuis's voice came out of the air as the holoprojic image of him bloomed a couple meters away: "You're a dick, Tin-man."

Dupuis was eighty, looked sixty, was fat, and had allowed himself to get wrinkled and bald. He circulated the basic LE nanos, so he was healthy enough, but he wasn't concerned with the package. Tinzen liked that about him.

"Nice to hear from you, Dupe, how's the family? Skies okay in New York? I hear the war is getting costly."

The current war, among twenty cities in the WestHem, had been ongoing for almost three years.

"Wars are always costly. Price of doing business."

"That, and all the dead people."

Dupuis shrugged. "I didn't create the concept, you play the cards you are dealt."

"Or scrap the game and start over."

It was an old argument; it wouldn't be resolved today.

"Speaking of man's inhumanity to man, you didn't have to shoot the kid."

"No, but, no harm, no foul. We didn't have to let him get within a thousand kilometers; we knew what he was. Just checking out your chops."

"How did you make him?"

"Really? Come on. If you are going to send ops, you have to do better than that. You think I'm an idiot?"

"Yeah, pretty much."

"Give it up, Dupe. It's not happening.

"Oh, look at the time. I have to run, the baby monks have a new hot air balloon they want to show off. If I don't get blown into the mountain, it should be a fun ride. You know, up to the Vault and all."

"I hate you, Tin. You just said that to fuck with me."

"Yeah, that's true. Hey, but it's just a bunch of seeds and shit, why all the fuss?"

"I hope your balloon catches on fire. I hope you fall to a flaming death."

"Nice talking to you, as always. *Chagpo nang*."

"Yeah, you take care, too. Dick."

Tinzen laughed. It wasn't personal, just business. They liked each other as much as they could, given their relative positions: rapacious titan of industry and warmonger versus the neutral Buddhist monk and bleeding-heart peacenik. Honored adversaries and all.

"Comm off," he said.

✶

The balloon was a science project, using faux-traditional materials, vat-silk for the bag, sixth-gen cottonwood saplings for the basket, some propane-ish gas they made from recycled garbage to fire it up, things like that. It had alternating panels dyed red or yellow, with the image of some Tibetan demon covering half of one side, all stitched together by tailor nanobots, quite striking.

Tinzen ooh-ed and ahh-ed over it, and the baby monks grinned in youthful glee as they showed him the ins and outs. Tamila, the new girl from Johannesburg, would be running the rig. She'd gone classic whole-monk, shaved her head, wore the crimson robes, tabi socks in sandals. She was, like all of them, augmented against the cold by circulating tumo-nano-demons who provided heat or air conditioning as needed. He himself had started on The Path when there were still a few of the old tumo monks around, and he'd learned the technique, passed the edge-of-a-frozen-pond tests, but it was convenient to flick a mental switch and crank the AC up or down in a heartbeat instead of having to meditate for half an hour to get there. Both ways made you equally hungry afterwards.

Welcome to the future, Tinzen.

The rise was fast and, given that the control was either more fire or less, smooth and right on target. He expected there was a magnetic guidance and grapple system built into the basket. Be bad business to lose the head of the monastery in an uncontrolled bag of hot air, though maybe somehow appropriate in his case. The monk at the dock was big, agile, and he hooked a line onto the basket and hauled them in. Tamila had already shut off the flame, vented a little air, and the basket settled with only a small thump.

"Greetings, Rinpoche."

"Brad."

He saw William approaching, the scanner in his hand.

"Tinzen."

"William."

William pointed the ancient scanner at Tinzen, waved it back and forth. It wasn't really necessary, the manual scan, the Vault had a shit-load of inbuilt nano-sensors and penetrating rays that would verify who he was, and what, if anything, dangerous might be circulating in his system, but William was a belt-and-suspenders kind of guy. The Seed Vault had been under his charge for thirty-three years, and nobody was going to sneak onboard and fuck with anything on his watch, by all the gods and Buddha's left nut, thank you very much.

Anybody who tried to storm the Vault? They'd be dining on a plethora of A2A spikes, with a side of heart-shredder lasers, brain-destroying ultrasonics, and green hellfire cookies for dessert. Assuming they got past the geosynch warsat's microwave cannons, riding shotgun out past the exosphere.

Quite the potential killing machine to be run by Buddhists, and the irony was not lost on Tinzen. At least they hadn't had to use any of the killware. Yet.

William looked at the antique scanner, satisfied.

"Come and see," he said. He gave Tinzen a tight grin, which for him, was like screaming and jumping up and down in front of a brass band. Of course, it was indeed something special.

As they walked for the first pressure door, Tinzen thought about his conversation with Dupuis earlier. The Vault was a lot more than a bunch of seeds, of course. The cutting-edge research on nanos and biologicals was second to none. It wasn't just a big floating box ready to go when the Earth got its shit together again; it was where improvements to life were in constant flux.

Pure science that could make things better for everybody, everywhere, was a 24/7/365 process, and the things they had found and developed in the last couple of decades were nothing short of miraculous. Not just plants and animals, but the fate of humanity had been postulated and begun, and when those results were made manifest, the next generations of genetically enhanced people were going to be superheroes, capable of things unrevised men had never dreamed were possible.

No wonder that people like Dupuis wanted to get their capitalist hands on it in advance of the rollout. Which made things trickier, but possible. William led him on a long and winding path through sterile, air-tight corridors, hallways that were aswarm with invisible nanoguards that would gray-goo anybody not properly in synch, and those codes were updated at random intervals, and complex enough that even a quantum computer couldn't break them in time to do any good.

There might be more secure places than here, but Tinzen didn't know of any. The Vault was small as floating cities went, more of a village than a town, but it always seemed bigger to Tinzen once he was inside.

They arrived at the research section called H-NXT. After due process, they were admitted. In a clear, upright cylinder full of hyper-oxygenated fluid, was the latest model. It—no sexual characteristics for the last couple of generations—was a meter and a half tall, probably fifty kilos, hairless, and could probably pass for a standard human in a dim light or from a distance.

"We're about to decant hir," William said. "Thought you'd want to see."

Hir. With the sexless ones, they'd come up with new pronouns. Zhe, hir, zem, zose, a couple others that were supposed to warm things a bit from "it." The new models were all improved, but this latest one was as cutting edge as was currently possible.

"Zhe have a name?"

"'Mahu.' Kind of lame, but you know the psychoscience team, they all think they are so clever."

Tinzen nodded.

"Bring hir out," William said.

Pumps sucked the fluid away, through a hidden opening in the cylinder's floor, and as it did, the vat-grown child's muscles flexed and took the weight. Zhe coughed fluid from hir lungs, and by the time the invisible panel slid open in the cylinder, zhe was breathing normally. Green eyes, that was different than the last round. Zhe stepped out onto the tile floor.

"Hello, Rinpoche Tinzen," Mahu said. Zhe pressed hir hands together in namaste and gave him a slight bow.

Born walking and talking, he thought. Looks twelve. How amazing is that?

Mahu smiled, Mona Lisa-like, and vanished.

Poof!

Tinzen blinked, startled.

"Want to not see it again?" Mahu said, from behind him. Zhe laughed.

Tinzen turned, sparing William a glance as he did.

"Monofocal psychedelics in hir exhaled breath," he said. "Only works at close range. It stalls the signal between eyes and brain, and one's sense of time, for nearly a second. Nothing magic, zhe just emits the chem, watches for the pupils to react, then steps around a watcher."

"To what end?"

William shrugged. "To give the psychochemists something to brag about, I suspect. Useful in certain circumstances. Won't fool a camera, but there you go."

"Why didn't my scanner nanos catch it?"

"New designer mix, they didn't recognize it. They will next time if zhe uses the same formulation, but zhe won't. Zhe can reformulate it slightly every use. It'll get past you six times before your nanos recognize the underlying pattern shift and nix it."

Mahu smiled. "Did you like my trick? Was it funny?"

Tinzen nodded. "Actually, yeah, I did, and it was."

He noticed that hir eyes were now blue. Interesting.

"I got some of my sense of humor from you, Rinpoche."

"My apologies," he said.

Zhe laughed.

Tinzen looked at William. "You think we are ready?"

"As ready as we can be," William said. "What about the Conclave?"

"What about them?"

"Um …?"

"Fuck 'em. We go. I'd rather ask for forgiveness, if it comes to that. What they don't know won't hurt them."

"Your funeral. How long, you figure?"

"Dupuis already has ops in the queue. A few days, maybe a week." He turned to Mahu. "You think you'll be ready?"

"I was born ready. Literally."

✶

The main trick was, it had to be hard enough so Dupuis would buy it. If it was too easy, he'd never believe it. He wasn't a dummy, you didn't get to be head of the second largest pharmaCorp in the world unless you had some serious mojo, and Dupuis had it.

Ultimately, it would rest on Mahu's shoulders, and if zhe was anywhere close to as realized as they thought, it would work. No guarantees, of course, but that was life in two words, wasn't it? Pay your passage and take the ride.

✶

The op was a monk-applicant from Hong Kong, and the background had been tailored to make him particularly appealing:

A former Jesuit, couple more degrees in religion and philosophy, a seeker who had run into a wall in his intellectually based journey to Oneness, looking for a new path. Dedicated, trained, smart, spiritually yearning, as fine a potential monk as one could hope for. Didn't get a lot of them this good, and there was just enough dross in the history so it didn't seem perfect, wasn't quite too good to be true.

Went by the name of "Lu," late thirties, average looks in a world where you could duplicate pretty much any holoproj star's face with cheap, outpatient nanosurgery you could get at any neighborhood clinic.

Tinzen had no doubt the investigators sent to poke around would find real people who would affirm Lu's personal history—friends, family, employers, lovers. Dupuis would be looking for the snoops, electronic and real, and it would sound alarms if they didn't go. It was a chess opening: move, expected counter, move again; certain things needed to happen to get to the end game. Small errors early got magnified later, so caution and by-the-numbers was the way of it.

He was looking forward to meeting this one, who would certainly have enough knowledge to make intellectual sparring about life, the universe, and the grand cosmic scheme of things interesting.

✶

In the course of a couple of months, Lu was as much fun as Tinzen had hoped, and his ersatz-Jesuit-trained mind a stimulating toy. Brought up a question: if the op had trained enough in something to fool an expert in it, was he not effectively the thing he pretended to be?

Over tea one evening, they got into the nature of change, and Tinzen carefully offered the idea of humankind's continuing evolution.

"Of course, with nanotechnology and genetic tinkering, we now can direct our own changes, speeded up considerably from what nature did with accidental sports."

Lu nodded. And just as carefully, simply said, "More tea?"

"Yes, please."

Lu poured, then sat.

A little herding began: "So are we become gods, to make such decisions?"

"Well, the Conclave worries that we think so. Why there are such detailed rules about how and why and when it gets done."

Lu nodded. "And what gives them the wisdom to decide?"

Tinzen shrugged. "The notion that a bunch of smart people in consensus are better equipped to offer world-changing conclusions than a few scientists in a lab somewhere who don't have the big picture or the long view."

"You believe that?"

"Generally, yes."

"I hear a 'but.'"

"You know the old saw about a camel being a horse designed by committee."

"Of course."

"A mob is only as smart as the dumbest members in it. The same holds for rooms full of smart people. Real progress needs a consensus, but it is almost always a single person, sometimes a couple, who have a vision that leads the way. Think of all the great advances in any field, and you will come up with a name, maybe a few names, that opened the door for others to follow."

"So, you don't think the Conclave is unlocking any new doors?"

"They mostly sweep the floor in front of the ones that are already opened."

Lu nodded and smiled. Either he was impressed with the metaphor, or thought it smart to pretend to be.

Tinzen made a small gesture, rubbing at his chin with a thumb and forefinger, and the hidden camera sent that image to the team waiting for it. In five seconds, the door behind Tinzen was going to open, and Kinsu was going to stick her head in and allow as how Rinpoche's next appointment was about to arrive. Behind her, just barely visible, would stand Mahu. Three … two … one …

The door opened.

Lu flicked a glance that way. Could not control the barely-perceptible dilation of his pupils as he saw who—what—stood behind Kinsu. And he would know what zhe looked like because that information had been carefully leaked. Data that cost a lot of effort and money tended to be valued.

Data stolen from somebody trying to hide it? Even more precious.

"Rinpoche, your next appointment ...?"

Tinzen responded, the door closed, and he stood.

"Well, I have enjoyed our talk, as always."

Lu stood, bowed, namasted, and left via the main exit to his rear. Doubtlessly alive with joy at having found what he had been sent to find, and believing that Rinpoche's next appointment was with the small miracle standing in the hallway. Here was the way: the Vault was impenetrable, but the monastery was not.

✶

A week later, he and Mahu met.

"This is the critical nexus," Tinzen said.

Mahu smiled. "Teach your grandparent to suck eggs."

Tinzen laughed. "I sometimes forget that you are smarter and wiser than your appearance. Forgive me."

"Part of the design, isn't it? Not to worry, Lu is patting himself on the back at how cleverly he has brought me along. I'll resist his blandishments but once more before I come see his truth. Two days from now."

Tinzen nodded. If Lu bought it, he would sell it to Dupuis, because Dupuis wanted to be sold. The man was a war-waging moneymonger, but he fancied that he had vision, and he would convince himself that he was Doing Good, which, in truth, he would be doing.

✶

The abduction, if it could be called that, began in the wee hours, when the staff was only a skeletal shift and energy was perhaps a little lower than in the daylight. Tinzen watched them on the network of hidden cameras that backed up the obvious security cams Lu had cleverly disabled. He and Mahu walked toward the exit where only a pair of guards watched the door, and before either of them realized what he was about, he pulled his dart pistol and fired.

Nice shooting, smooth, fast, accurate.

The guards went down, and Lu gave the door the codes he had swiped.

Moments later, Lu and Mahu reached the transport, a long-range hopper that he had carefully rigged for his escape.

Right about now …

Another pair of guards unexpectedly appeared from nowhere, waving their own pistols, and a brief shooting match ensued, with Lu winning—not before a couple of near-miss darts spanged off the transport close enough to make Lu nervous. The pair entered the hopper.

Seconds later, the craft came to life, lifting on the repellers. Four more monks arrived, fired their weapons uselessly at the hopper as it rose and spun away.

Somebody would throw a missile at it in a few more heartbeats, but it would be a near-miss that Lu would believe the hopper's radiochaff had misdirected. A glancing maser beam would paint the hopper's rear end, enough to bubble the plastic and make some smoke, but do no real damage.

He would drop the craft low, a few meters over the ground, until he was far enough away to lose any chasers, then he would eventually ditch the hopper, get picked up by Dupuis's security at a prearranged point, and they'd be home free. And Lu would likely be richer than Midas, too. Tinzen didn't begrudge him that. He'd played his part.

✶

On the Vault, Tinzen had tea with William in his office.

"I take it things went as planned?"

Tinzen nodded. "Yep."

William sipped his tea. "You think Dupuis will go for it?"

"Mahu is most convincing. Truth-scans will come up clean if zhe tells him zhe rode in on a pink elephant that sneezed fire. Lu will allow as how they barely made it. And zhe is a walking pharmacopeia of wonder. They can pull out millions in new tech without scratching hir, and a skin sample and a few drops of blood? Tens of billions more, if carefully marketed, and Dupuis absolutely knows how to do that."

"Won't be the most fun life for hir."

"Hir choice."

"Sort of."

Tinzen shrugged. "Zhe will be able to work the system to hir benefit."

"You think he will call to gloat?"

"Nah. He's not small-minded. At his level, you don't bitch much if you lose, and you don't need to crow if you win. He has the prize—he knows it, he knows that I know it. He can afford to be magnanimous."

"And so now we wait."

"Might live long enough to see it, if we're lucky." Tinzen sipped his own tea. It was good—William used extract, so no leaves to worry about.

Dupuis had the prize. A new human whose unique qualities, carefully parsed out, would make him the richest and most powerful executive on the planet, hands down.

He had gotten what he wanted. More, of course, than he knew. Because the most clever part of Mahu's physiology, and the very reason for hir being, was a submicroscopic and virtually undetectable bit of engineering, a tiny, tiny harmless proto-virus nobody would likely see even if they were looking for it. A shrug-it-off artifact. But, it was code that would, when it found its way into a new chem product to enhance orgasms, or change eye color, or add longevity, whatever—would replicate inside a user and eventually become a physiological moral imperative. A thing that would be transmitted through the air or by body fluids and would do nothing to cause any apparent adverse effects.

It would take years, decades, maybe a century to spread everywhere, but it would, and when it did, it would continue to thrive in the children and grandchildren and great-grandchildren.

An offshoot of the god gene, in essence. A Buddhist's dream.

Killing violence would become unthinkable. The notion that one human would willfully cause death to another would be replaced with a realization that we are all in this together, that the grand, cosmic dance and the all-encompassing song of the universe was what mattered more than anything. A fine piece of work, that. There would be no more war. True civilization would finally come to pass.

Om ... motherfuckers.

Om ...

✶

Steve Perry is older than dirt, has written and had published millions of words, and lives in the Pacific Northwest with his wife, two Welsh Cardigan Corgis, and a fussy cat. Find out more about Steve at his website, http://www.soulofacarp.com/sperry/.

TIPPING THE SCALES

MIKE RESNICK & ANDREA STEWART

Smoke swirled near the ceiling, while multicolored lights shone through the haze. Maria lingered near the entrance, the velvet curtain heavy in her hand. She really didn't have the time, but it had been months since she'd been back to Vegas Station, to the Cirque Fantastique and its illegal sideshow. The circus drew her like red drew hummingbirds, and she could only hover as she drank. There was always another job, always another place to be.

"You a cat? In or out?" A hefty man sat on a stool near the entrance, sweat beading his brow. He had a hand-axe belted to his right side, a rare handgun on his other hip. But then, everyone in Vegas carried a weapon. It wasn't the most reputable of floating cities.

Maria didn't answer. She stepped inside and let the curtain fall behind her. As soon as she did so, the bouncer's gaze slid away. She was not pretty, nor ugly, neither old nor young. Bland was what Maria was; bland as oats boiled in water and then put through a blender. She was ignorable, and sometimes—like tonight—that suited her.

An hour was what she had, if she timed everything right. In some cities, she had to wait days for her next shipment—but in Vegas she always had the next shipment lined up before her ship had even docked.

Her first mate had lifted an eyebrow when she'd told him she was disembarking, but he trusted her enough not to ask where she always went when they docked at Vegas. Or she filled his pockets enough to weigh down his tongue. It came to the same thing.

The Curiosités room was set up to look like the inside of a tent, striped cloth hanging from the ceiling and the walls. It smelled musty and musky, like the deck of her ship after a downpour—all sweat and metal and the earthy scent of damp wood. The cages were cobbled together from salvaged pieces of the Old World, welded and tied together in so many places that one couldn't tell where the construction had begun.

Maria wandered past the enclosures of a giant tiger and iridescent birds, toward the back. A tinny orchestral piece played over the speakers, the music bouncing off of the metal floors and being absorbed into the cloth walls. It brought back memories of nights in Texas City, when she and her friend Nicholas would take their meager allowances and go to the circus. It only stopped by in the summer, but she could still feel the stickiness of the cotton candy between her fingers, the bright, hot lights, the pervasive smell of caramel popcorn. They ran through the tents like mice in an abandoned kitchen, arms linked, pulling one another in every direction.

Nicholas would have loved this place.

He might love this place still, if he ever came to Vegas Station. And though her heartbeat quickened at the thought, Maria knew it was unlikely. He was a Scout. He'd never been the type to overindulge in anything.

The aquarium stretched across the back wall, casting blue, shifting light across her arms. Shadows swam in the depths of the tank—indiscernible shapes that only became clear as they moved toward the glass. A two-headed shark, a school of luminescent fish, an eel with teeth as long as each of Maria's fingers. The open air above the water was visible from a platform, a small shore jutting out from the wall.

A knock sounded, startling her.

She glanced up. One of the merfolk—a female, and hence a mermaid—had her webbed fingers pressed against the glass of the aquarium. The appearance of the creature always startled Maria, much as she tried to suppress the instinct. It was a little like looking into a funhouse mirror. Merfolk might have once been of human stock, but genetic modification had stretched and pulled them in unnatural directions. A frill the color of sea grass ran from the top of the mermaid's scalp to the small of her back. Barbs protruded from her elbows and forearms, as well as from her ankles. Maria remembered the first time she'd seen Talki in the tank, and had wondered, only briefly, if keeping such a creature was allowed. But this *was* Las Vegas, and Maria was a smuggler. Questions of legality slid off of her the way fingers slipped from the rubbery skin of a fish.

Talki knocked once more, pointed to the surface, and mouthed one word: "Up."

Maria nodded, stashing her tablet back in her pocket and heading to the stairs, her heartbeat becoming staccato. It wasn't fear. Despite her teeth and claws, Talki couldn't reach Maria through the glass.

Perhaps it was the sense of something forbidden.

"Hello." Talki's voice was muffled through the thick pane. Her tongue moved through her mouth roughly, as though the word were barbed with splinters.

"Hi," said Maria.

Talki smoothed a hand over her forehead in a remarkably human gesture. "You said you would be back again soon. It has been two weeks."

She thought about the shipment dossier in her pocket. More salvaged weapon components, to an unknown buyer. As long as she showed up at the right place at the right time, she'd get paid. It wasn't any of her business, no matter what Nicholas had said.

The Old World had fallen away after the Yellowstone eruption, leaving a new one to rise from the ashes. As a Scout, Nicholas might have the luxury of black-and-white morality. He was a head taller than Maria and possessed twice her strength. With his innate ability to sense changes in the weather, he had certain advantages Maria never would possess. He'd had a position on a ship lined up as soon as he was of working age. Maria had always had to scrabble for whatever she could earn, scraping a living from the sky

"I'm sorry," answered Maria, placing a hand over her heart as she spoke, hoping that could convey the sincerity of her words. Talking to Talki was occasionally like trying to read a book through a layer of gauze. "My work doesn't always take me in predictable paths."

Talki's eyes narrowed. "Smuggler," she said.

For a moment they just stared at one another, and Maria's throat closed. It was Nicholas, all over again. "The laws are there for a reason," he'd said to her. "I don't care if some officials turn a blind eye. People could be getting hurt because of what you're doing. My uncle died in a fight with a Ghost Fleet ship outfitted with Old World tech. Isn't there enough suffering? Why not do what I did—start from the ground and work your way up."

Oh, she'd wanted to slap him. He couldn't see that he hadn't started from the ground. He didn't know where the ground was. He'd started halfway up the mountain and thought he was at the base. Maria didn't have his damned genetics. She only had her wits and an ability to be beneath most people's notice.

But she hadn't mentioned any of this to him. She was too proud to ask for a hand up—and he'd never offered.

Talki's face relaxed. "I ... missed you."

And then Maria could breathe again. This wasn't Nicholas. This wasn't that conversation. "I missed you too," she said. She swallowed to clear the lump in her throat. "How did you know about what I do?"

The mermaid swept her head in a wide circle, taking in the entirety of the Curiosités room. "This place. Your schedule. You say you work with rare items. Someone like you brought me here from the ocean. I am not stupid. I can figure things out."

"I didn't mean to imply—" Maria stopped herself. It didn't matter. "Are you any closer to getting out?"

"Closer," Talki said. "The knife you brought me helps. I've been picking away at the wall. But I think the keeper suspects something." The frill on her head twitched, her fingers curling at the glass. "I want to go back to the ocean. I want to see my family again."

Maria didn't know anyone else who had spoken to the merfolk. Rumors spoke of underwater cities, of some social structure. But people mostly believed only what they could see, and what they saw were the rare merfolk out of the water, and the even rarer raid on seaside towns and cities. "Your daughter?"

The corners of Talki's lips strained, the tendons in her neck standing out, the points of her teeth visible. "Yes."

A pang of empathetic pain struck Maria. She hadn't seen her family in years, though she kept in touch. She sent money back to them, when she could. Her mother always asked after Nicholas—"You two were always so close. Why don't you still speak with him?"—but she was under the guileless impression that Maria captained a legal ship.

"You could always speak to the people here and ask them to free you. Speak to the other people that see you in the tank," Maria said. "Find someone to get you out."

"What, someone like you?" Talki's gaze slid away, as though she couldn't put the force behind the words she wanted to. She licked her lips, her gills flaring, the frill on her head settling against her scalp. "Tell me again of your friend Nicholas. Tell me about this city. Tell me about the people that walk through its corridors."

So Maria did. She used a pad of paper and a pencil when words failed, showing Talki what the city looked like from above, the way it had been so carefully planned. She sketched out the places beyond the circus. "Some people spend all day gambling. They sit in their chairs and only move to place bets or to lay down cards." She mimed a hand darting out and back in.

Talki laughed. "Like eels on a reef," she said.

They shared a smile, and Maria relaxed. And then, haltingly, she told Talki of Nicholas. The way they'd met as children, how she'd defended him from the other kids when they'd poked fun at his appearance. Their fast friendship—the way they'd clung to one another like two dinghies lost at sea. She'd never speak to her crew this way. They supported one another, but it was in the way that struts supported a bridge—there was no kindness in it, only necessity.

She'd sent a message to Nicholas, just after she'd first met the mermaid. Maria knew the name of the airship he served on, and she knew he docked back at Texas City every so often. He should have gotten her letter. But maybe he was still angry; she didn't know.

Talki's fingers curled to fists against the glass. "I wish I had a friend like that," she said. "There are those that miss me. Those that need me."

"I'm your friend," Maria said. She put a hand to the glass.

Suddenly her alarm buzzed. The shipment had arrived. They needed her back at the airship.

Talki shook her head. "If you are my friend, then get me out of here."

If you are my friend, don't walk this path, said Nicholas, his hand on hers. The only friend she had in the world, the person she trusted the most. *There are other ways to make a living.* And then he'd wrapped her in a hug and Maria could feel her world splitting apart. She didn't have the choices he thought she did. "I have to go," Maria said. "I'll be back soon."

"Maria," Talki hissed. She didn't dare raise her voice.

Maria strode away and did her best not to look back. The tinny music rose to a crescendo, and she passed another patron on her way out. Smoke clung to her as she burst from the entrance and back into the clear air of the city.

She'd already given the mermaid a knife. What else could she do? She'd gotten too close to Talki. At first it had been the thrill of having a mermaid choose to talk to her, in a language she understood. And then it had just been having *someone* talk to her, and having someone listen.

But Nicholas was wrong, had always been wrong.

Friends didn't ask more than one could give.

✶

She was back in Vegas in a week. If all roads once led to Rome, it seemed that now all flight paths—at least for smugglers—led back to Vegas Station. Another haul of presumably stolen or illegally salvaged goods. What did it matter to her? Let the cities and the factions destroy one another. If she wasn't supplying them with the means to do so, someone else would. At least this way she got paid.

She met the seller at a bar that doubled as a casino, like every establishment in Vegas Station. Maria had found the lights overwhelming at first, the press of people just going from one fix to another totally oppressive. But she'd grown accustomed to it, until it all just became something that hummed in the background of her mind—brought to attention only when someone mentioned it.

Like the seller did.

"Can't really stand the noise," the woman said, stubbing her cigarette into the ash tray. She glanced about the room, her nose wrinkled. "And the lights." She had the air of a stray cat—scruffy, skittish, and ready to scratch at the slightest provocation. Her jacket was frayed at the wrists, the elbows worn to a faded blue. She hunched into her collar as though she could hide in it.

"You get used to it," Maria said. She held out a hand.

The seller dug in her jacket and produced a slim leather clutch. Maria accepted it, opened it, and counted the money inside.

"I've got a buyer lined up already. He'll be meeting you on the docks at the Citadel. Ask for Felix." She glanced about the room. "I need you to pick up the goods from the earthside city before nightfall."

Maria paused, her hand still inside the clutch. "That wasn't part of the agreement."

The woman leaned across the table. "It's an easy job—you don't have to fence them yourself. Just pick them up from the ground, okay?"

It took longer to get an airship up off the ground than it did to fly away from the docks. It would cost her more helium, too. "I'm not sure why you can't just wait your turn and have the goods shuttled up to the station," said Maria. "Have you been flagged already? There aren't any checkpoints between the groundside city and the station."

"No, but"—the seller licked her lips—"my partner saw two merfolk last night. In the river."

Maria laughed. "Sounds like your partner didn't listen to warnings about cheap alcohol in Vegas."

"He was sober," the woman said. "He said they were mean-looking things, with barbs like teeth on their arms. He said one of them came out of the water, met a guy by the shore, and they exchanged something."

"They're a long way from home," replied Maria. She thought of Talki, wondering if they were here for her friend.

"They're not the first merfolk to be spotted here," the seller said. "Not from what I've heard. One of the residents found a mermaid drying out in the desert heat, like she was a whale beaching herself.

Rumor says she's in the circus sideshow now." She shook her head, her gaze going to the clock on the wall. "I've heard about merfolk raids, and I don't want to be in the middle of that. I don't know what the merfolk were trading last night, but knowing Vegas Station, it can't have been good. It's got my partner jumpy, and that's got *me* jumpy. We don't want to wait until tomorrow to offload. I can always find another smuggler."

Maria pursed her lips, and her insides twisted. Talki had said she was from the ocean. How had she made her way all the way up the Colorado River? And while leaving her daughter behind in the sea? It didn't make sense.

"Who is Felix buying for?" asked Maria.

The seller gave her an odd look. "Probably the Ghost Fleet. But what does that matter to you?"

What *did* it matter? Her family was too poor to be bothered by pirates, and Nicholas was long gone—she'd never see him again. She shrugged, trying to affect more nonchalance than she felt. "It doesn't. I was just curious."

"So?" The woman raised an eyebrow. "Are you in or out?"

The money would pay her crew for another few months and they'd recently refueled. "In," answered Maria.

✶

The sideshow of Cirque Fantastique was behind two doors and three sets of stairs. Maria had to pay extra to access the smoky room in the depths of Vegas Station. This time, Maria didn't hesitate in the doorway. The bouncer barely glanced up as she swept past.

Talki was nowhere to be seen. For a moment, Maria thought, *they must have come and taken her away*, but she rapped out their code on the glass. One heartbeat, two, and Talki emerged from the murky waters.

Neither gestured or said anything; Maria went to the stairs and Talki swam to the surface.

"Tell me about the city again," said Talki, pressing a hand to the glass.

Maria studied her face—the slitted nostrils, the large, luminous eyes. The face of someone she'd thought she knew. "They didn't capture you in the ocean. They found you drying up in the desert heat. Why didn't you tell me the truth?"

Talki's face closed up; she drew away from the glass. Both were subtle movements, but Maria noticed.

"Why did you swim upriver? Why did you leave your daughter behind? You claim to miss her."

The mermaid shook her head. "There's much you don't understand."

"Then tell me," insisted Maria.

"Someone made us this way," Talki said, gesturing to her spines, her webbed feet and hands. "We don't have old cities in the ocean to salvage from. We don't have Old-World tech that makes our lives easier and keeps us alive. What we have—we must make on our own."

Or steal it. She remembered what she'd said to Nicholas, the day before she'd accepted a position on a smuggler's ship. "No one ever saw any promise in me," she'd snapped. "I'm a fast learner, but no one cares. I'm a poor girl from the slums of Texas City—there are thousands like me. No one wants to hire me. You're a Scout. Some people call you Weather Mages. *Mages.* I don't have your inborn skills, Nicholas. I have to take what I can get."

"You've got a lot to offer," Nicholas had said, as though soothing a wounded child.

She'd backed away. "Well, no one else sees it."

Her throat ached at the memory. Talki was watching her, both webbed hands pressed against the glass.

Maria chose her next words carefully. "Merfolk have been spotted in the river. Someone saw them trading with a man on the shore."

Talki's frill rose just a fraction.

"Why do you always want me to tell you of the city?" Maria continued. As soon as she spoke the question aloud, a sick feeling filled the emptiness left behind. She tried to fill the space with more words. "Why do you want to know where everything in Vegas Station is? Why do you ask me to draw you diagrams of it? Is it really just because you want to be free of this tank?"

But of course she knew the answers already.

Talki ran a hand over her forehead, as though wiping away sweat or tears. "I have been lonely, Maria. I only just—"

"When is the raid happening?" Maria whispered the last question.

They stared at one another, the tinny orchestral music rising in the background. The giant tiger growled in its cage, the sound sending prickles up Maria's spine.

"Get out of the city," said Talki. "Do what you must and then leave."

Maria felt somehow betrayed. She wasn't a hummingbird drinking from a flower, she was a rat unable to resist the lure of a poisoned trap. First Nicholas, and now Talki. Her crew, who stayed with her only for pay, were the closest things to friends she had. "Tonight? A lot of people are going to get killed—on your side and on ours." *Ours*, like she had a stake in this game.

"And one of them might be you," said Talki. "I don't want that."

Maria's heart thudded in her chest, each beat like the shuddering of an engine not quite able to start. She'd told Talki where everything in the station was, she'd told her where the defensive gun batteries were. If the merfolk got a hold of the shuttles, they'd storm Vegas Station. "How many?" Maria demanded, her voice hoarse.

"Many," Talki said. And then she slipped below the surface of the water, fading back into the deep blue, leaving only ripples in her wake.

✶

Maria watched the passage of the sun from the gangplank; her crew loaded the boxes into the hold. A warm breeze swept across the ground, brushing past Maria's cheeks and rippling the vast balloon of her airship.

She felt like a hawk sitting in the grass. She should never have agreed to collect the goods from the earthside city. They should have been amongst the shining metal towers of Vegas Station. Instead, they sat close—too close—to the shining surface of the river. The sunlight reflected off its surface, though Maria imagined she could see into the water, see the teeming masses of merfolk waiting for dark to fall.

The horizon turned pale, the clouds cast in orange and pink.

"Last box." Her first mate, Alan, came up behind her. "I've got everything nearly ready. As soon as we've got it all settled in the hold, we can get in the air and on our way."

She hadn't said anything to anyone in the city about the raid. It wasn't her problem. Why should she care? If the raid was successful, they'd free Talki. If it wasn't, someone in the city would kill her for her part in things. The pain Maria felt was merely reflexive; the mermaid had used her, had betrayed her.

And she couldn't seem to stop thinking about Nicholas. He'd tell her there was another way. Even the thought seemed to taste bitter.

"Captain?" her first mate said. He had an eyebrow raised. "Should we finish preparations to get out of here?"

Out, or in?

She'd forgiven herself a lot of things, had given herself permission for a great many dubious acts. Maria blinked. "Get us off the ground," she said to her first mate, "but not to the Citadel yet. We need to stop back at Vegas Station first."

✶

The station security center had the air of a seedy bar, cleaned up hastily in anticipation of wealthier patrons. It stank of old sweat and the sour scent of dried-up alcohol. The man at the front desk glanced at her briefly when she walked in. Maria was used to this. She never could seem to hold anyone's attention for too long.

But this time she needed his attention.

"The merfolk are going to raid this city within the hour," she said.

The officer looked up again, and this time, his gaze lingered. "I'm sorry. What?"

"There's a mermaid in the Cirque Fantastique sideshow, and she told me the merfolk are raiding the city tonight. She's been getting information about Vegas Station to merfolk in the river."

He ran his hands down the stiff blue front of his uniform, straightening and licking his lips. "The Cirque Fantastique doesn't have a sideshow. And keeping a mermaid wouldn't be legal."

This was what he'd taken away from her words? Maria knew a liar when she saw one.

She slammed her fists down on the desk. "My name is Maria Ramos, and I'm a smuggler. I don't give a damn if you've taken any bribes. Merfolk are going to attack the city earthside, and then they're going to raid Vegas Station. They know its layout, including where the gun batteries are."

Her gaze flitted to the window. The sun had set, the horizon turning gray. "Get someone to secure the shuttles. Send out a distress call. You could save lives!"

There was nothing else she could do or say; she left the security center as swiftly as she'd arrived.

Maria made her way to the circus. Alan hadn't questioned her orders—they didn't endanger the crew or the cargo—but she knew he'd been curious about her motives. She'd owe him after this.

She waited in the ticket line, fidgeting, glancing at the darkening sky. At the front, she paid the extra money and said the pass phrase —"The circus is wonderful, but I'm interested in something more exotic"—and passed behind the curtain to the right. The stairs were narrow and dark, descending past the humming machinery that kept Vegas Station aloft.

When she drew near the bottom, an alarm clanged high above her, the sound vibrating through layers of metal and pipes. The merfolk had attacked.

Her breath catching in her throat, Maria ran down the rest of the steps and burst into the Curiosités room.

The bouncer wasn't there. The animals stirred in their enclosures, restless at the sound of the alarm. The tinny orchestral music still played. And there was Talki, floating at the surface of her tank, Maria's knife in hand.

"Maria!" Talki's eyes narrowed when she saw the smuggler. "You're not supposed to be here."

Maria took the steps to the top level of the tank two at a time and went straight for the access door. The panel was easy to rewire; she'd done it once before, when she'd given Talki the knife.

It slid open.

The second door, into the tank enclosure itself, was a trickier matter. The last time, she'd been able to slip her knife into the gap at the bottom of the door. If she tried to rewire this door, it would trigger an alarm.

But what was one more alarm?

As soon as she pulled the first wire free, a high-pitched wail joined the cacophony of orchestral music and the clanging station alarm. No one came to stop her, and she wondered just how bad the raid was. Her fingers slipped several times, her palms sweaty. But the door finally opened.

Talki stood on the other side, dripping water onto the metal floor. With her frill raised and the knife in her hand, she looked dangerous. "My people would have come for me," she said.

Maria backed up a step, giving the mermaid room to stride past her. "You couldn't be sure of that. Get out of here before someone has the presence of mind to blame you!"

Talki hesitated on the threshold for a moment before taking a step from her enclosure, and then another. "Thank you," she said. "I won't forget this."

When she brushed past Maria, the air smelled of salt and seaweed.

"I told the city about the attack," Maria said, not looking at Talki. She heard Talki's footsteps pause. "You don't have to raid us—there could be other ways. There's enough suffering in the world."

Talki laughed, and the harsh sound echoed from the metal walls. "What other ways?"

Maria said nothing, and she wondered if Nicholas had ever felt as helpless as she did now.

"I thought so," Talki said. "You cannot be on both sides, Maria."

And then she was gone.

✶

Vegas station was a chaotic mass of people, and Maria couldn't tell who ran toward the fight and who ran away from it.

"The merfolk docked a shuttle!" someone shouted. The station alarm abruptly ceased, and for one brief moment, silence reigned.

Through the crowd, Maria thought she caught a glimpse of blue-green skin, of frills, of flashing knives. People screamed.

She needed to get back to her ship, to give Alan the order to take off. There was still time. Maria shoved past sweating bodies, past old men and women simply looking to gamble, past families toting children in their arms, past others who looked a little disreputable, just like her.

Voices rose in panic behind her. Metal clashed against metal, mingled with the periodic sharp tap of gunfire.

The night air was cool when she finally reached the docks. Sweat tickled her neck. The press of bodies thinned. Some people still ran toward their ships, but most people had already either left or decided they were staying.

"Captain!" Alan's head swam above the crowd. "We need to leave!" he shouted. "The merfolk have swarmed the earthside city! Colorado River is packed with them! Reinforcements are on their way, but it's a bloody battle! If the merfolk take the city, it'll be bloodier still!"

All the men and women she'd passed on her way to the docks would be dead.

It wasn't like she had much choice.

She squeezed her eyes shut. "Alan," she said, and it felt like another Maria was speaking, "take the ship! Get to a safe distance. I've got things to take care of!"

Maria didn't wait to see if he obeyed. She drew her short sword, took a deep breath, and strode back into the city like a damned fool.

Oh, Nicholas, she thought wryly, *if only you could see me now!*

✶

There was nothing pretty about a fight with merfolk. Every time Maria hacked at a limb, she tried not to look, tried not to see if it was Talki. Her breath felt like it was laced with thorns; her arm burned each time she lifted her sword.

She barely felt the slashes across her shoulder—souvenirs from one of the merfolk's barbs. The lights of Vegas Station still blinked and whirled, making the battle into a multicolored nightmare.

If the merfolk had taken other parts of the station, if they had taken salvage, Maria didn't know. Her world was the flash of her blade, the angry eyes of the merfolk, the shoulders of Vegas citizens, pressed to hers in solidarity.

More than once she thought, *This was a terrible decision*, and more than once she brushed the thought aside.

When the reinforcements arrived, it was well past midnight. Everything in Maria's body ached. It took several minutes after the merfolk retreated for her to realize that she could put away her sword, and several hours for her to realize that they'd won.

They'd held the city.

✶

There was no reward, no commendation for her service. Alan brought the ship back to the docks once the fight was done, and she boarded, and they didn't speak of it. It was how things were done among smugglers. Perhaps she imagined an extra squeeze when her first mate clapped her on the shoulder. Perhaps she didn't.

They took their cargo to the Citadel and offloaded the goods to Felix, just as she'd promised. The crew took their bonuses and nodded appreciatively at the sums. She sent a little money back home.

But it didn't feel the same. It didn't feel *right*.

It wasn't until she received the letter from Nicholas that she realized what had changed. She waited until they were airborne before opening it, unsure what he might have to say to her after so long.

Maria,

I got your letter. I'm sorry I didn't respond sooner, but I had been thinking about the things you said when we parted. I did not want to write back to you with nothing to offer.

It took me seeing more of the world to understand. I know you accepted the job you did because you didn't have many choices. But here's a choice.

I spoke about you to the captain of my ship, and he's in need of a good first mate. I know you've the experience now, and it's honest work with honest pay. He's interested in at least meeting you and possibly hiring you on.

What do you say, old friend? Are you in?

—Nicholas

• • •

Her fingers trembled, the paper wavering. It was what she'd wanted and had been denied, so many years ago. A job with steady pay. No worrying about anyone breathing down her neck or getting caught and imprisoned.

There was another way.

Her thoughts swirled, and always they led back to Nicholas, and to Talki. One above her, and one below. She folded the letter and made her way to the observation deck.

She found Alan there, looking out over the landscape.

"Alan," she said, and he turned, "has anyone ever tried to trade with the merfolk?"

He lifted an eyebrow, and his expression made her stifle a laugh. "People don't speak to them much," he said. "It might be because they keep raiding our cities and towns."

"We have things that they want, and I'm sure they have things that we want. I'm not saying it wouldn't be difficult. But I've spoken with one of them and we're not all that different. I don't think they just want weapons. I think some of them would jump at the opportunity to get Old-World salvage without bloodshed."

"It would be dangerous," Alan said.

"Yes," she said.

"Profitable?"

"Very."

"And the goods we'd be taking to them and bringing out, well they wouldn't be exactly legal."

"No," she said.

He shrugged and turned back to the view. "Doesn't sound much different from what we're already doing."

Maria penned her answer to Nicholas that evening, though it didn't take very long. In the end, she only wrote one word:

Out.

✶

Mike Resnick won an impressive five Hugos and was nominated for thirty-one more. The author of the Starship series, the John Justin Mallory series, the Eli Paxton Mysteries, and four Weird West Tales, he sold sixty-nine science fiction novels and more than two hundred fifty short stories and edited forty anthologies. His Kirinyaga series, with sixty-seven major and minor awards and nominations to date, is the most honored series of stories in the history of science fiction.

Andrea Stewart is the daughter of immigrants and was raised in a number of places across the United States. Her parents always emphasized science and education, so she spent her childhood immersed in *Star Trek* and odd-smelling library books. When her (admittedly ambitious) dreams of becoming a dragon slayer didn't pan out, she instead turned to writing books. She now lives in sunny California, and in addition to writing, can be found herding cats, looking at birds, and falling down research rabbit holes.

JACK AND JILL WENT UP THE HILL

DAVID GERROLD

It's not going to work," he said.

"Of course not," she answered. "But we only have one tool. Failure. Every failed attempt teaches us something else that doesn't work. Eventually—"

"Please, I went to school, too. You don't have to quote philosophy at me."

"It's not philosophy. It's just what it is." She spread the ancient maps across the table, laying out the pages in their precise numbered order, creating a massive grid of lines and colors and labels.

"I'm going only as far as it's safe," he said.

She sniffed. "How courageous."

He shrugged. "I see no value in dying."

She placed the last page in the map array. "You have been ordered to go."

"My father didn't say how far."

"I know what your father said. You're going all the way."

He didn't answer, his expression was sour enough. His name was Jackalyn9 and he was pure-strain—another reason why some people regarded him as an ancestral freak.

The woman was tall and spindly, almost sexless, yet somehow imposing. She had strong features and a penetrating gaze. Her name was Brindayn1, she had been identified as the first of a new line.

"All right," she said. "Here's what we do know." She pointed at specific pages. "These are very old maps, they're from before the tsunamis. So, everything on this side of the black line was wiped out. Everything on this side of the red line is still underwater. These green circles are the islands that were left. We can sail all the way up to the Sea of Angels without much trouble. Most of these places are uninhabited. Not a lot of people want to risk living that close to the water walls, and those that still live out on the sea mostly keep to themselves. We won't be bothered. We'll land and leave the boat here, where the canyon meets the ocean, and we'll head up through here. There are three communities—here, here, and here. We have treaties with all of them, and they're going to provide safe passage all the way to Simi."

"I've been to Simi."

"Yes, I know. But this isn't a royal visit. You're traveling incognito. As far as anyone knows, you're an indentured, selling sperm to communities that are struggling with infertility."

"I find that insulting."

"It should be—"

"It won't work. As soon as they run a DNA test, they'll know who I am—"

"They're not going to, because you're not going to contribute anywhere. As far as anyone knows, you're under contract and I'm just delivering you. That's our cover story and I expect you to stick to it." She turned back to the maps. "There's an enclave of survivors here." She pointed to the mountains above a place that was once called Santa Barbara. "We can get there from Simi without too much trouble."

"I'm not going farther than Simi—"

"Yes, you are. You don't have a choice in the matter. There are things in this world that are far more important than you." She began gathering the pages, keeping them in careful order. When she finished, she slid them into a leather folder and returned them to her bag. "They can get us where we need to go."

"I'll tell you what I told my father. I don't want to go."

"Your presence, as a member of the family, makes it official." She saw Jackalyn9's annoyance and held up a finger. "Don't say it."

"I will say it. I resent being used as a prop."

"Get used to it, Prince. That's all you'll ever be." Then she added, "Unless you disavow your family and learn a real skill."

"I am loyal to my heritage," he said stiffly. "If we had all been loyal to our heritage, we wouldn't need numbers anymore."

"I've heard that speech before. It's boring. It's retrograde thinking. Now, give me your gear. I'm going to go through it..."

Jackalyn9 started to protest, then realized it would be useless. He lifted his case onto an adjacent table. Brindayn1 dumped its contents unceremoniously. She sorted through the items quickly, pushing most of them to the side.

"None of this is appropriate, most of it is either useless or unnecessary. You can keep your toothbrush." She went to the ancient steel shelf at the side of the chamber and pulled down a wooden box. "Here. Pack these. Hooded cloak. Pantaloons. Heavy socks. Soft boots. Loincloths. Hard soap. Armor-vest. Weapon-belt. Pick what knives you want. Nothing ceremonial—and nothing too threatening."

"We're not taking any guns?"

"We're traveling under a peace-bond. I'm going to respect it."

"My father never did. That's how we survived."

"That's how he put you all in danger. More than once. You survived because it would have been politically risky to take him out."

"You shouldn't talk to me like that."

"Why not? You have no power. You probably never will."

"What if you're wrong?"

Brindayn1 smiled wryly at the thought. "I expect that I will have to save your life more than once in the next few days. After that, you will be bound by your own integrity. That is, if you have any. Here, pack this gear. It'll be lighter now. Put on the travel robes and we'll go."

Jackalyn9 didn't answer. He inspected each item with distaste before pushing it back into his travel bag.

Brindayn1 watched with amusement. "Don't look so unhappy, boy. Would you rather be dancing the gavotte with your pretty polished companions?"

"The companions aren't rude."

"Neither are they honest," Brindayn1 said. "Change quickly. I'll wait for you on the boat. If you're not there in fifteen minutes, we'll sail without you. And I'll know you for a coward, afraid to come." The door thunked shut behind her.

Jackalyn9 didn't hurry, but he didn't keep her waiting either. The insult stung. The clothes she'd laid out were unfamiliar, but they weren't uncomfortable. They kept him warm against the cold bite of the wind coming off the sea. A thick blanket of dark gray clouds foretold of a storm. He didn't like the look of that, but it hid the floating city in the distant sky; he assumed they would be equally hidden from the surveillance of its inhabitants. No one knew who or what might live up there now.

He made his way down to the small boat at the end of the dock and stepped gingerly aboard, his expression revealing his distaste. Before he could say anything Brindayn1 pushed him toward the empty hold. "Go below," she said. She followed him down the steep ladder-like steps. The space reeked of fish and other smells, unfamiliar ones.

"We'll be down here for a bit. Make yourself comfortable."

A single lantern hung at the front of the hold. In the dim light, Jackalyn9 could see piles of nets and dirty canvas. He shook his head, but a few moments later when the boat started rocking, he changed his mind and flopped down on the cleanest looking pile. He'd been on boats before, but never so shabby.

After a while, the captain of the boat came down to check on them. He carried two wooden mugs of hot broth, some kind of fish stew. "Sorry it ain't tea. This is all we got. But it'll warm your bellies. Better drink it fast though. The storm is catching up with us, we're gonna get rocky for a bit. Not to worry though, we'll pump up our inflatables. Then it'll just be bouncy. Great fun, eh?" He slammed the hatch behind him.

Jackalyn9 looked across at Brindayn1. "Who is he? What boat are we on?"

Brindayn1 shook her head. "I don't know."

"Eh? What do you mean?"

"I mean what I said. I don't know and we're going to keep it that way."

Jackalyn9 thought about demanding more from her but decided to lean back instead and just glare. He sipped at his broth. It wasn't very hot, barely warm, but it was food, and he was hungry. There were bits of clam and potato in it. Almost before he finished, the boat began to roll. At first it was easy, but as the storm caught up with them, the journey became much more precarious. The boat rolled in the waves, rising precariously with the turbulence, then dropping down into the troughs below before rising again.

Jackalyn9 looked across at Brindayn1. "This will be uncomfortable."

"I know."

"You've been on a boat before?"

"You don't need to know."

"I know that you're a stranger to my people. I know that my father thinks he can trust you. But I don't know I should trust you."

"I don't need you to trust me. The real question is whether I can trust you."

"I will do what is required of me." Jackalyn9 added, "What I don't know is whether or not you should have that authority."

"That is your problem," she replied. "Don't make it mine." She turned away from him then, no longer interested in conversation.

They fell into silence. The boat bounced and rocked in the unseen storm. The lantern swung wildly, and frenzied shadows danced on the hull around them. The hull creaked ominously, straining against the elements. And then after a longer time, it got worse—the boat pitched violently, and splashes of water came drenching them from above.

Jackalyn9 wrapped his cloak tight around him, even pulling the hood as far forward as he could. He wasn't scared as much as he was annoyed. Even the smaller boats in the harbor had deep keels and high collars of inflatables to keep them balanced against the towering waves that regularly hammered the coast. But if the storm didn't let up soon, it would be impossible for them to dock safely. They'd have to stay at sea all night and wait for the morning calm. All he could do was endure.

But he must have fallen asleep. He came awake to bright light streaming through the open hatch and the sounds of squawking seabirds. Brindayn1 was already standing, her figure lost within the folds of her robe. She adjusted her pack upon her shoulders. She turned to see him watching. "Are you coming?"

Jackalyn9 wiped the sleep from his eyes. His hands and face felt grimy, he was hungry, and he ached all over. But he wasn't going to let her know it. She was an old woman; she must be hurting even worse. She showed no sign of it though. He shouldered his leather travel bag and followed her up the ladder, shielding his eyes against the glare of day. His hood had a darkening veil; he pulled it forward and let it hang in front of his face. He followed after Brindayn1 like a silent, dark specter.

Safe on land, finally, where his footing was solid again, he looked back to the boat. It was smaller than he'd thought. It appeared to be deserted. Whoever had piloted them north did not want to be seen—did not want to be identified. There weren't any cities visible in the sky, but that didn't mean there were no eyes above.

This was not the way he'd traveled to Simi with his family, many years before. That journey had traveled in daylight and with a great deal of ceremony. They had been met by official delegations all along the way.

But here—there was nothing, no one waiting to meet them. The shore was empty of life, only an old, abandoned building to indicate that humans had once settled here. It leaned precariously, having been knocked off its foundation by one of the relentless tsunamis that came west across the Pacific.

Further inland, he saw towering slabs of concrete, the remains of an ancient highway. The pieces had been broken and smashed against one another, some of them pushed upright, others smashed by time and weather, creating a wall of rubble impossible to cross. But there had to be a way, the dock was evidence of that.

He followed her north along the beach. She walked close to the water so that her footprints would be quickly erased by the waves. Brindayn1 walked fast, faster than he would have thought a woman her age could move. He had to quicken his pace to keep up. At last, she headed inland, under a thick canopy of broad leaves, wide enough to provide shelter from the warming sun and any possible observers in the sky.

Jackalyn9 realized that Brindayn1 was following a well-hidden trail. She had to be a frequent traveler along this route, probably many other hidden routes as well. At last, they reached the old highway. It had turned inland, away from the pounding storms. Here, it had stood as a series of high bridges. Some of them had fallen, knocked down by quakes, but there were still a few places where the roadway stood high above the ground, places where they could cross beneath.

"You haven't seen this before, have you?"

"I've seen ruins. Lots of them. The ancients built roads everywhere, but they weren't very good roads. They didn't last."

"Don't reveal your ignorance, boy. They built great roads. Highways filled with traffic beyond your ability to imagine. Their roads stood up to a daily pounding of thousands and thousands of vehicles every hour, everyone rushing from one place to another, without fear, without panic. Just hunger to go. All those people, all those machines. And most amazing ... they took it all for granted. Of course, why not? It was their everyday existence. That's why—oh, why am I speaking to you? You have the imagination of a tree stump. Come on. This way. And don't talk."

They walked through strange overgrown places, all of rectangular design. Walls of vines and flowers stood in regular ranks, everything right angles, everything perpendicular. But here and there, ancient trees had broken through the slabs of pavement, upending them in their ceaseless quest for sunlight. Thick vines grew everywhere, a sea of dark green ivy. Where the sunlight broke through the leaves, there were walls of color, deep crimson shading toward rosy-scarlet, blue, and violet, a dazzling display.

"Watch out," Brindayn1 cautioned. "Bougainvillea has thorns."

"Are they poisonous?"

"I don't know. Eat some of the flowers and see if you die."

He snorted in disbelief, but still stepped carefully around a sprawling grove of orange and yellow blossoms.

The ancient streets had been laid out in a gridwork. Jackalyn9 lost count of the blocks they passed. Brindayn1 did not stop, nor did she offer Jackalyn9 a chance to rest. When he did finally stop to empty his nagging bladder, she didn't even look back. When he finished, he had to run to keep up with her. He wondered how or when she managed herself.

"This isn't the way to Simi," Jackalyn9 called after her.

"You're right. It isn't. We skipped Simi."

"You lied to me."

"Had to," she called back to him.

"Tell me why."

Brindayn1 didn't answer. She kept walking.

Jackalyn9 stopped abruptly. "Tell me why," he called after her, "Or I'm not going another step." He dropped his pack to the ground.

Brindayn1 kept walking. A few more steps, then finally she stopped where she was and turned around to face him.

"You would have been recognized in Simi. I couldn't risk that. And if I had told you that we were going to sail north, all the way to Santa Barbara, would you have gotten on the boat?"

Jackalyn9 stared at her, too angry to speak.

"Would you?" she demanded.

He didn't answer. He just glared. The silence and the distance between them seemed to stretch forever.

Finally, Brindayn1 said, "You want to know why I lied? It's all on you. You said you wouldn't go past Simi. And I didn't have time to argue. Now you're here and there's no going back. The boat is gone, and you'll never make it past the hostiles if you try to go back on foot. So, you have a choice. You can keep on with me—or you can stay here in the middle of nothing and wait for the boogies to catch you. But I'm going on. I have a real job." And with that, she turned and started away.

Jackalyn9 picked up his pack and followed.

After a while, they were no longer going deeper into the perpendicular gardens, they were coming out the other side. Finally, they came to a crumbling road that wound around a long slope up toward the distant hills and the mountains beyond.

"Wait here," she said. "Have something to eat and drink. It's a long way to the top." She left him alone while she disappeared behind a moss-covered wall, all that remained of some long-lost structure.

Jackalyn9 dug into his travel bag. He had packed food and water for three days, hard sausage, hard biscuits, hard cheese, some dried fruit, and dried meat. Not his usual banquet, but he wasn't the dilettante that Brindayn1 believed. He gnawed at the sausage and sipped at his canteen, only a little though. He hoped he had brought enough. He had only packed for Simi, he didn't know how much farther they still had to go.

The forest around him whispered. The trees rustled uneasily. Bright winged insects fluttered in the woods. Others buzzed around him. Overhead, loud angry birds shouted territorial warnings to other loud angry birds. Off in the distance, a lonely wolf howled until other wolves began to answer. They weren't close—but they weren't that far either. He stood up and turned around nervously.

When Brindayn1 finally came back, still adjusting her robe around her, he said, "I heard wolves."

"Uh-huh," she said. "There are bears here, too. And mountain lions. Also, wild dogs and cats. Oh, and deer and rabbits, squirrels, skunks, raccoons, possums, and beavers, too. And a few things nobody has named yet. Did you see any?"

"No."

"That means they saw us. This is a hunting ground for the Santa Barbarians. The wildlife has learned to fear humans. Well, the edible ones have. And don't worry about the cats. Humans taste bad. Especially the variant strains. Let's move on."

They followed the road up into the foothills, but only where they could stay under the canopy of the forest. There were places where they had to circle around a clearing. They risked the open sky only once, when they came to an old bridge over a rushing stream. Even so, they waited an hour until the shadows of the encroaching forest lengthened across the span, providing the illusion of cover.

By the time the sun was dipping toward the west, turning the distant sky yellow and orange, they had climbed high into the foothills. Here there were fewer ruins, and most had already been reclaimed by nature, but occasionally they came to a moss-covered structure that had not yet succumbed to time. They took shelter in one of these. Not wanting to risk a fire, they ate a cold meal, wrapped themselves in their separate robes and bedded down for the evening. Disturbing noises reached them from the forest below, things growling and roaring and snarling in rage—and once a scream of something dying in violence.

The next morning, they were on their way as soon as dawn tinged the east. The road ended abruptly against a wall of foliage. The forest had overgrown an ancient mudslide and it seemed as if their way upward was now blocked. But Brindayn1 didn't seem deterred. She pointed upslope. It wasn't steep, only a short climb to a well-worn path that wound around the crest of the obstruction. They left the road behind and followed this trail toward the higher hills. In places, the climb was arduous and necessitated frequent breaks to catch their breath. Jackalyn9 said little and Brindayn1 said less.

Shortly after midday, they came to a steep cliff; it looked unclimbable. There were huge granite boulders scattered at its base, as if they had fallen from the heights above. A bed of loose rocks and debris surrounded them. Brindayn1 looked around, surveying the land. She said, "We'll wait here."

"How long?"

"As long as it takes."

Jackalyn9 sighed and shook his head. Talking to this woman was a waste of energy. He found a grassy slope and stretched out for a nap. The day was warm, and sleep came easily.

He awoke to the sound of voices, low and whispered. Sitting up, he saw Brindayn1 and a young man, barely in his teens. He wore the black pantaloons and brown leather vest of a worker. He spoke softly to Brindayn1, apparently giving instructions. Next to them, suspended from an arrangement of ropes and pulleys, a large basket-like construction hung just above the ground. Jackalyn9 stood up slowly, brushing the leaves and grass from his robe.

Brindayn1 noticed first. "He's awake."

The young man turned to look at Jackalyn9, studying him with a dubious expression. "He doesn't look like a royal."

Brindayn1 replied, "I tested him myself. The strain is pure."

"We'll test him ourselves."

"Do so, yes."

The young man stepped over to Jackalyn9, already holding up a white-tipped stylus.

"Open your mouth." He swabbed the inside of Jackalyn9's

cheek, put the swab in a glass tube and returned the glass tube to somewhere inside his vest. "I'll take this up," he said. "If the basket comes back down, we'll take him." He climbed into the basket and began winching it up the side of the cliff. It hung from a wooden frame that hadn't been there when they'd arrived at the bottom; it must have been moved into place just for this meeting. As soon as the basket was a man's height above the ground, it started rising faster. There must have been people up top, lending their own strength to the effort.

Jackalyn9 watched the ascent until the basket reached the top and was pulled out of sight. He turned to Brindayn1. "Are you going to tell me now? What's happening here?"

"If you pass—if you really are your father's son, that is—then they'll lower the basket again. If they don't ...." She shrugged.

"What do you mean? If they don't—then what?"

"Well, I guess you'll have a very interesting conversation with your mother."

"My line is pure. You said so yourself."

Brindayn1 shrugged. "I'm satisfied. But I can't promise they'll be." She nodded upward. "I don't know what standard they use for verification."

"How long until we know?"

"Not too long. Certainly before nightfall."

"And if they don't—?"

"Then we'll have one more failure to learn from, won't we?"

Jackalyn9 shook his head. "You're annoying. You know that?"

"One could say the same about you. Right now, I'm going to rest. You should do the same." She found a patch of grass under a willow tree, inspected it for insects, then arranged herself comfortably. Jackalyn9 watched her, skeptically. He returned to his own bit of grass and searched through his pack for something to eat, a bit of cheese perhaps, maybe half a biscuit and some dried meat, followed by a few swallows of wine. It didn't look like he'd be going anywhere for a while.

After he finished eating, he took out a small, ancient book. Its pages were frayed and some of them were stained, but most of the words were still readable. This one told of a troubled family and their desperate journey to the west. But many of the last pages of the book had long ago gone missing. In his mind, he imagined that this book might be a history of his own ancestors. But sometimes he wondered if he might one day find a complete copy of the work and what that might reveal about the eventual fate of that long ago family.

Sometimes Jackalyn9 admired the ancients for their storied triumphs. Sometimes he hated them for their disastrous failures. But mostly he wondered how they could have been so smart and so stupid, all at the same time. Despite the wealth of ruins and roads and artifacts they'd left behind, the people of the Old World remained a strange mystery. So much critical knowledge had been lost.

The wealth of the world's information had been stored in an electric cloud, billions of little drops of data—but when the electricity vanished, so did all that history and wisdom. And not too long after that, whatever had been stored on paper began to rot away, destroyed by fire or rain, nibbled away by rats, or simply dried into wind-blown flakes.

Yes, some libraries had survived the elements. Some private collections survived. Where the chambers had been sealed against the weather, there were still a few scattered treasures to be found. Those who studied the past were continually digging through the ruins, but the past remained defiantly distant, receding further into time with every generation. Every new discovery only reaffirmed how much had been lost.

What kept them digging was the hope of the ultimate discovery. The frozen cloud.

There were legends, a great many legends. Supposedly, ancients had engraved the contents of the entire cloud into thick glass plates that would last for ten thousand years. The legends told of great storehouses where rack after rack of these plates, hundreds of thousands of them were neatly arrayed, where ranks of magical devices could shine a light through the glass plates and retrieve whatever information one desired.

Some of the ancient maps that had survived suggested that there were storehouses of knowledge scattered all across the continent, some in the ruins of cities, some hidden in mountain vaults—but the greatest library of all was rumored to be buried in a series of vaults near the great inland sea to the north.

Lesser artifacts had been discovered, small silvery disks, but most had deteriorated so badly they were barely an intimation of what wonders they might have once revealed. They were discolored, pitted, and sometimes cracked. The few working machines that had been recovered had not been able to decode them. Nevertheless, the existence of these relics suggested that greater treasures had once existed and might still be found.

Jackalyn9 closed his book. He'd read the same page twenty times and still couldn't remember what he'd read. This journey annoyed him. Brindayn1 was clearly one of those obsessive souls who still believed in the legend of the frozen cloud. She'd been a frequent pilgrim through his father's domain, often bringing news and messages from the realms she'd passed through. For many years, her visits had been welcome. But not this time—this time, she'd whispered some fantastic tale to Jackalyn9's father and shortly after that, Jackalyn9 had been sent to join her next fevered journey.

The afternoon was already facing toward evening. He was beginning to doubt that the unknown people of the cliff were going to lower the basket, so he pondered his journey back south, imagining how he might follow the broken highway, creeping along beside it at night, hiding from hostiles by day, until he could reach one of the roads that would take him to Simi. From there, he could probably arrange safe passage—or at least get a message to his father.

He was already gathering up his belongings, stashing them in his travel bag when the basket came lowering down and Brindayn1 came striding over to him.

"Good, you're packed. Get in the basket. See that rope? Pull that one down, it works the pulley. Once you start rising, they'll start pulling you up. But you have to keep pulling this rope down to help. Got that?"

Jackalyn9 climbed into the basket carefully. It felt dangerous and unsteady. He lowered his bag to its floor, braced his feet, and put both hands on the rope. He took a breath, hesitated—

Brindayn1 said one more thing to him. "You don't have to thank me."

"Don't worry, I won't." For a moment, he wondered what she meant, but not a lot of what she said made much sense to him. He dismissed the remark as just another expression of her annoying manners.

"The hell with it," he said. He grabbed the rope again and began pulling it downward. The line was made of rough fibers and the pulley above his head squealed in protest, but the basket jerked immediately upward. At first, the work was difficult, but when the unseen workers above joined the effort, the task became easier, and the basket rose faster.

Jacklyn9 wasn't normally afraid of heights, but this was different. He focused on the rope directly in front of him and ignored the receding ground beneath. Occasionally he glanced upward to see how far he still had to go, but that was almost as unsettling. The wooden frame above looked uncomfortably like a gallows.

When he finally reached the top, two men pulled the basket sideways onto the rocky ground. Almost immediately, even before Jackalyn9 could climb out of the basket, they began turning the wooden frame so it was no longer visible from the ground. "Wait? What? Aren't you bringing up Brindayn1?"

One of the men was the youngster who'd swabbed his cheek. "She's not needed. Grab your bag. Follow me."

"But I thought she was—"

"Her job was to deliver you here. That's all. My job is to take you the rest of the way."

"The way where?"

"Where we're going."

Jackalyn9 suppressed his annoyance. This young man was no more courteous than Brindayn1. They didn't have far to go, but it was all open ground. He looked up at the sky, turning around slowly. He didn't see anything other than a few clouds, but that didn't mean much. "Aren't you exposed to the sky here?" he asked.

"Obviously."

"So how do you hide?"

"We don't. They know we're here. They just don't know everything. We lower and raise the basket several times a day for hunters and ruin-scavengers. There's always a few coming and going. They can watch, but we make it hard for them to know how many are here."

He followed the youngster into a nearby cluster of trees, behind them a higher wall of rock, but once under the branches the young man turned sharply left, keeping care to stay under the canopy. After a bit, Jackalyn9 noticed that the leaves above weren't real. Pale green banners, strung with darker ribbons fluttered softly in the breeze, creating the appearance of an even more verdant cover.

At last they came to what looked like two moss-covered boulders leaning against each other, with a space between them just wide enough for a person to enter.

"Watch your step, it's steep here."

Jackalyn9 followed the young man into the cleft—and almost toppled forward. A narrow stone stair led sharply down into darkness. Only a few small glowing panels illuminated the edges of the steps. At the bottom, they paused in front of a granite slab. Jackalyn9 didn't see what the other person did, but the slab rolled sideways like a giant wheel, and they entered a carved stone chamber.

"What is this place?" Jackalyn9 asked.

"Don't ask," said the other. "The less you know, the less you can tell." He pointed to a curtained alcove, barely lit by orange luminescence. "Wait here. There's food and drink and a toilet. And a bed."

"How long—?"

"As long as it takes."

Jackalyn9 bristled. "My name is Jackalyn9. I'm a prince of the Southern Realm. But even if I were only an ordinary, I would still be entitled to the courtesy given to a guest."

"You're not a guest," said the young man.

"Then what am I?"

"You are what you are."

"And what's that—?"

The youngster looked annoyed at the question. "You're the package. Nothing more."

"I am not a package. I'm an adult male and I won't be disrespected."

"You're a man. And while you are in our custody, you will be given as much respect as any man deserves."

"What about you? You're a man—"

"I am not a man," she said. "I am a variant, and I am nearly twice your age. I am a semi-mortal instance of a masculinized line of femmaloids. My name is Jillandra7 and my authority over you is an earned responsibility. You will cooperate—"

"And if I don't—?"

"That would be unwise. We are committed only to transporting your genotype. What condition it arrives in is up to you." Jillandra7 pointed again to the alcove. "You decide."

Then she turned and disappeared back up the stairs.

Jackalyn9 pushed back the curtain of the alcove and flopped down on the bed, a knot of anger growing in his chest as the realization sank in. His father had sold him into slavery.

No. There had to be a better explanation. He doubted he would find it here. Brindayn1 had been discourteous, but Jillandra7 was deliberately rude. Neither had answered any questions except the most immediate. The larger circumstance remained unknown.

Somewhere there was a frozen cloud. Maybe. He knew that much. And somewhere there might be a rainmaker. Someone wanted a rainstorm, a flood, a torrent, a fountain of knowledge, all the recorded history and wisdom of the ages. Someone had agreed to trade his genetics for a pail of water.

But not his father, no. His father would never have agreed to that kind of arrangement. Brindayn1 must have lied to him, must have promised some advantage that no Realm-Lord could resist. An alliance? That was the only thing that Jackalyn9 could imagine. But with who? One of the flying cities? That was impossible, wasn't it? But what if it wasn't?

And what about Jillandra7? Who was she?

He knew about variants. The genetic wars hadn't lasted long, but the viral reconstructions they'd unleashed had triggered widespread biological redefinitions of the human phenotype. The bipocalypse had also left the planet under-inhabited because most of the recombinations were much less fecund. Making a baby was no longer an accidental occurrence, so what was left of humanity was scattered in small tribal settlements across a continent gone wild. If that was not the case, that information had never reached the Southern Realm.

If anyone knew anything, it would have to be those who lived above—in the high castles that hung in the sky—distant and unreachable, ominous, and unknowable. There were stories, contradictory tales of magic and despair, abandonment and glory. No one knew for sure. No one Jackalyn9 knew, anyway.

Pangs of hunger reminded him that he hadn't eaten since dawn. A pitcher and a tray waited on a small table. He lifted the cover of the tray. A small loaf of dark bread, several unrecognizable fruits, a square of cheese. No meat. But the flask contained a bright apple-flavored wine. After he finished, he lay back on the padded planks that served as a bed and stared at the carved roof of the alcove.

He thought about leaving. As far as he knew, there were no guards. They probably weren't necessary. There was no way down from the cliff except by the basket and he was pretty sure he couldn't operate it by himself. There might be other ways down to the forest below, but he had no idea how to find them.

So, he was a prisoner—at least as long as he couldn't see a possibility of escape. But he wasn't foolhardy either. He was in a strange realm with unknown dangers. In fact, this whole journey had been structured to keep him subservient. Brindayn1 had limited his options from the beginning. She might have been exaggerating the risks between here and Simi, but even with a map of traversable terrain, it would have been a journey of a week or more. He didn't have enough food and he had little to trade—that is, if he could find friendly folk along his journey. Probably not. The Southern Realm was known to be rich in resources. That meant they were surrounded by envious adversaries, allies of convenience.

Even if he could get down the cliff or find another way off this mountain, he didn't know this realm. His captors here would certainly pursue. He represented some value to them. He just wasn't sure what kind.

So Jackalyn9 did what he usually did when there was nothing else he could do. He lay back and fell asleep. Perhaps it was the liquor, perhaps he was just tired, but sleep came quickly, deep and dreamless.

Jackalyn9 didn't know how long he slept. Deep in the silence of the cave, cocooned in the almost-darkness, he had no sense of time. He came awake with a start—Jillandra7 was shaking him awake.

Her manner was rough. When he sat up, blinking and complaining, she said nothing. She handed him a mug.

"Hot tea."

He took it warily, sniffed the brew and not recognizing the aroma put it aside on the table. "I have to pee."

Jillandra7 dropped a lightweight garment on the bed. He didn't recognize the fabric. It had a strange satiny shine. "Wear this under your cloak. It'll hide your heat signature. I'll be up top. Don't keep me waiting."

Jackalyn9 wondered what would happen if he simply rolled back into bed. Would Jillandra7 come back down and somehow force him up? Or did she truly mean what she'd said before? He decided not to test it. When he finally did make his unsteady way up the dark stairs, he came out to a fading day. Already the first bright stars sparkled against the dusk.

"This way," she said. She didn't wait to see if he followed. He had to pick his way carefully; the ground had an uneven slope. He couldn't tell how far they walked. Sometimes they were under the canopy of the trees, sometimes under the ceilings of nets and banners and ribbons. And sometimes under the open sky.

Eventually, they came to a path that wound downward through the hills, and here the going was easier. A half-moon gave just enough light that he could find his footing easily. By the time they reached the remains of the broken highway, the Moon was high in the sky. Here, they rested for a bit. They ate a light meal, and each took a mouthful of cold tea, the same flavor as before. It wasn't unpleasant, just unfamiliar.

They didn't rest long. Jillandra7 hurried him without explanation. "We have to get there before dawn," was all she would say. He followed without comment, without complaint. He had resigned himself to the journey—he hadn't given up the idea of escape. He just didn't see the possibility. He had to assume that the entire journey had been planned that way. Perhaps if he could get to a boat, he could sail it south to a more familiar harbor.

By the time they reached the edge of the wood, the Moon was lowering to the west. A broad plain lay before them, unnaturally flat. Perhaps this had been one of the legendary fields where vast crops had been grown. All those millions of ancient people must have had enormous appetites. But now, the field was a sea of grass, nearly as tall as he was.

"Be quiet," said Jillandra7. "I need to listen."

She put a small object into her right ear, then she unfolded a device like a collapsible fan, but broader; it opened to a concave disk. She held it aloft and turned around slowly, once, twice, a third time.

Jackalyn9 waited patiently until she finally collapsed the device again and removed the button from her ear. "Are we alone?" he whispered.

"Maybe. Maybe not." She packed away her gear. "Maybe they've found ways to watch and listen that we can't detect. And maybe they just don't care. Maybe we're not important enough to bother with."

"There aren't very many of you."

"That's what we want them to believe."

"How many of you are there?"

Jillandra7 looked at him, annoyed. "You don't need to know."

"Except for the other man on the basket-winch, I haven't seen anyone else from your tribe or community."

"And you won't. The less you know, the less you can tell. Now, be quiet and follow me." She didn't wait to see if he would. Keeping as low as she could, she moved southward, following the edge of the field.

Jackalyn9 followed.

Somewhere on the other side of this wide grassland, a dark smudge of green thickened the horizon. The grass whipped at them both as they circled the open plain. They picked their way slowly, avoiding the flat so as not to leave a track through the grass.

After what seemed like an endless time of slogging through the thick pasture, the darkness resolved into a line of ancient trees pointing south. A dense forest sprawled around a ruin of broken walls and fallen roofs. Towering frameworks of rusted metal beams loomed overhead, as if trying to escape the clinging vines and heavy moss that covered everything below. Exuberant bushes crowded every open space. Above, the twisted branches of the ancient trees filtered the fading moonlight, dappling the air with suggestions of midnight magic. Here and there, streams of clear water dripped from broken concrete tubes. They circled around the muddy patches.

But despite it all, Jillandra7 moved with careful precision. "We're late," she said. "You move too slow. I could have gotten here in half the time."

"But you need me. You said so yourself."

"No, not anymore. I have the swab. But yes, I'd rather deliver the meat. I don't know how much they'll need."

Jackalyn9 ignored the implications of that. Instead, he asked, "Who are you talking about?"

She didn't answer. "Here—" She pointed.

"Where?"

"Right in front of you."

"I don't see anything—"

"Good. Maybe they won't either."

"All I see are branches. And ropes. All bound together like you've woven a big nest—and then, I don't know, strung it with ragged green ribbons."

"Look closer."

Jackalyn9 looked closer. The entire construction was barely waist high. He shook his head. "I don't know what I'm looking at."

"It's the transport."

"That's no machine. That's just ... whatever it is."

"Machines don't have to be made out of metal. Climb aboard."

"Huh? How?"

Jillandra7 made a sound of annoyance. "Follow me." She scrambled up the side and perched momentarily on top of the wider construction that served as its body.

"Oh," Jackalyn9 said. He followed her up with an uncertain clumsiness. Once he got to the top, Jillandra7 pushed him down into a recessed well and dropped in beside him. There were two seats here and a set of wooden pedals and handles. He watched carefully as Jillandra7 began manipulating the strange controls. As she did so, the device came to life, unwinding eight spindly legs from around itself with deliberate grace. It uprooted itself from its nest and rose to its full height, taller than Jackalyn9 himself.

He half-stood to get a better view. Their nest was balanced in the center of eight wooden legs. The legs looked like untrimmed branches. The central nest could have been woven by a giant bird. The whole thing looked like an enormous leafy spider. Jackalyn9 sat down again, shaking his head in puzzlement. "What is this thing?" he asked.

"The technical term is perambulator. Or pedipulator. Or spider-van. Or whatever other words you want to make up. But most call it a walker."

"It walks?" Jackalyn9 asked.

"Right. Let's go." And as if the strange construction had understood her command, it began moving slowly through the wood, picking its footing with careful precision.

It did not move like anything Jackalyn9 had ever experienced before. It rocked but not uncomfortably. Mostly, their central nest stayed steady, even balancing itself when they went up or down a slope. The crawler made little sound, only a faint creaking and rustling as its various pieces moved against each other.

"I don't hear an engine? How does it move?"

"The same way you do. It has muscles."

"It's awfully dark. How do you see where we're going?"

"I don't have to. The crawler can see in the dark."

"Did you build this? Or grow it? I've never seen anything like this"

"No one has."

"Is this the only one? Or do you have more?"

"You don't need to know."

He wanted to say, "Yes, I do," but decided that would be unwise. He was already wondering if he could capture one of these constructions and ride it all the way back to the Southern Realm.

"You can rest if you want to. It's a three-day trip."

"This thing doesn't go very fast?"

"We're traveling in the dark."

That didn't answer the question he'd asked, but it told him something else instead—that the existence of this spider-crawler must be a closely-held secret, unknown to anyone watching from the sky. Well, maybe. Nobody knew just what skills the skylanders might have.

Jackalyn9 did the math in his head. In oldspeak, they would have to do at least 150 miles a night. So, possibly fifteen or twenty miles an hour, maybe faster across open ground. Thirty miles per hour, perhaps? Forty?

In klicks, that would be about a hundred klicks per night, at least ten per hour, maybe as much as twenty. He'd never traveled that fast before. It would be an adventure. He wasn't sure he would enjoy it. Not having a choice in the matter made him even more anxious.

At last they came out of the woods and approached what was left of the old highway. A long stretch of road remained unbroken here and the last glow of moonlight gave the concrete a faint ghostly appearance. Jackalyn9 sat up straighter. This would give him some idea of the spider's top speed.

The strange wooden machine lumbered over the broken terrain and up onto the long, straight course. Here and there, clumps of grass struggled to survive in ragged cracks and crevices, but most of the way was clear. And suddenly, the spider-thing wasn't walking, it was galloping. The pads that served as feet barely tapped the ground. To Jackalyn9, it sounded like the pattering of heavy rain. The ride felt so smooth it seemed as if they were flying. Jackalyn9 now had a better sense of the speed of the machine.

By the time the faint pink glow of dawn had begun to outline the hills to the east, they had covered thirty, maybe forty miles. Jillandra7 turned the walker inland, off the ancient highway and up a steep slope. The spider-machine picked its way toward a thickly wooded ridge. As soon as they were under the shelter of the trees, she brought the vehicle to a stop. Jackalyn9 noticed that there were more nets and veils above, adding to the cover of the canopy.

Jillandra7 let the walker settle to the ground. She climbed out of the nest and slid down quickly. She patted the flank of it and whispered something soothing. Then she unhooked a large flask from the side of the machine. Jackalyn9 couldn't see what she did next, but it looked like she was pouring the flask into the machine.

"What are you doing?" he called.

"Feeding it," she said. "Then we're going to let it sleep. We didn't run it hard, but it still needs to rest. Tonight is going to be long. Now climb down."

She unwrapped a small meal for the both of them, mostly dried fruit and nuts, the inevitable hard biscuits, and a few strips of dried meat. She also offered a flask of some dark fruity wine. He couldn't identify the flavor.

"You don't have water?"

"It's not always safe to drink. Even if we boil it, there might still be slow-poisons. Or worse, biologicals."

Jackalyn9 looked around. He saw no evidence that others had been here recently, but there was a small woven structure half-buried in the ground. "Is that where we'll sleep?"

"You will. I'll stay out here with the walker."

"Aren't you afraid I'll try to sneak away?"

"No. You're not that stupid." Then she added, "I could chain you, but then I'd have to leave you behind if we had to make a quick escape."

"From who?"

"From anyone. You don't know where we are. I do. Let's keep it that way."

Jackalyn9 considered her words. There might be hostiles on the other side of those hills. There might not be. But he was farther from home than he'd ever been before. He might not like this situation, but sneaking away might be a great deal worse.

He finished eating, stood up, brushed himself off, walked around the walker a few times, studying it carefully, trying to figure out how it worked, but without much success. Jillandra7 treated it like it was a living thing, but she called it a machine. It had to eat and rest, but it moved tirelessly and with a mechanical precision. The engineering of this construction was beyond the knowledge of anyone in the Southern Realm. Whoever had created this machine, it would be better to have them as allies than enemies. Who knew what other devices they might be capable of creating?

He relieved himself behind a tree, then returned to the woven structure, half nest, half cave. Its roof was a thick layer of grass and vines. There was a thick curtain across the opening. Inside, it was warmer than Jackalyn9 expected. The floor was blanketed and there were more layers of blankets to sleep on. A few clay pots of water were by the door. A pair of flasks and a leather satchel sat on a small table. Inside, Jackalyn9 found a bit more food. Supplies for tomorrow? Probably. Someone had known they would be stopping here and had prepared this place to be ready.

Jackalyn9 wondered about that. What kind of communications did these people have? They had certainly been in touch with Brindayn1 even before she had reached the Southern Realm. Why hadn't they established that connection with his father's domain?

Even more worrying, if they were using any of the old ways, were the skylanders listening in? No. With all the secrecy attendant to this journey, certainly this society of engineers, or whatever they were, would have applied the same caution to their channels of communication. Obviously, not all of the science had retreated to the sky.

He awoke midday to the smell of something roasting. He crawled out of the constructed cave to see Jillandra7 roasting two carcasses over a campfire. One was a rabbit, the other must have been a duck. She squatted by the flames, slowly turning the makeshift spit.

"You went hunting," he said.

"I have friends," she said. She removed the meat from the fire and started cutting slices off and laying them on a large leaf.

"Smells good," Jackalyn9 said.

"Eat up," she replied. "We're moving out soon."

Jackalyn9 sat. He reached for a slice of rabbit, but it was still too hot for his fingers. He decided to wait. "I thought you said we weren't traveling by day."

Jillandra7 pointed at the sky. "There's a heavy storm coming in. It'll give us cover."

"Um ..."

"What?"

"Don't they have ... what's the word? Orbit-eyes?"

"You mean satellites? Yes."

"Um,"

She stopped slicing the meat and looked at him. "They have to know what they're looking for. And then they have to know where to look for it." She stabbed a slice of duck with her knife and studied it for a moment before taking a bite. She chewed slowly, savoring the taste. "Try it."

"Duck is greasy," Jackalyn9 said.

"You've never had it roasted over an open flame. Most of the grease drips into the fire." She took another bite, then a swallow of wine from her flask. "We're staying away from the road. There are several fishing communities, very distrustful of strangers, because there are also bandits. We want to stay away from both."

She took another bite, chewed slowly. "On the eastern side of those mountains, there's a long flat valley and a lot of unbroken highway. We can't go that way either. There are too many floaters in the air and hunters on the ground. So ..." She popped the last bit of duck into her mouth.

After a swallow of wine, she wiped her mouth and said, "From here, we go north, staying high in the mountains. The walker is the only way to get across these hills. We'll stay under the trees, so even if their orbit-eyes are looking, even if they can see through the trees, even if they can see our residual heat signatures, they still won't know what they're looking at. We'll look like rabbits or deer. And when the storm hits, they won't be able to see anything—"

"Storm—?"

Jillandra7 pointed west through the trees, toward a darkening wall of clouds. "That storm. Now—" She pointed at the remaining slices of meat. "Eat your fill, wrap the rest for later. Then get ready to go." She rose, wiping her hands on her leggings. "It's going to be a hard day." She disappeared into the trees to attend to her personal needs.

Jackalyn9 ate a slice of rabbit. It wasn't what he was used to. At home there would have been a sharp dipping sauce, but he was hungry, and the meat was acceptable. He wrapped the rest of the rabbit and the duck in a broad leaf and grabbed the additional supplies from the woven cave, as well. By the time Jillandra7 returned, he had already seated himself in the nest of the vehicle.

Jillandra7 grunted a rough acknowledgment as she brought the wooden machine back to life. The spider-van rose up and began lumbering deeper into the woods.

The storm came in slowly, first as a steady darkening of the sky, then a slight dampness in the air, followed by a light drizzle—and then abruptly, as if announcing its oncoming fury, a flurry of crackling flashes across the whole western sky. Thunder boomed across the hills, it rolled and echoed, never quite dying away before the next sudden flash and bang.

Then the rain began, hard and furious. Even under the shelter of the trees there was no escape. Within moments, they were drenched.

They pulled their hoods on, pulled their robes tight around them, pulled a blanket over themselves, and huddled in the wooden nest. The eight-legged machine moved deliberately through the trees, choosing each step precisely.

The rest of the day was a wet gray blur, dark and gloomy, illuminated by frequent bursts of lightning. Water sprayed them both. It rolled off their robes and drained out the bottom of the woven nest. Despite the protection of his wrappings Jackalyn9 still felt cold and uncomfortable, but he said nothing. If Jillandra7 wasn't complaining, neither would he.

Mostly, they traveled along the sides of the hills. They stopped every two hours to rest the machine. Each time, Jillandra7 climbed down to feed it and reassure it that its efforts were appreciated. She spoke to it as if it had a soul. Maybe it did. Jackalyn9 still wasn't sure if it was plant or animal or construct. It seemed like it was all three at once.

The storm did not ease. If anything, they had traveled deeper into its wrath. But they kept moving anyway. Several times, the ground was so slippery that the walker nearly lost its footing and started to slide sideways down the slope, but each time it caught itself and resumed its steady pace forward. From time to time, the rain would ease, but each time it returned with renewed fury. The day remained gray.

Finally, Jillandra7 called a halt. She steered the machine toward a sheltering grove. "We need to rest. We'll wait here until nightfall, then move on. I want to get north of the Obispans as quickly as we can. They're not good people. They live under a sky-city. They claim its authority. It's probably a lie, but nobody wants to test it. So, they send out raiders with impunity and plunder the surrounding communities." To Jackalyn9's worried look, she added, "They won't be out in this weather. They're not that brave. And it's only going to get colder and wetter the further north we go."

Jackalyn9 grunted. After sitting so long in the cold wind, he ached all over. He wrapped himself tighter in his heavy cloak. Jillandra7 frowned at him. "You're shivering. Get out. Get down. Get out of the wind."

She helped him climb out of the nest, down from the top of the spider-machine. "Get under," she said, pushing him into the narrow space beneath the body of the vehicle. She crawled in beside him. The bottom of the machine radiated a soothing warmth. They were lying on cold wet grass, but their cloaks were thick enough to keep out the damp. This was almost comfortable.

"Thank you," he said.

They stayed together under the walker for a long time. Finally, Jackalyn9 dozed. Strange dreams troubled his sleep. A room with his father and several dark men, but the door was closed, he couldn't enter. Then he was with some people he didn't know, and they were taking him somewhere cold. He came awake realizing none of it had been a dream.

Hunger brought him awake and out from under the machine. The rain had stopped, leaving the trees sparkling in the moonlight. Jillandra7 was feeding the machine again. She looked over to him.

"Ready to go?"

"Can I eat first?"

"I left you the rest of the rabbit."

"Thank you."

Jackalyn9 climbed aboard the walker, found the travel bag with the food, and finished the last of the meat. He was still wiping his mouth when Jillandra7 climbed aboard. She didn't waste any time. She grabbed the handles and urged the machine forward. "Let's go, baby."

Here, the forests had grown tall and the undergrowth thick. The way promised to be uneven. The hills had been smoothed by wind and water and time, but erosion had opened gullies and arroyos that aspired to be canyons.

They climbed the easiest slopes but circled around the steeper ones. The eight legs of the walker kept them balanced no matter how severe the angle. Here on the rain-soaked ground, the steps of the wooden beast squelched in occasional patches of mud, but were otherwise almost inaudible, just a very faint patter beneath. The effect was soothing enough that Jackalyn9 drifted in and out of a light doze for much of the night, waking only when Jillandra7 stopped to give the vehicle a rest.

By morning, the rain had stopped, but the sky was gray with the threat of more downpours to follow. The wind remained strong, so if more rain was coming, it would be on them quickly.

"Where are we?" Jackalyn9 asked.

"A place called Kingland. There's a town down there, but I don't know if anyone still lives in it. So, we're staying in the hills. There's not enough tree cover here. Have something to eat, make a bed under the machine, get some real sleep. If we don't get enough rain to hide in, we'll wait until dark."

Jackalyn9 looked at her suspiciously. "You've traveled this way before. Up and down the coast." It wasn't a question.

Jillandra7 studied him. "Why do you ask?"

"I wasn't asking. You know things."

"True."

"Things you're not saying."

"That's true too."

"Why not?"

"I already told you. What you don't know, you can't tell."

"Who am I going to tell?"

"I have no idea." She took a breath. "Look, you're not stupid. But you're also not ..." Jillandra7 hesitated, unsure of the best way to proceed. "You're not very wise in the ways of this part of the world. Maybe you know how things work in the Southern Realm, but that is a very limited bit of knowledge, insufficient the moment you step outside those walls you've put up around yourselves.

"Your realm is just another isolated community tucked away on the edge of a chaotic continent. Nobody knows anything beyond their own borders, except what they know from traders and vagrants—most of it more fantasy than fact. My own people—we know just enough to know how much we don't know. We know enough to be skeptical and cautious and careful. That's it. But in the end, we're just as parochial as you are. So ..."

She spread her hands. "We make arrangements that we hope will be beneficial and if they're not, we don't make those arrangements anymore. What we're doing here—it's because of everything we've learned from the past."

"That explains nothing," Jackalyn9 said.

"That's correct," she answered. "But that's as much explanation as you will get from me, and even that much is a gift. Consider it a kindness. Unnecessary, but given freely. As much as you may disparage my manners—yes, I see it in your eyes—I am still committed to your well-being. I am not without, what is your word? Empathy?"

"I do not think you understand that word."

"Perhaps I understand it better than you."

"I don't believe that."

"What you believe is irrelevant. Now, go and relieve yourself, get something to eat, and get some rest. I'm tired and I'm through talking."

Jackalyn9 climbed down from the vehicle, his mind churning with all the things he wanted to say, all the resentment he wanted to express. But he'd learned in court never to speak aloud what he was really thinking. Whatever words are thrown, like pebbles into the pond of royal politics, spread ripples that cannot be recalled. In that regard, he was very much like Jillandra7—considering every utterance carefully.

So, he did as he was told, made himself comfortable under the walker again and tried not to imagine the larger circumstances. That, he had long ago been taught, is an avenue to madness.

When the rains resumed, so did their journey north. Most of it was an uneventful trek. Other than the encounter with the two bear cubs and the enraged mama grizzly that ripped one of the rear legs off the machine, the mudslide that nearly toppled the spider-van into a deep gully, and the attempted ambush by bandit-trappers, they made good time.

By then, Jackalyn9 was unsurprised to discover that the wood and muscle vehicle was not as fragile as it appeared. Contained within its woven frame were several very efficient crossbows. The two survivors of the ambush would tell how they encountered a giant spider in the forest that stabbed their fellows and ate them. The story—and the spider—would grow in subsequent retellings, likely establishing a new mythology about the fearful creatures that lived in the high mountains, and the mysterious little people who rode them.

Heavy clouds covered the sky for the rest of their journey. Sporadic rainstorms swept southward, drenching them until the next break in the storm gave them a chance to dry off. But the downpours made it possible to travel by day.

Not much was left of the realm that had once been called San Jose. Repeated tsunamis had scoured the land, turning the plain into a desolate wasteland broken only by scattered ruins. Now, creeping vegetation had overgrown those few walls that had survived. A young forest still struggled to establish itself here.

The walker came down out of the hills and limped inland, picking its way methodically through the gridwork of the broken avenues, the foliage-covered walls, and the unrecognizable moss-covered lumps of rusting metal that might once have been tiny dwellings. With all those open windows, Jackalyn9 couldn't imagine that they had been anything else.

"These little houses don't look very comfortable," he pointed this out to Jillandra7.

She didn't answer.

"They must have been for the servant class. Or perhaps the slaves."

"Shut up," she said, her voice suddenly hard.

"I was merely pointing out—"

"I know what you were pointing out. You were pointing out your stupidity. And your arrogance. Those aren't houses. They were vehicles. They had wheels. They could go hundreds of miles in a day. That's why the ancients needed all those broad highways."

"Why did they need to go so fast—or so far? Why didn't they have everything they needed close by?"

"Who knows why they did anything they did? Their world ended so ours could begin. We're better off without them. We'd be better off without your people too—" She stopped abruptly. "I've said too much."

"You hate me, don't you? So did Brindayn1. I'm not surprised. Most of the people who travel through the Southern Realm are jealous of our wealth."

"We're not jealous," she said.

"If it's not jealousy, then what is it?"

"You people keep slaves."

"Of course, we do. It's for their own good. Some people are not capable of rational independence. They need controls. They need structure. We take good care of our slaves and servants. It's a good life. They're well cared for."

"My mother was a slave," said Jillandra7 coldly. "She escaped from your realm. She hid in a trading caravan."

Jackalyn9 nodded. "Yes. That's why we don't allow caravans inside the realm anymore. They have to stay outside the walls. Because they steal slaves. They tell them they're liberating them. But what they really create are bands of hostiles, hungry and cold and desperate. Inside the Realm, we take care of our people."

Jillandra7's response was a single snort of disbelief.

"This walker," Jackalyn9 said. "Is it alive?"

"Why do you ask?"

"You treat it like it's a living creature. When the bear ripped its leg off, you stopped to treat its wound. You wrapped the end of the broken limb. You massaged the torn muscle and applied healing ointment. You spoke soothing words. You gave it the care that you would a living creature, a creature with a soul, a creature that can hurt."

"Of course, I did. It feels pain."

"That is precisely my point. This creature, whatever it is, is your slave. You use it as transport and in return you care for it. The caravans keep horses as slaves. Their slaves pull their wagons and in return they get fed and groomed. People everywhere keep slaves. Dogs to patrol. Cats to kill vermin. Unlike you, we are not hypocrites about it. We are honest about those who provide service. Why should we pretend that all humans are equal when it is so clear that we are not? In our society, the lesser people work to the limits of their abilities, and we give them our best care."

Jillandra7 stopped the walker and faced him. "Yes, from your side, it's a great system. You should try being a slave sometime. My mother was barely thirteen when she was taken as a bedwarmer for one of your bloodline nobles."

Jackalyn9 sniffed. "We don't take girls against their will. That's disrespectful. They come to that way of work on their own. It's always their choice."

"And if the choice is starvation? That's not a choice at all. My mother was hungry and cold and desperate. She was purchased like a piece of meat. A man bought her in the market. He took her and he used her. And when he was bored with her, he passed her around at celebrations and festivals. She wasn't a respected worker. She was just another convenient toy for selfish arrogant aristos."

"Perhaps there have been abuses, but I tell you that is just not the case for a licensed companion. I have been to many celebrations and festivals. The companions are always beautiful and gracious and as affectionate as kittens. They're pampered like royalty. They're well fed and well cared for. Their every need is catered to. Their only responsibility is to create pleasure—not just for men, but for themselves as well. Do you think I haven't spent time with them? They have repeatedly told me how much they enjoy their work, being with noblemen, entertaining them. It pleases them to make us happy."

Jillandra7 stared at him, astonished. "You idiot. What else would you have them say? They're stroking your delusions."

"Is that what your mother told you?"

"She told me the truth." Jillandra7 kept her voice cold and contained. "She told me everything. Those weren't festivals, they were excuses for rape! My mother was repeatedly raped by drunken slobs! The only time they left her alone was when she got pregnant with me. They said she was careless, she wasn't supposed to bear a child, they tried to beat it out of her, that's why she fled your wonderful, wonderful Southern Realm. And yes, one of your oh-so-noble celebrants was likely my uncaring sire. Perhaps it was even your father, that's how close my bloodline is to yours."

"I suppose I should be offended. But perhaps you should be grateful for your inheritance. It's why you're so workable..."

"Grateful?" Jillandra7 made no attempt to conceal her rage. "You arrogant jackass! I wanted to twist a knife in your gut the moment I met you. I wanted to watch you die in slow painful agony. I still do. But I've been holding my anger inside for three days now because this journey is so necessary, but not so necessary that I have to tolerate your ugly conceits."

Jackalyn9 bristled in response. "You know nothing of the Southern Realm. We are the most civilized of all the realms. You've shown me nothing that would cause me to question that. This entire journey, we've done nothing but run and hide. Your people have no friendly relations with any community, do you?"

Jillandra7 snorted and turned away. "You are so stupid. So ignorant. So blind. You've been living behind your little walls so long, celebrating your artifice and delusion, that you have no idea at all what lies beyond. You're surrounded by enemies who would celebrate your destruction. The hell with you and your fantasies. Believe what you want. I'm not obligated to educate you, only deliver you." She started the walker again. "We'll be there soon. And I'll be rid of you."

"You're not taking me back—?"

Jillandra7 said, "I'd rather sell you to the worst gang of bandits I can find and let you find out how much fun it is to be a slave. That's still a possibility. I despise all slaveholders. You should stop talking now. I don't want to get any angrier than I already am."

Jackalyn9 wrapped himself tight in his cloak. He pulled his hood over his head and tried to curl up inside himself. Jillandra7's outburst disturbed him. He had treated her with all the respect and courtesy that was due an underling. The entire journey, he had been as gracious as a prince could be. Indeed, he'd practically treated her as an equal. You did that when a worker was providing a necessary service.

This journey was a necessary duty—a task that his father had given him. He hadn't been told why this journey was so important to the Southern Realm, but the politics of it must have been critical or his father wouldn't have chosen him. So, he had endured the rudeness of Brindayn1 and the open hostility of Jillandra7 as a responsibility to his ancestors, his entire bloodline. These duties were a necessary part of being a prince, representing the royal family.

What Jillandra7 had said, the way she had said it—it annoyed him. She was wrong. Her anger was unjustified. He knew that. He had not failed here. No, the failure was very much Jillandra7's. She had never realized the privilege and honor that his royal trust represented. Someday there would be songs written about her. But now he feared they would not be songs she would appreciate. Very well then, he would stay silent.

The walker lumbered through the remains of the city. There were rabbits hunkering in the bushes, squirrels chittering in the trees, and even a few deer browsing the grass. Jillandra7 steered the machine carefully, avoiding the places where the ground had opened up in gaping sinkholes. They picked their way over the broken bones of a once-soaring highway, then up toward higher ground, places where the surging waters of the tsunamis had finally broken against the surrounding hills.

Abruptly, Jackalyn9 broke his silence. He pointed to the north. "Look—!"

Jillandra7 barely glanced. "It's the Sanfra city. We're not going near it."

It glimmered in the sky, a floating jewel against the dark gray clouds piled up behind it. Even at this distance, and in this weather, it sparkled—a magnificent ornament of spires and terraces. Vertices and lines, towers and terraces, everything blazing with light, bold and unafraid.

Jackalyn9 stared in wonder. He'd seen sky cities before, but never this big and never this close. Always before, they'd been distant lights, twinkling in anonymous splendor. It wasn't safe to approach—that was what everyone said. But just the same, he still wondered about the people in the sky. How did they live up there? Would it be as magical as it appeared? Or was it something far more sinister? There were stories of evil, but little confirmation, only stories.

"Has anyone ever been up there? Anyone you know?"

She ignored him.

"Are you going to answer my question or not?"

"What you don't know you can't say. Shut up."

He fell back in his seat and folded his arms. Her response crystallized his decision. The first chance that came, he would leave her. As dangerous as it might be to travel south on foot and alone, he really had no choice. No matter what she said, he could no longer trust his safety to a woman who had openly expressed her desire to kill him.

He had to think about this.

He was still thinking about it when she finally brought the walker to a halt.

They had wound their way around the nearby foothills, followed what was left of a wide avenue, and finally to the broken shards of what had once been a sparkling glass station. Now it was stained by time and overgrowth. The forest had not yet reclaimed it.

"What is this?" Jackalyn9 asked.

"It's where we wait," she said. "You can get down here. Eat. Rest. Relieve yourself. I don't care. My job is almost over."

Jackalyn9 did as he was told. He climbed down, stretched, and looked around, trying to get his bearings. He didn't have to be on the road to follow it south. As long as he stayed near to it, keeping it in sight as much as possible, he would eventually get home. Or perhaps he could head west to the coast and find a boat. Perhaps a fishing boat would take him directly home in return for the promise of a sizable reward? Jillandra7 hadn't said much about the fishing villages, but the people who lived there had to be rugged; they were the survivors of the ocean's wrath. Perhaps he could trade one of his jeweled knives for a boat. Or at least a journey.

"Don't even think about it," she said from behind his back.

He turned around to look at her. She was inspecting the walker's wounded leg. "I'm not thinking about anything," he said.

"That's another thing you're bad at. Lying."

Jackalyn9 decided she wasn't worth responding to. He gathered his personal gear and walked off to sit on a square flat rock. He nibbled at one of the remaining hard biscuits, but without much enthusiasm. It was simply something to do. He didn't have enough wine to get properly drunk, and that was probably a bad idea anyway.

"Is this him?" a voice said. He stood up to see a woman and two men. The two men were carrying tube-like devices. They might have been weapons. All three were dressed in loose garments that seemed to change color even as he looked at them, brown, gray, green, as if dappled from within. No, just black. Or not. He resisted the impulse to rub his eyes.

"This is him," Jillandra7 confirmed.

The woman nodded. She stood taller than the men. The men were stocky and muscular and looked dangerous. They must have been guards. The woman eyed Jackalyn9 with a calculating glance. She held up a flat device in his direction and studied it for a moment. "He's viable. But we still have to test him." She looked to Jillandra7. "You'll come with us. Until the tests are concluded."

Jillandra7 looked like she wanted to object, but she shrugged and grabbed her own travel kit. "Will my transport be safe here? It's been injured. It needs to rest."

"It will not be molested. This is a sacred space. The locals will not attend. We may be a while. Does your machine need to root? We can provide some care for it."

"Thank you for your offer, but the walker can manage its own recovery." She pointed. "I told it to root in that shadowed grove."

"Very good. Follow us then."

The woman led Jillandra7 and Jackalyn9 down a pathway toward an open gulley. The roof of a circular tunnel had collapsed, or perhaps it had been broken into. They stepped past the rubble into the long, dark tube beyond.

The interior of this long pipe was lined with rails, above and below. A little farther on and both of the guards brought out illumination devices. They gave off a sharp white glow, lighting up the tunnel as bright as day. Jackalyn9 said nothing. Whatever magic these people had, it was unlike anything he had experienced in the Southern Realm.

Just ahead, a simple dais blocked the tube, but it had seats on it, so Jackalyn9 assumed that this was their destination. It had short walls and high windows framing it, so it was clearly intended as a private space. Obviously, their host intended for them to sit there. Perhaps there would be tea. Or wine. But Jackalyn9 didn't see any refreshments. So maybe this was where they intended to test him? Or maybe this would be an interview of some kind. Or, he hoped, an explanation.

The guards stood to one side, holding their light-making devices high while the woman stepped up onto the platform. Jillandra7 pushed him forward and Jackalyn9 climbed up after. He seated himself opposite the nameless woman. She didn't look at him. She was busying herself with her device.

Jillandra7 parked herself beside him. She poked him. "Fasten your seatbelt."

"Eh?"

"Here—" She reached around him to something behind his shoulder, pulled a strap diagonally across his chest and touched the end of it to the seat back where it stayed as if glued. She found a similar strap behind her own seat and repeated the maneuver. Opposite him, the woman had done the same. The two guards remained behind.

Jackalyn9 frowned in puzzlement. He tugged at the strap to see if he could release it, but it resisted his efforts. "I don't see why it is necessary to imprison us—" But before he could finish the sentence, the platform began to whine—and then it *moved*.

It was a vehicle! It accelerated slowly at first, then faster and faster. Soon it was flying down the tunnel. The walls blurred around them, and wind whipped at his hair, tugged at his cloak. He had never experienced anything like this, and it terrified him. He looked to Jillandra7, wide-eyed—she was evidently enjoying this. She saw the terror on his face and laughed.

Jackalyn9 wrapped his arms around his chest, closed his eyes, and told himself, "These people are not afraid. They are familiar with this device. They know it is safe. I will count my breaths until this unholy machine arrives at its destination."

He lost count several times and had to start again, but eventually his heartbeat slowed and he dared to open his eyes again. The walls still blurred, the vehicle existed in a sphere of light, with the tunnel racing out of darkness before them and disappearing back into darkness behind them.

And then, finally, the platform began to slow. It coasted to a graceful stop at the side of an open chamber. More of that strange white glow filled the room. Jackalyn9 had never seen a space so brightly illuminated. He could see every corner clearly. The walls of this place looked old, but free of dirt and grime, another marvel.

Jillandra7 did something to the strap across her chest and it retracted back into the seat. She did something to his own strap as well and he was free of the encumbrance.

"This way," said the woman. She led them across a tiled floor and into a square alcove lined with doors. One of the doors was open, revealing a small square room. She ushered Jillandra7 and Jackalyn9 into the space and stepped in behind them. As Jackalyn9 turned around, puzzled, the door slid shut. Another marvel, yes, but why? This room was tiny. Just enough space for the three of them to stand—

And then ... then it dropped downward and Jackalyn9 gasped.

He grabbed for the wall. But they weren't falling, they were descending! Jillandra7 put her hand on his arm. "Easy. It's only an elevator." As if that explained it. But the gesture still calmed him. Despite her outspoken enmity, it was still an uncharacteristic moment of compassion.

The elevator thumped to a stop and the door slid open again. They stepped out into a very different corridor. It took him a moment to realize what had happened, then he smiled. Very clever. A device for traveling up and down. It seemed frivolous to him. Why build a machine for something so basic? But perhaps they had descended a great distance. That might explain it.

He followed the woman—she still hadn't introduced herself—through a series of passages, all lit with that same bright glow. It seemed to come from everywhere, but especially the ceiling. He'd heard tales of the magics of the ancients. He hadn't believed in them. If their magic had been that good, why had they died? But now, perhaps, maybe, it was possible that some of those tales might have some truth in them.

"In here," she said, pointing to an open doorway. She nodded to Jillandra7. "You wait with him."

This room was larger. It had a desk, a couch, and several padded chairs, but was otherwise empty. Jackalyn9 examined one of the chairs before he sat. It was as luxurious a piece of furniture as he had ever seen, with leather stitching so precise he could not imagine how it had been done. It would have been suitable for his father's throne. And there were five of these chairs in the room, all identical. What other riches did these people have that they could be so casual about such chairs? Jillandra7 didn't seem to notice. She paced back and forth as if she was looking for something.

"Are you all right?" Jackalyn9 asked.

"There's something wrong," she said. "This isn't the way it's supposed to be."

"How is it supposed to be?"

"I don't know. Just not this. They were supposed to—there was a promise of knowledge. They told us that the cloud was leaking. The cloud is information. It's in the air all around us. We know it's there, but we can't drink it. These people—they told us they had water. They promised water, a whole pail of water. My people—we need it to feed the fields of ignorance. We need so we can understand how to grow the old magic."

"And destroy the world again—?"

"Maybe we can do better. We have to. We're living in misery and disease. Oh, we think we're doing well—but we're not. We're hungry half the time. Our children die of ailments because we have no healing. The ancients could tell when storms were coming, when tsunamis threatened. They flew through the skies. They went to the Moon—"

"Nobody believes that—"

"Listen to me! When everything fell apart, the lucky survivors retreated to the cities. And all of us down here? Why were we abandoned? We have a right to the magic too, don't we? So here we are—wherever this is. These people, they say it's raining. And they have buckets and buckets of data. My people—we're engineers. We want a pail of that information, anything we can use. Anything at all—"

A new voice. "That might not be possible—"

Jillandra7 and Jackalyn9 both looked up. A white-haired woman stood in the doorway. She wore a plain robe. "May I join you? My name is Ballantine. No number." She was carrying a tray with three cups and a steaming pot of tea. She didn't wait for an invitation; she came into the room and sat opposite Jackalyn9. "You look healthy enough." To Jillandra7, she said, "Please sit."

She busied herself pouring tea and passing out cups. Jillandra7 sat, accepted the first cup. Jackalyn9 took a cup and sniffed suspiciously. It was an unfamiliar aroma, but not unpleasant. He sipped carefully.

Ballantine put her own cup down on the desk behind her and looked to Jackalyn9. "I don't know how much anyone has told you, but unfortunately, the situation has changed. Yes, we still want your X-chromosome. And possibly your Y-chromosome as well. As a courtesy, even if your bloodline is not as represented, we will still minimize the terms of your indenture …"

"Stop. Right there," said Jackalyn9. "I am not a slave. I am a prince of the Southern Realm."

Ballantine held up a hand. "Please—" She waved at the wall and suddenly it was a window. They were up in the air, flying over wooded lands. Jackalyn9 leapt to his feet and backed away.

"It's only a picture," said Jillandra7. "Sit down. It's not real."

"It is real—" he said, pointing.

Ballantine waved again and the picture disappeared. "I'm sorry," she said. "I had no idea."

Jackalyn9 sat down nervously. "What magic is this?"

"It's not magic, it's just technology."

"That word means magic."

"Yes, I guess it does mean that to you." Ballantine sighed. "I had hoped to make this easier."

Jillandra7 interrupted. "What is it you're not telling us?"

Ballantine held up a hand to quiet her. "Be patient, please." To Jackalyn9, she said, "Do you want to try again?"

"All right, yes. Please."

Ballantine waved the wall to life again. This time, Jackalyn9 recognized the landscape. "That's the Southern Realm," he said. "There's the fields, I recognize them, and wall, and the towers and wait—" He stood up again. "No! No! What is this you're showing me? This is wrong! The keep is burning! The whole realm—make it stop! Stop it!"

The wall showed horror. Men in leather armor swarmed through the streets, swinging their machetes with skilled precision. They left bodies in their wake, men, women, children—no exceptions. And fire as well. Thick clouds of dark smoke rose from the largest buildings.

Jackalyn9 cringed backward, flailing, slamming up against the wall behind him, desperately trying to get away from the images before him. His screams became incoherent—until Ballantine blanked the image. He collapsed to his knees, overcome by fear and rage. "I've got to get back," he managed to say. "I've got to get back—"

Jillandra7 came to his side. She tried to put a hand on his shoulder, but he pushed her away. He stood up. He couldn't find the words. He clenched his fists, his face was red. He wanted to hurt something—

"That was recorded three days ago," Ballantine said. "This was recorded earlier today."

This time the wall showed a landscape of burnt desolation. Nothing remained except a fragment of wall, a tilted Tower, a shell of a building. "There's nothing to go back to. The keep is gone. The Southern Realm has been wiped out."

Jackalyn9 stared at the wall, silent, unable to find the words. Jillandra7 led him back to his chair and eased him down. "Leave me alone," he said. "Why aren't you celebrating? You hate me—"

"I hate slaughter even more."

"Go away—"

Jillandra7 retreated to the couch. Ballantine blanked the wall and sat down opposite Jackalyn9. She waited patiently until he finally looked to her and said hoarsely, "Tell me."

"Are you ready to hear it?"

"Tell me," he repeated.

"Very well. The Southern Realm made enemies. Too many enemies. All those enemies had a common goal—free themselves from the oppression of the Realm. So, they made an alliance, a secret alliance of resistance. They raised an army, and they trained their warriors in secret, in many isolated places so they would look like bandit camps.

"Brindayn1 knew of the alliance. She knew the slaughter was coming. She tried to warn your father. She told him he should take his family and leave. That might save his people. He didn't believe her. He said the realm's defenses were strong enough to withstand any assault. He was wrong. He was given the chance to surrender. He refused. What you saw on the wall—that was the result." Ballantine stopped and looked to Jackalyn9 gently. "I know that this is a lot to take in."

"I should have died with my people—"

"You would have, if you had stayed. Brindayn1 saved you."

"She didn't like me."

"Why should she have? You are not likable, Jackalyn9. But she knew that your bloodline is unique, and for that reason, necessary. So, she invited your father to send you to us. She promised great rewards, because she knew they would never have to be delivered. But that's why you're here, Jackalyn9. You have a null-variant genotype. That's something we wish to preserve."

"Who are you?"

"Call us librarians. We're trying to restore the wealth of ancient knowledge that has disappeared from the world. But whether or not that knowledge should be returned to human beings—we are still arguing about that ourselves."

"The people in the sky—"

"We have no contact with them. For all we know, they may be savages of another kind, living among wonders they don't understand. Or they may be gods. We don't know. So, we have to make our decisions based on what we do know." Her tone softened. "We will keep you safe, Jackalyn9. There is nothing for you to go back to."

Jillandra7 spoke then. "May I remind you? My people still want the pail of water that was promised."

"Oh," said Ballantine. "Yes. Your people. I'm sorry about that—"

"Wait! What? My people had nothing to do with—with his people." She pointed at Jackalyn9.

Ballantine said, "You had an arrangement with the Southern Realm—"

"It wasn't an arrangement, we traded for food and supplies—"

"Even that much was perceived as cooperation. That is why your community was never told about the alliance of resistance, never invited to join. And that is why—" Ballantine hesitated. "I am sorry, Jillandra7, but your community was attacked as well."

"They'd have to find us first."

"They did."

Jillandra7 shook her head in denial. "No, they couldn't have. We're well-hidden and—"

"The resistance to the realm was assembling itself for almost a decade. They placed spies and observers everywhere. Where they could, they seduced information. Where they couldn't seduce it, they bought it. Where they couldn't buy it, they blackmailed for it—and where they couldn't blackmail, they resorted to kidnapping and torture. It was a brutal alliance, forged in hatred and rage. They infused their warriors with fury and turned them loose without mercy. I'm sorry, but we have yet to establish if there were any survivors among your people."

"No," said Jillandra7. "I refuse to believe it—"

"Shall I show you the pictures?"

"Pictures can be faked—"

"What benefit would we gain by such trickery?"

"I don't know, but why should I trust you?"

Ballantine shrugged, as if the answer was obvious. "Your genotype is 97% true. We can work with that. So, yes—you could assume that we would trick you for your genetics, and you would be justified in leaving. If that's what you want, we won't try to stop you. But you do need to know, if you try to return south, you will find out the hard way that we have not tricked you, and we would lose your genotype and you would lose your life. It would be a tragic waste. It remains your choice to make. But the Southern Realm is gone, and you have no friends anywhere in that region. Here at least, we can keep you safe. Both of you. And you can contribute your genetics."

Jillandra7 lowered her face into her hands, still unable to accept what she was hearing. Jackalyn9 remained in shock.

Ballantine faced them both. "You will need some time to process this shock. You are going to experience denial and disbelief, as well as anger and grief, perhaps even despair. But when you are ready to hear what else is possible, we can have a different conversation."

Ballantine left the room then. Jillandra7 stared after her, then abruptly, she began sobbing, great heaving gasps. Jackalyn9 approached her cautiously—but it was her turn to push him away.

"I am not unfeeling," he said. "And you're not alone."

"Yes, I am. So are you."

"Well, then—let's be alone together."

At that, she looked up, her face streaked with tears. "You're still an ass."

"And you're still rude." He sat down beside her on the couch.

And for the longest time they sat alone together.

Jack and Jill
Went up the hill
To fetch a pail of water.

Jack fell down
And broke his crown
And Jill came tumbling after.

✶

David Gerrold has been writing professionally for half a century. He created the tribbles for *Star Trek* and the Sleestaks for *Land of the Lost*. His most famous novel is *The Man Who Folded Himself*. His semi-autobiographical tale of his son's adoption, *The Martian Child,* won both the Hugo and the Nebula Awards, and was the basis for the 2007 movie starring John Cusack and Amanda Peet. His latest novel, *Hella,* will be published in June of 2020.

THE FLYING DUTCHMAN

JEFF STURGEON & STEVEN L. SEARS

The ship shuddered again as the winds tried to tear the vessel from the harpoons anchoring it to the ground. The frame groaned at the pressure, but the old airship refused to break apart. The *Havana* was a heavy frigate that plied the sky loop and its jump points across the old southern border of the USA, from Vegas City and UC Tower on the coast to Nawlins in the far south to New York in the east. Still flightworthy, still fighting the effects of age. But even the durable majestic ships of the past had their limits.

Crew members on the bridge glanced worriedly at their captain. Theresa Sebesta sat calmly in her command chair as if the buffeting wind was no more than a mild inconvenience.

"Have they made it back yet?"

Her question made the crew look hurriedly at their displays. Labrake, her exec, shook his head.

"Have they set out the beacon?"

"It's being put out now," Labrake said flatly. He was a seasoned officer and, like the captain, didn't show any emotion when in command. He was efficient and smart, someone Sebesta had learned to rely on in their years together.

Sebesta's mouth tightened. They should have already been back in the skies where this mother of a summer blizzard would carry them to Vegas City in record time with their load of riches. "They better hurry." It was all she had to say.

✶

"Where the bloody hell is Rockpile?" Crewman Ramirez asked for the twentieth time as she and her partner, Tanner, geared up to take the beacon down to the edge of the ramp.

Tanner stopped answering her after he pulled on a heavy parka and snugged the hood down over his face. He tightened the goggles over his eyes and shoved his big hands into his gloves. He adjusted his harness, cinching the straps firm, before grabbing the beacon.

Ramirez clipped the line to his harness and gave it a tug to be sure it was properly secured, then signaled him on. The big man edged out towards the hangar door and leaned into the wind. He was soon lost in the swirling snow; the only indication of his progress was the steady tug of the line she held. With his slow pace, she had plenty of time to grouse about their situation.

They had set down little over a day ago. How Captain Sebesta had known of the treasure under the layers of ash, stone, and rubble, Ramirez wouldn't guess. Whatever the case, the *Havana* now had a full load of treasure and salvage from an abandoned bank and casino, worth more than any salvage she'd ever seen before. The storm had set in just as they were bringing the last loads up into the bay and the weather had gone to hell from there. The captain ordered everyone to pack up and ready themselves to head back home. But one of the crews hadn't returned yet, Rockpile's crew.

The lights on the ship should have led them back. Rockpile's crew hadn't been too far behind her own. While the ship hadn't been easy to see until they got close, the lights could be seen from the tunnel entrance. No one could get them on the radio either. Not too surprising as the blizzard was wreaking havoc with the internal communications, as well.

She tried her comm link. "Bridge, this is Ramirez over ... bridge over ... anyone?" No answer. The comms had issues at the best of times, but with this storm it was worse than normal. Communication had to be done the hard way. The lieutenant himself had come down to deliver the order, to manually set a locator beacon on the ground.

Rockpile wasn't one to mess around, but some of his crew did.

Maybe they ran into trouble. But what trouble could they have stumbled into half an hour from the ship? If they had screwed off, well, the captain didn't tolerate BS when the weather turned bad. Ramirez passed the minutes thinking of punishments before the beacon ignited. It threw a flashing orange light that pierced the whiteout like a laser and was accompanied by a sharp horn blast. Its wail was quickly taken away by the storm as with anything else not tied down.

Five minutes passed as she watched the ramp and storm. Tanner's clip line ran down the railing, taut but shaking with the wind. She gripped the line as well as the railing, holding on as gusts of wind and snow swirled into the entry bay. She knew Tanner was waiting at the bottom, waiting to help anyone—if anyone could see the light and hear the horn to find their way back.

The beacon's orange light bathed the entry bay every couple of seconds, pushing back the glow from the ceiling light, the snow softening the brightness like a time lapse sun behind clouds. Again, the blast of the horn's alarm burst pierced the whistle of the wind, then was gone in a nanosecond.

The wind continued to scream and howl. Ramirez took a deep breath; she knew Tanner couldn't last much longer in these conditions. He was only wearing a basic work parka, not the long-term exploration parka the ground crews wore.

Tanner's clip line suddenly went rigid, like a load line goes when hauling up salvage. The vibration stopped. The cable began to pull through her hand, possibly ten feet before it suddenly wrenched to the side almost causing her to lose her footing. The line went slack as it recoiled, emerging from the maelstrom, sliding in the snow towards her like a snake. She dropped it and it returned to the railing as if nothing had happened.

The beacon continued to go off every two seconds as she stared down the ramp trying to see behind the wall of the blizzard. She felt extremely uncomfortable, the short hair on her neck standing up. Her eyes moved quickly across her field of vision as she backed up a step, pulling the glove off her right hand. She reached into her parka and pulled out a handgun, an ancient weapon called a Parker M77. It wasn't standard issue. Truth is, it was contraband she had found on a previous salvage. But she had kept it, appreciating its age and effectiveness.

Seconds passed as the beacon screamed and flashed its distress. Her hand was cold holding the weapon, but adrenalin overrode it. Her eyes strained to see through the maelstrom.

She noticed that the ramp had stopped its vibration, as if something heavy had been put on it like salvage, or someone had stepped onto it. The light of the beacon no longer flashed in her direction, though she could see it flashing in other directions. Something was blocking it.

She looked at the main bay doors behind her. They had not been opened since Rockpile's crew went down over five hours ago. She then looked at the stairwell door where it seemed like an eternity ago, she and Tanner had emerged. The door blurred in the swirling snow. The whistling wind in her ears played with her senses, imagining voices, malevolent and threatening.

Her instincts screamed *move*. With a glance down the ramp at the storm, she quickly moved to the stairway door, grabbing the latch and opening it, slamming it shut behind her, spinning the lock handle and, for added measure, dropping the steel lock bar into place.

Her breath came in short bursts. *I'm just being paranoid* she thought. Still, nothing could come through the big hangar doors or this door unless opened from the side she was on. Her breathing slowed as she silently chastised herself, thinking of the laugh Tanner would have when he found out she had run from the bay like a scared rabbit.

Still … something bothered her. Where was Tanner?

There was a small security window at eye level. She opened it and looked into the entry bay, the snow swirling with the wind, her tracks already gone. Ramirez pulled her hood back and goggles off to see more clearly. Snow stung her eyes as she waited and watched, her heart pounding.

✶

Electrical Engineering Officer Walter Jones rushed down the main bay hallway toward the ancillary communications panel next to the massive bay doors. Jonesy, as the crew called him, slammed his fist on the main access to pop it open as he flipped up the plastic guard plate and turned the comm volume up. He cursed silently as he heard only the rush of white noise. He knew he'd have to re-establish the comm system before he could open the doors for the side ramps. Rockpile and his crew finding the main ramp was a longshot in this storm. Normally, the side ramps would be opened as well, offering more options for their safety. That would also open the interior bay doors, but that wasn't usually a problem. As usual, though, there had been a misfire somewhere in the wiring and Jonesy was sent to save the day.

But first, he had to establish communications. The wiring ran side-by-side anyway, so fixing the comm should help him fix the remote for the bay doors and the ramps.

The system was ancient at best, and the storm didn't help. On the lower level, in the bays nearest the surface, the comms only worked half the time. Here, at Aft L6, the port where Ramirez and Tanner were working, the connection was far worse. The ground and storm created too much static electricity. He ducked down to drop the access panel for the relays. The comm unit was a hodgepodge of collected materials; sometimes wiggling the wires helped.

Jonesy would have to see if any spare parts were to be had once they made it to Vegas City. That was where the deals were done, the best prices for salvage bought and sold. With this huge haul, they should be able to afford some upgrades.

He began to hum to himself as his fingers worked among the wiring and relays, a nervous habit that helped him focus. *It would be good to be home,* he thought. Most of the crew had family there and the captain's family had headquartered there for decades. It was a neutral city. It was a dangerous city for those not wise to the street, but it was home.

Any place was better than this freezing hell hole, he mused. At this moment, the *Havana* hung above an old, ruined city once called Reno. How the captain knew of this place, he didn't know, or particularly care, so long as they made it back. Reno had been a place much like the mythical city of Las Vegas, from which Vegas City was born, but they hadn't taken to the skies before YE. The ruins of old Las Vegas were still giving up its salvage, its fabled wealth, the treasure. This place, however, had mostly been unexplored. Its distance, the weather, the danger, the stories that were told about the north by the crews and ships of the Loop, kept it isolated.

But the trip had been worth it. The holds of the *Havana* were already filled with gold and other treasures they had discovered below. If it weren't for Rockpile and his group of slackers, they'd be heading home by now.

Jonesy twisted two wires together and pulled back his hand as a spark snapped at his fingers. The radio crackled suddenly.

"Bridge, this is Ramirez over … bridge over … anyone?"

The comms unit squealed and static broke over the line. Jonesy flipped the microphone switch.

"I hear you," he replied, trying to re-establish contact. "It's Jonesy, I'm in the main bay and—"

A loud squeal made him spin the volume knob down reflexively. "Damn it!" he exclaimed as he thrust his hand back into the panel, cursing Rockpile's name and lineage.

✶

The storm screamed and howled as it whipped around the *Havana*. The bridge crew could feel the vibrations and sudden movements as she fought to remain oriented upright. The harpoon anchors held firm as the torrents of wind tried everything to rip them free.

Captain Sebesta tapped her fingers on the armrest, the only indication of her growing concern.

The crew tried to focus on their instruments and duties, but their eyes often wandered to the storm outside the curving window of the forward bridge.

The ship faced into the fury of the wind and snow, giving the illusion of the ship moving. It was disorienting and unnerving. Though unspoken, every officer knew there was a point when a decision had to be made; whether to give up on the Rockpile's lost ground crew or risk the entire ship holding out for a dwindling hope that they might still be alive.

The captain knew their thoughts. She was well aware that if she left them in this storm, it was a death sentence. What she didn't know was if she had already sentenced the entire ship to the same fate.

She glanced at Labrake. He nodded and headed off down the hatchway. Her fingers tapped faster on the armrest.

✶

Pellets of snow stung Ramirez's eyes as she stared through the eye slit, her eyes straining to see to the right, towards the ramp. The orange light of the beacon still cast pulses of ambient light that moved and swayed from a shadow that seemed to grow.

The spectacle was mesmerizing, and she found herself imagining images in the swirling whiteness. She blinked her eyes hard, jolting herself into clarity and coming back to focus.

For a split second, she thought she had made out a figure at the top of the ramp. It disappeared and she searched for it again. She pulled herself from the slit and rubbed her eyes hard, to clear them, then looked back.

The figure was there. A huge man-shaped thing swaying at the top of the ramp; reflected light shone from where its eyes would be. She caught her breath and reached for the latch, but stopped herself. The figure was Rockpile's size—he was a big man—and another vague man shape was behind it, possibly more on the ramp. Most details were lost in the dim light, but something told her this was not right. She slammed the eye slit shut and turned, slumping against the wall.

She had heard stories, had seen things herself, even though she had been aboard only for a few seasons. There were stories of things, monsters, mutants that had once been men, but were no longer. Twisted by genetic mutations, experiments long ago, before YE, that had bred for generations, haunted the wastelands and ruins of a long dead people who had ruled the world.

Her breath came quickly again, steaming around her in the cold as her mind struggled. She needed to calm down.

Was that Rockpile? If it was, she had to open the door immediately, to save his life and the lives of his crew. But security protocol demanded an absolute identification before opening any security door; the risk to the entire ship was too great to ignore.

No, her gut told her. That was not Rockpile or any of his crew. What did they do to Tanner?

She tried the comm link in her ear. "Bridge, or anyone, do you copy? It's Ramirez at Aft L6. We have *intruders;* Tanner has *disappeared* along with Rockpile's crew. *Things* are in the entry bay! Over. Help! Anyone copy?"

Something clanked on the stairwell, startling her. Ramirez turned to see Labrake coming down the stairs from the second level. Glancing at the gun in her hand he asked, "What's the situation? Where's Tanner?"

Shaking her head, she stepped away from him, turned and looked at the door, pointing with the handgun, "Someone is in the entry bay, and it isn't Tanner or Rockpile. I think they're dead. I have a bad feeling about this, sir."

He stepped up to the door, leaning forward as he slid the eye door open. His head jerked back as a bloodied hand reached through the opening and the door shuddered as something slammed against it. Inhuman growling rose against the howling wind. Labrake struggled to close the eye slit, but the hand kept clawing at him.

The fingers were human; the index finger and thumb were gone, as if bitten away, frozen blood and shards of bone showed. But on the pinky finger was a ring, Ramirez recognized it immediately; it belonged to Rockpile. It was his hand.

Ramirez slapped at her comm again. "Bridge, this is Ramirez! We have a situation!"

The hand pulled back through the slot as Labrake slammed it shut. He pulled his sidearm and yelled to Ramirez, "The comms are out! Get your ass up to the bridge and tell them what's going on!"

She turned to go but stopped. "Tell them *what*, sir?"

He looked hard at her. "Tell the captain the crew have come back but … but something has changed them … to that," glancing at the door as he said it. The door was under full assault as heavy pounding jarred the corner bolts loose. That was impossible. Labrake backed up slowly with his side arm.

They can't get through that! They can't get through that! Ramirez babbled internally.

He glanced quickly at her; his eyes dark and hard in the warm, heavy breath hanging in the cold air.

"Go! Now!" he yelled.

She turned and ran up the stairs, heading toward the command center. As she passed the second bulkhead door, she heard the overhead comm crackle to life. *"Okay, folks, I had to bypass the direct relay,"* she heard Jonesy announce. *"You can't talk to each other yet, but I think I fixed the bay door remote. Stand clear, ramps and inner bay doors opening now."*

Her eyes widened as she screamed "NO!" into the comm. She felt the dull vibration of the gears operating, the huge ramps being lowered and the bay doors sliding open. Releasing whatever was in the main ramp into the ship. Gunshots and screams of rage echoed from behind her. She ran up the stairs as fast as possible; she had to get to the bridge, to report to the captain. The sound of gunfire reverberated up the stairwell, then the horror unfolding over the comm fell silent.

✶

The comms between the aft bay and the engineering section were fully open thanks to Jonesy. The bridge crew listened, their eyes scanning above them as if imagining the carnage unfolding on the lower deck. Then the silence.

The shock was only momentary before Captain Sebesta stood.

"Prepare to blow the anchors. Open ballast three, four, and seven, spin us into the wind. Thane, I want you to go to the mezzanine and see what the hell is going on. Take some of your people with you and arm yourselves. If it's a Code Four, we need to seal the bridge deck ASAP."

She looked around at the officers staring at her from their stations. "Was I misunderstood? Move!"

The crew did as ordered, barking out commands to their individual stations, fighting to calm their fears, and hoping like hell they could save the ship and themselves.

✶

The ship-wide emergency lights began flashing just as Ramirez reached the second deck. Opening the door to it, the ringing in her head was coupled with yells and the distant sounds of weapons firing. She was nearly pushed back down the stairs as crew filled the deck, running and shouting as they ran to assigned stations, adding to the chaos. She flattened herself against the wall. The weapons fire was coming from the right—the deck mezzanine that overlooked the hangar.

"Ramirez!" someone yelled, sliding up beside her. It was Tober and his unmistakable Cajun drawl. "What the hell? Someone just said the captain called a Code Four! This is some *weird* voodoo bull-shit if you ask me." His voice came and went as his head spun like a swivel.

Tober was from back east; from dark and mysterious Nawlins that had been ruled for centuries by a queen. Reportedly, she was a priestess of the dark arts who had long ago sold her soul. Or so they said. His comment about voodoo wasn't just the result of adren-aline, he meant it and he was scared.

Her rank and training kicked in; she was bridge crew after all. "Where's your Code Four station, Tober? Get to it, now!" She turned, heading towards the ramp and up to third deck and on to fourth and the bridge. The ship was big but, right now, seemed helplessly small as she fought her way past men and women rushing to their stations.

Ramirez was thrown against the wall as the ship lurched violently starboard. The familiar concussive sound through the hull told her the harpoons were blowing free. The last one held the ship for a moment before being released. She felt a wave of vertigo as the *Havana* turned in line with the wind. She nodded in satisfaction. The captain was going to use the blizzard, to put as much distance between here and Vegas Station as possible.

She passed the security officer and two of his detail heading towards the mezzanine on this deck where the sounds of a battle still echoed. The smell of gunpowder, ozone, and smoke filled the ship.

Third deck was for storage for various things; equipment for the ground crews and support materials for maintenance of the ship. Ramirez took a moment to lean against the wall and catch her breath as she looked around at the caverns of crates and lockers. If whatever those things were made it to this level, it would be next to impossible to push them back. The captain would have to lock down this level completely and try to make the trip back on minimal supplies.

Pushing off from the bulkhead, she ran past door after door heading up the ramp to deck four and the bridge as more of the security team headed in the opposite direction, down towards the unfolding fight against whatever had come aboard. As they passed, she caught the eye of Keisha, her best friend. Keisha was also Rockpile's daughter. Ramirez reached out and they touched hands as they passed. Keisha was scared, she could tell, but she pushed on without hesitation.

The image of Rockpile's hand grabbing through the eye slit at Labrake screamed through her mind. Keisha had to know her father was dead. And that she, soon, might be joining him if Captain Sebesta had to seal off the lower decks.

Ramirez turned and continued running. Until Jonesy got two-way communication repaired, the captain was operating in the dark. She had to get to the bridge to tell her what she saw. Labrake might be dead, but she still had her orders.

The emergency lighting of the ship suddenly turned red. The captain had raised the threat level to Code Five. Ramirez heart sank as she realized the bridge was now on lockdown, there was no way to get to the captain.

But even worse, Code Five was the highest on the threat scale. After that was a rarely used self-destruct order intended to prevent disease and contamination from spreading to the floating cities.

✶

Ramirez made the choice to bypass the bridge; it was pointless now. The darkness of panic began to surround her. She had to focus, to get to safety. She ran past the crew quarters and a small galley to the stairwell. She paused for a moment, weighing her options. Below her, second deck had storage and supply rooms, somewhere, maybe safe to hide, to hold out until security regained control of the ship. She headed down the stairs.

Crewmembers with fear-filled faces passed her going up toward level three as she edged past them and entered second deck.

Weapons fire and screams echoed through the ship as she pulled open a door to a small storage room.

The cracking sound of a body thudding against the bulkhead made her look back toward the stairway. A crewman struggled into view around a bend fifteen feet away. She recognized his face, though she couldn't recall his name. His right arm hung limp, broken at the elbow. His eyes were wide with fear as something held him from behind.

The crewman screamed, his voice echoing off the metal walls. He tried to escape his attacker and pulled the creature with him into the hallway. It took too long for Ramirez to realize the creature was Tober. His face was pale with crazy eyes rimmed in red and black like bruises. His mouth wide and gleaming red, he leaned forward, biting, ripping away the ear and part of the scalp of the hapless crewman. The man's scream was beyond terror and pain.

Tober looked up and saw Ramirez.

His eyes widened, crazy with glee as he saw her. Ramirez was transfixed with the horror unfolding before her as Tober suddenly pushed forward, toward her, the screaming, struggling crewman still in his grasp. The bloodied ear still visible in a mouth now smiling with red, white teeth trailing strands of dark hair. He tried to say Ramirez's name, but only a guttural version of it came out.

Whatever monster Tober had become, it recognized her. It *wanted* her.

She backed into the storage room and slammed the door shut behind her. It was an interior storeroom, so it didn't have the sturdy metal bulkhead doors found between compartments. It was made of wood, and she knew it wouldn't last for long. She looked around wildly, searching for something to push against it, to block it. The room was stacked with extra empty pallets for the bay and coiled bundles of rope and old salvage, tables, chairs, junk. Ripping the tarp aside, she found mechanical parts and pieces and part of an old-style engine. Nothing.

She grabbed one of the chairs and wedged it against the door latch, then turned her attention to pulling one of the large pallets from the wall. She could still hear the screams of the crewman, the sound of someone being eaten alive. Then it abruptly ceased as if a switch had been thrown.

Ramirez knew that whatever Tober had become would now turn his full attention to her.

The door shuddered and groaned from impact as the Tober-thing began pounding on it. She fired a round from the Parker blowing a hole through the thin wood, the noise incredibly loud in the small storage room.

The thing on the other side made a gurgling noise akin to laughter and in another layer of horror she could see its insane eye peer through the hole at her before pulling away. Then the pounding began again, the door began to crack from the impacts as the Tober-thing sought to reach her.

✶

The bridge went to Code Five: Lockdown at all check points if possible, including the bridge. The ship shuddered as the vessel lurched hard to starboard as three of the four massive harpoons pulled free, swinging the ship clockwise like a giant arm, sweeping through the storm before the fourth blew, launching her like a missile. The sudden burst of speed pushed the crew back in their seats. Others had to grab for the railings.

Captain Sebesta ordered that all lockdowns had to hold in place, but there was no way to know if Jonesy had succeeded in reestablishing two-way communication. Even if it had, the orders were probably lost in the chaos unfolding across the ship.

Five crewmembers made it onto the bridge before the Code Five lockdown. They reported on what they had seen, but it was still too incomplete, too confused. All Sebesta had to make sense of were the sounds crackling from the overhead speakers. The weapons fire and the screams and orders from a lieutenant in the mezzanine indicated a last stand there. Others with comm links from other decks could be heard franticly firing weapons that seemed to do nothing.

There had been pounding on the heavy bridge door since the Code Five, but there was no way to know if it was the sound of the intruders or that of her crew seeking safety.

Captain Sebesta listened to her crew die as her ship was taken over by something she had never before encountered. The crew on the bridge listened with her, their faces covered in fear and shock.

She paced the deck as the ship's horrors played out, then slowly went quiet. Her mind was processing the options—the few options left. Every eye was on her, every person on that bridge knew their fate depended on her decision.

"Comm, do we still have outside communication?"

"I think so," the comm exec responded. "Yes ma'am, the exterior nodes are working."

Captain Sebesta nodded. "I need you to contact Vegas Tower Inbound," she said with a voice much firmer than she felt.

✶

The door to Ramirez's room splintered and broke as the Tober-thing pushed the remains aside. His terrifying visage excited to see her as she unloaded the powerful handgun into it. The heavy rounds of the ancient weapon hit their mark, blasting flesh from the creature's chest and face, staggering it back, but did little beyond making him look more horrifying.

He looked down for a moment at wounds that no longer mattered, slowly shaking his head from side to side as he looked back up at her. He stepped into the room reaching for her as she stumbled back desperately trying to fit another magazine into the gun.

Behind him, the man he had killed moments before, stood up. Part of his face was gone but one eye gleamed beneath dark hair matted with blood; his teeth shone white with a ghastly smile. He entered the room, following behind the Tober-thing.

Ramirez backed against the wall. She was trapped. There was nowhere to go. Her hands shook with fear, the Parker M77 fell to the floor.

"Oh, God …" was all she could whisper as Tober's clawed hands grabbed her.

Ramirez screamed as her flesh was ripped open.

✶

The HQ and Port command for all Vegas traffic was in the dominant north Tower with subsequent dock HQs for designated slips at the many docks located at various levels in both Towers and main city.

The Sebesta family called Vegas Station home. They operated three frigates—the *Havana, Santiago,* and the *Augustine*—all based in the mighty city. Currently, the *Santiago* was in dock and the *Augustine* was somewhere east, on a long run back from Texas City.

Lady Apollonia, the matriarch of the Sebesta family, was awakened in the middle of the night. The call was from Vegas Headquarters. It was urgent and requested her immediate presence in the docking Tower. As she quickly dressed, she learned that the captain of the *Santiago* was summoned as well as other people who had family members serving on the *Havana.*

Arriving at the docking Tower high above the city, she was told that the *Havana,* cloaked and hidden in the blizzard, had come within range of Vegas Port twenty minutes before. Visual assessment showed the obvious damage from the storm, with one of its loading ramps hanging loose and broken. However, Captain Sebesta had requested no quadrants for docking and refused the approach of any maintenance or rescue vehicles.

The communication transmission was spotty at best. The *Havana* was in range but keeping still, fighting the storm, as it attempted to maintain a fixed position. The late summer blizzard fought to sweep the vessel toward the canyons of the southwest.

As the family was ushered into the top conning spire for port control, they could hear the voice of Captain Sebesta, crackling in the static from the storm.

"Theresa ..." Lady Apollonia said, recognizing the voice of her daughter.

"No control," Sebesta's voice was fading in and out as the storm ravaged all local comm links. *"It ripped my guides off .... Alt 6 open were at ten degrees starboard ... holding."* Harsh static ripped through the room. The comm officer's hands quickly compensated on the board. Sebesta's voice returned. *"... during salvage in old Reno ... were boarded by something ... creatures ... taken over the ship and killed most of my crew."*

The families reacted in shock. Some cried out loud. Lady Apollonia took a deep breath, her throat tightened. Reno. She was the one who had suggested Theresa should investigate Reno and the rumors of untouched treasure still trapped in the ruins. Her daughter hadn't been sure it was worth the effort to chase rumors of lost treasure, but Apollonia had insisted.

"I do not know how long we can keep them from the bridge," Sebesta's voice cut through the white noise. Then, static again.

The Port Master reached over the comm exec and toggled the microphone open.

"Captain, this is Port Master Freas, we copy. Please repeat your request. You do not want an attempted rescue? Please confirm, you do not want us to come for you?"

Sebesta's response was clear and immediate. *"Negative, no rescue. Do not approach the* Havana *under any circumstances. We can't risk the Tower, these things are overrunning the ..."*

Her voice faded into the background noise.

Port Master Freas turned to the assembled group. Lady Apollonia steeled herself. She knew what he was going to say; her daughter had already said it.

"It's her call. It's her ship. They're on their own with ... whatever is with them."

Lady Apollonia closed her eyes as the families could no longer hold back their grief. Freas toggled the comm switch open again.

"*Havana,* if you can still hear us, we'll register last known nav projection. Let's hope your fins hold."

"Affirmative," Sebesta's voice came back. *"If we can retake the ship, we'll ... try ... otherwise, I repeat, do not attempt a rescue!"*

"We'll make sure every ship and Tower knows," Freas responded. "May the winds be with you, *Havana.*"

The white noise continued for a moment, then Sebesta's voice came through one last time. *"Tell my mother we found it. A fortune, beyond imagining ... a cursed treasure ... we found it. And the curse came with it. Tell her I love her."*

Lady Apollonia, the matriarch of the Sebesta Empire, mother to the great Captain Theresa Sebesta, collapsed to the floor as the *Havana* drifted off, into the storm.

✶

There are legends from the Old World, myths, rumors. Ghost ships seen that were long lost by whatever fate befell them. The *Havana* has become one, a combination of *The Flying Dutchman* and the Lost Treasures of King Solomon's Mines.

She is seen from time to time, the *Havana.* On an endless loop of the old southwest. Most ships avoid her, as is due the superstitious nature of airship crews. Some ships look for her, the temptation of a rumored treasure too hard to resist. And others have found her, never to be seen again, except maybe as ghostly companions, flying by her side and sharing her curse.

DIAMONDS IN THE SKY

MARK TEPPO

They had been out for eighteen days—*feesheeing,* as Tonker liked to say in that sing-song way of his, even though the catch basin of the *Peculiar Anecdote* was busted, and they couldn't hold anything larger than a wash of tuna. Eighteen days without a haul, and the mood on the scrudder was as dark as the thunderswell shunting them north.

Ain't no rock this far north, Fairboy had muttered that morning. If they couldn't refuel, the pokies would run down and then they'd be like all the other floaters—dead in the sky, chanting and wailing for the wind to save them.

Hash voiced the idea of hitting the swells, taking in seawater for fuel, and his idea had nearly caused a mutiny right there. Sure, you could put seawater in the pokies, but that wasn't much better than trying to put out an oil fire with pisswater. The salt-heavy go-juice would flense the core and chrome something fierce. Once the engine burned out, the ship'd be nothing more than a metal rot box at the mercy of the trade-chasing zephyrs.

Cap had to threaten violence to make herself heard over the bitching and moaning. *It's an option,* she said. *It ain't like the* Anecdote *hasn't kissed a wave before.*

When the need to feed all those mouths at 10Tower outgrew a day's sail, the old pretties—all those school-chasing, wind-catching, sea-slicking water babies—got overhauled. Deck-runners broke up clean keel lines with banks of A-G pods. They swapped out sails for sheets of solar cells. 'Gineers hauled lots of cable, linking cells to pods, and *rightee flightee!*, scrudders weren't wave-kissers anymore. They could go higher and farther. The cells juiced the pods, and pods let the crews go sky-scraping, where all manner of salvage could be found. There was no need to run the waves.

But a crew couldn't move these sky-sailers without fuel. The pokies had to be fed, and while the mass converters would pulp anything thrown in them, the old rules still applied. Mohs. Brinell. Vickers. The harder the material the better.

Cap flicked the edge of the holo-topo floating in the ready room. It spun counterclockwise, its summary data flickering wildly. "Find us some *terra firma*, Elpheie," she said, cutting to the quick.

Elpheie used her articulate to stop the map's rotation. In response to her intent, it redrew itself. It zoomed out a magnitude, and then another. There wasn't any difference in the display. "Wide water, Cap," she said. "Ain't been nothing here since the Blow."

"Wasn't anything here before the Blow neither," Malark said.

"Here" was a tiny triangle showing the *Anecdote*'s orientation and heading, along with Mercator Markers. No one outside of UC headcanon wonks gave much credence to Mercator Markers anymore. There weren't enough high-eyes to ping for ace confirmation, but that didn't stop the software from guessing. Elpheie had patched the soft with emoji-script, though, giving the viz a reliability scale. This position was rated two ducks, out of a possible five. Which, given all the light show hijinks the thunderswell had been venting, was pretty good.

It was Fairboy—golden-haired, nimble-fingered, slick-licker Fairboy—who drew them out of their viz funk. "Cap," he shouted down from the nav-conn. "I got a sparkle."

Everyone scrambled for a looksee. Cap and Hash squeezed into the narrow blister topside, forcing Fairboy to lean forward over the control sticks.

"Where?" Cap demanded.

"Four low," Fairboy said. Crowding the nav-chair even more, Cap and Hash peered into the lower righthand quadrant of the storm-darkened sky. There, sunlight flashed.

"Range?" Cap asked.

Fairboy shrugged. "Can't say," he said. "That swell is messing my scale."

Cap grunted. The *Anecdote* had range-finding systems, useful for aquatic echo-locating and aerial topo-mapping, but atmospheric disturbances like the storm system thrashing along the horizon tended to make a mess of active echo. Which left them with Fairboy's bright eyes that could track a silver fin at three klicks, but even he needed something to judge scale and distance by.

Down below, pressed against starboard portholes, Malark and Tonker squinted through the wavy glass. "It sure do sparkle," Malark said.

Tonker wet his lower lip with his tongue. "It's a hab," he crowed. "We got ourselves a right prize."

"Ain't no hab," Malark countered. "It's just a shearspire. That sparkle is coming off sun-panels. We'll be lucky if there's any go-juice at all."

"It's a hab," Tonker insisted. "VeeCeeFundee."

"Ain't none of that left," Malark snapped.

"I tell ya, it is," Tonker argued. "It's got that gleam."

"You wouldn't know VeeCee gleam, boy."

They continued to bicker as the captain told Fairboy to set a course for the floating object.

✶

When they got close enough to get cleaner data from the range-finders, Hash officially marked it as a 'hab,' and Elpheie filed the information in the ship's log.

Malark was hot in the mouth after that, havin' to fetch a handful of ruby-colored shards to pay Tonker, as they'd wagered about the object. Tonker didn't gloat outright, but he played with the shards for a while, tossing them back and forth between his hands.

He dropped one, and before it could settle on the deck, Ollie scurried across the floor. Tonker shouted at the water dog, and when that had no impact—*respect my tonalatee, water hog!*—Tonker started yammering at Hash.

Ollie perched on the knob of the driftee near Hash's watch

station and spun the red shard in his paws. *Querk! Querk!* It wasn't quite a bark.

"Give it back," Hash said quietly to the water dog.

Querk?

"He's gunna keep hollering," Hash said. "Might make Cap unhappy."

The water dog's black nose wriggled. *Quonk?* Hash looked at him with a raised eyebrow, and Ollie popped the shard in his mouth.

"Take that out," Hash said.

Ollie shook his head.

"Cap might make a hat out of you," Hash said.

A corner of the shard slid between Ollie's lips. "Just give it back," Hash said.

The water dog made a noise like a baffle flooding with water, and then he slithered down the driftee and disappeared. A few moments later, Hash heard Tonker yell in surprise. "It's slimee!" the 'gineer shouted. "Your water dog slimed my treasure!"

"Batten it," Cap shouted from her station. "We're on approach."

Elpheie finally managed to render a holo-topo of the floating habitat. Scale notation rendered it about a quarter acre—broad by beam. Hash didn't see any obvious life rings, but judging by the arrangement of iridescent solar panels, he thought it was at least a three slicer. It trailed a slither of snaky cables and exhaust tubes.

Fairboy found an auto-slip on the port side, and he put the *Peculiar Anecdote* down with a tiny shiver that ran tip to stern in the old scrudder. Hash felt a sympathetic shudder run up his spine, and he tried to shake it off as a twitch from having been at sea too long. Ollie cocked his head and went *pop! pop!* with his mouth.

"It's gunna be fine," he said, scratching the water dog behind the ears. Ollie nuzzled his hand and went squirmy down the driftee. Hash sighed, and with a final glance at the viz snapshot he had taken, he got up from his station and went aft to gear up with the rest of the crew.

✶

The auto-slip was gauged for narrower craft than the *Anecdote*, which meant the *Anecdote* was perched peculiar on the extended tongue of the dock. Auto-locks fussed and popped along the forward edge of the hull, unable to get a solid lock. Hash could feel tiny tremors in the deck under his feet as Fairboy kept nudging the sticks to keep the ship in contact with the hab's auto-slip.

"Up and over," Cap called up to Malark at the front of the line at the forward hatch. "No dallying."

Malark spun the access wheel and pulled the panel open. The crew shuffled for an instant, and then they were scrambling forward, like the sure-footed deck-runners they were.

They tumbled onto a wide porch that stuck out three meters or so from a set of shallow steps. The steps led up to an entry port, set beneath a curved arch. The portal itself was oblong, taller than it was wide. Hash noted there were no hard corners on the structure. It was all curves and slopes. "Some sort of flex fiber?" he wondered out loud.

Tonker kicked at the bottom step. "Ain't no seams," he said.

"We could use the cutter," Malark said, patting the rig hanging from his belt. "Carve ourselves a slice."

"It's all one piece," Tonker said. "Modeled and made. You ain't going to carve shit. This is—"

"Let's get inside before we start slicin' and dicin'," Cap said, cutting the 'gineer off. Keeping her slugthrower ready, she went up the steps and ducked into the alcove. The rest of the crew stayed down-step, spread into a formation that presented eyes forward and to the sides.

A brief play of pink and green light came from the alcove, and Hash brought up his weapon in alarm. But the light vanished nearly as quickly as it had come. In its wake, he heard a shush of escaping air.

"Door's open." Cap's voice floated down. A sputtering yellow glow flushed out from the alcove, and as if summoned by the light, Tonker rushed up the steps. Malark squawked in annoyance and hurried after him, leaving Elpheie and Hash at the base of the stairs.

Elpheie gave Hash a familiar look. *Those two are going to get us all killed.* Hash responded with the same shrug he always did. *As long as it's just them and not us, who are we to get in their way?*

"Elpheie," Cap called down. "Eyes and brains up top."

Hash jerked his head, letting Elpheie know that he was fine with bringing up the rear. As she went up the stairs, he took one last look around the porch. It was too clean and too shiny for his liking. Print-to-order, he thought, but on a scale unlike any he'd ever seen.

He caught sight of movement on the *Anecdote*'s bow. "Stay there," he said to the water dog, who was peeking over the rail. Ollie went *pop! pop!* with his mouth, and Hash just shook his head at the animal's response.

Hash hurried up the stairs, unwilling to be the last one on the porch. He ducked through the low threshold in the alcove and found himself in a cramped vestibule. The walls were as slick as the porch, and some sort of light source behind it made the material glow.

There was a panel at the front of the room, and when Hash peered around Tonker to get a better look, his breath caught in his throat. The panel was like a window, but he didn't understand what he was seeing. There were tall posts scattered around a long room, and each was festooned with knobs and ledges at various heights. Tubes ran complicated courses across the floor and along the walls.

"What is it?" he wondered.

"Fab factory," Tonker said. "Extrusion molds."

Malark shook his head. "Tubes ain't straight," he said. He pointed at an opening at the end of one of the tubes. "Stuff comes out there, but it ain't molded."

"What kind of stuff?" Hash wanted to know.

"Stuff with teeth," Malark said. Behind him, Tonker rolled his eyes.

"Look at this," Cap said, breaking up the routine between the two before it could start. There was a circular opening near the floor, and as Cap moved her foot near it, an icon flickered on the wall beside it.

Elpheie nudged Tonker out of the way so she could get a better look at the symbol. "It's some sort of eye-dee sigil," she said.

"What kind?" Cap asked.

"Looks like a water dog," Tonker suggested.

Hash squinted at the glowing symbol. It looked like a pair of concentric circles with two triangles stuck on top. "Ears are wrong," he said.

Elpheie wasn't looking at the floor. Her eyes were up, and the tip of her articulate was flicking back and forth. She was accessing databanks on the *Anecdote,* flicking through UC reference charts Hash had swiped for her seasons ago. "Fauna iconography," she muttered.

Tonker, bored with waiting for Elpheie to finish her data run, got down on his knees. He grabbed a wiggle light from his belt and aimed its beam into the hole. "There's something shiny in here," he said.

"Squids," Elpheie muttered. Her eyes were flicking back and forth in time with her articulate. "How far back is this...?"

"I can reach it," Tonker said. He clenched the stem of the wiggle lamp in his teeth and put himself flush with the floor.

"It's a cat," Elpheie said, her gaze coming back into focus. "But this sigil is pre-Blow."

Tonker put his hand in the hole, grunted slightly, and then edged closer to the wall. "I ... almost ..." He jerked suddenly and let out a yelp.

"Tonker!" Cap put both hands on her slugthrower and took a step back. The rest of the crew instinctively tried to get out of the way, which was almost impossible in the crowded vestibule. "What are you doing?"

Tonker strained and pulled. "I can't pull it out," he whined.

Malark dropped to his knees and scrabbled at the wall around Tonker's arm. "It's tight," he said.

"Why did you put—?" Cap didn't bother finishing her question.

"I can use my cutter," Malark said, reaching for his rig.

"I wouldn't do that," Hash said.

Tonker blinked. A sheen of sweat covered his face. "Wh—what?"

"It's too trig," Hash asked. "You can't do a spin without slicing Tonker."

"Dunk that," Malark said. "I can."

Hash shook his head. "No one cuts more true than you, but you ain't got the angle."

Malark's face darkened. "I'll short the beam—"

"Hash is right," Cap said. "You'll still cut Tonker."

Tonker started wailing, making noises that weren't quite words. His face got redder and sweatier, and then he suddenly rolled away from the wall. A wide stroke of blood splashed across the smooth surface.

There was pandemonium for a minute. Tonker, missing the lower portion of his right arm, thrashed about the vestibule, spraying blood everywhere. Malark tried to get hold of him, but Tonker was like a slippery eel. Cap kept waving her weapon about, and Hash stepped on something—maybe it was Malark's foot—as he tried to stay out of the line of fire. Elpheie managed to pull a patch from her field kit and slap it over the end of Tonker's arm.

As Tonker quieted down, everyone backed away as best they could in a room without any corners.

"It took my arm," Tonker sniveled. He was trying to get the backing off a second patch but was having trouble.

Malark, whose face and chest were stained with the 'gineer's blood, finally snatched the patch out of Tonker's hand. "Hold still," he grumbled, and Tonker let out another agonized wail when Malark slapped the second patch in place.

"Oh, batten it," Elpheie muttered.

"I got no arm," Tonker shouted at her. He shook his arm—well, he would have, if he still had it.

Elpheie gave him a fish-eyed stare. "You'll live," she said. The tips of her articulate clacked like an oyster shell. "I got a spare you can borrow."

"Dunk you," Tonker slurred. His face was a mess of blood and tears. "Ain't going to be no gimpee. I'll get a regrow." He focused on Cap. "You owe me a regrow," he said. "I got assurance."

"We're not on the ship," Cap said. "And I didn't tell you to stick your arm in that hole."

"I was on duty," Tonker argued. "I'm assured."

"Look," Hash said, interrupting Tonker's lamentation. He pointed at the wall. The hole was open again, and there was script next to the cat icon. "What's that say?"

"'Incorrect physiology,'" Elpheie said. She could translate the script easily, now that she had found the right reference set.

"Incorrect what?" Malark asked.

As if in reply, the icon on the wall transformed into a profile image—something with four legs and a tail. The icon blinked three times, and then reformed into the original circle with two triangles on top.

"Tonkers wasn't a cat," Hash said.

He scooped up the 'gineer's wiggle lamp and leaned over the hole. "There is something shiny," he said. He shifted the light back and forth, and then he looked at Tonker. "It's a lure, you shrimp," he said.

Elpheie was standing at the window, and she shook her head. "It's a way in," she said. She waved Cap over. "You can see his light."

Hash swung the wiggle lamp back and forth, and Cap nodded. "I see it," she said. She chewed on her lower lip for a moment. "You think this opens if we pull that lure?" she asked.

"Can't see no other way in," Elpheie said.

Malark patted his side pack opposite his cutter. "Got sappers," he offered. "Could blow a gap."

Hash straightened up and put his back to the wall. "This's moldflow. Might even be adaptive."

"It ain't that flex," Malark said.

"You don't know that," Hash countered. "You—we—don't know whale piss about this hab."

Tonker, usually one to throw himself into an argument about tech, stayed out of the discussion between the deck-runner and the ship-thinker. Cap stared at the 'gineer's ruined arm, seemingly lost in thought.

"We need fuel," Elpheie said gently, trying to nudge Cap toward a decision. "Gotta have something to squeeze for the pokies."

Cap nodded. "No sapping," she said, and Malark's mouth firmed into a hard line. "We don't know what synth or sys this is running," she said. "We keep it blue." She gave the deck-runner a stern eye. "You clear?" she said.

"Clear," Malark said. "We keep it blue."

Cap nodded toward the hole. "Elpheie says that's the way, so if we have to jig that lure, that's what we do."

"We don't have a cat," Elpheie said.

"Maybe we don't need one," Cap said.

Hash shook his head. "No," he said. "We're not putting Ollie in that hole."

"Why not? He ain't crew," Tonker snapped. He waved his shortened arm at Hash. "I'm owed."

"You went shrimp shit on us," Hash shot back. "You ain't owed nothing."

Tonker fumbled with his belt, and it took Hash a moment to figure out what the 'gineer was doing. By the time, Tonker got his holster pulled around enough to get at his gun, Hash had pulled his own weapon. He pushed the barrel against the side of Tonker's head.

"Forestall," Cap said. There was no emotion in her voice, and her hand was snug against her slugthrower. "There will be no shrimping. Everyone ease off."

Tonker's eyes stopped jamming. Malark's hand moved no further. Hash slid his thumb away from the safety on his weapon.

"We need fuel," Cap said, directing her tone toward Hash. "You keep crying us off from marking this place, but I haven't heard no better idea from you yet."

Hash licked his lips. "We can surf," he said. "Maybe we can find some tuna. Or a black-and-white. That'll be enough for the pokie."

"We'll get swamped by a dozen more before Malark can carve it up," Cap argued. "You know as well as I do about bloodslick."

"He'll have to work faster, is all," Hash argued.

Cap inclined her head at Tonker. "We're already down one hand," she said. "I'm not losing more." She watched Hash closely. "It's my ship," she reminded him. "It's my call."

Querk! Querk!

A sinuous shape slipped into the room with them. Tonker let out a strangled chuckle as the water dog darted around his legs. Ollie stopped near Hash and stood on his hind legs. His whiskers were stiff, and his dark nose trembled. *Querk?* He looked at Hash, and then Cap, and then Elpheie, and then back at Hash. *Querk?*

Hash lifted his gun away from Tonker's head, and keeping his fingers clear of the trigger, slid the gun back into its holster. "Your—your call, Cap," he said.

"Awfully polite of you," Cap said. When Hash glared at her, she met his stare with one of her own. The hard-edged one. The one that said he would take whatever she offered, and he would say 'Yes ma'am.'

"Yes, ma'am," Hash said.

With a tiny nod, Cap relented. She let the barrel of her slugthrower dip as she looked down at the water dog. "Yo, scupper," she said. She snapped her fingers. "Eyes on me."

Ollie looked up at Cap, his whiskers twitching. He made the noise with his mouth. *Pop! Pop!*

"Need you to do a run and tug," Cap said. She pointed at the hole in the wall.

Ollie's head went up and down. *Querk?* He held his front paws up. *Querk querk?*

"Run and tug," Cap said. She jerked her head at the hole. "Can you do that for me?"

Ollie looked at Hash, who nodded without making eye contact with the water dog. Ollie dropped down to all fours and lowered his head until he was nearly flat. His feet scrabbled on the slick floor, and he rotated like a compass arrow until he was pointing at the hole. He surged forward, having spotted the lure in the back.

The hole in the wall sealed up after the water dog, and Hash bit back a cry of alarm. The icon above the hole started to blink, each pulse coming faster, and then it stopped. The icon changed to the side view of the cat, and a notification scrolled along the wall next to it.

Physiology match: 85%.

The panel peeled away like a rind. They had access to the hab.

✶

They went in, spreading out across the courtyard of tunnels and posts. Hash caught a glimpse of Ollie here and there as the water dog darted through the tubes. Malark examined the posts and ledges, trying to find one that wasn't as seamlessly extruded as everything else. Tonker staggered along behind him, his face waxy. There was a shiver in his step, a sign he was floating on painblockers and neuro-stims. Cap stayed near the door, letting her crew do their assessment.

Elpheie stood near a wall on Hash's left. She was looking through another transparent panel. "Look at this," she said, waving him closer.

The window looked into a cold store. There were rows and rows of elongated capsules. Each one was over a meter long, and they were cradled in suspension grippers that held them close to thick posts. There were status displays marbled on each post, though Hash couldn't make sense of what the displays were showing.

"It's all autonomous," he said, realizing the extent of the tech.

"Has to be," Elpheie said. "That cat sigil? That's pre-Blow iconography."

"Pre?"

Tonker had wandered near enough to hear their conversation. "I tole yee," the 'gineer tittered. "VeeCeeFundee."

"Venture Capital," Elpheie explained, reading Hash's expression. "From the Valley."

"This is a one-per hab?"

Elpheie shrugged. "It's all fancy and shiny," she said. "And thinky. What else?" She nodded at the capsules. "What's in those?" she asked. "Is this a big brain store?"

Hash shook his head. "Maybe," he said. He glanced around the courtyard again, trying to reconcile the tubes and posts with the hanging capsules. He watched Ollie scramble up one of the posts and circle around twice on the flat pad at the top. The water dog lay down, resting his paws on the edge of the pad.

"It's not heads," Hash realized.

"What's not?" Cap asked. She joined Elpheie and Hash at the window.

Hash was about to tell Cap his theory when Ollie went *pop! pop! pop!* The water dog's head went up, and his attention was on the far side of the courtyard. Hash looked, and he grabbed Cap's arm. "There," he said.

A white-haired creature had wandered out of one of the tubes. The creature wasn't much larger than Ollie, but unlike the water dog, this animal had long legs that kept its belly off the ground. It had a sinuous tail that flicked from side to side.

"What is that?" Cap hissed.

The creature strolled along the top of a tube, and the narrow collar around its neck flashed and twinkled. It didn't appear to be worried about the strange intruders, but when Tonker clicked his tongue, it froze.

Hash started to say something, but held the words back. The creature had stopped moving. Only the tip of its tail still twitched.

Tonker clicked his tongue again. "Hereyee," he said. "Nicee nicee." He took a step toward the creature.

"Don't—" Hash started, but that was as far as he got.

The creature darted into a nearby opening. A flash of light from the creature's collar acted as a signal to the crew, throwing them all into motion. Tonker clawed at his belt for his gun. Malark brought his weapon up and swung it back and forth, looking for a target. Cap stepped away from Hash and Elpheie, her slugthrower ready. Up on the perch, Ollie let out a tiny *querk!* and lowered himself so that he couldn't be seen from the ground. Hash stayed close to Elpheie, his gun in his hand.

Elpheie's articulate cycled. "Holo-topo rendering," she said.

There was a flash of white fur near the middle of the room. "Hurry," Hash said. "It's in the tubes," Hash said.

"Just a few more spins," she said.

"Where is it?" Malark called out. His gun drifted back and forth. Tonker had managed to draw his weapon, and the 'gineer drifted toward one of the tube openings.

"Got it," Elpheie said. She opened her articulate, and a three-dimensional projection of the courtyard spumed from her palm. Blue dots indicated the crew of the *Peculiar Anecdote*, and a red dot—

Tonker let out a yelp of surprise, and his weapon clattered to the floor. He thrashed about, trying to beat himself with his remaining arm. The white creature—the *cat*, Hash mentally corrected, because that was what it was—had come out of a nearby tube. It was on Tonker, and not in a friendly way.

"Get it! Get it!" Tonker shouted.

Cap raised her slugthrower, but she didn't fire. The white cat was a blur of fangs and flash. She was as likely to hit Tonker as she was the cat.

Malark lumbered over, and he spun Tonker around. Tonker got a hand on the beast, slowing it down, and Malark wrapped his enormous hands around the ferocious cat. There was blood on its muzzle, and Malark grunted as one of its hind legs swiped at his forearm.

Tonker, bleeding from the neck and face, reeled against a nearby tube. "This is bonks," he snarled, and he scooped up his weapon from the floor. He pointed it at Malark and the squirming shape in the deck-runner's hands.

"Not at me!" Malark shouted.

"Hold it still," Tonker shouted back.

Machinery whined, and something made a popping noise. It wasn't like the sound Ollie made. This sound was colder, like a vacuum filling. Malark froze, a surprised look on his face, and then his eyes rolled up. A thin thread of smoke drifted from a neat hole in the center of his forehead. The cat shot out of his hands as Malark collapsed.

"Mishandling of Miz Suzee Diamond is a violation of acceptable use policy," a polite voice informed the surprised and shocked crew of the *Peculiar Anecdote*.

Near the ceiling, the slick-steel barrel of a military-grade railgun protruded from a nearly opened slot in the seamless hab.

The cat sat on the floor near Malark's dead body, utterly unperturbed by the sudden violence visited upon the deck-runner. It licked its paw and wiped at its face. At first, Hash thought it was cleaning itself, but then he realized the cat was lapping Tonker's blood *off* its paw.

Tonker came to the same realization. "Dunk this," he snarled. He brought up his weapon, and amazingly, managed to get a shot off before the railgun punched a hole through his head—ear to ear.

Even more amazingly—given that he was using his off-hand—his aim was true.

Miz Suzee Diamond left a smear of blood on the floor as she went tumbling. When she came to a stop, she looked like a discarded clump of dingy gull feathers.

"Gross negligence toward Miz Suzee Diamond is a flagrant violation of acceptable use policy," the machine intelligence said. Its voice was still polite, even with the additional adjectives. "As per section four, paragraph seventy-two, categorical violation of the acceptable use policy results in a forfeiture of deposit, and allows for immediate remedy at the sole discretion of the policy owners."

The portion of the wall through which they had entered the courtyard closed as neatly as it had opened. They were sealed in.

"Squids," Elpheie said. She looked up from her holo-topo

display, which was showing more red dots. "They're waking up," she said.

As if summoned by Elpheie's words, a black cat wandered out of a tube. It yawned, and Hash shuddered at the number of sharp teeth revealed by the yawn. Almost nonchalantly, it padded over and started to lap at the pool of blood spreading around Tonker.

"They're going to eat us," Elpheie whimpered. "That's what it means by 'remedy.' It's ..."

"Not all of us," Cap said, cutting her off. Cap slid her feet across the floor, incrementally heading toward the place where the door had been. "We're getting out of here."

When neither Hash nor Elpheie moved, Cap hissed at them.

Hash tore his gaze away from the sight of the cat drinking. "Wh—what?"

"We need an egress," Cap whispered. Without turning her head, she indicated the bodies. "Malark's sappers."

Hash started to shake his head, but tensed his shoulders instead. He took a careful step toward his dead shipmates. He started when the black cat jumped onto Tonker's shoulder, but it wasn't interested in him. Hash took another step as the black cat bit at what was left of Tonker's ear.

Out of the corner of his eye, he saw more movement, and when he looked, he saw a third cat—an orange one, with white tips on its ears. It mewled at him, a sound intended to be heart-melting and cute, but in a room full of corpses, it caused a shiver of revulsion instead.

The orange cat joined the black one, and they both gnawed greedily at Tonker's—

Hash's stomach did a flip, and he looked away. He didn't need to see that.

He looked up at the railgun instead. The barrel of the weapon was trained on him. If it was going to fire, it would have, he reasoned. As long as he made no threatening motions toward the cats, he wouldn't be in violation of whatever administrative contract that was governing the railgun. They were in *remedy* right now—as Elpheie has sussed—which allowed the cats to gorge themselves. *When they finish there, they'll come after us,* he thought.

Hash reached Malark's body without issue. Four more cats had tumbled into the room, and they, too, swarmed Tonker's body. Hash crouched by the dead deck-runner and, fingers trembling, carefully undid the clips on Malark's side pouch. He started to pull it free, and then froze when the orange cat climbed onto Malark's chest.

Hash froze.

The cat cocked its head and looked at him with its big eyes. *Mewrr?* it said. A bloody stripe down its chin belied its innocent expression.

Hash tightened his grip on the pouch and pulled slowly. The orange cat batted at one of the straps on Malark's rig. The leather strap flapped back and forth, and the cat batted at it again.

Hash stared at the orange cat's collar. Like the one Miz Suzee Diamond was wearing, it sparkled. Up close, Hash could see why. He ducked his head, suddenly afraid that the cat would see the gleam in his eye.

The pouch came free, and with an ache that he felt all the way down to his toes, he duck-walked away from the cat and the dead deck-runner.

"What?" Elpheie asked when he reached the two women who were crouched near the wall.

"The sparkle on their collars," Hash said thickly as he grabbed the shapeable putty from Malark's pouch. "It's bling."

"Bling? Like Mohs-style?" Cap asked.

Hash nodded dumbly as he molded the putty into a long strand.

"Diamonds," Elpheie whispered. She sank to the floor next to Hash. "They're wearing diamonds."

Hash made a circle on the wall with the putty. He thumbed the ends together and stuck a charge stick in it. "Clear," he muttered to Cap and Elpheie, and both shuffled along the wall until they were several meters away. Hash flicked the fuse tip, and then scrambled to his right, bumping into Elpheie.

She grabbed his wrist with her articulate, and hissed in his ear. He looked, and his blood went cold in his chest. The black cat and another one with gray stripes were staring up at the panel at the top of a post. Their tails were flicking back and forth.

A small brown head peered over the edge of the panel.

"Ollie—" Hash started.

The charge went off, making the room quiver. There was a lot of smoke, and Cap's slugthrower coughed. The railgun made its sizzle-pop noise, and Cap's slugthrower coughed once more.

Elpheie shoved Hash. "Go," she shouted, though it sounded like she was much farther away than she was. He tumbled against the wall as she plowed past him.

The sapper charge had worked. There was a hole in the wall, and he could see shivery blue beyond. The ragged edges of the hole twisted and smoked, and Elpheie cried out as she touched the edge, but she made it through.

Hash stumbled toward the hole, leaning heavily against the wall. The hole was already getting smaller—the habitat was, in fact, capable of repairing itself. Some of the smoke cleared and he caught sight of Cap slumped against the wall on the other side of the hole. There was a hole in her chest, and her gaze was fixed at something distant and beyond his apprehension.

"Hash!" Elpheie shouted at him from the other side of the hole.

He turned and thrust himself at the gap. The self-repairing wall burned against his clothes as he scraped over the sizzling material. He flailed at Elpheie's outstretched hand. She caught him and pulled, and with a desperate shove of his feet, he forced himself through. They tumbled across the vestibule, knees and elbows knocking.

Hash extricated himself from Elpheie and started back toward the hole.

"What are you doing?" Elpheie shouted at him.

"Ollie!" Hash slammed against the wall. The gap was the size of a human head now. The edges crackled and smoked.

The railgun fired, and he flinched, even though part of him knew that if it had been firing at him, he would have been dead before he heard the report. He spotted a flash of orange and a glitter of bling. "Ollie!" he shouted again.

The water dog came out of the smoke, humping along the floor. There was something in his mouth, something that almost tripped him up. Hash cried out, his voice breaking into a sob of panic.

Behind him, the black cat came—fang and fury—and when the water dog slithered widdershins, the black cat overshot.

The gap—closing relentlessly—was the size of Hash's hand.

The black cat pivoted adroitly, almost as if it had planned such a maneuver. It was closer now. Almost within reach.

Ollie leaped, and like a water squirt from a clam, he was through the hole. Hash fell onto his back, laughing and sobbing and trying to hug the water dog all at the same time. Ollie squirmed free, slippery as ever.

Behind him, a black paw extended through the wall. It flexed once, thrusting out bloodied claws, and Hash scrambled back, getting farther away from it. The paw fell to the floor, neatly severed as the wall completed its self-repair, and Hash stared at it dumbly. *Was it going to keep—?* But it merely twitched once and then went still.

Querk?

Ollie bounced up and down when Hash rolled toward him. He dipped his head and dropped what he was carrying into Hash's outstretched hand.

"Bling?" Elpheie was peering over his shoulder.

Hash nodded. "Aye," he said. He held the cat collar up, and the diamonds mounted on the leather strap sparkled in the afternoon sunlight. "The hardest bling there is."

They weren't big stones, but that didn't matter to the pokie. They were hard—top of the Mohs scale, in fact—and the converter would chew on them for months, giving the scrudder a near-unlimited supply of go-juice.

Querk?

Hash rubbed the water dog's head. "You did good, boy," he said. "You did real good."

✶

Mark Teppo is the author of more than a dozen novels. Recently, he's published *Solitaire* (a weird western), *In the Mansion of Madness* (a horror adventure), and a pair of books on writing. He's the publisher of Underland Press.

URSA MAJOR

JIM WRIGHT

"Bears!"

The watch's panicked shout echoed down the entrance tunnel.

Bears.

As if the situation wasn't already bad enough.

Huff swore a profanity foul enough to melt hoarfrost. He gestured sharply to the two airmen near the entrance, "Go! *Go!* Secure the ship!"

"I told you, we should have kept her aloft," Stiles said without thinking.

Huff whirled to face the Quartermaster, his face twisted in a furious snarl. Stiles shied back, regretting his impulsive words. Huff didn't handle criticism well. *Captain* Huff, Stiles reminded himself, self-promoted from Machinist's Mate.

"Go!" commanded Huff again.

The men drew swords and went. Reluctantly, Stiles thought. They were afraid of Huff, but nobody wanted to face the damned bears. The great beasts were ghosts, cybernetic nightmares with ten-centimeter fangs and titanium claws, fast, cunning, and nearly invisible in the blinding snow. They'd already taken three crew. Men simply vanished from their posts, disappeared into the white land, leaving behind nothing, no tracks, no blood, no trace.

Their blades were pitifully inadequate against the monsters.

They were afraid of Huff, but no one wanted to be eaten alive by bears.

Huff balled up his hands and Stiles braced himself. There was metal in those fists. But instead of the Quartermaster, Huff danced a step to the right and buried his punches in the old man's stomach. Stiles heard a sharp *woof* of air expelled from massive lungs. Hot breath steamed bright in the frigid air and trailed behind as the tall figure crumpled, dropping to his knees, ragged wings falling around him like the folds of a broken umbrella.

"Damn it, Hu ... *Captain*," Stiles corrected himself. "If you kill him, we'll never open the vault. It'll all be for nothing! We go home with *nothing!*"

Faint shouting echoed down the tunnel.

Stiles could hear the old navigator-scout sucking freezing air through swollen lips, but he didn't dare look away from Huff's wild gaze. The man was dangerously close to murder. More murder.

"He's tougher than he looks," Huff kicked viciously at the old man, but he relaxed his fists. "You get your pet parrot to open that door or it's on *your* head." And then the mutineer whirled and was gone up the tunnel, pulling the exec's ancient pistol from his belt as he ran. Huff's pistol now.

Maybe the weapon would stop a bear, maybe not. As he listened to Huff's boots echo up the tunnel, Stiles wasn't sure which outcome he preferred. He waited, head cocked to one side, listening, for screams, for the ring of steel, for gunshots, for the howl of airship engines spinning up in emergency lift. But there was only faint shouting and the ghostly moan of never-ending wind.

"C'mon," he turned to the old man. "Get up."

Longsoar raised his head and looked Stiles in the eye. Even on his knees the old man was taller than the Quartermaster by five centimeters. If the cold bothered him, he didn't show it; his people were engineered for the frigid skies. Irises of deep violet threaded with veins of gold, like lightning in thunderheads, the Scout's gaze held steady and unflinching. Huff was right, the old man looked fragile, but he wasn't.

"You're a mutineer now?" The old man asked. "You've thrown in with Huff?"

Stiles turned away in embarrassment, wondering at what the

Scout might see in his own ordinary human eyes. "Not by choice. And I got them to spare your life, didn't I?"

"They don't trust you any more than they trust me."

"They trust me enough to watch you. Now, get up," Stiles repeated. "Get to work. Finish this so we can get out of here."

"You know he'll kill us both," Longsoar said, rising easily to his clawed feet. "Just as soon as he gets what he wants. He can't bring us back to Vegas Station. Not after what he's done. The other crews would throw him from the docking ring for striking a Scout. The captains will have him shot for mutiny. He can't take us back."

"He can't take *you* back," Stiles corrected. "All I have to do is keep my mouth shut and go along. I'll be rich."

Longsoar said nothing.

Stiles could feel the Scout's strange eyes on the back of his neck. Those eyes were the result of long-lost biotechnologies, the genes of the ancient Navajo merged with that of condors and organic nanocomputers. They saw things ordinary men did not, far into the infrared portion of the light spectrum and further into the ultraviolet, electromagnetic lines of force, gravitational flux, wind currents, and maybe deep into a man's soul.

"But," Stiles allowed, ashamed, "that doesn't mean I might not help you find *another* way home. What happened after that, if your people caught up to Huff, if the captains somehow found out ..." The Quartermaster shrugged. "None of that matters if we don't get this vault open. And soon. We can't stay here. Summer is over. There are more bears every day, Dread Cthulhu knows where they're coming from. We *have* to go." Stiles gestured to the vault door. "You have to finish. Please."

The old man's strange eyes held Stiles's gaze for a few more moments without blinking. Then he nodded and stepped forward to touch the walls. Under his long fingers, the crystal began to glow, and the brightness spread outward from his touch around the chamber like a dawn.

In that pearly light were ghostly tracings of the ancient constellations, the familiar Zodiac of the long-ago Greeks. And below those skies, the walls of the chamber were etched with images of the old north, scenes of life now buried under hundreds of feet of snow and ice, lost when the Yellowstone supervolcano erupted and plunged the polar regions into endless winter under skies forever dark with clouds of dust and the ash of human civilization.

"What do you see?" The wall glowed beneath Longsoar's fingers.

A band of arcane symbols, the mathematics of long forgotten sciences, at eye level like a horizon between the old skies and the ghosts of that long-lost civilization.

There were gaps in the band. Empty spaces.

A combination, perhaps.

Fill in the blanks, solve the puzzle, and the vault would open.

That was the theory anyway—the one Huff had staked all their lives on. The one he, and his cronies, murdered the captain and the ship's officers for.

And what was behind that door, a single massive slab of impenetrable synthetic diamond which dominated one end of the antechamber? No one knew. Its very construction was a fabulous treasure, dating from the time of high technology before war and Yellowstone, before the cities went aloft and civilization fell. No one could make anything like it today. They kept the surviving technology of their ancestors running where they could. Some cities could still build the simpler things, mechanical engines, radio tubes, basic medicines. But resources were buried under hundreds of feet of ice and cubic kilometers of volcanic ash. Computers and thinking robots, genetic machines and advanced technology had died five hundred years ago. No one could make a three-meter-tall slab of solid diamond today. They'd never breach it, not with the tools they had, four thousand kilometers from home. They would have to open it and behind that door could be anything, lost technologies, weapons, gold, even the ancients who had built this place, frozen in suspended animation.

Riches beyond comprehension.

That's what the crew of *Narwhal* had come seeking. Treasure.

That's why they were here, in a frozen vault carved into the living rock of a mountain buried in ice, a place that had once been the foundations, the anchor, of a flying city. That's why Stiles had signed up to journey beyond the known—*safe*—edges of the map. That's why they all signed on. A dangerous expedition of discovery in search of the fabled lost city of Anchorage, deep in the old state of Alaska.

A place only fools would go and a voyage from which no airship had ever returned.

"What do you see?"

"Stars, numbers, letters, I don't know," Stiles shook his head. "I'm not a cryptologist. You've been at this for a month. Summer is gone. Haven't you made *any* progress?"

"You plot the ship's course," the old man countered. "Find her location. Follow the terrain below. Read the old charts, looking for lost landmarks. You're responsible for the ship's clocks and instruments. Navigation. What's that then, if not a sort of code that must be broken? Look again, what do you see?"

"I don't ..."

"When Huff kills me," Longsoar said steadily, as if they were discussing wind currents during a training flight, "you will have to get the ship home. You helped get us here, *Quartermaster*. You have the skills and the education. You can do it. Look again."

Longsoar's people, *Homo Avis*, were born to the skies, engineered for it in more ways than wings and carbon-fiber bones and nanotech enhanced muscle. *Scouts*, his people were called, or sometimes *Weather Mages*—because what they did seemed like magic. Where unmodified men looked to crude instruments and ancient charts to find their way through the murky skies of the ruined Earth, Longsoar could look into the storm and *see* which way to go. Superior senses, genetic memory, faultless instinct, the old Scout's abilities were a testament to the desperate brilliance of those who had created his race centuries before.

Longsoar's confidence suddenly meant a very great deal to the Quartermaster.

The old man touched the vault door with his long fingers and a grid appeared there, a crosshatch of lines making up empty squares.

"Nine by nine," Stiles said, counting. "I've seen this before. A puzzle. Some of the pilots play this game. They trade books back at Vegas Station. If it's a code pad, to unlock the door, nine digits per line. Assuming base ten, that's a billion possible combinations. Times nine, that's eighty-one *billion* possible combinations. It's going to take a while to check each one," Stiles said sarcastically.

"You did the math wrong," Longsoar grinned. "It's *much* worse than that."

"Hell."

"Maybe not." The old man removed his hand from the diamond and the grid disappeared. He gestured to the room. "Look carefully."

Stiles looked again. Carefully, as instructed.

Eventually he had it. "Nine."

Longsoar nodded. "Yes."

Nine gaps in the equations banding the room.

The Scout pointed to the first gap. Lost stars above, lost civilization below. "What is that?"

Stiles stared at glowing lines. He saw people, strange machines, a surface city, ocean, mountains, trees, *green,* a warm red sun setting between distant mountains, a scene from the history books, a world that no longer existed.

"The North," Stiles answered slowly. "As it was before."

"Now, look up. What do you see?"

"Stars."

"How many?"

Stiles stared in exasperation at the pearly dome glowing with a thousand pinpricks of light. "I don't know. A lot?"

"Given clear skies, perhaps six thousand stars are visible to the unmodified human eye," Longsoar's voice took on a familiar lecturing tone and he left unsaid that his own eyes saw considerably more. "Long ago, navigators chose fifty-eight of those stars as the basis for celestial navigation. So far as I can tell, the Alaskans who built this place recreated that sky faithfully. You're a quartermaster. You know how to use a sextant, in the south when the skies are clear. Look carefully."

During the long voyage north, Quartermaster and Scout had passed many hours on watch just like this. The old man didn't teach so much as push you to learn for yourself. Stiles was a patient man, and a fairly intelligent one. But he was often frustrated at those sessions, left feeling like he should know more than he did.

After the mutiny, the newly self-promoted Captain Huff made Longsoar a prisoner and appointed Stiles as his jailer.

That should have changed their dynamic.

But it hadn't.

"Dammit!" Stiles swore. "Just tell me!"

The old man's smile wasn't a pleasant expression on his hawkish face. *"Look."*

Snarling in frustration, Stiles looked.

And then he saw it.

Some of the stars were brighter than the rest. Brighter than they would have been in the real sky up above this buried vault. One brightest of all.

"Polaris?"

"That's right. The *North* Star. The Guide Star. That's the clue. That's where it must begin. Now, in celestial navigation, there are eleven Northern Stars, including Polaris, in eleven constellations to help you remember."

"That's right."

"How many do you *see*?"

Stiles counted, Polaris, Capella, Cygnus, Vega ... He shrugged. "Eleven constellations. Eleven guide stars. As it should be. Brighter than the rest. Brighter than they should be in the actual sky."

"Yes."

"So?"

The old man laughed, "That's what stumped me too. For a long time. Misdirection. But it's obvious when you finally see it. Tell me, of those stars, which one do you think represents the scene below, the North as it was? That symbol that fills in the gap?"

"How the hell would ..."

The old man smiled his unpleasant smile again.

Stiles looked at the scene, the old north, people, strange machines, a surface city, ocean, mountains, trees, green, the disk of a warm red sun setting between distant mountains ...

"... wait."

"Ah, you do see it."

"*That's* the Old World, the old north, before the eruption. Twelve stars, not eleven, and it's the *sun*, of course. Celestial navigation is a function of star position and *time*."

"And the sun is the oldest clock. They called this place 'the land of the midnight sun' because in the summer, in the old days, there was never any darkness." Longsoar stepped past Stiles and traced a disk in the first gap. Under his spider finger, a circle glowed, blood red like the disk of a setting sun.

"Press your hand flat on the vault door," the old man commanded.

Stiles did so and the grid lit again, only this time a number of red circles illuminated seemingly random squares.

"As you said, it's a puzzle. A grid, nine by nine, divided into sub-grids of three by three. Base nine, *not* ten. Nine symbols. Nine rows. Nine columns. Nine sub-grids. Fill the grid with the symbols so that each column, row, and sub-grid block contains all of the symbols without duplication. It's an ancient logic puzzle, called a *Sudoku,* once a fetish among airship pilots—and sometimes, as you noted, it still is."

"Sure. My instructor pilot made us do number puzzles when I was an apprentice. But," Stiles said, "this is giving me a headache. I understand the basics. Nine symbols. Nine scenes give you the symbols. Put them in the grid, solve the puzzle open the door. I get that. I think. Maybe. But, why puzzles, games ...?"

"Civilization collapsed. There was war before Yellowstone. More people died in those years than are alive on the whole planet *now.* Then the eruption. Nuclear winter. Everything fell apart. The cities went aloft. More war. Humanity fell into savagery and feudalism. These people, these northerners, they were cut off by thousands of kilometers of snow and ice. Even the sun was lost to them. The government of that time abandoned them. Their own nation abandoned them. Abandoned the north completely. These people, they must have known they couldn't survive here. You've *seen* it."

Stiles had seen it, all right, fallen, frozen, and ruined in the ice. Eaten by bears.

They'd come seeking treasure and found only bitter disappointment. That was the seed of mutiny and murder.

"The North knew they wouldn't survive. But they must have hoped the skies would clear one day, that the world would thaw out and civilization would find its way North again."

"So?" Stiles shook his head. "*They* would be long dead."

"You're still young," the old man said. "You don't feel it yet."

"Feel what?"

"Mortality, Quartermaster." Longsoar smiled his strange smile again. "These people weren't just facing their own deaths, but the murder of their entire *culture*. Yellowstone didn't just kill them; it erased all that they ever were from history and buried their bones out there under ash and ice forever."

"The whole damn planet is buried under ash and snow...."

Stiles was a child of the ruined world.

He'd never given much thought to history or his place in it.

But there was something in Longsoar's voice. Something in those strange eyes. And in that moment Stiles saw a glimpse of history handed down from one generation to the next, again and again, a thousand times over millennia. Longsoar was old, battered by age and scarred by violence but still defiant. Suddenly Stiles saw in that determination more than just a single man, but rather a proud and resourceful people who had literally remade themselves, encoding their history and culture into their very flesh, rather than allow their tradition to perish.

"People want to be remembered?"

"Just so."

Stiles looked around the vault. "They buried this place in the foundation of their city so that it would be found even if the city fell and they themselves were long dead."

Longsoar nodded and waited for the Quartermaster to go on.

"Okay. I get that. I guess. But, but, why *this*? Why a puzzle?"

"Don't you see? In a hundred years, or thousand, they must have hoped an expedition from the South would come. Whatever is in there, they didn't want graverobbers to have it. They didn't want *Huff* to have it. This place was designed specifically to be unlocked by a navigator, an airship pilot. Someone with a specific education. By *you*."

"Or you. They didn't want Huff to have it," Stiles said. "But we're going to give it to him anyway."

Longsoar shrugged.

From there, it should have been easy. The first symbol, the sun, was simple, obviously designed to explain the puzzle to those with the necessary skills to solve it.

The rest should have been easy.

But it wasn't.

If it had been, Stiles thought, Longsoar himself would have

solved the puzzle and opened the vault weeks ago. They'd be on their way home now with the treasure and there might never have been a mutiny.

Narwhal had left Vegas Station in spring, tracking north along the Rockies. The airship was old and had been refitted many times over the centuries. A freighter turned explorer, she was now equipped with heavy insulation against the deep arctic cold, oversized fuel tanks, spare parts and extended stores, survival equipment, medical bay and machine shop, explosive mooring anchors that would let them set her down in the wilderness without a ground crew. The trade-off, of course, was crew size. More self-sufficiency meant less airmen, fewer officers, more work and less rest for each.

By the time they reached Alaska they were cold and exhausted and afraid they'd never return home, desperate to find *anything* that would make the trip worthwhile.

Yellowstone had brought a new ice age, causing the seas to freeze and retreat. Snow fell every year and under the ash clouds there was no summer warmth to melt it. Glaciers advanced and the very landscape changed beyond recognition.

It took too many weeks to find the site of old Anchorage.

The city had once stood on the edge of the Cook Inlet, at the base of the Chugach Mountains, but the sea was now tens of kilometers distant and the shape of the very mountains had changed beneath the weight of the grinding ice.

Their ancient charts were nearly useless, but eventually the near magical skills of their Scout Navigator brought them to the right place.

In the South, nations on the brink of extinction had worked to construct the flying cities and send them aloft. Great, graceful, self-sufficient spires took to the skies on gravity engines, where they might ride out the coming centuries above the ruined Earth below.

The North was abandoned, left to its own cold fate.

But Alaska had always been a harsh land, had always forced its people to be resourceful and tenacious and to make do. Cold was nothing new to Alaskans. And so, they had taken what was at hand, oil rigs and mining equipment and the massive machines of their world, and built their own refuge. New Anchorage, squat, angular, and defiantly different from the southern cities. Final broadcasts, before communications failed and the corpse of civilization was buried beneath the ash, showed the city aloft, tethered to the granite of the Chugach, riding the fierce winds above a mountaintop that had once long ago been a fortress defending the land below from attack.

"But the war came anyway," said Longsoar sadly. "And worse."

They had come seeking that final image from the North: a city on a mountaintop, built by a people smart enough and resilient enough to survive in a place where no one else could.

What wonders would such a city hold?

What knowledge might such a people share?

But New Anchorage had fallen long ago.

The wreckage lay below the mountain, shattered buttresses protruding from the ice like the yellowed bones of some great whale, and it seemed the people they had come seeking hadn't survived after all.

All that remained of them was this vault.

Maybe nothing waiting behind that door, or maybe treasure beyond imagination.

There were hints. Longsoar was certain that the equations banding the chamber were genetic code. A blueprint for human modification, biotechnologies long, long lost, like those which created his own race. Similar, and yet very, very different.

Or perhaps it was something else.

Stiles and the old navigator were making progress, but it was taking too long. Every time they made a mistake, the puzzle reset. New scenes appeared which had to be interpreted, a new lesson from a lost people to be learned, new constellations chosen as the key symbols. They *were* making progress, but summer was over, and Huff was dangerously close to murder.

Another day, Stiles told the mutineer. Maybe two.

They were so close.

That night, without warning, the first winter storm hit. A maelstrom of ice and snow, powered by winds crossing eight thousand kilometers of frozen ocean.

Then, in the whiteout, came the bears.

And suddenly *Narwhal* was out of time.

Stiles and Longsoar had been returning to the airship for a meal and rest when the attack came. Stiles had been dreading the inevitable confrontation with Huff, and it was almost a relief when they heard the shouted alarm.

In the murk and swirling snow beneath the airship, Stiles couldn't see a thing. He could barely keep his eyes open in the stinging ice and cold.

But not Longsoar, of course. The old man saw just fine.

"The watch!" the old man shouted. "At the mooring!"

Stiles drew his blade and yelled his own warning to the ship. He heard confused shouting in response and the heavy thuds of armed men and women running.

Over the creaking of the airship and howl of the icy wind, he heard a deeper roar, and a nightmare came at him out of the storm. Its white fur blended perfectly with the snow and all Stiles could see was a sudden flash of enormous fangs set in black gums, running bright red with blood.

He swung wildly with his blade, missed, and felt Longsoar grab him from behind, throwing them both backward.

The monster disappeared into the snow.

Stiles heard the ring of steel and men shouting in fear and bloodlust.

"I can't see anything!" Stiles shouted. "I'm turned around! Where are they?"

"It doesn't matter," Longsoar said. "If they cut the mooring, we'll lose the ship. You're the pilot! You have to get to the controls! This way."

Suddenly, there were bright flashes in the gloom and Stiles heard the report of the exec's ancient pistol. Forward. They were trying to defend the mooring anchor.

"We have to help Huff!" Stiles cried.

"Leave him to the bears!"

"No!"

"Give me your sword then, Quartermaster," the old man demanded. "I'll do it. If you want to save your crew, get to the ship!"

Huff's pistol roared in the darkness again.

"Goddammit!" Stiles shoved the hilt of his blade into the old navigator's hands. "Help them!"

Longsoar's strange eyes flashed like lightning in thunderheads and held Stiles's own for a moment longer, then he spread massive wings like great black scythes and pointed into the storm. "That way. The ramp is ten meters!" And suddenly the old man was gone and for the first time in his life, Stiles heard the keening deadly cry of a Weather Mage flying into battle.

Stiles fumbled blindly through the storm. The wind gusted and he could feel the mass of *Narwhal* shifting overhead in response. And then, for just a moment, the snow eddied in the lee of the airship and he saw the gangway an arm's length away. He grabbed at the rail with nearly frozen fingers and was dragged across the ice as the airship swung in the wind like a pendulum from the pivot of its anchor. He managed to pull himself onto the ramp and crawled on hands and knees up the gangway into the back of the control car.

Stiles climbed to his feet and tumbled across the lurching deck into the pilot's station. He twisted control switches and outside the storm was suddenly lit brilliant white with the landing lights. He glanced at the forward windscreen, towards the mooring anchor, as he reached for the engine controls ...

... and froze.

The battle was over.

The actinic arcs of the airship's powerful forward spotlight cut through the snow.

What was left of *Narwhal*'s crew, those still alive, huddled in a forlorn knot around the anchor. The rest lay scattered on red-stained ice already turning white with new drifts.

Beneath the nose of the ship, Huff stood with pistol drawn.

But the weapon wasn't pointed at the *hundreds* of great ursids, even now barely visible in the snow, which surrounded the ship.

No, Huff's gun was pointed at the old navigator.

Stiles shouted "No!" as the weapon barked, a single bright flash. There was no expression on Huff's face as he watched Longsoar fall.

Then Huff calmly put the pistol to his own temple and pulled the trigger.

✶

Like so many others over the centuries, they had come to Alaska seeking treasure.

And like many of those adventurers, their expedition had found hardship and death.

"But for those of us who survive," Stiles said to *Narwhal*'s crew, a handful, barely enough to fly the ship home, "there is still a chance."

The vault room was crowded with the surviving airmen and a dozen of the massive ursids.

Stiles glanced to where Huff stood, defiant and furious, his hands bound firmly behind his back. The Quartermaster still savored the expression on the mutineer's face when the hammer of his stolen pistol had fallen on an empty chamber.

"What do we call you?" Stiles asked.

An ursid, fully half again larger than the rest of the great creatures, standing on hind legs and tall enough that her massive head brushed the ceiling of the chamber, snorted steam and said, "Whatever you like."

Her words were distorted by metal teeth as big as a large man's hand and a mouth not designed for human speech, but Stiles understood her well enough.

"Why did you attack us?"

"Because you attacked us. Because you attacked each other. Because you came to take what we would have given freely but we will not allow you to steal."

Stiles, glancing again towards the mutineer, said, "We were misled."

"And now?"

Stiles raised his voice, "A people want to be remembered." He was speaking to the crew now, as well as the bears.

Stiles stepped past the great creature and began to draw on the wall of the chamber, demonstrating what he and Longsoar had learned.

"This place was once called Alyeska, *Alaska,* The Great Land. The history of the people who once lived here goes back to the last ice age, 25,000 years. These were *their* stars," Stiles pointed to the sky overhead. "These were their constellations."

Stiles sketched the symbols he and Longsoar had worked out:

wolf, salmon, whale, fox, crow, walrus, eagle, moose. And, at last, the bear.

"Others came and went, sometimes this place belonged to one nation and sometimes another. But *they* remained, part of this land. They fought the invaders for their history, for the right to be remembered as a people. When Yellowstone happened, and a new ice age, Alaska and the North were abandoned. Cut off. Those people, they weren't facing just their own death, but all that they had ever been. As if they had never existed. They knew they couldn't survive here, not as human beings."

"So, they built New Anchorage and sent it aloft, to give themselves time to make a race that *could*. Their ancestors," Stiles went on, "told stories of men who could shapeshift, became animals, birds, fish. Technology gave them that ability for real."

Stiles turned to face the bears. He gestured to the band of genetic equations wrapping the chamber, dividing heaven and earth, between the Old World and the new. "You're their children."

If she could have smiled, Stiles suspected the huge ursid would have.

Symbols glowed in a grid on the great slab of diamond. Stiles stepped forward to solve the final puzzle, but she stopped him.

"A people want to be remembered," she said.

She placed a massive paw flat on the surface and crystal began to glow.

Stiles nodded in satisfaction. The puzzle had never mattered. History was the key. He watched words and numbers flow across the surface, an index, a card catalog, technology that hadn't been seen in half a thousand years. Over his shoulder, he said, "If you had waited, Huff, if you had been the kind of man who used his brain instead of his fists, you could have been rich."

"I don't ..."

"This isn't a door to some vault. *This* is the treasure. It's a classroom. It's a library. It's all the knowledge that we lost when Yellowstone erupted. History. Science. Medicine. Technology. Literature. The ability to rebuild this world and rebuild ourselves to fit in it. Wealth beyond imagination. *This* is what we came for."

"What good is that?" Huff shouted. "We can't take it with us ..."

"No. We'll have to come back. With specialists, engineers, scientists, historians. We'll have to build, *rebuild,* the tools to understand. We will have to remember those people who left us such a gift and forge a friendship with their descendants. We'll have to return to the North *our* ancestors abandoned."

"You're a fool!"

"Perhaps." Stiles turned to look the mutineer in the eye one last time. "It will take years, decades, maybe centuries, to rebuild what we've lost. It will take a dozen ships, more. A thousand voyages. You would have been one of the only airmen to come this far in five hundred years. You could have led them. You could have been legend. You could have been part of *history.* Instead, you'll be forgotten as if you never were."

Captain Stiles turned to face his crew. "But for now … let's go home."

✶

Jim Wright is a retired US Navy Intelligence Officer turned political analyst and writer. If there's a place in the world you can name, he's probably been there. He lived longer in Alaska than anywhere else and misses it terribly, but circumstances forced him to move to the fetid swamps of the Florida Panhandle, where he lives now in an ancient Cold War bunker of a house surrounded by alligators and Spanish moss. He's the mind behind the political blog, *Stonekettle Station.* You can follow him on Facebook and Twitter.

SCOUT'S HONOR

RAVEN OAK

I never wanted to work with the cartel.

Mi abuela wanted better for her little Pia Fernandez. Before the Yellowstone eruption sent fire and ash into the sky, *su abuela*, her grandmother, studied weather, and *su madre* was a doctor. A long line of women with more to their name than a few scraps of food. But all of that changed with *mi padre*. He had connections and influence—at least before the Ghost Fleet murdered him. The day I inherited his airship, *La Hermana del Bendito Sol*, or *The Blessed Sun's Sister*, I inherited everything else, including his *mala suerte*, or bad luck. Now, only fools would be willing to crew *La Hermana*.

Knowing that, I ignored the usual haunts of those looking for work and set off for *el último muelle*, the last pier in Mexico City, where broken-down fools waited on broken-down docks for fools like me to hire them. Only thrill seekers and thieves, their desperation smelling as strongly as their sweat, would take a chance out there. Before I could open my mouth, a shadow rose before me, and the fools lining the old pier scattered down a nearby alleyway. Only two people could make us turn to dust—Jefe, or his second in command, Two-Cross.

"Oye, chica. ¿Qué pasa?" Two-Cross's gravelly voice mixed with the creaking planks beneath his heavy boots as he stepped up beside me. Like most cartel *familias*, he wore a gold cross, but Two-Cross

wore his in both jewelry and skin, as black ink marred his face with the ornate holy symbol.

"I need work," I said.

"There's no work for you here."

"Mierda." I removed the plastic board from my backpack and set it in front of him. "You posted this job yesterday, and I know it ain't been filled 'cause it was still marked available when I removed it."

Two-Cross leaned close to me, his breath a mix of booze and decay. Much as my feet wished to tumble backward, I remained still, my nose almost touching his. "Lucky for you, Jefe has a task he wants done."

I let loose a string of profanities in *Pocho,* or Spanglish. There was work, and then there were Jefe's *tasks*. "And am I meant to survive this?"

Two-Cross shrugged. "You know Monterrey Tower?" he asked.

"You know I do. It's where *mi padre* was killed."

"*Sí. Tu papá* was there to get tech for Jefe. He failed. Now *you* get tech for Jefe."

I nodded, my tongue thick in my mouth. "What will I get if I do this?"

"You get to live. *Maybe* you get your honor back."

"I'll need a crew."

He raised his hand—the one missing an index finger—and waggled it in the air. Two men and a woman slinked out of the shadows as they eyed me with suspicion. All human—or as human as any of us were these days.

"These three owe Jefe. They'll be your crew."

"Three ain't enough to crew *La Hermana,* and you know it."

When he wiggled his fingers in the air a second time, another dozen or more shadows became solid as they stepped into the sun. "They all owe Jefe, so they'll listen to you if they know what's good for them."

With no other choice, I nodded. Jefe says *saltar,* you jump. I set off down the pier with lean fools trailing behind me. My skin crawled from Two-Cross's gaze on my back as I stepped over places where planks had long since dropped away from the pier. He was probably wishing I'd fall through and save everyone the trouble.

La Hermana del Bendito Sol lay at the pier's end—there was nowhere else I was allowed to stow her—but from her spot in the city, *Teotihuacan* stretched out across the land beneath us like a promise that there were still things of beauty in this world.

I set my jaw firmly in place as we steered away from our floating city and towards my future, whatever it would be.

✶

The half-finished, half-flooded Monterrey City lay to the north, and to the east lay what little remained of old tropical forests and their pyramids. We flew over the Avenue of the Dead as we approached *Teotihuacan*, the Pyramid of the Moon, while to the west of us rose a lengthy mountain range with its own unpredictable weather system. Somewhere along our path traveled the powerful Ghost Fleet, with airships that could hide amidst both cloud and sun, and attack before a captain had done little more than gasp. Or so it was rumored.

Mi padre's death brought few details as no crew members survived. One moment, he'd reached Monterrey and the next, he was gone. When he didn't return, I bartered the last of my savings to the cartel, which had found his battered ship downed in a valley. No other ships could make burn marks like the Ghost Fleet, so when Jefe reported to *mi abuela* that her son and his crew were lost to the ghosts, rumor became solid. Became fact.

An inexperienced captain would take the forest route, but the ghosts would expect that. Something I kept in mind as I ordered my crew to the west.

"Captain." Juan pointed in the distance where the gray haze of rain lay. Like the rest of him, his arm sported enough ink to be more black than brown. "We goin' through that?"

"We are."

"It's monsoon season."

Pamella, a woman who resembled *mi abuela* in both stature and attitude, frowned. "That a problem?"

"You'd no more fly a plane than an airship through that kinda wind. As much as we got engines and rudders, this thing still follows air currents." When I furrowed my brows, Juan added, "Been running crew for Jefe long time. I know how a ship works."

Pamella's eyes grew wide as she turned to face me. "No offense, but flying through that sounds like a bad plan, and we're here to make sure Jefe gets what's his."

"It's either that or face the ghosts," I said as I pointed at my map. "You knew the risks when you walked on board. Make sure we've got enough lift. Wouldn't help us to snag ourselves on *Cerro*'s peak."

Around us, grand waterfalls dumped torrents of water down the rocky mountainside, and in the distance, the familiar saddle shape of *Cerro de la Silla* appeared through the haze. As the clouds darkened, rain splashed against the bridge's windows.

"Hey, Captain," said Pamella. "Something on the screen."

I scooted over to where she manned the reverse periscope, and she pointed to airship remains a dozen meters ahead. If I hadn't been sailing *La Hermana del Bendito Sol,* I could almost swear I was staring at my ship's remains, right down to the scorch marks on her bow.

"Let's check it out."

"You thinking there might be something worth salvaging?" asked Pamella.

"Maybe. Could be the weather took them down. Could be the ghosts. Either way, they weren't expecting to land in that basin. Take us lower, Juan."

A retort shone in his eyes, but the words rested on his thin lips and remained there as our approach revealed the shadow of someone or something moving near the ship itself.

"What is it? Could it be a bear?" asked Juan.

"Doubtful. Could be a survivor. Maybe someone willing to pay for their safe return to Mexico City." I watched through the periscope as we drew closer to the ground. My bino-glasses zoomed in, giving me a grainy image. There was no mistaking the lengthy shadow that moved among the debris. Too tall for a human. Too tall for anything but a Scout.

Our ship light reflected off purple-gold eyes, painting an eerie mask on a rather gaunt being. Rather than hide, they stood tall as the rain poured down from the sky. "Stay behind me," I said as I slid my arms through my raincoat's sleeves. "It's a Scout, and they're fairly jumpy. If there's something worth salvaging, they could be the key to finding it."

"Is it true that Scouts have magic?" asked Juan.

I shook off the greedy look in his eyes and scowled. "It ain't magic. Just something different is all."

The wind buffeted my small airship and me, once I opened the doors. In the downpour, I couldn't see but a half meter in front of me, and I tapped the focusing dial on my glasses, and the lens zoomed in on the Scout and the wreckage behind him. Plastic and metal framing mixed with the balloon's torn fabric, while random personal effects lay scattered in charred piles.

"Maybe he can tell us what happened."

I spun on my heel to glare at Juan, a look he couldn't see with my bino-glasses in the way.

He held up his hands. "I didn't mean nothing by it. Not magic, just what happened to the ship. If he was here when it went down."

My insides quaked more than I liked, and I took a deep breath to steady myself. Jefe's fools, dangerous though they might be, needed me to find *mi padre's* tech. Rather than expecting a knife in the back, I returned to the scene before us, a forced smile plastered across my face.

"Hello? *¡Hola!*"

There was nowhere to take shelter in those remains, so I gestured for the Scout to approach my ship. At first, his eyes grew shadowed as he glanced over my head, but when the wind buffeted us all with a wave of water, he darted forward with much longer and faster strides than I could make.

Mi padre's Scout had been reclusive. Too busy to interact with a kid like me. This one didn't seem to be the same, which gave me pause. The four of us settled in my ship's tiny dining space, where we gathered around a lone table. I wiped a clump of hair from where it had plastered against my face, then smiled at our visitor.

"I'm Captain Pia of *La Hermana del Bendito Sol*. We were heading toward Monterrey when the crew spotted ship remains. From the debris pattern, it appears to have smashed against the rocks, after getting hit by … something. Was this your ship?" I glanced up at him, craning my neck with his great height, and gestured for him to have a seat.

The gold in his eyes softened until only purple remained. "I am Diego Aparicio of Veracruz, though some to the north call me Doug.

Captain Hendricks out of Texas piloted the ship, *The Strong Birds*. The weather spoke of a creeping cloud that spread across the mountains between thunderclaps, but Captain Hendricks would not hear of it. 'The weather does not speak,' he said to me before the ghosts arrived."

Rather than folding himself awkwardly into a seat, he perched on the chair's back. The membranes between his arms and ribs folded in on themselves, leaving long gaps at his leather vest's sides. While he talked, I poured hot water into mugs and splashed dried tea leaves into my own. His smooth face spoke of youth, but with so little known about his kind, I wasn't ready to assume it. "What do you know of this area?" I asked.

"Not much. Honestly, I have not been to Mexico in a long while."

Making it unlikely he'd heard of *mi familia*. That could work in my benefit. "Were there no survivors in the crash?" I asked, and he shook his head.

"So, how'd you live? Do you have ma—"

I kicked Juan beneath the table, and his brows furrowed.

"The captain, he was mad. Something about the storm confused him. When I told him the storm would see us crashed along the mountainside, he refused to listen. I had no choice but to leave."

"You mean you abandoned your ship," I said.

The Scout nodded as he settled his hands around the warm tea mug.

"You said you chose to serve with *The Strong Birds*, but where were you before that?" I asked.

"With my tribe. *The Strong Birds* was my first ship."

I nodded confirmation, but Juan stood and tossed his cup toward the waste bin. "Captain, he ain't nothing but a *pendejo*, a coward. We should leave him here to rot with the rest of his crew. He'll only bring trouble."

Purple met my brown as Diego looked at me expectantly.

"Anything worth salvaging from the remains?" I asked.

"Beyond damaged framing? No, nothing survived the fall down the mountain. Less survived the ghosts," he said and closed his eyes. "Scavengers cleaned the bodies down to the bone, then dragged those off soon after, and the balloon cloth was too shredded to even use as a shield from the storms."

My glass's lens sharpened when I glanced at his gaunt frame, made gaunter by the way his ribs protruded at weird angles from his torso. "When's the last time you ate?"

He shrugged but took another sip of warm tea.

"Look, you ain't a coward. I know from *mi padre* that Scouts carry more than weather-sense with them, they carry honor. No one messes with a Scout or their crewmembers, so if you're willing to help get us to Monterrey, I'll feed you and make sure you get back to Mexico City. From there, well, where you go is entirely up to you."

"You're heading to Monterrey?" he asked, and it was my turn to nod. "The dead lay between here and there, sheltered in invisible metal that rains fire across the sky."

"The Ghost Fleet," I whispered, and beside me, Pamella shuddered. "Will we make it to Monterrey? Can we?"

"I do not see the future, Captain Fernandez."

Heat spread across my cheeks. "My apologies, Scout Diego. The storm's severe. I only meant to inquire after its progress through the mountain range. And please, Captain Pia if you will."

He glanced off to his left as if my ship's walls were see-through, then cleared his throat. "We should hurry."

I was moving before my mind caught up with my legs. "Pamella, get him something to eat. Everyone else, bridge," I called as I ran.

Perhaps the coward would cost me everything.

Or perhaps *mi padre's* spirit was with me after all. Perhaps he'd placed the Scout in my path so I could find my way home again.

✶

Rain battered my ship as we approached Monterrey, though the water more closely resembled fists than tiny droplets. With each mile passed, I held my breath tighter as Diego and I scanned the skies for the Ghost Fleet. Thunder rumbled in the distance, then approached like one of Jefe's moods—all sound and fury.

If the Ghost Fleet was out there, they hid themselves well, and I turned to Diego. "Can … can you see the Ghost Fleet? When they're hidden?"

He gave the briefest of nods, and behind us, Juan gasped.

"Juan, pay attention to steering the ship," I shouted over another bark of thunder. Up ahead, a clump of gray hovered and as we approached, my lenses focused enough to display the city of Monterrey. Its base, a mess of metal construction debris and overgrown moss, was a fifth the size of Mexico City. A handful of buildings reached up like fingers, their incomplete tops a gnarled mess of rebar and concrete. It didn't float so much as rest against the ground, its lowest layer crumbled into the mountainside.

"Take us to the right," I said as I pointed. A long wooden pier stuck out, complete with a metal anchor point. "You can anchor it but keep an eye out. That anchor's stuck in nothing but rot."

"Is it safe to dock there?" Juan gestured as the pier swayed with the gusting wind.

"If we land near the base, we'll have to climb over that mess. I don't know about you, but I don't wanna try that in this downpour. We'd slip and impale ourselves on rebar before we'd made it twenty feet."

As the ship brushed against the dock, wood creaked, and I winced as I locked the airship's controls. While the others stared at the developing lightning show outside, I slid the key into a hidden pocket in my shirt seam.

"Juan, go tether us, please. Preferably somewhere secure."

He cocked an eyebrow but set off to follow my commands. I turned to the rest of my makeshift crew and forced my shoulders to relax.

"Scout Diego comes with me. You all will remain here and keep watch." I handed a short-range radio to Pamella. "If you see anything, call me on Channel One."

"You trust us to stay with the ship?" asked Pamella, and I smiled.

"Jefe wants his tech. Without me, good luck finding it. Besides, you'd still have to escape the Ghost Fleet. I *might* be able to talk them out of killing us painfully. But you all? Let's just say they like their victims rough around the edges."

Her lips pursed together as she stared at Diego. "Separating a Scout from their ship is bad luck, but it's on your head, Captain."

"What isn't?" I muttered.

Hard rain pelted us as Diego and I stepped outside. Juan had tied us to a metal hook bolted into a long pillar, and I leaned over to check his knots. "Good enough?" he shouted over the weather.

"They'll hold better than the pier will!" Ship secure, I gestured for Diego to follow me toward the city.

A low moan escaped the pier as another gust of wind rocked it, and he flinched.

"My redemption is necessary, Captain—maybe yours is too, considering this fool's errand—but this storm is nothing to trifle with." He pointed to the tallest Tower towards the city's center. "Why enter a building in danger of collapse at any moment? What do you wish to prove?"

As we trudged through the rain, debris littered the streets as the wind screamed through mostly hollow buildings.

"I can't go back empty-handed," I shouted over the storm. "Otherwise, it's not worth going back. The cartel isn't forgiving."

"No, they are not."

The way he said it rang of pain and truth, and I asked, "So, what would a Scout know of the cartel? No offense, but you ride around on airships, reading weather, right? There are so many rumors surrounding you Scouts, it's hard to know what's truth, but people revere you. You're sought after like a prized piece of tech, while people like me, well, we're lucky if we live long enough to die, let alone have a *familia*."

The Scout blinked at me, his eyes rapidly cycling between their purple and golden hues. "You are not the only one to know loss and pain. What use is there in flying if it is in service to a—never mind. There are many types of shackles, Captain Pia."

A chunk of cement building lay across the cracked road we followed. While I crawled through a hollowed-out square at its corner, Diego leapt over the pillar with ease.

"Once with *mi padre*, his Scout leapt off the ship and rode the air currents down below us. There ain't any shackles on you that I can see. You could fly away right now, and I'd never find you. Me? My chains are forged by Jefe and the cartel. There's no where I can run that he wouldn't find me."

"Do not presume to know everything about Scouts and their lives, Captain. To you, we are a commodity to use. There's a reason my people avoid Mexico City in favor of the Arizonas to the north."

The walk forward remained silent except for a few grunts as we hiked toward our goal. Thunder rattled the buildings a few times, sending small cascades of stone down the building's sides. Our eyes remained skyward as we waited for something larger to loom overhead, yet nothing more than storm clouds darkened our path.

Had it been finished, the building that stood before us could've been beautiful; stretching high above the other buildings by double, its stone columns were carved with intricate line work. It wasn't the line's maze-like formation that caught my eye, but the delicate tulip sketched beside the door.

"What is it?" asked Diego.

"*Mi padre* was here." I laid my hand against the mark, allowing its roughness to scratch my palm. "Jefe used to give him grief for having such a girlie mark, but *mi abuela* loves tulips. He said every time he drew one, it reminded him of her sacrifices."

I tugged on the door, which remained stuck, and, after a good wrench, it flung open with the wind's assistance. If *mi padre* had left that mark, he had meant for me to find the tech.

"Is it safe to go inside? The building … she leans."

One corner of the building had sunk into the ground below, giving the building a noticeable tilt. I shook the door, and when the building remained standing, I shrugged. "She's solid enough."

Three feet inside, debris blocked our forward momentum. Muscles hid beneath Diego's slender frame, and I couldn't help but admire the efficiency in which he cleared a path for us toward a second set of doors.

These led to a windowless hallway that made my skin crawl. There was darkness and then there was this. I reached up to touch the side of my glasses, and a light beam shot forward, illuminating the area. Wider than I'd expected, the hall held three doors and a sitting area. Green moss covered what at one time must have been furniture but now had slickened into uselessness. Diego sneezed.

"Onward we go," I whispered as we passed through the first door.

A larger room, perhaps one that had served as storage, was empty of all but small rodents who fled my light for the various holes in the walls. The faint smell of mold tickled my nose, but its source remained unknown. Another storage room met our exploration, but the third door led to another hall, with more doors leading us deeper into the building.

"If you are determined to find something, let us find it and be gone from this graveyard." Diego shuddered as he eyed the crumbling walls.

At first, several rooms we passed through were like the first, a mixture of mud and green moss, cracked from plants and animals that had reclaimed the areas as their own. Sometimes holes allowed a trickle of rain to find its way in, and soon we slogged our way through knee-deep water as we approached the sunken corner.

"There must be something important in this building. Why else would the Ghost Fleet be protecting it?" I asked.

"Who says they are protecting it?"

"Look, trust me. There's something here. If there was nothing here, then *mi padre* died for nothing. They killed him to keep him from it." I turned away to keep him from seeing my tears.

"If there is something of value here, where would it be?" he asked.

I pursed my lips. Where had *mi padre* looked when searching for goods? I glanced around the next room, but nothing popped out at me. No wall coverings at odd angles or lock boxes tucked beneath furniture. "Maybe we're on the wrong floor. I mean, the ground level isn't exactly where one hides important items."

"Or maybe there is nothing here. This city was never finished, so would your ancestors have kept anything of value here?"

He wasn't wrong, and I balled my hands into fists as we slogged through yet another waterlogged room. "There must be something. *Mi padre* didn't leave his mark for nothing," I whispered and then flinched as he heard me.

"Where does your cartel keep its valuables?" he asked.

"Most of the tech running the Tower is at the city's inner core, in the lower levels. If the makers of this city were anything like the cartel, I assume they'd keep their goods in the basement like Jefe does." I shrugged. "It's not like they'd tell me. But unfinished? Maybe they kept their building libraries here."

"Building libraries?"

"Knowledge. On how they made the cities in the sky."

The Scout pointed at a sign on the wall. Its stepped iconography indicated the stairs, and we followed them down two floors where the water reached my chest. "I don't think I can go down another level. This will have to do."

At a height of seven feet, water didn't bother Diego, and he pried open the door with ease. Metal shelving, bolted to the walls, stood stripped of anything useful. A few old, rusted wires draped from the ceiling, but otherwise, the room held more water than goods.

"Damn," I muttered.

"I have to ask, why bring me along, Captain? I could be—*should* be watching over the ship rather than searching for the unknown."

"I can't trust my crew, well, Jefe's crew. Backstabbing thieves, the lot of them. I certainly can't trust them to have my back."

"So, I am here to guard you and open doors?" When I nodded, he continued, "What makes you think your crew will not steal your ship?"

"Take *La Hermana del Bendito Sol*?" I laughed, and the sound echoed across the emptiness. The next room was stripped bare as well, as was the next, and I blinked back tears.

"Why is the thought of theft funny?"

"My ship's famous, Scout Diego. At least in Mexico. *Mi padre* captained her for twenty years, the whole time, running salvage for the cartel. Any man stupid enough to defy *mi padre's* wishes for me to fly her is a man looking for a cursed life."

One moment there was ground beneath me, and the next, the floor sank, and I tumbled into cold, murky water with a gasp. My head broke the surface as I tread water, while a current tugged at my clothing. My light flickered in and out, then failed, leaving me in sudden darkness. Panic rose from my belly, pushing out my air too fast, and I took too large a gasp. Water flooded my mouth as slender hands grabbed me by the shoulders and pulled diagonally until I stood on solid floor.

"Thank you," I said with a cough, then pointed back the way we'd come. "Perhaps we should go up a floor. Might be easier than drowning. Besides, anything under that much water is useless to us."

"It will take a while to return to the stairs. Especially in the dark like this."

I removed my glasses and blew on them in an attempt to dry their insides. After a moment or two, the light flickered on, weak but working. The pale beam illuminated a pile of plywood and metal bars in the corner, and I asked, "Could you break a hole in the ceiling with any of that? Maybe we could climb up as a shortcut."

The Scout tilted his head as he examined the beams, then tested two metal bars. He thrust the heaviest into the ceiling tile several times as water poured forth, and wriggled the bar back and forth to expand the hole large enough to squeeze through. He lifted me through it easily before pulling himself into yet another room that had been stripped of tech.

Both of us sat on damp concrete to catch our breaths, though I suspected we rested more for my benefit than his.

"How did you end up in possession of your father's ship?" he asked when we crossed into a room that had served as an office space.

I tugged open drawers and cabinet doors, searching for anything and finding nothing. A few scraps of paper and a dead mouse. "*Mi padre* was killed by the Ghost Fleet while ... well, while searching this Tower. He made it out, but they took down the ship. Cost me my entire savings to convince Jefe to search for him. Jefe's crew returned with the damaged ship. I ... I owe him for her repairs."

The Scout's eyes grew wide. "Your father was Thomas Fernandez."

"He was."

"And his ship was *La Hermana del Bendito Sol*?"

"*Sí.*"

The way he paled, I figured the Ghost Fleet was outside, and I reached for my radio. "Pia to Pamella." The signal crackled before her response reached me. Assured that only the weather threatened us harm, I turned my attention back to the Scout.

"I did not mean to alarm you, Captain, but I never knew the ship's name. I met *su padre* once. You greatly resemble him," he said.

"I've been told that a lot."

Diego pried open another door. Another empty office space, and he growled in response. "There is nothing here, Captain. This Tower is nothing but a ghost town."

"Perhaps. Or perhaps not." Next to the last door—one I thought to be a closet—a tiny tulip was carved beside the doorknob, almost hovering above the water line. I stepped away to reveal the discovery to Diego when the Tower rumbled, raining water and debris down on our heads.

"What was that?" I asked as I brushed a clump of moss from my hair.

"If that was the Ghost Fleet, I suspect we would be falling to our deaths. A strong wind may have knocked something loose." When Diego followed me into the room, his sigh was almost as strong as the wind outside. "Book chips? That is your treasure? I thought you mentioned plans for building these great cities in the sky."

"This is a library. An actual *biblioteca*! I thought they were just rumors." He frowned, and I added, "I know Scouts prefer the oral tradition, but not me. Before the Yellowstone eruption, people kept stories in places called libraries. You could learn about anything at all. Books are worth their weight in gold, *mijo*. Somewhere in here, we're bound to find those plans, too."

A few storage cases lay underwater or cracked, rendering them useless, and I ignored them as I moved across the room.

"When the Event happened, those too poor to move up into the skies made do where they could with whatever they had. No electricity on the surface meant no access to books. What use were book chips if you had no way to read them? *Mi bisabuela* talked about the 'fancy folks in the cities' with their tech. They had no idea what life was like down in the ghettos surrounded by frigid storms of dust and ash. You ever tried fixing an airship's engine?"

He shook his head.

"Me neither. These boats will last longer than we will. But occasionally, they break, and when they do, it takes someone with Old-World knowledge to fix it. Books, they've got Old-World knowledge." I picked up a case holding a dozen chips. "Each chip holds more knowledge than our brains. Much more."

I shrugged out of my backpack and once open, shoved cases of chips inside.

"Does Mexico City have the ability to read these?"

"*Sí*, but even if we didn't, that's what this is for," I said as I scooped up a small earpiece. Others lay strewn across the table, and I swept them all into my bag. Diego picked up a handful of cases, and I shook my head. "See the green tab? Those are fiction. Made-up stories. We need science. How-to. *Information* with value. Shout if you see any gold tabs."

"There is knowledge in storytelling, too."

Something about his sharp tone sent a chill across my arms. "Fine, toss 'em in. Leave anything cracked or submerged. Won't do any good."

Between the two of us, we filled my backpack to the brim. It wasn't until I turned to leave that I saw the glass case built into the wall behind the door. A dozen, gold-tabbed book chips lay behind it, and I grinned. "Woosh! This is what *mi padre* died for."

My hands trembled as I slid the glass open and shoved all twelve chips into my pockets. No way were they going in my bag—too easily stolen. Someone would have to kill me to take them from my person.

As we trudged back through the building, Diego remained silent as he watched the walls. Like the floor below, this one had been stripped of most everything, but the way his eye colors shifted, I wondered if he could see through the walls themselves.

"I'm guessing *mi padre* left me clues to find these in case he was interrupted. Anyone else looking at a tulip wouldn't know it for a pirate's mark. Win for us." *Thank you, Padre.* I crossed myself as something slammed into the building again, sending bits of wood down into the water we waded through.

"Captain, we've … got—" The radio at my side crackled, then whined sharp enough to make me wince.

The Scout didn't have to say a word. His haunted face said it all. Water splashed up to my thighs as I trudged up the stairwell and down the long hall. Upon reaching the entrance, only one door remained attached as the other lay in a charred mess nearby. Something had blown a small hole in the wall.

"Were they aiming at your ship or the towering building?" Diego asked.

"The Ghost Fleet doesn't miss. That was their warning shot."

"They don't miss, but they warn? I thought they killed without question."

I stepped outside, where the rain battered against my skin. "They do that, too, but they want us to know they're coming," I shouted over the rumbling thunder.

"Why? What good does that do?"

"So we can make our peace with the spirits before we die."

"How merciful of them."

Electricity danced around us as we half-ran, half-crawled our way down the road. Both of us huddled as close to the other buildings as we dared in an attempt to keep from the sight of anyone watching. Another crackle, then silence from my radio as we reached the pier.

Lightning struck a nearby lightning rod, and, momentarily blind, I slid on the slick wood. Thin railing collapsed under my sudden weight, and I pitched forward, stopped only by Diego's hands as they grabbed me by my jacket.

"Thanks," I said as he tugged me back to the dock.

Each lightning strike illuminated the sky, which pinpointed the Ghost Fleet's location. Unfortunately, it also betrayed my ship's location. I tumbled through my ship's door as the wind gust threatened to rip the wood from its frame. The crewmembers stood directly inside, arms across their chests.

"Did you find the loot?" asked Juan.

I took the key from my pocket and stuck it in the control panel. When no one moved, I said, "*Sí*, get us out of here."

"Not until we see the goods." Pamella gestured toward my backpack.

"Are you insane? That's the Ghost Fleet out there. You'll kill us all with this foolishness."

"We ain't moving 'til we know we're gonna get paid."

I snatched off my backpack and tossed open the flap. "Happy now? Get us outta here."

Up ahead, the Ghost Fleet's ship rumbled, and I turned toward the window. Something dark moved beside me, and I spun to find Juan holding the backpack in one hand. My fingers wrapped around the dagger's hilt clipped to my belt. Holding the backpack in front of him as a shield, Juan retrieved his own dagger.

No way was I waiting for him to strike. I threw my dagger, and a sliver sliced through his loose shirt sleeve but missed hitting meat. I feinted, and when he moved to block, a few chips scattered out the doorway. With a curse, he dropped the bag and dagger in front of him, scooped up the chips. Wood slick in the deluge, I stepped toward him carefully.

Juan grinned and lunged.

A shadow to the left caught us both off guard as seven feet of lithe muscle hit Juan, sending him across the pier and over the edge. Juan's wide eyes stared up at me in shock before the storm swallowed him in gray. Diego gathered up my backpack as I cut the ties anchoring us to the pier.

The remaining crewmembers flinched as two drowned rats returned instead of three. "Get us out of here. Or does anyone else wish to fly off?" I asked.

Seeing them scamper, I turned to Diego as my facial muscles warred between relief and fear. "That's thrice you've saved me today. I am in your debt."

He shook his head. "Now I have fulfilled my debt to your father."

My brows shot up at his words. "If we escape the Ghost Fleet, you have some explaining to do."

"On my honor."

I tucked the information away for another time and took my place before the wheel. Rather than steer away from the city, I waited for us to gain lift before bringing us closer to its tallest building.

"Captain, may I ask why we do not flee?" asked Diego.

"No one outruns the Ghost Fleet. If we can't run, we must fight."

His eyes flashed a dangerous gold as he shook his head. "That would be a bad idea. This storm is dangerous enough, Captain."

I didn't steer us away. Instead, I waited. Would he abandon this ship as he had the one before? Or had he regained his sense of bravery along with his honor?

He smiled suddenly in the bright lightning, his fingers stretching through the air as he breathed deeply, nostrils flaring. When he wrested control of the wheel from me, I opened my mouth in protest, but he didn't turn east as expected. Instead, he moved west. Closer to the towering building.

"Wha—"

"If we wish to lose them, it is not enough to hope lightning strikes. We must call the weather to us and *make* it strike. This is what a Scout can do."

As my ship neared a lightning rod, the electricity hummed in the air around us, and my crew crossed themselves before closing their eyes in prayer. The cross around my own neck warmed as the Ghost Fleet pulled up beside us.

A man with short, spiky hair pointed at me and yelled something lost as a bolt struck nearby and thunder nearly cracked open our eardrums.

My short-range radio squealed before a strange voice came over the line. "You should be dead!" the male voice yelled.

Beside me, Diego laughed as I stared at the radio in my hand. "With your hood up, you look so very much like your father. Perhaps you are his *fantasma* or *espíritu*," he said.

I couldn't help the grin that split across my face in the lightning glow, and I pressed the button on my radio. "I will never die! *¡Viva La Hermana del Bendito Sol!*"

Ghost Fleet or not, the idea spooked them as they maneuvered in front of us. "Slow us down *un poco*. Let them reach the lightning rod first," I said.

"I know, Captain. Get ready for brightness."

The rudder shift slowed us as the sky filled with branches of light that wove their way around our ship as if we were made of rubber. I glanced at Diego, whose eyes glowed in the eerie light around us, and goosebumps crawled across my skin.

"*Santa Madre de Dios*, holy mother of God," I whispered.

The lightning and thunder warred for dominance above Monterrey City, but never had I felt safer as Diego steered us in circles 'round the building. The Ghost Fleet might've been scary on most days, but as they tried to navigate the storm, their fancy ship attracted the storm like the rod on the building's roof.

A bolt struck the lightning rod, then reached out its tendrils to strike their balloon's metal frame. The lights inside their bridge vanished as their ship ceased moving, and I punched the air. "Their ship's inoperable—at least for a while. Let's move before we join them."

"*Sí*, Captain," said Pamella.

Diego stepped aside to give her the wheel, and when I touched his shoulder, a small zap of electricity transferred to me. My fingers stung, and I nodded to him. "Good job, Scout Diego."

As we pulled away, my gaze remained on the skies. The storm could take us down, as could another ship if anyone else was fool enough to be out here. Beside me, the Scout watched with eyes that saw more than my mechanically enhanced ones, and I smiled.

Perhaps *mi padre* had been right. A good Scout *was* worth dying for.

✶

Once we'd escaped the worst of the storm, a gentle rain carried us back to Mexico City where my crew followed me through the pier and into the marketplace. As I approached the three-story building that served as Jefe's place, Two-Cross stood outside, a smirk on his face. "Look who's back."

Rather than get roped into a verbal tug-of-war, I removed one book chip from my pocket and held it up. "Take me to Jefe."

Two-Cross's gaze lingered on the chip a moment before he allowed himself a look at the Scout. He shifted his sight to my remaining crewmembers. "Looks like ol' Juan got greedy. Figures."

I clapped my hands together. "Jefe. Now, Two-Cross."

"Oh-ho! *Chica* returned with some *cojones*!" He yawned as he stretched. "Jefe's waiting for you at *su casa*."

My skin prickled. I'd been hoping to avoid *mi abuela,* at least until I'd gotten *mi familia's* name back, but to have Jefe there … *Dios sea misericordioso.* God be merciful.

Diego and I left Two-Cross standing in the rain, a crooked smile on his slimy lips, as we set off for my home on the city's fifth level.

While closer to the core than I liked, the fifth level gave us plenty of space and the cartel's protection. Pamella trailed behind us while the rest of my "crew" remained with Two-Cross. As we moved through the Tower, people looked twice as they passed, especially once they spotted Diego keeping step with me. I wasn't getting the *mal de ojo,* the evil eye from folks, but they weren't exactly smiling in welcome either.

Two of Jefe's thugs stood outside my door, their stance screaming for a fight, but when they spotted me, they parted to allow us entrance. The moment I stepped inside the dim front room, *mi abuela* was on me like a snake on a rat.

"*Chica,* what were you thinking? *¿Tienes un deseo de muerte?* You planning to follow *su padre* into the afterlife?"

Her voice trailed off as she caught sight of the Scout. "*Bendición de Dios,* you're Scout Diego."

"How'd you know that, *abuela*?" I asked.

"This is the son of Tiega Aparicio, the Scout *tu padre* saved! I'd know *su familia* anywhere."

The Scout knelt before *mi abuela* and kissed her wrinkled hand. "I have thrice saved Pia's life. Have I repaid the debt my family owed yours?"

Mi abuela nodded, and Jefe stepped forward from the shadows. Despite expecting his appearance, I couldn't help but flinch.

"Charming as this is, I hear you have something for me, Little Pia."

Even when *mi padre* had been alive, Jefe's voice made me want to disappear. Like an airship meeting the side of a mountain, the crunch in its depth would have anyone running. Beside me, Diego bristled.

"Or perhaps you bring me something better."

Jefe reached out to touch Diego, who retreated with a headshake. "I am not for trade."

While Jefe relented, something in his expression told me the discussion wasn't over. *Mi abuela* crossed herself and began whispering prayers as she lowered herself into a chair. Before tempers got the better of us, I shrugged out of my backpack and passed it to Jefe. "This is what I brought you."

When Jefe flipped it open, he let loose a string of Spanish that made *mi abuela* pray all the harder. "*Bonita* Pia, this—this is unexpected. What a wealth you have brought me."

I emptied the remaining chips from my pockets into his free hand. "I will gladly trade for the spoils of my trip."

"Why would I trade that which is already mine?"

The prayers in the corner grew louder as *mi abuela* pried one eye open to watch us.

"Everything in Mexico is Jefe's to give or trade as he sees fit, but not even Jefe can control where I go and what I bring back. Maybe, next time I'll take my goods to *Tejas*. I hear they deal fairly across the border wall."

The way his eyes narrowed, I'd pushed things—maybe too far—but there was no other way to gain respect in the cartel, a lesson *mi padre* had drilled into me as a child.

"I'm not asking for anything not rightfully mine, Jefe," I said as I glanced over my shoulder. "A better crew, my name back, *mi familia's* honor. Enough of a share to feed *mi familia* and pay the crew that came with me." At that, his eyes flashed, and I added, "One always pays the crew, *sí*?"

Jefe tilted his head in thought. He held up a chip to the room's lone light. "You got any readers with these?" he asked.

"A dozen or so."

He stepped closer to Diego to better look him in the eyes. For an uncomfortable moment, no one breathed. Then Jefe returned his focus to me.

"You have a deal, but one of these days, you'll have to tell me the story of how you escaped the Ghost Fleet."

My skin prickled. How'd he know about that? Unless …

When he snapped his fingers, the two men from outside entered and gathered up the loot. My shoulders tensed as I suppressed the urge to leap on Jefe. Sensing my anger, Diego whispered in my ear, "Live to fight another day, Captain."

Jefe nodded once to *mi abuela*. Before he left *mi casa*, he glanced over his shoulder at the Scout. "Keep him, *chica*. Maybe he'll keep you in line. Keep you alive."

My partial crew followed Jefe, leaving me alone with Diego and *mi abuela*. And my temper.

"That *bastardo* killed *mi padre*!"

"Hush, Pia. He might hear you!" said *mi abuela.*

I waved a hand to shush her. "He sent the Ghost Fleet after him, just like he did me today. I don't have proof, but someday I'll find it."

"I'd like to help with that."

At Diego's words, *mi abuela* sent up prayers again, and I laughed before gesturing for him to take a seat. "I'm going to hold you to that, Scout Diego, but first, *mi abuela's torta de tamal* is the best this side of the mountains. If you're going to be my Scout, you're going to have to get used to *mi abuela's* cooking ..."

He flushed at the attention, and I smiled.

My honor, my name, my ship, a crew, and a Scout. That's all I needed to discover the truth. Then, one day, perhaps I'd be as free as my Scout. But for now, *mi padre's* spirit was smiling down on me.

I had all that I needed.

✶

Multi-international-award-winning speculative fiction author and artist **Raven Oak** is best known for *Amaskan's Blood* (2016 Ozma Fantasy Award Winner, Epic Awards Finalist, 2019 Reader's Choice Award Winner), *Amaskan's War* (2018 UK Wishing Award YA Finalist), and *Class-M Exile.* She has multiple short stories published in anthologies and magazines, and she's even published on the Moon. (Raven spent most of her K–12 education doodling stories and 500-page monstrosities that are forever locked away in a filing cabinet.)

When she's not writing, she's getting her game on, indulging in cartography and art, or staring at the ocean. She lives in the Seattle area with her husband, and their three kitties who enjoy lounging across the keyboard when writing deadlines approach.

To learn more, visit www.ravenoak.net

SNOWFLAKES

CAT RAMBO

Standing in the bunker's antechamber, Young Hettie shrugged on the costume's bulky upper half. Inserting her arms, she let the torso covering obscure sight and sound, pushing her head into the darkness and up before she could squint through the eyeholes.

She was not a small woman, broad-shouldered and well-bosomed, not to mention a little paunchy. Nonetheless, the costume made her take up space in a way she didn't usually, large and uncomfortable, unready to step into the outside world.

Her companions, Young Jolene and Young Amy, seemed less reluctant as they put on their own costumes. Old Jolene fussed around, stroking at chips in the paper mâché skin, tweaking ringlets of snowy beard hair into place, adjusting the crown of real deer horn and artificial holly. Finally, she stood back and considered the trio.

The costume's heavy layers were already making Hettie sweat, but she knew it wouldn't last, out in the snow and wind. The first time she'd made the trek, sixteen years ago, it had overawed her, but the time stretching between eighteen and thirty-four years old had made her considerably more jaded about the nonsensical demands of machines from Before.

She frowned at Old Jolene, even though she knew the woman couldn't see her expression and said, "Well?"

"Ain't frowning at you," Old Jolene said. "Try again to get some materials we can repair those with. Once they're so far gone he doesn't recognize them, we're sunk."

Young Hettie shrugged. There was time enough. The older sisters worried too much, that was their main trait. Jolene was maybe the worst among them. Plenty of years left in these, even if they were the last. The old bot would produce something they could use, sooner or later, and life would go on in its limited way as it always did. Which was, to Young Hettie's mind, the main problem.

They'd already climbed the long ladder up from the bunker —no sense in doing anything in costume until the appointed time, which didn't officially start until they stepped out the steel door.

Outside the sky was the color of dirty steel, dull gray clouds trying to scour it clean. To the south was Rainier with its perpetual black smoke, and to the west the floating city of Seattle rode the clouds, its upper limits hazed with grayness that made it look like a rain-washed chalk drawing.

Young Hettie paused to watch it, feeling that fierce ache she always did. What would it be like to go there, or anywhere, for that matter? What would it be like to be able to actually interact with the outside world, rather than just skim into it at intervals, able to see it and then having to retreat back into bunker life?

A glint on the horizon, a sliver of copper light. An airship, headed somewhere.

What would it be like to board that ship and head somewhere else?

Young Jolene said from behind her, "No use in pining over it, Hettie."

"It's just not fair," she muttered, but moved along.

Underfoot the cold white snow had different colors in the sharp-edged shadows, hints of violet and chilly blue, and the trees stooped, encased in grayish ice coats. Many wouldn't survive this cold snap; the women would spend some time this summer replanting as many cold-hardy ones as they could, but the weather of this world was not as suited for trees as it was in Before.

Young Hettie's hand was stretched around the staff she held, the ridiculous one that made all the Olds go off into ribald jokes whenever the New Year rolled around and it was brought out. She was lead Wise Man; at least there was that.

She frowned back over her shoulder at Young Jolene and Young Amy, but didn't say anything, just set off at a rapid, punishing pace that left them all breathless after ten minutes, so she relented and slowed.

It was good to be out of the shelter at least. Most of the winter meant staying indoors where it was warm, doing the work in there that there would not be time for during the short growing season they were so dependent on.

She had a list in her pocket of seeds that they wanted. Lately they'd been trying a new strategy, listing lots of different kinds, rather than the usual strains. The machine seemed to pick from among the offerings when they did that, rather than swapping in something bizarre and usually unusable of its own choosing. She had a list in her pocket with a lot of things, and no way to steer the machine into picking one thing rather than another. Old Amy still tried to track the numbers, to discern a pattern that would let them manipulate the erratic, idiosyncratic machine that produced many of the supplies needed for their sheltered existence, but she had yet to be successful.

It was early morning. Their footsteps crunching over the snow, the whistle of the wind over the ice-covered trees were the only sounds. Young Hettie's boots were cracked; snowmelt seeped into her socks within a few moments, but she kept walking. They had a long way to go.

✶

In 2085, billionaire Georg Thomas Nagle, reacted to events in his own way. His outlook on life was libertarianism, informed by the poet Robert Bly and the writer Robert Heinlein, and his own peculiar brand of Puritan-flavored hippie nostalgia led him to create an underground compound on the slopes of the Cascades and people it with his own creations, retreating there rather than into the sky.

Many years later, Nagle was long dead, while his clone-wives lived on.

✶

The place they were bound bordered on Microsoft territory, and those folks didn't kid around. Scavengers aplenty on the east side of Lake Washington as well, hunting through the old houses and buildings.

But the solar panels that powered the machine were up at the top of the small mountain, and there wasn't anything for it but to make the trip on Winter Solstice. That was the only time they could coax supplies out of the old machine, by asking for presents, and who knew how much longer even that would last. Old Jolene kept muttering about the limits of 3-D printers. Old Jolene had never been the same after they'd tried Education on her, and she was why they'd never try that again, no matter how desperate they became.

"You checked the weather, right?" Young Amy asked for the third time.

"I did," Hettie said with more patience than she felt.

Young Jolene said, "It don't matter, they can't predict the storms."

"Sometimes they can," Young Amy insisted. Technically she was Young Young Amy, because her predecessor had met a Fate, not died naturally the way they usually did. The others had a decade on her, but they tried not to be bullies about it even when she was being silly, which did seem to be most of the time.

"Storm can come out of anywhere," Young Jolene said darkly. "Or bees. Or anything winter-hungry ..."

It was true, but Hettie gave her a look anyway. They didn't need to be wasting time comforting Amy. Jolene scowled but nodded and they kept crunching on through the snow. Dead trees rose all around them, bulked up by the living vines choking them, enrobed in snow.

Hettie kept her ears peeled for any sounds.

From here they had a different view of the sky island that was Seattle—and far away, the gleam of the sound's water, and the distant bubbles of artificial islands, like froth. There were people there, real people, not made.

All of the problems with the machine would be over if the Olds would let them go and trade with the other group, but they refused the change of tradition. That didn't make sense to Hettie. It wasn't Before anymore, and acting like it was wouldn't change that.

"There's songs we could sing to pass the time," Young Amy said as they trudged along.

Young Hettie bit back the first remark that came to mind, which was if Young Amy wasn't so bent on singing all the time, she'd be easier to live around. But that was the sort of remark that was best bit back and kept to oneself, even if it seemed to be true to the point where you knew it was. You could glance over at Young Jolene and know that she was thinking exactly the same thing.

So instead she said, "Which songs would you like to sing?" even though she knew which ones Amy was thinking of. But listening to her list them, "Lil' Town o Beddleham," for one, and Silence Night, an' …" gave Hettie a little bit of time in which to think about how to keep her from singing them, how she could best object to it without actually seeming to object to it.

When Young Amy took a breath, Young Hettie held up a hand without saying anything more than "Shhhhh, do you hear that?"

All three of them listened. The pines brushed the dry and lonely wind. Young Hettie could hear the breathing of the others. She held her own breath, but she still heard—or felt as much as heard—the thudding of her heart in the cup of her throat. She kept her hand upraised, making the others be still, and drew the moment out as long as she dared, to the point that she heard Young Amy inhale in order to say something. Only then did she speak.

"I heard something," she said, keeping her face intent. "But seems like it's gone. Best stay quiet and keep our ears open."

It was an obvious enough ruse to her, but Young Amy just sighed and followed along obediently enough, although, every once in a while, Hettie could hear her mumbling one of the songs to herself. The litany of those was for the weeks like this, when the deepest snows lay on the ground, and it made no sense to go outside. That was, she thought sourly, the reason they were supposed to make their trek to the mountain, to cater to some Before way of thinking about things.

Like so much in life, it made no sense and seemed arbitrary and counter, not indifferent so much as deliberately constructed to impede one's joy in life.

As they rose in elevation, the snow underfoot grew dryer and fluffier. Some of it had laid where it was now for years, but none of their footsteps from the previous year had survived. They trudged onward, and their breath puffed damply in the air, exploding out of their lungs as the air grew thinner and they were forced to concentrate on it, keeping their heads down despite the awkwardness of the costumes and the ways the overhead branches dragged at them.

By the time they got to the mountain's top, they were all winded. Most of the time they spent indoors, inside the tunnel system that Georg had built so long ago, and no matter how much one walked on the treadmill there, it was never the same as being on the outside.

✶

After checking the solar panel array to make sure it was still in working order, they paused just outside the cave where the Machine lived. Young Hettie looked the two over. They were a little worse for the wear, the costumes at any rate, but they would pass.

"How am I?" she asked in turn.

"Good enough," Young Amy said without looking, but Young Jolene did her the courtesy of a once-over before nodding and pronouncing her fit enough to enter.

The entrance to the cave was always free of snow; she didn't know how. The ground itself was warm, steaming just a little in the air. They stepped inside.

The air inside, too, was warmer than it should have been. One year they had surprised two animals inside the cave taking shelter. Young Hettie remembered the pair's frantic scramble to get out, how the women had pressed themselves back against the walls of the cavern.

Things were much drier than she thought they should have been. Underfoot was dry sand, with no sign how it might have come there, and a regularity to the cavern walls, a feeling of tameness that reminded her of Home and its walls, some of which pretended to look natural but were not.

The hole in the back of the wall of the cave ended in concrete stairs leading down into the darkness. This was one of the more difficult parts of the trip; the bulky costumes were unwieldy in the narrow staircase. There had once been lanterns but those were long dead, and now the only light was that of the glowstones at their belts, giving back the light they had absorbed above ground.

Young Hettie led the way, Young Amy behind her, and Young Jolene bringing up the rear. After they had been going for about ten minutes, they could see a dim luminescence up ahead where the stairs came to a landing. Music seeped from the tinny speakers, bleeding out a tune Hettie didn't recognize.

The landing was bland, its former furnishings long ago crumbled into dust and debris. There were no signs of animals down here, not even small ones or insects. That always made Hettie a little wary. Even Home had spiders, and you weren't supposed to kill them, because they ate bad insects.

The music stopped and the Machine spoke.

"Gentlemen, is it the Solstice already?" Its big booming voice rolled like thunder and made Hettie glad for the costume covering her ears. "Have you donned your sacred apparel and come to greet me, to exchange tidings of the season?"

"Ho ho ho," Hettie said. "Ho ho ho. We have our wishlist, this joyous Yuletide. Perhaps you will give it to Santa?"

The Machine's voice was wheedling and sly suddenly. "Perhaps. Have you been good children, all this time?"

"We are men, not children," Hettie said uneasily. She didn't like it when the Machine deviated from the established script. All of them knew it was a bad sign when a machine started to be inaccurate or go awry. Particularly a machine that one depended on, as they did this one. She held out the shiny envelope with its list contained, folded three times over. "But our children at home have been good and they deserve the things that we request."

This was also not in the script, and she heard the muffled, indrawn breaths as both Young Amy and Young Jolene reacted. But she pressed on. If it could change things up and adjust the configuration, then so could she. Things were desperate enough as it was, and someone had to do something. Otherwise they'd just fade away. Maybe those old women back home were happy enough with that, but she was not.

"You have children at home," the Machine said slowly, and she could have laughed to hear how surprised it sounded by the notion. "But you said you would be men of purity."

Her breath caught in her throat again. "Children people have brought us," she said with a smoothness that belied how hard her heart was racing. "They leave them at the door to our compound. We take them in out of charity."

"Ah," said the Machine. A drawer extended and she put the envelope inside it. It slid closed smoothly, ingesting the missive. She waited politely for the Machine to process it.

The waiting for the Machine to answer was the part that had always irked Young Hettie. It was like being stabbed with pins, waiting was. There was always something else useful—or at least entertaining—that you could be doing with whatever part of the day you'd been presented with. Making someone wait was pure egotism as far as she was concerned, a way of building oneself up. Nonetheless, it always took the Machine four or five minutes to process the list, so it surprised Young Hettie when it popped back after thirty seconds with the envelope, unopened.

"First a holiday game," it said. "If you want Santa to help you out, you have to make sure that Santa's in the right mood."

Hettie's idea of Santa had always been rough, but she didn't know that she thought he was unfairly demanding, the way that the Machine seemed to be implying. Still, she played along. "What sort of game?"

"Go chop down the tallest tree in the forest ..." it started, and then broke off, speaking in a slightly different voice. "No, no," he said. "That's copywritten material." He focused on the two of them for a moment before saying, "Greenery. Can't have a holiday without a little greenery to spruce up the place." It paused and barked out three notes of mechanical laughter "Classic dad joke, right?"

It was not what she expected him to say. The Machine had never been particularly kind or sympathetic to her, had never seemed like anything except an annoyance from Before, a creature that had been left behind to inexplicably torment them, as with so many of the machines at Home.

There, it seemed as though everything had been set up for the convenience of the ghost of the founder, the ghost of the man who had used to live there before he had succumbed to disease. Young Hettie was not entirely sure what kind of disease he might have had. The older women refused to speak of it, and they dropped their voices when doing so, when they thought that the younger women couldn't hear them, a soft and hushed conversation that was maddening in the way it was hard to hear but even more so in the attitude that it displayed.

She bit her lip as a familiar worry chewed at her. When would they be just Hettie and Jolene and Amy, without the "Old" and "Young" in front of the name? Why was there no one in between?

Was it that the women who should have occupied that slot had somehow gotten away from Home and its demands? She had a sneaking suspicion that those women didn't exist, that they never were.

Maybe one day a young one realized that they were old, looked up from one of the innumerable tasks of the shelter, one of the many tasks of home, and they asked themselves, what sort of world it was that they lived in? What sort of world was it where they pandered to machines pandering to the idea of an old and ancient man?

She said, "Can you clarify what you want?"

"Sure," the Machine said. "Actually, I've changed my mind. Go and find something that defines the meaning of Christmas."

"You have got to be kidding me," Young Hettie said. There was a pause and she realized she'd said the words in her natural voice. She hastily dropped it by an octave and blustered on. "What do you mean by the meaning of Christmas? We are busy men, with little time to waste."

"Are you now?" the Machine asked. "Are you now? Because when I listen to the voices in the heavens, the voices that used to speak back and forth and back, so quickly it was almost as though they were all speaking at the same time, nowadays all but a few are silent and those sing to each other, or perhaps to themselves, I cannot tell which, but not to me. And if they are not busy, if the world is not regulated and monitored and made to run, then how can you be busy?"

It was not a good sign that the Machine had begun questioning the state of the world like this, Young Hettie knew. In her experiences, and in the stories of the women that had come before her, when machines asked questions like that, they were usually on the way to breaking down in some spectacular fashion, and no longer providing whatever it was they were depended on for.

That, or else they were about to assert their independence, usually by ceasing whatever function they had previously fulfilled, which had the same result.

Hettie had seen this happen twice in her lifetime, but the stories of the other Hetties that Old Hettie had passed along to her were full of instances of such things.

She said hastily, still in her deep voice, "Very well, we will go seek the thing you wish us to."

The others would have said something, but once again she gestured them to silence and was grateful that Young Amy did not choose this moment to rebel, the way that she had previously. They trudged back up the steps in silence and did not speak until they were back into the darkness and out of the dim luminescence of the below-world.

She'd thought that Young Amy would be the one to break the silence, but instead it was Young Jolene, voice measured and reasonable, who said, "Do you have any idea what he meant by something that defines the meaning of Christmas?"

"We all know what Christmas is," she said. "It's presents and sacrifices and turkey-flavored loaf. Used to be wine, too. How hard can that be? We'll find something that seems like a present and bring it back."

"You have no guarantee that he will accept whatever it is that you bring him back," Young Jolene pointed out.

"Something festive," Young Hettie said. "Something merry."

They emerged from the stairway and into the cavern. Outside its mouth, fluffy white flakes danced in the air as they stepped out into the open space around the entrance. Sunlight was fighting its way through the thickening clouds.

"If I could bring him snow, I would," Young Hettie said. "That's festive and pretty."

"And about all there is," Young Amy said. "Snow and twigs. Icicles maybe."

"They'd melt before you got down to him," Young Jolene said. "That's such a long walk. Hettie, can't we take a rest now? We brought food and we're probably going to have to sleep here overnight as it is. It'll be long dark by the time we find something and bring it back. This isn't in the ritual, so I say we could take these off, rest, and then go look."

"Alright," Hettie said. "But no more than half an hour or so, and then we go out and spend some time looking before we come back and dig in for the night."

Back inside the cavern, she rubbed where a strap had cut too tight, while Jolene helped her off with the back piece and then was helped in turn, before they both moved to assist the waiting Young Amy. Underneath the costumes, they were all sweaty, and the crisp air cutting in through the cavern's entrance was welcome.

The food bars were one of her favorite flavors, a nutty sweetness called peanuts, though Young Amy wrinkled her nose and said she didn't like the way they smelled.

"Well, run on down and see if he'll print you out a steak," Hettie said peevishly.

"I don't think he still could," Young Jolene said before Young Amy could snap anything back. "Maybe this whole quest is just his way of stalling us because he can't deliver on any of our requests."

"Any of them?" Young Hettie said dubiously. There'd been at least a dozen items on the list, maybe more. Previously the Machine had sometimes been unable to supply an item or two, but it was unheard of for it to decline every single thing on a list. Young Jolene knew that as well as she did. Did she really think things were that dire or was she trying to stir up trouble in her own way? Young Hettie tried to read her expression across the way, but it was inscrutable, as though she hadn't pulled off the costume.

They started to go back out into the world, but the strength of the winds and the cold snow it flung at them swiftly drove them back, resolved to look in the morning, when the storm had died down.

There was wood stacked in a corner of the chamber along with blankets, a gift from past iterations of themselves. They built a little fire in the cubby that had been shaped to hold such a thing and direct its smoke outside. Crouched down around it, they used the bulky robes of the costumes like blankets, drying them out over the fire before piling them into heaps to sleep on.

But they sat awake for a while, trading ghost stories and speculating on what it had been like to live in the Before and who and what they would have been, if they had been born back in those days.

Hettie woke in the chill hour before dawn. The doorway formed a black arch, showcasing the scudding of thinly wrung clouds trying to scrub the Moon's smudged face clean. Some billionaire, decades ago, had written her name on the side of that white world. Later terrorists had blown up the project, so all that was visible now were the letters "che" trailing off into uneven marks. She went to the door and looked out.

From this vantage point, she could look eastward to see the mountains, and westward to glimpse the Sammamish marsh, its water only an invisible glimmer of ice now. Here in former East Side, creatures left over from corporate campus security ruled the wilderness and the resources that the Sammamish represented, primarily fresh water.

There were humans still here, the scavenger tribes who gleaned from the tech company ruins, but for the most part this area was deserted, and that was how the Hetties and the Jolenes and the Amys had always preferred it. They'd been made to serve a human, so long ago, and they had no desire to go back to that sort of existence.

At the same time, the world as it had emerged nowadays was often savage, and rarely cooperative. There was supposed to be a settlement big enough to have a trade market up near the old Redmond Town Center, but Young Hettie had never been able to talk the others into letting her travel there.

Maybe when she was old.

There was something about the day … a chiming in the distance. She held herself on tiptoes, trying to hear it. Was it going farther away, as it seemed, or—

The wind shifted, carrying the music with it, even louder. Even closer.

There was one thing she'd learned about the world, and that was not to assume benevolence. She faded back into the cavern, motioned the others to silence, cutting Young Amy's objections off in her throat, and then, they all settled back to wait. By now all of them could hear it, or perhaps Young Amy would have said something. Instead she stayed silent, listening to that music, which sounded like it was made of breaking ice, ice so cold it had no sense of wetness about it, ice as brittle as glass.

Then the first flake of metal appeared in the doorway.

They all held their breath. Machines could be tricked, if they were primitive or eccentric enough in their algorithms, and who knew with this one? If they held still enough, perhaps it would go away, and that was best. Avoiding things was always best.

It hovered in the air about three feet off the ground, turning, chiming softly to itself. Then another joined it and another. They chimed to each other, turning in the air, seeming to pay no attention to the women holding still as they could manage, breathing shallowly when they breathed at all, nor the three large upper torsos stacked against the side of the cavern wall.

Hettie had never seen anything like these before; they were the size of a small coin and made of silvery metal.

More and more of them appeared, filling up the entrance. Young Hettie thought about making a dash for the hallway leading downward but there was no door to be closed, not until you were far, far down in the earth.

Young Amy, presented with the same situation, did not reach the same conclusion. She rose and ran for the exit

The flakes moved through the air, and they moved faster than anything that Young Hettie had ever seen before. Faster than a knife slicing through the air. They wove a cage around Young Amy and three sliced across her, one across her cheek, and another across her shoulder, and the last one across her hand. Not deep cuts, not to the bone. Warning cuts.

Young Amy heeded the warning and held still. Young Jolene and Young Hettie maintained their own stillness.

They waited, expectantly, but the metal snowflakes seemed content enough with the way things were. One would emit a passage of sound and others would echo it sometimes, and other times change it, and other times create an entirely different sound sequence, with no predictable pattern, as far as Young Hettie could tell, as to which one said what and when. She thought of it as *said* because the phrases were about the length of human sentences, varying in the same way.

But where she would have thought she'd be able to catch some emotion or tone from the way that they made their sounds, there was nothing of the emotional about it, only the musical, and that music, a careful and considered logical one, not like the thump of rock (forbidden but still known to all of them) or the inane wheedle of the Christmas carols that Young Amy loved so much.

"Perhaps they want us to make the next move," Young Jolene said in a low voice.

Young Amy and Young Hettie both flinched at the sound of her voice, but the snowflakes didn't seem to react at all, the cadences of their music unchanged by what Young Jolene had said. There was a hint of ozone in the air, a metallic smell.

"What sort of move would you suggest that be?" Young Hettie asked. "It seems to me from the way that they're acting that they don't want Amy to move."

"Well, she was moving fast, and meant to run away," Young Jolene pointed out. "Maybe if she moved slower, they wouldn't have reacted."

"Are you suggesting she try this experiment?" Young Hettie said with interest, curious to see exactly how cold-blooded Young Jolene could be.

"Well, she's the logical one," Jolene said. "And she can't keep on standing upright forever, you know that as well as I. Sooner or later she's going to need to sit down. So, the question is, really, whether we find out in a controlled way or whether we find out when she just crashes to the ground out of pure stubbornness."

"Well, I never," Young Amy said, but did not elaborate on what it was that she never.

Young Hettie had to admit, it took guts for Young Amy to do what she did next. She lowered her arms, with excruciating slowness, to her sides, and moved in small and circumscribed steps to sit down beside Young Hettie.

As she did so, the cage gave way before her, sliding apart like a zipper, to allow the motion. It did not re-form around her, but continue to hang in the air, vaguely Amy-shaped. A few sparkled here and there through the air, drifting to investigate cracks and crevices, which they seemed more interested in than anything else.

Another handful hung in the entrance where the steps led down, as though considering.

"What do you want?" Young Jolene finally said, directly to the flakes.

"Jolene!" Young Amy said as though scandalized, which struck Young Hettie as oddly funny. She wanted to laugh but muffled it by biting down on her sleeve

The flakes whirred and dipped and buzzed, almost lazily in the air. The ones that had formed the cage drew in further, made Young Amy's shape more clearly as they clustered. A buzzing came from them, not from the area that would have been the other Amy's mouth, but rather from all of them at once, as though they were all emitting the noise.

"Analysis: meat. Analysis: meat. Communication initiated. Communicate scarcity, class carbon. Communicate scarcity, class polymer. Analysis: meat, initiate communication."

"I don't understand," Young Jolene said.

"Communication means talking," Young Hettie said. She stared at the snowflakes intently.

What were they? Old tech for sure, and old tech in nowadays shape. That meant either made new and recent, which seemed unlikely, or more likely self-maintaining, the way the tanks that made the young ones when they were needed. "Communication means they're smart, too, like us."

"I'm not feeling so smart right now," Young Amy muttered.

After a few seconds, the flakes sounded again. "Communication affirmation I don't understand. Communication means talking. I'm not feeling so smart right now. Communication analysis: unclear. Analysis: meat, continue communication."

Hettie's mind scrambled through the words, trying to make sense of it. "We're meat," she said. "Are we?"

"Communication We're meat. Are we. Communication analysis complete. Communication initiated. Communicate yes. Communicate scarcity, class carbon. Communicate scarcity, class polymer. Analysis: meat, initiate communication."

"You need things," Young Hettie said. "That's what scarcity means. We need things too."

This time the flakes did not hesitate in their answer or repeat the words. "Communication initiated. Communicate query needs. Analysis: meat, initiate communication."

"We need something that shows Christmas," Young Hettie said.

"The meaning of Christmas, to be exact," Young Amy said primly.

"Don't split hairs," Young Hettie said in her direction, and they would have started an argument, but the snowflakes were already moving into an ordered but intricate pattern like a larger version of themselves. They glittered with music, an unearthly chiming that echoed one of the songs that Young Amy had been singing on the way over. The song went on through a full iteration, and then the snowflakes settled back into more irregular clumps. The voice came again. "Communication initiated. Communicate Christmas display default executed single loop. Communicate query. Analysis: meat, initiate communication."

"Well now," Young Hettie said, mind still racing. Surely this would be better than anything they could scavenge. "That's very well indeed. But we need you to do it somewhere else. We need you to come down that staircase with us."

She rose to grab her costume and began hauling it on. Young Jolene stooped to interrupt the motion, but Young Hettie shrugged her off and addressed the snowflakes. "Is that agreeable?"

✶

As they descended further and further, the snowflakes gave off their own chilly luminescence. Young Jolene kept trying to catch up with Hettie. Finally she did, hissing through the mask, "Do you really think this is a good idea?"

"Do you have a better idea, Jolene?" Young Hettie said. "Or are you just second-guessing so if it all goes wrong you can stand in the middle of disaster, going *I told you so, Hettie*?"

"I just don't know what's going to happen, that's all."

"Like I do? All I'm doing is going with the flow, Jolene. Seems to me that if you have two problems, sometimes the thing to do is to introduce them to each other."

"All right," Young Jolene said.

They had forgotten to lower their voices by the last of this. The

Machine's voice came floating up the stairway towards them, "Who is that?"

Hettie lowered her voice. "We come, but were speaking of the children we teach," she equivocated. "We have brought you your marvel."

Behind them, the snowflakes said nothing.

Down and down they went, the air warming, the stairwell ringing slightly underfoot. When they emerged in the chamber, the Machine said, almost greedily, "What have you brought me?"

Young Hettie thought to herself, what must it be like, being here at this mountaintop, with us visiting once a year?

She had always wondered why the Machine did not see through their costumes. Now it occurred to her for the first time that perhaps the Machine did see though them but chose not to acknowledge it. To deny them would be to deny the only commerce that it had. It had been put into place long ago by the same person who had created Hettie and her sisters, and was as much a slave as they were.

She said, "It is a Christmas song." She beckoned to the snowflakes.

They floated forward in the air, coming to rest in the chamber's center.

"Execute Christmas default," came the message. They began to sing.

The song had been beautiful up in the chilly air of the cavern. Here it took on a muffled discordance, a resonance that made the hairs on Young Hettie's arm crawl. She shifted uneasily from foot to foot but otherwise stood still for the performance, as did the others.

The song came to an end, its sound lingering.

"That is …" the Machine began, but what it was, Young Hettie was never to learn.

Every flake turned sideways in the air and slashed forward at the console in front of them. They sank into its plastic and netting like hot razors cutting through snow. Where they had passed, there were now thin slits of light in the material, showing the sparks behind them, bright blue and actinic.

The Machine shrieked something. The agonized claxon sent the women reeling, sinking to their feet, trying to clutch the costume heads tight enough to keep away the sound.

The sound went up, higher and higher. Young Hettie thought that her ears must be bleeding with it, that she could stand the agony of it no further. She screamed out loud to let the agony out of her head.

Then, suddenly the alarm cut off. There was only the pop of sparks. Smoke roiled from the slits in the material and seeped down to the floor. It curled around their ankles, smelling of burned plastic and something that singed the back of their throats.

A single snowflake came forth from the console. Was it the one that had originally spoken with them? She had no way of knowing. It said, "Initiate communication. Resources are abundant. Trade is accepted. Communication is now at an end."

"You've destroyed it!" Young Amy gasped.

It repeated, "Initiate communication. Resources are abundant. Trade is accepted. Communication is now at an end."

The smoke was rising. Young Hettie said, "Come on. We have to get out of here."

"But our list!" Young Amy turned to the console. "You owe us! It's not fair!"

But the console continued to silently seep smoke. The snowflake retracted into it and was no longer visible.

"It's not fair," Young Amy said again, more quietly this time.

"That we can all acknowledge," Young Hettie said. "At least we don't have to wear these things anymore. Come on, before we all suffocate."

"Maybe you *should* suffocate," Young Amy said. "You've destroyed our world without even asking. What will the Olds say?" She turned to Young Jolene as though for corroboration and for a second Young Hettie knew a real moment of fear.

But Young Jolene shook her head.

"Don't be silly, Amy," she said. "Few enough of us as it is without you talking about leaving any of us behind. Come on." She started back up the stairs.

The way up was long, but they were all silent as they went up.

Young Hettie thought about what all of this would mean. They'd have to tell the Olds what had happened, face the recriminations, the blame, and the "you should have done things differently"s.

But she also thought about the fact that while they'd followed his dictums all these years, they'd never tried bringing him back, never created a Young Master to follow the Old.

Amy started a song. They walked forward unencumbered, singing it quietly, over the placid, witnessing snow.

✶

Cat Rambo lives, writes, and teaches somewhere in the Pacific Northwest. Her 200+ fiction publications include stories in *Asimov's, Clarkesworld Magazine,* and *The Magazine of Fantasy and Science Fiction*. She is an Endeavour, Nebula, and World Fantasy Award nominee. Her most recent works include *Hearts of Tabat, Exiles of Tabat* (novels, WordFire Press), *Carpe Glitter* (novelette, Meerkat Press), and *You Sexy Thing* (Tor Macmillan, 2021). Forthcoming is the conclusion to the Tabat Quartet, *Gods of Tabat* (Wordfire Press, 2022).

For more about her, as well as links to her fiction and her popular online school, The Rambo Academy for Wayward Writers, see http://www.kittywumpus.net

FOLLOWING ICARUS DOWN

KEVIN J. ANDERSON & SAM KNIGHT

In the golden rays of the setting sun, Aponivi climbed onto the balcony rail of the second largest Tower, wavered, recaptured his graceful balance, and did what no one else in Vegas Station would have considered.

He jumped.

A startled cry from somewhere within the crowded, glittering casino behind him was lost to the rushing wind as he plummeted, headfirst, toward the jutting spires far below. The outer wall of the needle-like Tower flowed beside him as he dropped. He felt the gentle nudge of the great city's anti-gravity generators pushing him outward, away from the immense floating construct they supported high in the air. As the smaller spire loomed below, threatening to impale him, Aponivi spread his arms and legs, lifted his head, stretched his membranes … and caught the breezes.

His people believed that wind flowed through their veins, as much as blood did.

Aponivi soared out over the sharp skyscrapers, away from the floating city and toward the warm sun. The late afternoon sky, unusually clear of murky clouds, let the golden rays shine across the desert to the canyon walls beyond the Hoover Dam. There, the sheer rock caught the light, calling to him, reminding him of home.

The temperate air felt good as it stretched taut the skin connecting his arms to his sides, turning the membranes into wings.

He flew for miles, toward the immense reservoir created by long-lost aspirations and the clifflike concrete wall, like a gate against a barbarian invasion.

He smiled. His father and his teachers had told him many legends, stories, and possible history of the human race, long before the eruption and disaster changed everything....

As Aponivi passed over the water held back by the titanic dam, the cooler air made him adjust his glide angle so he would not lose altitude. He lowered his legs to catch the air with the membrane between them, slowing and lifting him at the same time, and he veered to the right to bring himself back over the dry, rugged land.

He rode the warm updraft from below, and with a joyous heart, he let it carry him upward into the sky instead of deep into the canyon as he'd originally intended.

As he turned back into the sun, he thought of the myth of Icarus, another fascinating story he'd collected only last year when his airship had docked at UC Tower. Aponivi understood the human desire to soar high enough to touch the sun, and he was still human ... mostly. Being a glider, bound to the whims of the winds, he sometimes wished for true wings, strong wings, that could carry him anywhere, maybe even closer to the sun.

But for now, this was more than enough. This was everything. This was what a Weather Mage lived for.

The other crewmembers on the airship could spend their leave and money inside the flashing casinos or dim-lit brothels, but Aponivi relished the warm air under his wings and the warm sunlight on his face. Both things were rare in this world of cold storms. He took a moment to cherish it all.

As he flew over the perfect gray curve of the battered dam, preparing to dive into the river canyon below it, something gave him pause. His sensitive membranes were vibrating, a faint change in the air, but it was not the normal vibrations by which he judged the environment around him. No, this was not a natural sound of the desert and sky, but rather a rising and falling rhythmic *thrum* that should not be there.

He scooped his arms and slowed his glide. Then, spreading his fingers wide, he exposed all of the sensitive webbing; the better to feel details. Something was happening down by the lake, the dam.

The vibration came from below. The steady flow of water over the spillways to either side of the dam filled the air with a fine mist that turned into rainbows as he circled, but the mist and the roar also masked the strange thrumming.

Aponivi turned in a wide circle, studying the dam like a vulture investigating a carcass. The upstream side of the dam, which held back the great lake it had created, had only air and water, and Aponivi could discern nothing unusual there. The western, downstream side glowed amber in the setting sun, magnificently haloed in rainbows and reflecting light back up the canyon, removing all but the deepest shadows. Even with his eyes, which were much more acute than any normal human's, he saw nothing out of the ordinary.

But the strange vibrations grew stronger as he circled lower.

At the edge of the waterline, near the central point of the graceful curve of concrete, he spotted a white bloom of disturbed water, something splashing on the glass-smooth lake.

As he turned his attention, Aponivi felt a sudden, quick spike in the vibrations, a threat, and he instantly reacted. He twisted away just as a deadly arrow streaked past him, hissing as it went by. The razor-edged point missed him by only inches. It had not been a warning shot.

Trying to put immediate distance between himself and whomever had shot the arrow, he banked away in his glide. Something was out there, in the air above the dam, unseen. Someone had attacked him! Maybe it was a camouflaged ship of the Ghost Fleet ... but why would they fire on a Weather Mage? He was flying alone, no threat to them, and his people were neutral among all the airships and the floating cities. The Mages were regarded as invaluable, often even sacred, to the airship captains and crew who needed them as Scouts.

Sensing another change in the air, Aponivi dove to avoid a second arrow that flew past him. He still couldn't see the ship, but they were firing on him, trying to bring him down.

If this invisible airship was merely stealing a resupply of fresh water from the reservoir, they could have done it anywhere on the lake, not so close to the dam. No one would have needed to fire upon him, but they had tried to kill him! They were up to something terrible. Perhaps they were readying an attack upon Vegas Station itself.

He needed to get out of here, back to Vegas Station. He needed to find his own captain, to warn—

A third arrow whistled toward him, and Aponivi twisted to the right so that the deadly projectile streaked past his ear—but before he could exhale in relief, the next arrow sliced through his left wing membrane and nicked his arm. Pain flared as the wind tore the wound even wider, ripped the thin, sensitive skin.

Aponivi dropped rapidly, drew his wounded arm close so he would fall in a tight spiral, while he tried to control the descent with his legs and good wing. As the vast dark lake rushed up to meet him, he folded himself up, braced himself, and dove into the icy water. The impact jarred him, and he lost his bearings, but his light frame quickly bobbed to the surface. He gasped for breath, coughing.

The lake's frigid water numbed the immediate pain, but he knew the tear in his wing was bad, a widening hole that would keep him from flying … perhaps forever. He kept his arm tucked close to his body. The only way such a tear would ever heal—the only way he would fly again—was to protect the membrane, keep the tear from ripping wider. If he did not get help, he would never soar on the winds, never glide with the freedom of a Weather Mage.

First he had to get out of here, find safety and shelter. A place to hide. Someone had tried to kill him!

He heard a splash in the water, not far away, someone coming close. His mysterious attackers were not satisfied with merely knocking him out of the air. They had spotted where he'd crashed into the water.

Taking a deep breath, Aponivi dove under the water, using his leg membranes like a fish tail to propel him down and down. A Weather Mage belonged in the air, but for generations his people had sustained themselves by fishing out in the desolation, and water was not unknown to them.

Trying to outwit his attackers, he swam deeper and moved in the direction from which the mysterious arrows had come. With the powerful boost from his leg membranes, he nearly reached the dam barrier before his breath gave out. A Weather Mage's lungs could subsist on the thin air of the highest reaches of the sky, but he still had his limits.

Desperate for air, Aponivi let himself gently float up to the surface. Though he was starving for air, he forced himself to be calm, careful not to break the water hard. He didn't dare make a splash in the deepening twilight. Letting only his face emerge, he took a slow breath and looked up into the sky above him. It shimmered, ever so slightly, in the last fading light. Directly above the dam, not much more than a blur, he could make out the shape of an airship floating thirty feet overhead, but it was indistinct ... camouflaged.

"He has to come up for air sooner or later," a muffled voice said from seemingly out of thin air.

"Maybe he's dead."

"No. Those Weather Mage Scouts are tough bastards. Hard to kill. They might look scrawny, like they'd snap in two, but they don't. They're strong as hell and twice as dangerous. Keep your eyes open. No witnesses, no warning. He could fly back to Vegas Station in time to cause us trouble."

A deep voice chuckled. "I've still got more arrows, boss."

Aponivi took a full breath and calmed his pounding heart, then slipped back under the water, trying not to think of his wounded wing. His light, lean body couldn't stay submerged in the deep cold for much longer. He had to get to the dam, or to the rocky shore.

As he stroked through the chill, dark water, he detected the strange vibration here, too, even stronger than in the air. As cautiously as he could manage, Aponivi swam in an arc until he located the vibration. Gently drifting up for another lungful of air, he paused to listen again.

This time he heard no voices, but that did not mean he was safe. The Ghost Ship must still be there.

Tucking his wounded arm against his chest, he swam toward the vibrations. His legs and his good arm began to fatigue, and he needed to get out of the water as soon as he could. But the attackers were still out there.

Who were they? What kind of people would not only fire on a soaring Weather Mage, but would do so with contempt? And what were they doing in their camouflaged airship? *No witnesses, no warning.*

Aponivi had to find the answers ... but he had to survive first.

His strokes became more labored, but he continued moving toward the source. The vibrations became louder, stronger, until they were nearly unbearable, suffocating. The pressure waves not only affected his sensitive skin membranes, but his ears as well. He surfaced again, no longer worried about the sound of a splash over the noise, but the mysterious attackers in their airship could still spot him in the waning light.

His head broke water mere yards from the great concrete barrier of the dam. It held back the entire lake like a gigantic fortress wall. From this low angle in the water, he now spotted something he'd not been able to see when he'd glided overhead. A tight group of men were gathered on top of the dam, twenty-five feet or so above the waterline, and they were partially hidden by some kind of stealth technology. The strange camouflage field erased the people from the waist up, blending them with the sky as if they'd been cut in two, and he could see only their legs walking. Two more people hung in rope baskets just above the water.

From above, when he'd soared overhead on his other flights, this part of the dam had looked like much of the rest, where chunks had broken away, damaged by time and environmental upheaval. Here from the waterline, though, he could see that this part of the dam was actually whole, and sturdy.

These people were doing something to the dam itself. Considering that they had shot him out of the sky to hide what they were doing, to prevent him from warning Vegas Station, he knew immediately that he had to stop them. That was all the answer he needed.

His sharp eyes focused on the figures. These men did not wear the type of uniform he had seen on formal airship crews. Their piecemeal clothes were instead ragged and worn, in the way of scavengers and pirates, people who seemed more at home in the surface desolation than in the floating cities like Vegas Station.

Suddenly the vibration stopped, and Aponivi's ears rang in the oppressive silence.

One of the dangling men shouted up. "That's it! Bore hole is finished!" He held a piece of equipment in his arms, like a strange cannon loaded with a heavy spearhead. Someone on top of the dam began pulling it up by an attached rope.

"Ready for the payload! Lower it down," called the man hanging in the other rope basket. "And be careful—unless you actually believe the new stuff is completely stable!"

A ripple of nervous laughter answered him.

As the camouflaged group on top of the dam lowered something down, the two dangling men shifted positions, spreading apart. From the waterline, Aponivi saw that they had drilled a hole in the concrete wall—that was the vibrations he had heard. The bore hole was deep and wide enough to stick an arm into.

Now a package was lowered down to the men in the rope baskets, a long and narrow oilskin bag shaped to fit into the newly made hole.

"I can't see a damned thing," one of the dangling men complained. "It's too dark already."

"I told you we should have done this earlier," answered a half-visible man up on the dam.

"Shut up and send down the torch! Let's ignite this and get away from here. We'll watch the show from above."

In dismay, Aponivi realized they were trying to blow a hole through the dam and the satchel was apparently filled with explosives. He had no idea why anyone would want to do such a thing, but as the fuse was lit, he had no doubt.

He stroked backward to get away from the area of the blast, but he had no place to go. Fortunately, the sinister men were making so much noise of their own, they did not hear his splash.

The two dangling men frantically pushed the lit fuse inside the bag and knotted the top, then shoved the entire oilskin satchel farther into the hole. The second man tamped it in with a stick, pushing it as deep as it could go, while the other began filling the rest of the hole with mud-like cement or epoxy from a bucket hanging on another single rope.

"Done! Pull us up!" The first man tried to climb up the rope as his companions above started hauling him.

The other man tamped down the mortar one last time, then tossed his stick into the water below. "Hurry!" He tugged on the rope and began climbing rapidly up the concrete wall of the dam, like a fish on a line.

The camouflage field suddenly vanished, and the entire sabotage crew was revealed. Together now, they ran along the top of the dam toward a rope ladder that appeared as if by magic, falling out of the shimmering blur in the sky above. The Ghost Ship was still enclosed in its stealth shroud.

"Full speed!" a voice called from somewhere above. "We've got less than five minutes!"

The men hastily seized the ladder and began scrambling up to their hidden airship, one at a time in a frantic rush. Even as the last man grabbed hold of the ladder, the invisible craft began moving away, pulling him along as he hopped on one leg.

Unseen in the cold water, Aponivi looked from the dangling airship ladder crowded with climbing figures to the dark spot on the dam wall, where they had patched in the explosive. His instinct told him to swim to shore with all possible speed, to scramble up the rocks and get as far away from the blast as he could, limp up to higher ground. Five minutes? The crude fuse could not be very accurate, but if the explosive technology was anything like the stealth field these pirates used …

This was about more than just saving himself and getting away from the blast. What would his father and his teachers say? Aponivi knew that if the already damaged dam were breached, the seismic spilling of the enormous reservoir would cause incalculable harm. Yes, Vegas Station levitated safely above the ground, but the epic flood would obliterate the fledgling settlements that had just started to spring up along the river, kill all the people who were now living down there, just barely eking out a living. If the dam broke, how many would die? And for what purpose? The aftermath would damage all trade and disrupt the vital routes. Was that what the marauders wanted?

Five of the saboteurs were still climbing the ladder up into the invisible shroud, swinging wildly as the camouflaged airship began to cruise away from the dam. The other men had already vanished onto the floating vessel.

Aponivi felt a surge of renewed anger. These people had shot him out of the sky. He would not let them succeed in this barbaric attack. Setting his jaw, he made a decision that might cost him his life, but in exchange for so many, his life—and his death—would gain great value indeed. He was a Weather Mage. He remembered everything his mentors had taught him. Their honor code was as strong as the wind.

He could not let this go.

With powerful strokes, blocking out thoughts of the increasing damage he was doing to his wounded membrane, he shot forward to the dam. He no longer bothered to remain hidden as he swam. There was no time to cover the sound of his splashes.

An angry voice called down from the cloaked airship above. "What's that?"

"It's that damned birdman!"

Reaching the huge cliff of concrete, Aponivi pumped his legs to hold him afloat. He pushed his torso far enough out of the water so he could reach the plugged hole.

"He's going after the charge!"

"Dammit! Archers!"

The mud-like epoxy or cement they had used to seal the hole was already hardening. Aponivi's good arm, fatigued from all the swimming, was so weak he could barely raise it over his head, let alone dig at setting mortar. His long fingers scraped at the partially dried mud, but he couldn't clear enough of it. His hooked nails bled.

"Take him out."

Once exposed to the air, the torn wound in the membrane burned with pain. As he lifted his arms to claw away at the setting mortar, he felt his thin, sensitive skin rip even more, widening the wound. But there was no point in nursing the tear. With a grimace, Aponivi raised his other hand, using both to dig.

Inside the bore hole, the fuse would be burning down. Five minutes? How much time was left? He gritted his teeth and ignored the cutting pain to claw harder, faster, tearing his nails in the setting mortar. He grunted, kicking his legs to remain above the water.

With a sharp report, an arrow struck the wall just to the left of his head. The sharp steel tip sparked against the concrete, a brief flare in the thick shadows of evening. He closed his eyes and kept digging.

As he pushed his arms deeper into the clogged hole, his fingertips brushed against something that felt more like oilcloth than rock.

He managed to hook another long finger into a chunk of the hardening mortar, and broke out a large chunk that fell into his face. The heavy shard smashed his nose with a flash of pain, and his nostrils filled with the quick smell of iron.

Another arrow ricocheted off the concrete just to the right of his cheek. The next one might strike him between the shoulder blades. …

His muscles were all lead and pain. He couldn't keep pumping his legs. He couldn't keep digging, but just when he thought he couldn't pull for one second more, he snagged the knot at the top of the oilskin sack. He grabbed it and pulled, dragging the sack partly out of the hole, then he let himself slide back. Gravity would do the rest of the work.

An arrow pierced his other wing as he fell away from the dam, tearing the membrane with a thin scream of pain, but the prize was in his hand. He fell, taking the knotted sack with him into the water.

"I got him! He's done now!"

"He got the damned charge!"

Aponivi sank into the water, floating, vulnerable. With his torn fingers, he yanked at the knot, tugged, and tried to untie it, but his hands were bloody, and the tight oilskin folds refused to yield. He submerged it, but the water would never extinguish the fuse. The bomb would go off at any time. He didn't even know what kind of explosive it was.

Even if he managed to get far enough away to save the dam wall, the blast would tear him to shreds.

Aponivi kicked away from the wall, hugging the package close. His ruined wings were agony, and he felt numb and sickened with the knowledge of how badly he was hurt. Even if he got away, he would never recover from this, never be whole again. But his first mission was to stay alive, get away so he could report to Vegas Station, warn them of these terrorists, even if he stopped the bomb this time.

He had to survive the next minutes.

An arrow pierced the surface above him as he swam, plunging down like a viper, but it missed him in the water. These marauders had casually fired upon a Weather Mage. Aponivi hadn't attacked them, hadn't threatened them, hadn't even seen them. Weather Mages didn't attack others. They were as calm as the winds, as open as the skies. Aponivi likely would never have realized what they were doing had they not shot at him.

But the hatred of these people seemed to run deep. Maybe they were just murderers and did not give bloodshed a second thought. They had no concerns about blasting the dam open and sending a deadly flood-hammer across the settled lands.

More arrows hit the surface, but he swam deep with his dangerous package, and the water stole the weapons' efficacy. The men on the airship had to know they couldn't harm him. Why were they wasting arrows, as if driving him away?

Thirty feet from the dam wall, he finally surged back up to gulp a breath. As he flung cold water out of his eyes, he spotted the last man on the rope ladder still struggling to board the invisible airship —directly above him. The rest of the craft was hidden behind the stealth field. Several more arrows peppered the water around him.

He realized they were trying to keep him away, even if they didn't kill him. He had the sack with the explosives, and he didn't know how powerful the blast would be. But the lumbering Ghost Ship had drifted over the lake, where Aponivi was. The airship moved, trying to gain speed.

He realized that the magnitude of the bomb's destructive power had to be incredible, since no mere blast could crack open the behemoth of Hoover Dam. What kind of technology did these people have? Once the bomb did explode, it could well take out the nearby Ghost Ship, even in the air above.

Grim satisfaction crept over Aponivi's face as he realized what he could do. This would be better than just sitting under the cloaked airship.

Diving deep with his burden, swimming down until the pressure squeezed his eardrums, Aponivi tumbled in the water, reversed direction, and raced toward the surface hard as he could. He used his membranes to push against the water, not caring how much more he tore them. Accelerating, rising, it was like flying again. When he broke the water, he shot into the air like a cork popping from a bottle. In the brief moment of weightless freedom, he kicked desperately, using his ruined wings to gain even a few feet of additional altitude.

Right overhead, hands seemed to magically appear around the last man climbing the ladder. The upper half of his body vanished as his crewmates hauled him aboard.

At the apex of his jump, Aponivi flung the wet oilskin package after the man's feet. And then he fell away, dropping back down to the lake.

The plunge seemed slower than any glide he'd ever done. Two more arrows whistled past him just as he saw the charge vanish into the camouflage field.

Aponivi struck the water with his back, landing hard. Two arrows from the shower of projectiles bit him, sliced past as he fell beneath the surface, sinking to imagined safety.

There was nothing more he could do. The airship was gliding away from the dam, gaining altitude.

He surfaced, ignoring the burning pain of his numerous wounds. He struck out for the shoreline and the concrete dam, dredging more energy from his exhausted muscles. He noticed with odd detachment that an arrow protruded from the meat of his arm, and without thinking, he grabbed the shaft and snatched it out. The cold water did little to lessen the ripping pain. Discarding the arrow, he began swimming again. He no longer even felt cold.

A surge of light from above was like a flash of rare sunlight reflecting from a mirror. An instant later, the shockwave shoved him under the water. He stayed under as the roiling fire and debris swept over the surface, and then flailing, he swam up to air again. He broke the surface to see the flaming airship, its camouflage gone, the ungainly and mortally wounded vessel slowly falling to the lake. It was a large, hodge-podge marauder, flying no colors that he recognized. Debris rained down, components of the levitation engines, great hunks of the hull, flaming support struts. Burning human figures also tumbled out like debris.

Better the pirate airship was destroyed than the dam.

He began swimming again, sluggish with pain, bone-deep weariness, and shock. Only now did he feel the drag of another arrow shaft, and he found another a projectile stuck into his thigh, but not deep. He plucked it out, as if it were no more than a splinter.

The flames of the burning, crashing airship lit the water, and he could see a swirl of blood surrounding his pale body, leaking from all his wounds.

It didn't matter.

He drifted, floating, imagining himself aloft on an open breeze, free and weightless. On normal days, the skies were much warmer, and smelled of flowers and fruit.

Aponivi nearly lost consciousness, ready to fall … just to sink, but he shook his head and forced himself to swim farther, aiming for the rocky shore at the far end of the battered dam. The dusk had deepened to the edge of full night by the time he reached the smooth, water-stained rock where the concrete ended and the natural shore began.

The Hoover Dam had been damaged by time, nature, and the apocalypse from the great eruption. The titanic structure might not last for centuries more, but it would endure for a few more years. For today. Thanks to him.

At the edge of the concrete dam wall, he found stairs leading down to the waterline, an ancient maintenance access from the old road across the dam. He pulled himself up, staggering one step after another, climbing to a flat landing, where the stairs turned to go someplace higher. He collapsed on his back, gasping, and looked up at the stars that had come out between patches of returning clouds.

Aponivi was glad to see the stars. They were so rarely visible from the ground.

He remembered a flight as a young boy, when his father had taken him above the near-perpetual storms to see the stars. So bright and clear, so pure and pristine, they made his heart hurt to look upon them.

He paid no attention to the burning wreck of the Ghost Ship he had destroyed. Flames still roiled across the floating debris, orange and sputtering on the surface of the water.

As he huddled on the landing, throbbing with pain from a dozen wounds, a chill wind brought cold mist from the spillway across his body. He closed his eyes, listening to the distant roar of the spillway waterfall, and just waited for his spirit to join the stars cycling endlessly in the heavens above.

Voices woke him, nearby voices and the sound of splashing

water.

"I know he went this way," one said. "I saw him. Bastard!"

"He could be anywhere, boss," another responded. "We should get out of here while we can. Vegas Station might've sent flyers out to investigate already."

Aponivi couldn't make himself move, as if parts of him were already dead. Collapsed on the landing halfway up to the roadway above, he managed to roll on his side and look out across the dark lake. Two forms, clinging to floating debris from the doomed airship, were approaching the shore.

"He took my ship! I'll kill that flying freak. I'll kill every one of those damned birdmen!"

Aponivi just wanted to close his eyes and be done. He heard the man's words with his heart, and he believed them. This murderous man had shown no compunction about shooting at an innocent, neutral Weather Mage out on patrol. The evil airship captain would do the same to any Weather Mage he encountered, Aponivi's people, his family. The man's hatred was irrational and deep. If the man lived through this night, he would kill more.

He had to be stopped.

Rolling to his belly, Aponivi used numb and bleeding hands to force himself up, to stand upon numb feet. His wounds, the only things he could truly feel, ached like cold fire. Reaching inside himself, he focused on the sensation and pulled himself out of his torpor. He lowered his head, turning away from the stars he wanted so desperately to join.

He was not done here. Not yet. Not with that violent man still out there.

With no weapons and no strength, a creature of the sky with clipped wings, Aponivi's only advantage over these men was that he could see in the night better than they could. He had to find a way to use that before his body failed him.

A clack and scrape below told him the men's improvised debris raft had reached the shore edge of the dam wall.

"Up there! I see him on the steps!"

Realizing he stood silhouetted against the sky, Aponivi hobbled up the second flight of stairs from the landing. Many of the steps were broken and missing after so much time, and he stumbled to his knees more than once. A warm streak ran down his arm and leg, and he realized it was blood mingling with the water on his skin. His torn wing membranes opened up like a gasp of pain each time he reached out to catch himself, but he pushed on.

A Weather Mage was meant to fly, and now he was trapped here on the ground, just out of the water. He would rather have faced a terrible storm.

At the top of the landing, he found an open expanse partially covered in the hard black paving the ancient peoples had used on their roads. Aponivi searched for any place to hide, any weapon or tool he could use, but his vision was obscured by the spillway mist that rose high into the air around him.

He turned toward the roar of the artificial waterfall, where the lake overflow gushed and drained around the dam to the river below. A force of nature, a different kind of explosion than anything the Ghost Ship marauders could create. Maybe that was a weapon he could use....

He stood on top of the dam, well above the lake surface on one side of the concrete wall and the sheer drop-off and spillway to the canyon on the other. Behind him, the men were still climbing the first flight of stairs, panting and cursing as they reached the landing where Aponivi had held onto a peaceful moment and stared at the stars. He could hear their voices but could no longer make out the words over the spillway's crashing water.

Aponivi stood tall against the sky where he knew they could see him, luring them. The vile airship captain spotted him, shouted. Aponivi moved, trying to outrun the pain as well as the men in pursuit. He headed toward the spillway.

Jagged stones tore at his feet, shoving aside the numbness. Limping, leaving a trail of blood, he looked back only once to make sure the men still followed, then let himself become lost to them in the misty air.

In the smokescreen of the spillway spray, he slipped away from the cracked roadway and worked his way to the very edge of the drop-off to the deep canyon downstream of the towering dam. Here, the roar of the overflow water was deafening, the cold spray thick and blinding, like a dense fog. With his sharp eyes, he kept watch for his pursuers.

He had circled overhead many times, looking down like an angel on the crashing water, the tumbling and graceful gush that thundered down into the canyon. He had never come this close before, though. The sheer force of the spillway made the ground tremble beneath his feet.

When shadowy figures came closer, hunting him, he watched them stalk forward, but they continued moving along the remnants of the road. All but blind in the night and deafened by the roaring water, they did not even look his way.

Aponivi stooped and picked up a fist-sized rock. His nails were cracked and torn, and his arm throbbed with pain from the arrow wound and the torn wing membrane. He hurled the rock at them, missed.

The two men spun in his direction, and he saw that they brandished clubs or swords, some kind of weapons they had salvaged from the crash. They came closer, taking each step cautiously as they tried to find him. Aponivi waited.

They hesitated, aware of the danger he might pose. One bent down and scrabbled around on the ground before grabbing a rock. He flung it in Aponivi's direction, but it missed by a wide margin.

Warm blood dripped down Aponivi's arm, thick and wet, but it cooled by the time it reached his fingers. He could feel his time waning, his strength, his soul. These men only had to wait him out. Did they know that? He fought the urge to slump to the ground and just give up.

Instead, he picked up another rock and threw it. This time, he grazed the shoulder of the airship captain. Cursing, both men turned, more accurately facing him now. Aponivi heard angry voices, but could not make out the words. He didn't need to. They were closing in on him. He threw another rock, but his arm was shaking. The effort nearly made him collapse. His head spun.

As they closed in on him, though, he stumbled to the side, camouflaged by the spray and the darkness. He was sure they could neither see nor hear him. With awkward movements, Aponivi circled behind them, tripping on unsteady feet. When both men stood between himself and the spillway, looking for where he had gone, Aponivi crouched, mustered the last of his strength. They were at the edge, looking toward the spillway below, trying to find him.

Instead, he found them. Aponivi charged, his arms wide, his tattered membranes like scoops to catch them both.

The marauders turned at the sound of his bestial roar, which was loud enough to be heard over the roaring waterfall, but they were too late to do more than scream. The demon-like shape of the altered human flung himself out of the mist, wrapped them in his wings. He carried them over the edge and into the abyss and the embrace of the colossal waterfall.

Aponivi flew again, for one last time.

✶

The morning was cloudy and cold, but the water was even colder as Aponivi's crew pulled him from the sandbar where he had washed up, a mile downriver.

He heard their words from a distance, familiar voices in an endless roaring nightmare. They talked as if he wasn't there, and he could barely cling to the last thread of consciousness. They said his wings were completely gone, they speculated he wouldn't live, they muttered disbelief and admiration over his single-handed victory against a ship of the Ghost Fleet. Other search parties had been dispatched from Vegas Station.

But none of it mattered.

Aponivi closed his eyes as he felt his body lifted up, taken somewhere. He had already known he would never fly again, but that was all right. He remembered the story of Icarus, the tale his father and his teachers had told him again and again, and he finally understood something else about the story, something a man named Wilde had written about Icarus.

"Never regret thy fall, O Icarus of the fearless flight

"For the greatest tragedy of them all

"Is never to feel the burning light."

Aponivi had flown for all his life, something so few others would ever do, and he had flown one last, vital time. He had sacrificed everything for the lives of others who would never know. Countless others. The great fortress wall of the dam remained, and would remain, with the huge, light-filled city of Vegas Station hovering nearby, high overhead.

He felt the pure, burning light of the sun behind the ubiquitous clouds. It shone down upon him in approval, calling upon Aponivi to join the sun, to soar in the heavens, burning bright.

What more could anyone ask for?

✶

Kevin J. Anderson is an international bestselling author with over 23 million copies in print. He has written novels for Star Wars, X-Files, Batman, as well as novels in the Dune universe with Brian Herbert. His original work includes the Dan Shamble, Zombie P.I. series, the Saga of Seven Suns, *Spine of the Dragon,* and *Clockwork Angels* and *Clockwork Lives,* both with legendary Rush drummer Neil Peart. As an editor, he has put together numerous anthologies, including the three bestselling science fiction anthologies of all time. He is a professor at Western Colorado University where he is the director of the Publishing MA program. Kevin and his wife, Rebecca Moesta, are the publishers of WordFire Press.

A Colorado native, *Sam Knight* spent ten years in California's wine country before returning to the Rockies. When asked if he misses California, he gets a wistful look in his eyes and replies he misses the green mountains in the winter, but he is glad to be back home. As well as having worked for at least three publishing companies, Sam is author of six children's books, six short story collections, three novels, and around five dozen short stories, including two media tie-ins co-authored with Kevin J. Anderson: "Wayward Pines: Aberration" (Kindle Worlds, 2014) and "Of Monsters and Men, Planet of the Apes: Tales from the Forbidden Zone" (Titan, 2016).

A stay-at-home father, Sam attempts to be a full-time writer, but there are only so many hours left in a day after kids. Once upon a time, he was known to quote books the way some people quote movies, but now he claims having a family has made him forgetful, as a survival adaptation. He can be found at SamKnight.com and contacted at Sam@samknight.com.

WARRIORS OF THE RAINBOW

STEVEN L. SEARS

She started to feel warmth on her back from the friction of the air. Flaming debris was still falling from the wreckage, much at the same rate she was, giving the illusion they were all floating in space together. At a certain point, when she hit terminal velocity, Gerita knew she would relax. She had spread her body evenly, slightly bent in the middle, facing up toward the fireworks in the sky as the wind from her rapid descent played in her ears.

"There it is," she mumbled to herself as she hit her maximum speed and the air resistance became like a cushion. It was her first good chance to examine the strange Dreadnought that had rammed her airship.

It was big, perhaps twice as much tonnage as the *Leif Erickson,* and that was saying a lot. *The Erikson,* or *Big Red* as the crew called her, was a full research ship with several onboard laboratories. As one of the top environmentalists of the UC Tower she had flown on it often; it was the perfect platform for her studies into Mother Earth's efforts to return to balance after the devastation of the Yellowstone Event. But with heavy duty gas bags designed for lifting and stabilization, it wasn't built for speed. As research vessels frequently came under attack by the Ghost Fleet and pirates, it was solid and had the most current defensive systems that the UC Tower could provide. None of that seemed to matter as the strange Dreadnought pushed forward through the superstructure of *Big Red,* fracturing it and creating multiple onboard explosions.

It was the strangest vessel she had ever seen. The main envelope housing the gas bags on the attacker was narrowed to a point in the front and wider, rounded at the stern. The weaponry, usually located at mid-height or under the main bag on most warships, was located on metal racks over the top; at least twenty 35mm cannons with rocket pods on the side. There was no sign of a command gondola but, instead, small bubbles affixed to the front. Gerita assumed they were pilot houses of some sort.

Whoever the captain was, he or she was a master of the sky. The Dreadnought slammed into the *Erikson* just as the cumbersome research vessel was turning to bring its own guns to bear, splitting it in two and bending it back upon itself. The stabilizing engines had blown, sending fireballs up and around the main envelope. Everyone above C Deck had, most likely, been incinerated immediately.

Gerita had been on the lower deck, using the ground scopes to survey the canyons below, memorizing the topography for her mission. The Dreadnought had pushed its way into the corner of her view when it popped up through the clouds. She barely had enough time to get to her cabin and pull on her squirrel suit. The retaining braces next to her window had just started to bend with the impact when she jumped through the shattered glass and into the open sky.

Flying on vessels like *Big Red* always came with a certain amount of danger, as much of the work meant exploration in uncivilized areas with no protection from the predations of the Ghost Fleet. An attack from them would not be unusual.

But this ship was not from the Ghost Fleet, she knew it without a doubt. For although she was one of the top environmentalists from the UC Tower, she was also a spy for the Ghost Fleet; a saboteur and assassin. A very good one with a stellar, if secret, record. Being a naturalist allowed her a certain amount of freedom in her travels. After all, who would suspect this young red-haired girl who was obsessed with nature to be the mysterious spy and killer known as "Koala"? It was a perfect cover and it served her well.

She would write up a full description of the strange vessel when she reported back to the Grand Admiral. She was still on a mission, and despite this minor interruption, she had her orders. To fail could mean the greatest destructive event since the Yellowstone eruption.

Small objects seemed to detach from the Dreadnought, dropping, then moving quickly through the air. *Search Drones* she thought, though she couldn't see them clearly. More likely, Search and Destroy Drones. She had to drop within the safety of the clouds before they picked her out of the debris.

With a toss of her shoulder, she allowed the air supporting her to escape around her right side, turned easily, and pushed her upper body down. She flattened herself, tilting forward, pulling the lanyards on either side of her squirrel suit. The flaps snapped free as her arms moved away from her body. The wind caught the material and filled the pockets, expanding it and increasing the flat surface area of her body until the glide areas were completely open and she was back in control.

Her eyes scanned the horizon. The tops of the Appalachian Mountains peeked through the canopy of clouds to her right, which meant her target was somewhere to the left, far below. With a slight shift of weight, she turned easily and smoothly, dodging the fireballs of her former vessel as they continued their descent to the earth.

This was the easy part. The hard part, always the hard part, was landing. She couldn't see the ground through the clouds, but from her research, she knew it would be rocky and uneven. It was going to be a controlled crash at best. She could only hope that her broken bones would be minor.

Gerita dove toward the clouds, determined to complete the mission the Grand Admiral had given her when she had met with him.

✶

Gerita sat in the Tribunal Hall of the Council, fumbling with the sleeve of her utilitarian jumpsuit. It was a standard issue, designed to make sure no one could bring any contraband or weapons into the highest offices of the Ghost Fleet.

The room was large and, like the suit, utilitarian. A row of thirteen seats ran along one side where the Command Council usually sat. Above them, on a raised level, were the three chairs of the Wolves; the godlike commanders who ruled the Ghost Fleet. Their history went deep into the past, before the Yellowstone Event changed the world forever. That they were not present didn't surprise her. It would have been remarkable had they been there to brief her on her mission in person. She was here to meet with the Grand Admiral, the one person who, many believed, was destined to replace one of the Wolves when the time came. Or, as some whispered, to replace them all.

The fact that she had been pulled from her cover at UC Tower to come to Groom Lake in person was a major departure of protocol. The UC had noticed her absence and was committing resources to her recovery in the northern Rockies. She already had her cover story and, truth was, it wasn't uncommon for Gerita to go off the grid in her research. As soon as this meeting was over, she'd be returned to her base camp, contact her fellow academics, and return to her work at the UC Academy of Environmental Research.

At least she assumed so. That would depend on the purpose of this meeting with the Grand Admiral. Despite being one of the greatest military tacticians and strategists in history, little was known about his actual background except that he rose quickly through the ranks as his daring and unconventional tactics captured the attention of the Wolves. The Grand Admiral now served directly under them in overall tactical command and no navy in the world wanted to go up against him. He was that universally feared.

She took a deep breath and turned in her seat toward the transparent wall that overlooked the Groom Lake berths. The number of warships being supplied told her something was up. The Ghost Fleet, as feared as it was, did not usually deploy in large numbers as a single unit. The preferred tactics were to travel in small groups, taking opportunities when they came. Actual grand fleet movements were rare, usually when one of the City-Tower fiefdoms attempted to expand their power base. But here were the makings of a full fleet close to deployment. She recognized the USS *Harrison,* a mid-size airship transport and the USS *Whipple*, a destroyer. She had seen them in action during the Rio Grande attack. Both were instrumental in repelling the attempts by Mexico City to claim control of the air space favored by the drug cartels. It wasn't that the Ghost Fleet had any interest in the cartels, they sometimes traded with them. Mexico City was looking to reassert the Spanish Empire by pushing north and splitting North America into two regions. To do that, they would have to take Groom Lake.

Gerita had been researching the mud flows of the Madrid earthquake post-YE in her UC Tower guise when the war broke out. Though it spanned an area of several hundreds of thousands of square acres, the major part of the battle had occurred directly over her camp. Outnumbered fifteen to one, the Grand Admiral had brilliantly used deception and envelopment to wipe out the Mexico City force and secure his reputation in the western hemisphere.

The force she could see assembled from her seat in the Tribunal room would make that action seem like a small incursion. She had no idea where this fleet was headed but whoever was in its way was not going to be long for this world.

She hoped it wouldn't be the UC Tower. Though her real profession was spy and assassin, she actually *was* an accredited naturalist. Her love of the environment was real and was the major reason for her secret profession. The world was in disarray and the danger of another environmental disaster was too much to risk. To rise from the ashes, the various nations and Towers of the world would have to come together, under one banner, to preserve humanity and civilization. The Ghost Fleet, with the wisdom of the Wolves and the Grand Admiral in charge of strategy, was the most likely to do so.

The entry door behind her slid open and Commander Vin Moseli walked into the room. He was the head of the Ghost Fleet Intelligence Network and she had reported to him many times. Tall and imposing, his sharp features were what one would expect from his position. The web of spies and assassins under his command spanned the continent. It was said that he had agents in high positions in every City-Tower of the Americas. Time bombs waiting for him to light the fuse and kill on command. Gerita was one of them.

"Koala," he said as he nodded to her. Of course, he would use her code name; even here, her identity was known to only a few. "Nervous?" he continued.

She took a deep breath. "I never thought I would meet the Grand Admiral in person."

"Well, you won't be meeting him this time," he responded with a dry laugh. "At least, not face to face. The threat of assassination is too high. He'll talk to you from his office, behind the blast doors."

He indicated the large double panels at the end of the chamber, the door to the Admiral's office. The well-being of the Grand Admiral was central to the success of the Ghost Fleet and all precautions had been taken to protect him. "Have you met him? In person?" she asked of Moseli.

"Once," he responded. "Many, many years ago."

Silence followed. Gerita watched him as he stared off into the distance. Finally, he turned and walked to her. She started to rise, but he gestured her to remain seated.

"Listen carefully," Moseli's voice just above a whisper. "No matter what is said here, this meeting never happened. Do you understand?"

Gerita nodded, a bit confused. She had already assumed the secrecy protocols would be observed. She was a spy, after all.

"Beyond your training," he continued. "This means no one, absolutely no one, is to know the contents of this conversation. When we leave this room, we will not discuss or acknowledge anything about it except as the Grand Admiral requests, do you understand?"

The emphasis he put on the last few words made it clear to her. Any violation and she wouldn't just die, she would die slowly and painfully. She glanced toward the three chairs of the Wolves. Of course, they had to know about this meeting, didn't they?

"I had not expected a woman." The voice of the Admiral boomed into the room. The biometric lock on the doors glowed and pulsated with energy, but she wasn't sure if that was a function of the voice or just an effect, something for people to focus on.

Moseli shot a look to her and indicated she should respond. "Koala," she said. "I serve the Ghost Fleet." Her voice was stronger than she felt.

"Commander Moseli has told me of your work. Commendable. He assures me you are the best at what you do."

She took a deep breath of pride but tinged with fear that she couldn't possibly live up to the accolades. "I do what I can, for the Fleet and for our world," she replied, lowering her eyes.

"You are aware of The Dark Zone?" he continued. Gerita shot a look toward Moseli. The Ghost Fleet rarely acknowledged the existence of The Dark Zone, a no-fly zone along the Atlantic coast that had mysteriously claimed many airships. All Towers and nations steered clear of it, and the Ghost Fleet was no exception. Most rumors described it as a Bermuda Triangle, with strange, mutated beasts that preyed on all foolish enough to enter it.

"Yes," she replied. "I've actually studied it a bit."

"Do you know that it's growing?" the Grand Admiral's voice was flat.

"I did not," she acknowledged, hearing the shock in her own voice.

A screen lowered itself from the ceiling to her right. It flickered to life, showing a map of the Atlantic Coast of the former United States, an area from old Boston to the ruins of Jacksonville. To the side of the coastline was a shaded region, The Dark Zone. As she watched the screen, the shaded region began to move slowly, a timer in the lower right indicating the passage of months. It didn't move as a weather pattern would, but it seemed to move with purpose. A small finger of The Darkness probed toward the northern bay areas, then retracted. Another appeared in the middle, also retracted. Then one at the bottom, near Old Georgia, moved inland. This one didn't retract and, slowly, it began to expand, covering more territory, pushing farther toward the base of the Appalachian Mountains, then moving northward.

The image froze for a moment, then reset, repeating the movement. Fascinated, Gerita rose and walked closer to the screen, examining it.

"This is … not random. It's not a product of nature," she said out loud but more to herself. She touched the screen, tracing her finger along the boundaries of The Darkness as it moved.

"Explain," the Grand Admiral commanded.

"These sections here," she continued. "In the north and the middle … they aren't moving for meteorological reasons. No wind patterns would account for that." She paused, thinking. Suddenly, she leaned back. "They're probes. They're probes! The two, here and here, probing for weaknesses, and retreating. But down here," she stabbed her finger at the lower probe as it expanded again. "It found something. It's moving in force around the southern mountains and ..."

She stepped back in full realization. "It's ... an invasion."

"Commander, your faith in this agent is well-founded." The Grand Admiral sounded almost relieved.

Gerita didn't hear him, she was still examining the screen. "Wait, what's this?" she asked as she pointed to a small flickering light in an area near the southern coast that The Darkness had moved around but not encompassed.

"It's a radioactive signature," Moseli stated.

"Impossible!" Gerita reacted. "There are no natural radioactive deposits in the Appalachians except for the old missile silos, and those have all been accounted for and destroyed."

"Still, it is there," the Grand Admiral responded. "And that's why you're here. You're going to go in and find out what it is."

Gerita reacted in shock, eyes widening. "That's Cherokee territory."

"Which makes it all the more imperative," Moseli said. "We wouldn't risk your life if it wasn't."

Gerita sat down again. Not much was known about the Cherokee Nation except that it was a secretive society that wasn't very tolerant with outsiders. It wasn't just made up of Cherokees but was an amalgam of many tribes that had concentrated themselves in the Appalachians after YE. The Nation had at least three Towers operating in those mountains but, with the exception of heavily regulated trade, contact with them was almost non-existent. And the very few incursions into their lands had been bloody failures. A squadron of the Ghost Fleet itself had been turned back in the Battle of the Mists when they tried to force a trading route across Cherokee territory to the Atlantic. It was not mentioned in the official records but was, like The Dark Zone, a well-known secret.

Despite the obvious military abilities of the Native Americans and the technology they possessed, it was believed that most of the Cherokees had reverted to their 'savage nature.' Popular depictions had them as barbarians, eating the raw flesh of hapless creatures and torturing outsiders with impunity. Cannibalism was often cited as an example of their cruelty; the idea of capturing the soul of their enemies by devouring their hearts.

"Our security services feel that those subhumans might actually be the cause of The Dark Zone," the Grand Admiral stated.

"Not confirmed," Moseli interjected. "But strongly indicated. If you'll notice, The Darkness moves around their territory as it heads inland, but not through it."

"How are we detecting this Dark Zone?" Gerita asked. "Does it have substance? I mean, this isn't just a map of missing airships."

"Ozone," Commander Moseli replied. "An intense amount of ozone in the atmosphere. We don't know why, but it also means a huge potential for electrostatic energy. Which could explain the disappearances of the airships."

"That's strange," Gerita pondered. The scientist in her had kicked in again. Weather patterns created ozone traces, but not to the extent that was shown on the screen.

"The Cherokees have been somewhat tolerant of environmentalists," the Admiral said. "Your cover, as I am told, is in that arena."

"Yes, it is," Gerita acknowledged. "But that area is a complete wasteland after the Ridge Tsunami of YE 38. Even a naturalist would look suspicious just walking in."

"You won't be walking in." Moseli handed her a folder, ripping off the dissolve tab as she took it. "This outlines your procedure but, basically, you'll be aboard the research ship *Leif Erickson*. It won't cross their boundary, but it will move south along the border. You'll do an air insertion near the objective."

She took the folder. "One moment," she said as she scanned the documents, memorizing every detail. Standard operating procedure required a solid memory as all documents were designed to dissolve within minutes after the tab was pulled. "Got it," she said as she tossed it on the floor. "It didn't mention a time element. What do I have?"

"Two weeks," the Grand Admiral told her.

"Equipment?" she asked.

"None," The Admiral replied. "We can't afford to have anyone suspect our involvement."

"A good agent will always find the tools she needs when she needs them." Moseli added.

"I need to know what that radioactive signature is coming from," the Admiral went on. "If it's a weapon, I want it. If it's a power source, I want to know what it's for and if it has anything to do with The Dark Zone."

Gerita nodded. Though in possession of the mightiest navy in the world, the Grand Admiral knew the value of patience, strategy, and maximizing your resources before any venture. Any unknowns that *could* be known *had* to be known before taking action. Something monumental was about to happen and she was in the middle of it. *No,* she thought, *I'm crucial to it.*

The documents at her feet were already hissing as they dissolved. "And, if I'm terminated?" It was an audacious question to ask, but her curiosity got the best of her.

"I send in the largest Ghost Fleet the world has seen and we destroy it all, including the redskins and their nation." The Grand Admiral's voice was firm and resolute. "And if we don't hear from you at the end of two weeks, we'll assume you are dead."

"At that point, events are unstoppable," the Commander said. "We will be forced to invade."

Gerita realized such an action would mean war with every Tower in the Americas as they all scrambled for advantage. No doubt the Grand Admiral was anticipating that eventuality. He might even be counting on it, creating conflict between Towers in order to weaken them.

"You understand how crucial this is. You are to report only to me. No exceptions. Go." The pulsating glow of the lock went dark.

The doors behind her hissed open. Moseli merely gestured toward them.

This meeting was finished. Had never happened.

Gerita exited without pause. She had her orders; she had her mission. And the possible fate of the world on her shoulders.

✶

It wasn't the fall that almost killed her when she burst out of the clouds. It wasn't the change in air pressure, the abrupt rise in temperature, or the wind shear she hit while passing through the thermal layer. It was the view that almost did her in.

The rolling hills and mountains of the Appalachians spread out as far as she could see. Lush, fertile, green, and teeming with vegetation. A canopy of oaks and pines covered the landscape. Areas where the trees did not obscure her view of the ground were covered with flowering plants and grasses.

This was totally unexpected. It went against all the predictive models, including her own. This section of the Appalachians had been destroyed when the southern section of the North American Plate had violently subducted under the African Plate. The resulting earthquake had created a series of oceanic waves reaching heights of forty feet or more which scoured the coastline for miles inland. The effect of this disaster was believed to have rendered the region almost completely lifeless and desolate.

Her body tilted forward, anxious to get in among the flora and fauna. She had dreamed of ecosystems like this, in full recovery from YE. Once the Ghost Fleet established control of North America, it was her hope that organized reforestation and terraforming could take place in all areas.

This was exactly what she had always envisioned. She could only wonder how it had happened and wanted to study it. Her smile faded as she remembered that she wasn't here for regional study. There would be time for that later. Somewhere, down there, hidden among the leaves and animals she loved so much, was a radioactive source of power that could be the difference between the rebirth of Mother Earth and the completion of the destruction begun in Yellowstone those many years before.

Concentrate! she thought as she bit her lip and focused on her immediate situation. The location of the radioactive source was nearby, the contours of the mountains matched the topographic readings from the map. Her eyes searched for a place to land.

She saw what she was looking for toward the east. A small opening in the trees, following the approximate path of a stream winding amongst the rocks. There was a bare stretch of grass that she could shoot for. The angle would have to be steep to clear the treetops, but she should be able to make it. Even if she couldn't deploy the suit's membrane on time, she was hopeful that the grass would be soft, and the soil would be muddy. If Gerita got it wrong, even by the slightest degree, she would snap her spine just above the hips and separate every joint in her arms and legs.

Taking a deep breath, she pulled her right elbow into her body and instantly angled toward the opening in the trees. The immediate loss of altitude increased her speed; it was coming up faster than she had calculated.

The brush of the topmost branch was her signal to tuck her knees forward and begin her rotation, bringing her feet forward in anticipation of hitting the ground. She pulled the drawstring along her waist and spread her arms. The small braking flap ejected from the back of the suit, and she felt the tug of the wind pooling within it. She was almost to the ground. She readied herself to hit and roll forward, as she had been trained to do.

An abrupt movement to her right startled her. Something punched into her chest, flipping her backwards, slamming her hard to the ground on the back of her neck. She rolled, her limbs flailing and unresponsive until she tumbled into a tree trunk, leaving her in a sitting position, sagging limply like a rag doll.

The reason for her crash landing was tall, perhaps three meters or more. Biped, covered in matted fur, definitely a primate but much stockier. Its limbs were disproportionate to its body, bigger and longer. Its right arm had the remains of one of her suit's membranes dangling from it. Obviously this was an opportunistic attack; the creature taking advantage of her arrival and vulnerability on landing. Even in her dazed state, she reflexively analyzed the creature.

"Predator ... apex ..." she mumbled to herself as it reached toward her, grabbing her arm and pulling her. The flesh under her suit ripped and she was aware of warmth spreading down her sleeve from the blood. "A lair feeder ..." She recognized it wasn't going to eat her here, in the open. Her eyes closed and she started to fade.

Explosions shocked her awake. The creature screamed in pain, dropping her face first onto the rocks. *Roll, roll!* She urged her body as the dirt erupted in impacts. Something tugged at her leg, and she found herself being dragged face down across the ground to the protection of a boulder.

She could see the beast, staggering under the barrage of fire from above. The creature fell to the ground, its body twitching from the impacts.

Gerita blinked tightly, clearing her eyes of the blood pouring from her head wound as she tried to raise herself up. A hand pressed against her back, gently pushing her back down. It was a man, kneeling next to her, keeping her prone under the boulder. In the shadows, she couldn't make out much of his features except that his hair was long and wrapped with a leather band. He put his finger in front of his lips for silence, then pointed up. She glanced toward the sky, her eyes adjusting to the fading sunlight.

A Drone hovered just above the tree line. Gerita immediately calmed herself, slowing her breathing. It was undoubtedly one from the Dreadnought. It must have followed her down.

Gerita studied the Drone as it turned slowly, scanning the area. It was a strange design, almost like a combination of mechanics and organics. Even from twenty feet away, she recognized the advanced technology meshed with the flesh of the creature. By comparing it to the surrounding branches, she estimated its size at about seven feet in length, three or four feet wide. It had the profile of an insect, with six legs pulled up underneath a segmented body bristling with hair. Large optical bulbs protruded from the front on stalks, pivoting independently as they searched the surroundings underneath. The wings, if you could call them that, were mounted on the dorsal area, quietly generating lift by rotation. This would make sense, she thought, as many insects rotated their wings in a "figure eight" movement, although attempts to replicate such an ability in aircraft had eluded the best engineers.

There was no mistaking the dual cannons just underneath the eye stalks. They moved with deadly purpose, shifting aim from shadow to shadow, searching the brush and rocks for a target.

On the other side of the stream, no more than thirty feet away, were two more men dressed in tan hide, buckskins, with leather strap leggings over moccasins. Their long dark hair was wrapped with leather bands, like the man next to her. *Cherokees,* she thought to herself.

One of them held a bow with a full quiver of arrows slung on his back. He was stocky with broad shoulders and crouched behind a small mound of dirt, unmoving. The other man, tall and muscular, stood upright behind a tree, armed with an atlatl, a spear already locked into its throwing base.

She returned her attention to the Drone. The slow rotation from side to side indicated that it probably relied on movement to detect prey. The Cherokees remained frozen in place; obviously this encounter wasn't new for them.

A flurry of movement in the brush farther up the gully resulted in a barrage of exploding shells from the Drone. The hapless deer was shredded in place, pieces of the animal flying against the rocks. The man with the atlatl suddenly stepped from behind the tree and drew back his arm, preparing to launch the spear. The other man reached to him, grabbing his shoulder, stopping his attack, and shaking his head.

The whir from the Drone's rotating guns faded, replaced once again with the low hum of the wings and the sound of the drifting breeze against the leaves. The pitch of the wings rose slightly as the Drone began to move farther up the ravine until it launched itself skyward and disappeared.

Still, no one moved. Gerita understood and waited; this could just be a feint to draw them out, with more Drones waiting to pounce.

She glanced over to the beast that had attacked her when she landed. It was an Eastern Sasquatch, no doubt about it, the first she had ever seen in person. Stories of their existence had gone from crackpot legend to absolute fact after YE. Unlike the extinction of their hominid cousins, the Western Sasquatch, these had taken advantage of the ecosystem disruption and reclaimed their environmental niches, swelling in numbers and no longer needing to hide. But, as their territory was encompassed by the Cherokees, very few examples were available for study. She so wanted to crawl over to it, to take measurements and blood samples. *It would make a great addition to the UC museum,* she mused.

It was then that she noticed the intense pain in her right arm and that her leg seemed to be numb from the knee down. She heard a low whistle as the Cherokee next to her signaled to the men across the gully. The man with the quiver walked toward them. The other man, with the spear, walked toward the remains of the deer and knelt next to it, touching it, stroking its bloody fur, his eyes closed as if praying.

Gerita attempted to say something. She had learned some of their language, but what came out of her mouth was a bloody cough. The man waited for her to clear her throat then pointed to himself, "Watashi." He pointed to her, then opened his hand in a questioning manner. She understood. "Gerita," she said, then coughed again.

"Move not." Watashi turned his attention to his friend with the quiver. Gerita attempted to listen in, but her understanding of Tslagi, their language, was sparse and her focus was wavering. Watashi gestured toward her. "English," he said.

The other man nodded as the man with the spear joined them. There was a long pause as they looked to her, then back to each other. Gerita could tell there was an unspoken decision being pondered. Whatever it was, her life was at stake. She knew that her wounds were serious and that she would die if she didn't get help soon.

Watashi put his fist out in front of himself. The fist of the bow man joined it. A long moment passed before the other man put his fist into the circle. A decision had been made on her fate.

✶

Her mind fought for the light. Bits and pieces coming through, images of pristine white walls, lights moving overhead, voices speaking some unrecognizable dialect, flashes of a journey her memory only retained in fragments.

Fire seemed to flare within her left arm, from the shoulder to the elbow. The dull throbbing in her chest intensified with every breath she took. Something was wrong with her right leg, but she couldn't move it to determine the extent of the injury there. Her eyelids fluttered and opened.

She was lying on her back, a large device hanging over her. Rectangular in shape with lights along one side that flickered in steady sequence.

She turned her head carefully, inspecting her surroundings. The room was pristine. White walls, white inset panels, a few empty beds with similar devices hanging over them without any discernible attachment to the ceiling. A table seemed to float near the wall, smaller devices protruding from the top, like an array of tools. A panel of flat glass floated near another wall, a medical console of some sort. *Portable anti-grav units?* She thought. The technology was known, but the cost was prohibitive. Even the UC had nothing like this.

A door on the other side of the room opened into a hallway and she could see the movement of people through the translucent door. The smell of alcohol and antiseptic reaffirmed the obvious; she was in some sort of medical facility, but more advanced than any she had ever seen.

"Awake is good." A soft, highly pitched voice made her turn her head.

The woman was next to her bed, examining a panel on one of the floating tables. She was tall, much taller than Gerita, with dark hair, dark eyes, and skin the color of copper. She was Native American, no doubt about it. *She's beautiful,* Gerita thought. "Florence Nightingale," she said out loud in a cracked voice. This made the woman smile, which made her look more attractive. "You're beautiful," she repeated her thoughts out loud unintentionally.

The woman laughed. "Your tongue dances with the medication. It is normal." She returned her attention to the panel on the tabletop. "But, Nightingale," she seemed to consider it. "Yes, I rather like that. Use it, please."

"What happened?" Gerita felt the back of her throat rasp with breath as she tried to wrest control from the fuzziness in her brain.

"Darkness attack your airship," she replied. "Sasqua attack you on land. The Great Protector said no to your death, so you here with me; Nightingale." She shook her head lightly, enjoying her new name. "And you? I call you what?"

"Gerita. Gerita Alta," she replied. "How long have I been out?"

"Two, three day," the woman responded offhandedly, then paused, thinking. "Definitely three day."

Gerita felt a shock of adrenalin go through her. *Two days on the* Erickson *plus three days lost here,* she calculated. Assuming at least one day for extraction, she saw her two-week mission reduced to a mere eight days. Eight days before the Ghost Fleet flew into the region, blind and ignorant of what might await them.

"You speak English?" Gerita said, her mind still trying to find stability. "I can speak Tslagi if you want."

The woman laughed again. A lilting, almost melodic sound. "No, Gerita, you cannot," she said. "You tried. It was very funny."

"What did I say?" Gerita smiled despite herself. She had rushed the language course out of necessity.

"It matter not," Nightingale responded. "We speak English. Long ago, all my people knew your language. It has not been spoken for many passings, but easier we speak your language than you try ours again." She paused to put on a glove. "And, no, we do not have rabbit hats, to answer your question earlier."

Gerita had no recollection of being conscious since crashing in the woods and encountering the Cherokee, nor of inquiring about a hat. *What was his name again?* she pondered.

"Pain here? To here?" Nightingale traced her finger along a path from Gerita's elbow to shoulder. Gerita nodded. The woman pulled a pen-like instrument from the floating table and pressed the point into Gerita's elbow. A sharp pain pierced her bone like a nail. Nightingale lifted the instrument and a small arc of energy, like a sustained static charge, leapt from the elbow to its point. It followed the instrument as the woman traced a path to Gerita's shoulder, planting the instrument firmly into the socket area, the electric arc settling into her skin and fading.

The pain suddenly dissolved into numbness and disappeared.

"What was that?" Gerita reacted in surprise.

"Rerouted your neural circuit to bypass damaged area," the woman answered casually. "Still need to heal, though, so no." She wagged her finger at Gerita, indicating she was to keep the arm immobile.

"Has she her wits yet?" came a comment from the doorway. It was the Cherokee who rescued her, the one whose name she couldn't remember.

"Where am I?" Gerita asked.

"You are in our care," he answered. He was no longer in the buckskin he wore in the forest, though the attire he wore now had a similar style. He also seemed taller, his features sharper, his dark hair pulled back into a knot. He spoke to Nightingale in Tslagi, something about Gerita's health.

"I'm feeling fine, thank you," Gerita said loudly. She wanted them to know that she could, at least, understand some of it. More out of pride than expediency.

"Not completely fine, but she will be," Nightingale said to the man. "Needs more rest, but very strong, this one." She then returned to the medical console.

"Watashi!" Gerita exclaimed. "I remember your name. I am Gerita."

He smiled and nodded. "Yes, you told us. When you asked for the rabbit hat."

"I ... don't know what that was about," she replied. "Is this a hospital?"

"It is," Watashi replied. "You are in the Cherokee nation. But I assume you knew that."

"My ship was attacked," she replied. "I barely escaped. I didn't know where I was going. I didn't mean to land here, it wasn't my fault." In fact, the attack had done her a favor. Since the story was true, she didn't need to create a false one for being in their territory.

"Yes, we understand," he replied, touching her arm as if to reassure her. "Our people saw your ship come down. We are sorry for the loss of your friends."

"Thank you," she said, then leveled a stare at him. "Unless it was one of your ships that attacked us."

Her comment was blunt, deliberate, and calculated to get a response.

Watashi suddenly stiffened as Nightingale gave him a look. "It was not us," Watashi said without emotion. "We talk later." He turned and walked from the room.

If it wasn't their ship, they certainly know something about it, she thought to herself.

"You sleep now, Gerita Alta" Nightingale said.

Gerita started. "I don't want to—"

Nightingale pressed her finger on the panel, the device over Gerita's head sprayed down a mist and blackness found her again.

✶

The food they fed her wasn't completely without taste. She imagined it was something designed to help her recover, not necessarily to please her appetite. The attendants, all Cherokees of course, were pleasant, but refused to answer any of her questions. She had lost yet another day and still hadn't had a chance to begin her investigation. Still, she had to have patience and wait it out. Everything depended on her playing her cover perfectly.

Nightingale had come to get her, helping her into a floating chair and pushing her through a busy hallway. People moved about with purpose; all Native American but from many different tribes. As they moved along, she noted everything and committed it to memory, especially doors that seemed to have extra security and locks. Most of the doors were open and she peered into them as they went past. Offices, rooms with pristine equipment, manned by men and women who worked with efficient purpose. The idea that the Cherokees were mostly 'subhuman savages' as the Grand Admiral had described them was the result of old prejudices, ignorance, and, Gerita had to admit, deliberate propaganda manipulation. Even then, no one would have expected what she was seeing now. This facility was as advanced as any at UC. More so, in her opinion.

Their destination was a classroom of sorts. Chairs lined one side facing a podium which was placed in front of a ceiling-to-floor curtain extending the entire length of the wall. The decorations in the room were representations of the ancient weapons of the Native Americans, many mounted in frames, others hanging from hooks. She recognized the atlatl throwing spear, similar to the one the Cherokee in the forest had wielded. Next to that, several tomahawks and knives.

"You still use these?" Gerita gestured toward the weapons. "The men that rescued me had some of them."

"Mostly ceremonial, from many tribes," she responded as she pushed Gerita's chair to the front of the room. "Using them on a hunt is a way to honor our ancestors and respect the animal's spirit."

"Wouldn't guns be more efficient?" Gerita asked.

Nightingale smiled and shook her head slightly, as one might do with a well-meaning child who just doesn't understand. "Yes, they would be," she said. "If killing was the reward." She pressed a button on the wall and Gerita heard the curtain behind her start to open.

"You wait here, Gerita Alta," Nightingale said and left the room, shutting the door behind her.

If killing was the reward, Gerita pondered, staring at the closed door. Even as an assassin, her targets had always been those who harmed others or whose work threatened the future of the world. *Restoring our world, protecting our environment is reason enough,* she thought, taking a deep breath. *Yes, there has always been a higher reason. Otherwise it would just be … murder.*

She heard the click as the curtain stopped moving, revealing a panorama window. Gerita's eyes widened, her mouth dropped open. There, through the window, she saw a vast lake nestled between two mountains; a valley at one time, now filled with deep, blue water that extended into the distance, surrounded by a lush forest.

Her mind began to process the information, trying to explain it. *The Ridge Tsunami,* she thought. *The water had moved farther inland than anyone suspected, probably coursing through the many canyons along the Appalachian foothills.* What she was looking at was so unlikely, and yet there it was. *A simple collapse of canyon walls farther up would have trapped the water and created the lake!* It was the only theory that she could conceive of; the only one that made sense.

That it existed at all was amazing enough, but what had her leaning forward in her seat were the shores of the lake. Like the view that greeted her when she plunged out of the clouds, it was green and full. Pine trees, maples, oaks, and a few strange mutations lined the shoreline. The brush underneath them was pure and pristine. Brief movement amongst the leaves told her that wildlife thrived here.

She wasn't aware of the smile on her face, so taken as she was by the view. Certainly, in her role as an environmentalist, the UC Tower had sent her to areas where life was returning. This, however, was something from an era before YE. It existed only in the history books and papers of long dead naturalists.

A bird flew low across the water, skimming the small wind ripples, searching for fish. Gerita pounded her fist onto her knee in excitement. *A golden eagle!* They were thought to be extinct, but there it was. Her eyes followed it to the center of the lake and as it flew past the platform city above the surface of the water.

To call it a Tower would be an overstatement; probably no more than a few hundred people could live there. It floated about fifty feet above the water and the central building was only three stories tall.

Though it seemed to be there for a specific purpose, it looked totally at one with the lake, a perfect union of technology and nature.

"You wait long, I apologize," she heard from behind her. She turned as Watashi entered the room carrying an electronic pad.

"No," she responded, her eyes drifting back to the view. "It's so … beautiful. I've traveled all over and never seen anything like this."

"The work of the Great Protector," he said. "We are blessed to be in service to Her."

"Great Protector?" she asked. Nightingale had mentioned this as well. Watashi gestured toward the lake. "God, Gaia, Spirit, the Great Protector of all," he said. "In you, in me, in everything, the Great Protector is one."

A deity or combination of deities, Gerita noted to herself. If not the savages she had been led to believe, they were still superstitious people. That might be useful information to the Admiral.

"Wait," she started as a thought occurred to her. "In service? You don't mean to say that you're responsible for terraforming all this?"

"Merely tools in great hands," he said, walking toward the window and looking out. "The Great Spirit created the lake but the rest, yes, the work of many generations. My ancestors, the Warriors of the Rainbow, fulfilling their duty."

She leaned forward, peering at him. "Warriors of the Rainbow?"

Watashi smiled. "'*When the Earth is sick, the animals will begin to disappear. When that happens, the Warriors of the Rainbow come to save them,*'" he recited, then looked back to her. "The words of the mighty Chief Si'ahl, who lived many, many passings ago."

"Wow," was all she could respond with. She was determined to research this Si'ahl and this concept of "Warriors of the Rainbow" when she returned to UC Tower.

"How do you feel?" he gestured toward her leg.

Gerita stretched it out, flexing it and wincing in pain. "It's hard to walk or move much." Though she still had some residual pain along the side of her leg and her elbow, she was much better than she let on. Having them believe she was debilitated by her injuries could be useful later. "I can't thank you enough for saving my life."

"To be fair, it was for selfish reasons," he said. "We plan to eat you later."

Gerita reacted, her eyes opening wide. "What?"

Watashi returned her stare, then burst into laughter. "No, no, little one," he gasped. "Of course not. We are not cannibals. Truth, most of us are vegetarians. You have no reason to fear."

She smiled despite herself. This man was intriguing. His people were fascinating. A war with them would be pointless. And, based on the advanced technology, possibly dangerous. She still had a mission to complete but the Admiral needed to know the truth, the Admiral needed to know he was wrong about them.

"So, it is time for questions, time for answers," he sat down in the chair opposite her. "This place is called Tova. It is under the ground, in the mountain of the ancient land of the Appalachee. You call it Appalachians. When the United States ruled here, many tunnels and complexes were built. All underground, to protect from a war that never happened. As the Event approached, much of this was abandoned as your people took to the sky. My people, the people of the land, we took it back."

"But the Cherokee Towers?" she asked.

"Yes, we have Towers. Three large cities and many more villages like this you see here." He gestured to the small floating community in the center of the lake. "We were one with the Earth long before your people arrived. We have come home." He leaned forward and peered at her. "Now, you tell me, who you are. Why you are here."

The interrogation has begun, she thought. *Don't get complacent with his demeanor, this man is smart,* she reminded herself.

"My name is Gerita Alta, I'm an environmentalist working out of the UC Tower." She paused, then said "I don't mean to be insulting, but do you know what the UC Tower is?"

"No insult, little one," he returned. "A western Tower dedicated to preserve western knowledge and to educate. Close?"

"Basically," she nodded. "I'm one of the leading naturalists in the Division of Environmental Research. My original assignment was to stay west of your nation and ... well ... to map the southern border with The Dark Zone."

He looked at her and frowned. "The Dark Zone," he said.

"There have been reports in the North of new mutations appearing," Gerita explained. "We wanted to know if that was regional or if there were new forms in the South as well."

There was a long pause as Gerita awaited a response. She cleared her throat. "I can give you a high-level access code to communicate directly with the UC Administrator to verify my identity. We would love to establish scientific and cultural exchanges with—"

Watashi waved his hand, dismissing her thought before she expressed it.

"I guess you'll just have to take my word for it," she said, then laughed. "It's not like I'm a spy or anything."

Watashi glanced at the pad in his hand, reading from it. "Gerita Alta. Twenty-eight, orphaned at three years old when abandoned at Community Center of Salt Lake Tower. Parents deceased. Admitted to UC Tower after passing full testing in top two percentile at age of nine. Only student to earn all three UC Letters of Achievement. Degrees in Advanced Genetic Mutation, Reactional Environment Responses, Symbiotic Relationships of Closed Systems, Ecological Collapse and Recovery, and many more." He looked up from the pad. "You are very impressive, little one."

Gerita was taken back. Not just because of his general knowledge of her, that was something that he could have come by easily. It was the knowledge of her percentile ratings, a seemingly small thing, that caught her attention. Those were classified, kept in a secure server at UC. The Administrator felt such things created an atmosphere of elitism. Gerita only knew them because of her intense curiosity and her other ability as a spy. *The Cherokees have spies as well,* she realized. *Even at the UC. Of course, it would make perfect sense.*

But there was something else, something more personal. "You said my parents were deceased. I was abandoned, even I don't know who they were. How could you know what happened to them?"

"We decoded your blood genome and compared it to our database." He frowned. "I understood DNA coding is done at UC Tower."

Genome coding was, indeed, done at UC using the most advance computers with the most accomplished experts. The UC Tower manufactured medical equipment which it exported to all the Towers. At the same time, they had been using the equipment to create a genetic database by sampling the populations, to track the mutations post-YE.

But, again, this was all a carefully guarded secret. No one except the highest echelons of the Tower Leadership knew about it. Or so she had thought.

"Who were they?" It would affect nothing, she had buried any feelings of abandonment years ago, but she didn't like unanswered questions in her life.

Watashi paused as if considering whether to answer or not. Finally, he cleared his throat and returned to the information on the pad. "Your parents, Olga Simkopf and Alexander Cole," he finally responded. "Missionaries of the Tower Salt Lake."

In that one instant, the mystery of Gerita's past was laid out before her. The Mormon Church had built the Citadel Tower at Salt Lake and continued the practice of missionary outreach. Her parents would have been a part of that, traveling to remote areas to spread their gospel. The Church had also begun the practice of communal upbringing, keeping children in the Tower instead of risking them outside. Her parents had left her there to fulfill their obligation to the Church.

"How did they die?" The words slipped from her lips before she could stop them. *It's a reasonable question,* she argued with herself. *To not ask it would be suspicious.*

"Cedar Creek," was all he said. Gerita sat back in shock. The Massacre of Cedar Creek Tower was well known, a small trading post Tower in the northern reaches of the Appalachian Mountains that was completely wiped out. By the very people who were now caring for her. Her eyes darkened.

"I'm sure the books of your history tell of the battle differently," he said.

"There was no battle," she said, controlling herself. "You wiped out a neutral trading Tower."

"You know of the Ghost Fleet?" he replied evenly. "The Tower was theirs, not neutral."

"You massacred an entire community," she shot back. "No less than that one on your lake!"

"That is not what happened," Watashi's voice became firm with restrained emotion. "We sent envoys to tell them they must go. They sent airships so we sent ours. We think they will attack us, but no.

They do not attack us, they attack their own Tower. We did not understand, we watched the Tower crash with all those people. Then we realized; the Tower, it was the weapon. It spilled poisons into the waters, fire fell around the trees to burn for years. To destroy our land, our crops, our animals, to force us to bend to them."

He stood up and walked the room, angrily speaking in his own tongue, then suddenly turned back to her. "Those people, your parents, the Great Protector cried for them. Today, we do not build there, we do not farm or hunt there. The trees still cry for their loss; the animals will not walk on the graves of innocents."

She couldn't believe the Ghost Fleet would attack a peaceful outpost, especially one of their own. But there was something compelling about Watashi's recounting of the event. Gerita fought to contain her own emotions; to stay focused on her mission.

"There is a lot about each of us that the other doesn't know." She chose her words carefully. "Ignorance and misunderstandings can be tragic. On both sides."

He nodded, staring at the floor. Finally, he took a deep breath and sat down again.

"The Darkness," he said, changing the subject, much to Gerita's relief. "You wish to know about it."

"Yes," she replied. "What is it? Ships have been sent to investigate it, but none have returned. It's thought that there might be something in the actual atmosphere that is responsible. Some think it's poisonous, but my observations disagree with that." She was deliberately being vague to draw him out, to find out if the Cherokee were complicit in The Dark Zone as the Admiral believed. "I think it might be some sort of lingering abrasive in the air," she continued. "Perhaps volcanic residue from YE?"

"No," Watashi said. "The Darkness is not a weather pattern. Or leftover debris. The Darkness is alive. It lives and creates."

"Alive?" she asked. "Creates what?"

"The airship that destroyed your vessel, the death bird that attacked you," he replied. "The Darkness thinks, it plans. It has forced mutations, horrible and obscene combinations of metal and animals, as an army against us."

"You mean, like, bionics?" Gerita responded.

Watashi shook his head. "Evolved from organic and metal. Carbon life and metal. From their own DNA."

"That's impossible," she blurted out. "You're saying that Drone that attacked me, that damn airship that destroyed my vessel, those were ... living creatures?" She shook her head; the thought was too incredulous.

"We have studied this, little one. You have not."

"I've studied mutations, I've catalogued them. I've tracked the changes and done predictive modeling!" Gerita allowed herself a bit of defensive pride. "We've seen no evidence of anything like this."

"No, you wouldn't." He shook his head sadly. "You Westerners spend so much time trying to rebuild your house that you ignore the wolf at the door."

"But why did it attack my ship?" she was at a loss. "Why did it kill my friends?"

"It is evil. It exists to kill us all," he replied.

They were interrupted by Nightingale at the door. "It is time for rest, now. No more talk."

Watashi nodded, stretched his back, and took a deep breath. "Enough for now, little one. We begin your lessons tomorrow." He stood.

"Lessons?" she asked. "I need to get back to UC. I must tell them about this!" This was both Gerita and Koala speaking now, with one voice. If this Darkness was what Watashi said, then it was, in fact, the wolf at the door. "You obviously have advance knowledge of it, we could work together."

"No," he said firmly. "Your people, they hate, they argue, they kill each other. You forget, we have history with them. My people fight The Darkness because the Great Protector demands it. Our duty as Warriors of the Rainbow."

He stood and walked toward the door, pausing to turn back to her. "Your knowledge, your love of the Great Protector's work, it has value here," he said. "Perhaps the day will come, you will not want to leave."

And he was gone.

✶

Gerita had been lying in the darkness for hours, her mind trying to digest and process the knowledge she had acquired the previous day.

The Grand Admiral needed to know exactly what was going on here. If he were to order his fleet into the Cherokee territory, there would be no telling what the result would be. Or, worse, like Cedar Creek, a tragedy because of a misunderstanding.

This idea that The Dark Zone was, somehow, a sentient creature that was bioengineering life forms was just too incredible to believe. Could it be true? Why would they lie?

And the other work they were doing, the beauty that she had seen, the restoration of the environment; that had captivated her. They were already terraforming while the rest of the world was still competing for the remaining resources. What techniques were they using? How had they redeemed the topsoil? How complete was the fauna restoration? She had so many questions.

First things first, she reminded herself. By her calculations, she was very near the source of the radiation signature, and she had a pretty good idea of where to look. "Let's see what we're up against," Gerita mumbled to herself.

The hallway outside her room was empty with the exception of a bright light at one end. She could hear voices from the nurse's station around the corner. Stepping carefully, Gerita moved in the other direction, toward a pair of double doors which led to a wider corridor.

The door she was looking for was all the way at the end. It had signage next to it that warned "RADIOACTIVE" in Tslagi, one of the Cherokee words Gerita had made sure she memorized before she left. Beneath that sign were a pair of boxes, set into the wall. One was a locked box, made of heavy metal, with a slit in the top. For disposal of something, she assumed. The other box had a hinged lid on the top that appeared to be unlocked.

Crossing to it, she opened the lid and looked inside. Her breath caught as she reached in and took out a small badge with a pin on the back. There was no mistaking its purpose, it was a safety device to measure the amount of radiation the wearer received. She knew she had found what she was looking for.

She dropped the badge back into the box and turned her attention to the heavy metal door. The electronic lock near the handle had a large flat screen keypad with Tslagi numerals. There were ten of them placed in a block enabling her to assign a standard number layout to the keys. Carefully exhaling on the pad revealed the dull areas, where fingers had repeatedly pressed. Three, six, eight and nine were the parts of the code. She didn't know the sequence or the numbers that repeated. Worse, if this keypad had a limited number of failed attempts, it would alert their security.

Gerita figured she still had some time before her absence would be noticed, so she quickly ran across the hall to another doorway and slipped inside. She left the door open a crack and waited.

It didn't take long before she heard footsteps approaching. She watched as a man walked up to the box and removed a badge. He affixed it to his shirt and turned to the lock. Gerita watched intently as he keyed in the code. *Three, three, six, eight, three, nine, six,* she repeated to herself. The door clicked open, and the man entered, pulling the door behind him, the lock engaging again.

She waited for several minutes in case the man exited again. Satisfied that enough time had passed, she moved to the door and quickly entered in the code. The door clicked open, and she slipped inside.

There were two more doors in the small room, across from each other. One had no lock, the other had a large handle on the side which operated a series of security bolts around the perimeter of the frame. She approached the door with the handle and pressed her ear against it. Closing her eyes to concentrate, she thought she heard the vague rustling sounds of air or wind. It took a bit of effort to pull the handle, but the bolts disengaged, and she opened the door. An orange ray of early dawn sunlight pierced the darkness from the outside. *Probably an emergency exit,* she thought. *Now I know how I'm getting out of here.* She shut that door and moved to the other one. There was a dull humming vibration and the sound of distant movement. Gently, she pushed it open and slipped through.

The door led to a long walking bridge, suspended from the ceiling, connected to the rocky face on the other side of a large cavern, perhaps twenty feet across. The lighting here was artificial, casting harsh shadows across the walls. She stayed within the cover of the surrounding rock and peered over the railing of the walkway.

Her legs almost buckled from what was laid out below her. A vast cave, most of it naturally formed, hundreds of feet across and receding into the distance. The entire space below was well lit where men and women worked, attending a huge cylindrical object three or four stories high and running the length of the cavern. Huge sections of it had been removed to accommodate access for equipment. She recognized the object, even though they didn't exist anymore. She had seen pictures of its kind in history books; history books about war.

It was a nuclear submarine.

Her mind reeled. *The Atlantic Tsunami!* It must have been washed ashore and been buried in the same collapsed mountainside that created the lake.

This had to be the source of the radioactive emissions. From the stacks of transformers and equipment cabled into the submarine, it was obvious the reactors were working, and the Cherokees were using it to power the entire facility.

A nuclear submarine. With a nuclear reactor. Gerita took a deep breath. *And, most likely, nuclear weapons,* she realized. *Have they made those functional as well?* There was no time to waste, she had to escape now and get this information back to the Admiral.

A dull rumble shook the room. She paused, waiting. Another rumble, this one louder. Dust and dirt fell from the above. The room shook again, the walls thudded with the sounds of repeated impacts, getting louder. It was unmistakable and she recognized it immediately as artillery explosions. The Cherokees were under attack.

Sirens went off as she moved quickly back through the door to the emergency exit. *I can use this distraction to cover my escape,* she thought as she pulled on the handle and bright sunlight filled the room. The way out was clear, but she paused. The vision of the Dreadnought that attacked the *Erickson* formed in her mind. Could this be The Darkness? She had to report to the Admiral, but was this her chance to learn more about this creature, this wolf at the door?

The hallway was filled with people, running back and forth as the sirens urged them onward, so preoccupied with their calls to station that no one noticed her as she merged with the crowd. From the sounds of the impacts, they were being attacked on the eastern side, the area with the lake.

She headed for the classroom and pushed through the door. The room was empty, but the window encompassed the entire panorama.

Four airships, moving high above the lake, their cannons pummeling the area. Water splashed up from explosions. The small Tower in the lake was firing back but taking a hellish beating. From hidden bastions along the mountainside, the Cherokees fired their main batteries at the attacking vessels, the tracer rounds arcing in trails of light to explode upon contact.

"The Dreadnoughts!" she whispered hoarsely. They were all identical to the ship that attacked the *Erickson*. They moved in coordination, like a pack, calculated and with deadly intent. She saw it now; they didn't move as machines under command, they moved like *predators*. They were alive!

Suddenly Drones separated from the center Dreadnought and dove straight down toward the Tower, cannons blazing. Gatling gun defensive weapons, known as Vulcan Defense Systems in the old books, lit up from around the Tower's perimeter and rapidly poured fire into the Drones. As many of them as they picked off, more dropped down to join the attack.

One of the Dreadnoughts suddenly dropped from the sky, seemingly crippled. "Yes!" Gerita screamed in delight. But just before impact, it leveled out, releasing several Drones at once which created trails of mist in their wake as they headed directly toward the Tower. Caught by surprise, the Cherokees attempted to redirect their fire onto the new threat. One by one, the Vulcans targeted them, dropping many into the lake. But many more made their way to the target, some impacting on the structure itself, exploding in massive balls of flame.

Gerita recoiled reflexively as a shell burst against the window, leaving a dark mark across it. "You're safe here," a voice said. "The glass is carbon H3." She turned and found Watashi standing behind her. He glanced at her, his jaw clenched, breathing deeply, then turned his gaze back to the battle outside.

The firepower of the base seemed to be taking its toll and Gerita could tell that the invaders weren't going to win; they couldn't win. It was a hopeless attempt; the facility was too well defended.

Then she saw it, she saw the strategy. *They aren't trying to win the battle!* While the Drones attacked individually, pulling most of the return fire, the Dreadnoughts had been pummeling the forest surrounding the lake. It was an inferno! The trees were ablaze, ignited by multiple impacts of incendiary shells, the entire shoreline engulfed in a growing firestorm. *They weren't going after the town … it's the forest,* she realized in horror.

Small animals tumbled into the lake, their fur burning brightly. Deer ran back and forth in fear, not certain where to go, only to be engulfed by the flames. Gerita saw a fawn looking toward her; she imagined that it could see her, its eyes pleading for help, then lost in a flare of incineration.

Her heart filled with anger and pain. It wasn't just an attack on people, this was an extermination of the living; deliberately destroying the ecosystem, the very basis of life.

Suddenly, as if of one mind, the Dreadnoughts rose directly up into the air, the Drones following them. They were retreating, their damage done. One by one, the mighty guns of the Cherokee ceased fire. The attack was over.

The floating Tower was smoking, its axis tilted and slowly submerging into the lake. She watched the people jumping into the water, now covered with a sheen of fire.

The trees along the lake continued to burn. The animals continued to scream, even if she couldn't hear them within the silence of the room.

Silent, that is, except for soft sobbing. She looked toward the tall Cherokee near the window. His back was to her as he stared across the water and watched the carnage. His shoulders shook.

Watashi was crying.

✶

The Cherokees were too busy with the aftermath of the attack to pay much attention to her as she made her way out of the emergency exit and headed down to the river. At one point, she thought she could see figures in the distance, along a ridge. Too far away to capture her, but close enough to show they had finally realized her escape.

When she had presented her credentials to the Captain of the *USS Whipple*, he had immediately assigned guards to her, and they had escorted her to a private room on the destroyer. No one was to talk to her or interact with her in any way except to deliver her to Groom Lake. She had no doubt that the guards were authorized to use lethal force on anyone who attempted otherwise. And, probably, on her as well.

Back in the Tribunal Council Hall, Gerita looked out over the Groom Lake Tower berths again, this time empty except for a few logistical transports. It was almost completely quiet and still. The Admiral's fleet was already assembled, somewhere, awaiting his command.

Again, she had been stripped of all her gear and was wearing the plain jumpsuit. Commander Moseli stood nearby with the two armed guards who had accompanied her from the moment of her extraction.

As before, the Tribunal was missing from the great hall, as were the Wolves. She began to nurse a suspicion that, perhaps, this plan of the Admiral's was a secret to more people than she thought.

"The woman has returned." The Grand Admiral's voice boomed as the lock on his office doors glowed again.

"I have," Gerita responded. "I am here to report my findings."

"And yet, I have received no report." The Grand Admiral seemed to be annoyed. "Commander Moseli?"

Moseli cleared his throat, stepping forward. "Agent Koala refused to log one." He shot her a firm look. "Against my urgings, I will add."

"I don't intend to withhold any information, Grand Admiral," Gerita responded. "You made it very clear that the mission you were sending me on was one of crucial importance. Something that could determine the future of Mankind. And you were correct. The things that I have seen, the information I have, it is just as important as you expected. And more."

She stood and walked directly to the doors, addressing the glowing lock. "Does the Grand Admiral think that I would dare commit the destiny of the world to a report? One that would have to pass through others before reaching His Excellency? No, sir. Not in a report, not to a glowing lock. You and you only, as you ordered. 'No exceptions.' Your words, sir."

Again, silence fell over the room. For the first time, Gerita considered the possibility that she might have overstepped herself. She knew he wanted the knowledge she had in her head, but she also knew Moseli had other ways to get to it. Methods that would leave her no more than a vegetable.

The doors in front of her shook then began to separate revealing a long hallway with lights running along its length. Gerita glanced to Moseli. He took a deep breath, then nodded toward the passageway.

Gerita entered the corridor as the doors behind her rumbled and shut. Another door opened at the other end of the hallway. She took a deep breath then continued walking forward.

The Admiral's office was sparse, just a few pieces of furniture. A large desk in the middle with chairs on either side. Behind that, a small crease in the continuous wall was the only suggestion of a second door, probably to the Grand Admiral's private quarters. An indentation midway down the crease indicated a biometric DNA lock.

The Grand Admiral himself stood behind the desk, leaning forward on it, smiling. He was taller than she expected, and much more youthful. His bright blue eyes seemed to twinkle. His uniform, if you could call it that, was similar to the jumpsuit she wore. The only real difference being a pair of metal bars on the shoulder indicating Admiralty.

"Koala," he said, as if greeting an old friend. "Enter. Sit down."

Gerita walked carefully toward the single chair in front of the desk.

The Grand Admiral chuckled. "It's not booby trapped, there's nothing to fear here. Do you think I would allow any weapon in this room with me? Especially with someone of your capabilities?"

The desk was, like the room, purely functional, though she didn't see any indication of drawers. Three buttons were to one side and a small bulge in the center of the desk glowed yellow as she settled into the chair. She recognized it, she expected it. It was a polygraph, a lie detector. Like the machines of old, it wasn't one hundred percent accurate, but enough to be useful to someone who knew how to read people. The Grand Admiral was just such a man.

"Do you think I'm going to kill you?" he asked.

The question didn't surprise Gerita. "Yes," she replied, "I think that's a good possibility." She glanced at the polygraph; it turned blue. She had no reason to lie and no intention to do so.

He laughed as he sat in his chair and leaned forward on the desk. "What you discovered must be incredibly important."

"It is," she replied. She began to understand part of the power the Grand Admiral had over people. His demeanor was casual, almost welcoming, somewhat seductive. But her training allowed her to look beyond the façade. This man commanded absolute power over life and death, and he knew it.

"So important, so earth shattering, that the destiny of our world hinges on it?" he went on, glancing down at the polygraph. It remained a steady blue.

"Perhaps," she nodded. Her throat was dry.

"And you think that once you tell me, I'd be a fool to let you leave this Tower and risk telling someone else, correct?"

Gerita said nothing.

"I'm not going to say it isn't a possibility. I assumed one of the reasons you wanted to talk directly to me was to plead for your life."

"One of the reasons?" she tilted her head in curiosity.

"Well, your devotion to duty is another reason. Or your intent to extort money or position, those are legitimate reasons as well." He leaned back in his seat. "Do I need more? With your life in my hands, do I need anything? Commander Moseli can get the information I want out of you and leave you a vegetable in the process."

She lowered her head in submission, leaning forward, bowing in her chair. "I live to serve. That's my reason."

"Good. Very good. So, tell me what you've learned from your time with the savages."

"They are much more advanced than we suspected," she told him. "Our assumptions are all wrong. I didn't manage to inspect all their weaponry, but what I did see was formidable…"

"The radioactivity," he interrupted her. "Did you discover the source of that? Do they have it?"

"Yes," she responded. "They have recovered a nuclear submarine and have managed to repair the reactors. It powers their main facility."

For the first time, she saw a flicker of surprise in his eyes. He glanced back to the orb to verify what he had just heard. The blue glow was unwavering.

"A nuclear submarine." The Admiral frowned, leaning back in his chair. "I would not have suspected that. Missiles? Are those functioning?"

"I don't know," she responded. "Doubtful. It looked as if they only had it rigged for power output."

"This changes the schedule," he said. "We have to move fast, before they can activate those weapons."

"It will be difficult to surprise them, sir," she responded, "They have early warning systems and fairly sophisticated defenses in place." She paused, then continued. "They haven't forgotten Cedar Creek."

"They shouldn't," he laughed dryly. "We taught them a lesson there."

"What lesson was that, sir?" Gerita asked, deliberately leading him. "The history books tell it as a massacre of the trading Tower. The Ghost Fleet drove the Cherokees off, but we had already lost hundreds of colonists."

"Yes," he smiled. "The history books do tell that version. But I can assure you, the savages know the victory was ours."

Gerita nodded her head. The Admiral had confirmed Watashi's account without even knowing it.

"This next victory will be even more convincing," he continued. "I don't care how good their defenses are, we're going after that nuclear sub, we're going to take it out first."

"The radioactive fallout would poison the entire area, for hundreds of miles," Gerita said.

"Even better." The Admiral stood, leaning on his desk, staring down at her. "These people live off the land, they trace their entire heritage to dirt. If we destroy that, we destroy them."

"I understand," she replied meekly.

"Once we take out that reactor, the fleet moves north and takes out their Towers, one by one." The Admiral clapped his hands together in satisfaction. "The entire mountain range is ours. And, with that, control of the Atlantic trading routes!"

"And The Dark Zone?" she asked. "What about that?"

"We'll worry about that once the Cherokees are gone," he replied and walked around the desk, leaning over to touch her on her head. Fatherly, gently, he brushed her hair. "You've done well, Koala. Your mission is complete."

Gerita looked up at him, putting her hand gently on his. "Not yet," she said softly.

Her eyes turned steely as she launched herself to her feet, slamming an elbow into his jaw, her other hand sliding up his arm and ripping the metal bars off his shoulder in one motion.

With a graceful pirouette, she spun her arm around, her hand slicing across his neck.

Blood sprayed from the Grand Admiral's wound. Gerita stepped back, the Admiral's bars still in her hand, dripping red.

He fell to his knees, reaching out across the spreading pool of crimson on the desk, slapping at the buttons. His eyes were wide, staring at her in complete incomprehension. His mouth moved, bubbling, soundless except for a pulsating gurgle. "Why"?

"Because life goes on, it must go on," she said. "And there is no difference between you and The Darkness."

The last glimmer in his eyes was one of confusion. The Grand Admiral, the greatest mind the battlefield had ever known, the bringer of order and the one to lead the world from anarchy, trembled once more, then fell to the floor, dead.

Gerita's breath slowed. She swallowed, cleared her throat.

"Well, this isn't very timely." The voice came from behind her. Gerita spun around, still holding the metal Admiral's bars as a weapon.

Commander Moseli and the two guards stood near the open hallway door. The soldiers had their weapons trained on her, there was no way she could disarm them at this distance. Moseli walked to the lifeless body of the Grand Admiral, kneeling to inspect him.

"Sir?" One of the guards spoke. "Shall I get a doctor?"

"No need. She was very efficient."

"My God," the other guard muttered under his breath. "We screened her!"

Moseli walked toward her, holding out his hand. Gerita placed the Admiral's bars in it. He examined it and grunted. "A good agent will always find the tools she needs when she needs them."

"You trained me well," she replied.

"I did," he responded. "But how were you going to escape?"

Gerita didn't respond.

Moseli nodded. "A suicide mission," he stated flatly. "Why? What did you see out there?"

Gerita dropped slowly, sitting on the floor with her head down, the last bit of energy leaving her body. She had accomplished her mission. She had given them all some time; a chance to fight back against The Darkness; a chance for the Cherokees to protect their land and continue their work.

She closed her eyes and breathed in, trying to remember the feel of the Appalachian air, seeing the verdant hills of green and the wildlife in her mind for one last time.

Moseli took the gun from one of the soldiers and walked back toward her. "No one can know what happened here. No one."

Moseli turned the gun toward the guards and pulled the trigger, hitting the guard who still had his weapon. He doubled over from the impact, his broken body slamming to the floor, his gun sliding toward the desk. The unarmed guard turned to run down the hall, but a second shot slammed into his back, splitting him in two.

Satisfied, the Commander turned his attention back to Gerita.

Her heart froze. Was Moseli going to allow the attacks to go forward? She had expected he would convene the Council immediately, to recall the fleet and reconsider. Did he think he could take the Grand Admiral's place? *Why hadn't I considered that?* She cursed herself.

"Commander, don't," Gerita implored. "You can't launch these attacks. You don't understand what's happening out there with The Darkness. What the Cherokees have done, for all of us!"

Moseli shook his head, then turned back toward the Grand Admiral's body.

Gerita took her chance. She dove for the remaining gun on the floor. Grabbing it, she rolled to her feet and leveled it at the Commander. His back was to her, seemingly ignoring the threat. He had dragged the Admiral across the room to the hidden door.

She paused, not certain what to do; not certain what he was doing.

Moseli lifted the Grand Admiral's hand and pressed it against the small DNA lock in the wall, opening the hidden door.

"There is another keylock on the other side of his bedroom," he said, dropping the Admiral's hand and kicking the body. "The code is 6-6-7-8-3-2; enter it. His personal aircraft is at the end of the tunnel. It's unmarked, no one will know it's his. Go."

Gerita's mind was in overload. If he wanted to take the place of the Admiral, why would he let her leave?

The Commander seemed to read her confusion. "You have no place here," he said. "Return to your new friends and serve the Great Protector."

The impact of the realization hit her full in the chest. *He's one of them!*

"The Warriors of the Rainbow. It is up to us to save them all," he continued as he pushed her through the door. "Go!" he repeated and shut the door behind her.

In a daze, Gerita found herself running past the late Grand Admiral's luxurious bedroom, into the tunnel beyond, and toward the safety of escape.

She felt fear, but not the fear of capture or death. It was the fear of confusion, the fear felt when all the things you've taken for granted have been ripped away. When the very foundation of your life shifts, realigns, and you suddenly realize that you've been traveling the right path, but heading in the wrong direction. The absolute terrifying fear one feels when they discover who they really are.

Tears ran down her cheeks. The fear dissolved into joy as she recalled the words of the wise Chief Si'ahl and recognized her real purpose.

When the Earth is sick, the animals will begin to disappear. When that happens, the Warriors of the Rainbow will come to save them.

ACKNOWLEDGMENTS

This book was a labor of love and determination. A six-year journey down paths and over obstacles I could never have imagined. But for dreams to succeed you must not give into the doubts or the stress of making a project and world like this come to life. Without the help and support of my family and my friends, it wouldn't have been possible.

I'd like to thank my parents for their love and support; my brother, David, who gave me my first science fiction novel to read; my sons, Duncan and Corwin; and their mother, my friend and ex-wife, Barbara, who helped me through some dark times. Thank you especially to my wife, Leslie, whom I believe would not have made this book you hold possible without her strength and love.

Thank you to John Pitts, my creative partner, who was another cornerstone to the success of this project. Sadly, we lost John in 2019, but his guidance and wisdom I still follow.

To the Redding gang: John Law, who also created the two exceptional videos for the Kickstarter campaign for *Last Cities;* to Matt Davidson who brought us all together; Jerry Gifford; Biff Bishcoff, my brother; Jeff Fennel; Misha and Jerry Griffith; Jim Sherman; Owen Smith; the Howells; Theresa Wood; the McKennas; Scott Heckinlively (RIP); and to Doug Herring who took me to my first con, gave me my first Rapidograph and water colors, and photographed some of my paintings over the years—thank you, Doug.

Todd Lockwood, thanks for your help and friendship! Steve L. Sears, BIG thank you for many things, deciding to collaborate and dive into my world without hesitation when your plate was already full—thank you! And to the authors who bought into my idea about this world and who waited patiently for me to gain my footing after my surgeries.

Thank you to my team—who are amazing—editor Jennifer Brozek; Danielle Ackley McPhail; Mike McPhail; Raven Oak; Manny Frishberg; and finally to Kevin J. Anderson, my publisher, one of the authors, and my friend. Thanks, Kevin.

There are so many others. I can't name everyone. Finally, a big thank you to the fans.

—Jeff Sturgeon
December 2020

ABOUT THE EDITORS

Jennifer Brozek is a multi-talented, award-winning author, editor, and media tie-in writer. She is the author of *Never Let Me Sleep* and *The Last Days of Salton Academy*, both of which were nominated for the Bram Stoker Award. Her *BattleTech* tie-in novel, *The Nellus Academy Incident*, won a Scribe Award. Her editing work has earned her nominations for the British Fantasy Award, the Bram Stoker Award, and the Hugo Award. She won the Australian Shadows Award for the *Grants Pass* anthology, co-edited with Amanda Pillar. Jennifer's short form work has appeared in Apex Publications, Daily Science Fiction, Uncanny Magazine, and in anthologies set in the worlds of *Valdemar, Shadowrun, V-Wars, Masters of Orion,* and *Predator.*

Jennifer has been a freelance author and editor for over fifteen years after leaving her high-paying tech job, and she's never been happier. She keeps a tight schedule on her writing and editing projects and somehow manages to find time to volunteer for several professional writing organizations such as SFWA, HWA, and IAMTW. She shares her husband, Jeff, with several cats and often uses him as a sounding board for her story ideas. Visit Jennifer's worlds at www.jenniferbrozek.com.

Jeff Sturgeon is a Northwest artist known for his beautiful, award-winning metal paintings. Jeff's career spans over thirty years, coming up through the ranks as a young fan artist in the 1980s to being hired in the first wave of computer game artists in the late 1980s and early 1990s. A long career in the 1990s as an artist, animator, concept artist, lead artist, game designer, and art director most notably for *Electronic Arts*. He continued to paint and display his work at science fiction conventions around the country and created new cover and interior work for clients such as Harper Collins Publishing and NASA JPL.

Jeff left the game business behind and went to painting full time with aluminum as his new canvas—though he did not give up traditional canvas completely. Through the new millennium, Jeff's work became nationally known with increased appearances as an art exhibitor, guest, panelist, and Guest of Honor at conventions around the country and as an award-winning illustrator and cover artist.

Jeff's work is much sought after by art collectors—whether one of his classic SF/astronomical pieces or his beautiful renderings of the American west. The last few years, Jeff has been concentrating on his shared world, *The Last Cities of Earth,* resulting in this very book. You can follow the efforts put into this anthology, and Jeff's upcoming projects, on his Facebook Pages, Jeff Sturgeon's *Last Cities of Earth* and The Art of Jeff Sturgeon, or from his personal website, www.jeffsturgeon.com, which includes links to all his social media accounts.

IF YOU LIKED ...

If you liked *Last Cities of Earth*, you might also enjoy:

Beasts of Tabat
by Cat Rambo

Strong Arm Tactics
by Jody Lynn Nye

Clockwork Lives
by Kevin J. Anderson & Neil Peart

ADDITIONAL COPYRIGHT INFORMATION

OTHER WORDFIRE PRESS TITLES

The Dark Lady
by Mike Resnick

The Silver Ship and the Sea
by Brenda Cooper

War of the Worlds: Global Dispatch
Edited by Kevin J Anderson

Our list of other WordFire Press authors and titles is always growing. To find out more and to shop our selection of titles, visit us at:
wordfirepress.com

facebook.com/WordfireIncWordfirePress
twitter.com/WordFirePress
instagram.com/WordFirePress
bookbub.com/profile/4109784512

CPSIA information can be obtained
at www.ICGtesting.com
Printed in the USA
LVHW061530190122
708888LV00018B/620/J

9 781680 572551